He appeared black-haired and black-eyed and black-clothed.

She could make out none of his features, just that tall, dark presence – broad of shoulder, slim-hipped. He might be dangerous, given his size and the shadowy darkness swallowing him from her view – but now, at this moment, she felt lured by him. Entranced. Captivated.

Their eyes locked. He knew he had her attention. And in that moment, she desperately wanted to walk off the stage, across the room, close enough to see if his face was as handsome as his shadowy form hinted. Then closer – to see what truths lay in the mysterious depths of those inky black eyes.

D1589845

"You want inside the house, right? Maybe we can make a deal." Dario's voice was husky.

Cassidy couldn't hide her desperation to search for the jewels. "Yeah."

"And my dad wants you to drop your claim on the place."

"True," she said, wondering where he was headed with all this.

"Sex."

She blinked. "Sex?"

He nodded. "You can stay in the house all week and search to your heart's content, but only on the condition that you'll be my love slave."

Her heart was beating a fast tattoo, and it had very little to do with the fact that the world's best-looking man was standing a mere foot away. "Are you serious?"

"There's one more thing."

His gorgeous dark eyes had settled on the bed. The hotel room seemed dimmer now, but only because night had fallen. Moonlight was streaming through the windows.

"What's that?" she asked in a whisper.

"The sex starts now."

OVEREXPOSED

BY
LESLIE KELLY

&

COLD CASE, HOT BODIES

BY
JULE McBRIDE

MILLS & BOON
Pure reading pleasure

*First published in Great Britain 2008
by Harlequin Mills & Boon Limited,
Eton House, 18-24 Paradise Road, Richmond, Surrey TW9 1SR*

*Overexposed © Leslie Kelly 2007
Cold Case, Hot Bodies © Julianne Randolph Moore 2007*

ISBN: 978 0 263 86726 8

14-1108

*Harlequin Mills & Boon policy is to use papers that are
natural, renewable and recyclable products and made from
wood grown in sustainable forests. The logging and
manufacturing processes conform to the legal environmental
regulations of the country of origin.*

*Printed and bound in Spain
by Litografia Rosés S.A., Barcelona*

OVEREXPOSED

BY
LESLIE KELLY

Dear Reader,

It's been a couple of years since I first worked with Julie Elizabeth Leto and Tori Carrington on THE BAD GIRLS CLUB series. So when Blaze® invited us to bring the mini-series over, I jumped at the chance, and was thrilled that Tori and Julie did, too!

Obviously, if you read all three of THE BAD GIRLS CLUB books, you will see a "shared" scene that appears in each. That was so much fun to write, and I have to tip my hat to Julie for creating it and including my heroine, even before I'd started on my own book!

Happy reading!

Leslie Kelly

LESLIE KELLY

A two-time RITA® Award nominee, eight-time *Romantic Times BOOKreviews* Award nominee and 2006 *RomanticTimes BOOKreviews* Award winner, Leslie Kelly has become known for her delightful characters, sparkling dialogue and outrageous humour.

Honoured with numerous other awards, including a National Readers' Choice Award, Leslie writes sexy novels for Mills & Boon® Blaze®, and single-title contemporary books. Keep up with her latest releases by visiting her website: www.lesliekelly.com, or her blog, www.plotmonkeys.com.

To a couple of my favourite "bad girls" –
Julie and Lori. And to one fun bad boy, Tony!
Let's be bad together again sometime!

Prologue

THEY CALLED HER the Crimson Rose.

As her name was announced in sultry, almost reverent tones at Leather and Lace, an exclusive men's club, an awed quiet began to slither through the crowd. The room stilled, noisy conversation giving way to quiet expectation.

Businessmen in open-collared shirts stopped their whispered flirtations with waitresses wearing tiny black skirts and skimpy tops. Attendees of an entire bachelor party returned to their table, elbowing the groom to watch and weep. Single men who came every week just to see *her* sat back in plush leather chairs and stared rapt at the stage through hooded eyes. The ice tinkling against their glasses was soon the only sound in the lushly appointed room, even the servers knew better than to interrupt the clientele when the Rose was on stage.

She danced only twice a week—on Saturdays and Sundays—and since the night she'd started, the Crimson Rose had become one of the hottest attractions in the Chicago club scene. Because while the jaded city had long been used to hard-looking dancers taking off their clothes and gyrating to the heavy beat of sexual music, they simply hadn't seen anything like *her.*

She wasn't hard-looking, she was elegant. Her delicate features and natural curves made every man who saw her wonder what it would feel like to touch her creamy skin.

She didn't strip…she undressed. Slowly. Seductively. As if she had all the time in the world to give a man pleasure.

She didn't gyrate, she swayed, moving with fluid grace. Every gesture, every turn an invitation to gaze at her.

Her sound wasn't sexual, it was sensual, erotic and soulful enough to make a man close his eyes and appreciate it. Though, of course, when she was onstage none ever would.

While her job might have diminished some women in the eyes of those around her, the Rose *owned* it, embraced it, lifted it up to a level of art rather than pure sexual titillation.

She liked what she did. And they liked watching her.

The low, sultry thrum of a smoky number began, but the stage remained dark as the workers put final placement on a portable red satin curtain, used only by her. It had been a recent addition by the management, who'd realized that the high-class, stage performer feel was part of the Crimson Rose's appeal. As was the mystery.

While most of the other dancers at the club performed under bright overhead light and full exposure, the Rose danced in shadow and pools of illumination provided by precisely timed spotlights. Her red velvet mask never came off. Most figured the management was playing upon the popularity of the aura of secrecy surrounding the Rose.

Finally the music grew louder, the gelled spotlights, ranging in color from soft pink to bloodred, illuminated the stage, dancing back and forth, each briefly touching on one spot: the seam of the closed satin curtain.

"Now, for your viewing delight," said a smooth male from the sound system, "Chicago's perfect bloom, the Crimson Rose."

No one clapped or whispered. No one *moved*. All eyes were on the center of the curtain, where a hand began to emerge.

It was pale. Delicate, with long fingers and slender wrists. A colorful design—painted-on body art—began at the tip of one finger, with a tiny leaf. It connected to a vine, which wound up her hand, around her wrist. As her arm emerged, more of the leafy vine, complete with sharp thorns, was revealed. It glittered, sensuous and wicked, alluring and dangerous.

Sinuous, slow, unhurried, she emerged from the drape, until she was fully revealed. But her head remained down, her long reddish-brown hair concealing her face.

The tempo throbbed. The dancer stayed still, as if completely oblivious to the crowd. Finally, the spotlights changed color, the vibrant reds giving way to a soft, morning yellow. And, as if she were a tightly wound blossom being awakened by a gentle dawn, the Rose began to move.

Her head slowly lifted, the delicate beauty of her pale throat emphasized by more body art. Her hair fell back as she turned toward the light, as if welcoming the morning.

Her full lips—red and wet—were parted, sending vivid images and erotic fantasies into the minds of every man close enough to see their glisteny sheen…. This was a woman made for the art of kissing. And sensual pleasure.

There the view of her face stopped. A soft red-velvet mask covered the rest. The mask glittered with green jewels like those in the vine, leaving her audience certain that the temptress's eyes must be a pure, vivid emerald. Most already knowing the mystery of her face would not be revealed, her admirers refocused their attention to the rest of her.

She wore layers of soft fabric, cut in petal shapes. Still like the flower being awakened by the sun, she began to indulge in the spotlight's warmth. Swaying, she stretched lazily like a cat in a puddle of light. Her movements were unhurried, revealing a length of thigh, a glimmer of hip.

Then the tempo picked up. So did her pace. She arched and swayed across the stage with feminine grace. But to most, she appeared lonely—removed from her surroundings—reveal-

ing a sensual want that begged for fulfillment that would
never come.

Anyone in the audience would have fulfilled it for her.
Anyone.

Every move she made set the billowing layers of her
costume in motion, until the petals nearly danced around her
on their own. They parted to reveal her slender legs, provid-
ing a peek here and a glimpse there.

And then they started to disappear.

Every man in the place leaned forward. Wherever she
turned, another bit of fabric hit the floor. Her hands moved
so effortlessly that the layers seemed to fall by themselves.
The light pinks and puffy outer veil went first, followed by
the heavier satin pieces. Soon her long, perfectly toned legs
were revealed up to the thigh. A drape of satin covering her
stomach fell next, torn away from the strings of a bikini top.

She continued her siren's dance as the fabric fell away, the
tempo pushing harder, her hips thrusting in response. Finally,
when she wore nothing but a sparkly red G-string and two
tiny, delicate pink petals on the tips of her breasts, she glanced
at the audience, deigning to give them her attention.
Normally, at this point, she would offer a saucy smile, pluck
the petals off her nipples, then duck behind her curtains.
She'd give them a glimpse—quick, heart-stoppingly sexy—
then disappear into the dark recesses of the club until her
second performance of the night. But tonight…tonight, she
hesitated. No. Tonight, she *froze.*

Because as she cast a final glance at her audience, seeing a
number of familiar faces in the crowd, her attention was
captured by a shadowy figure standing in the back of the room,
beside the bar. Ignoring the expectant hush from those familiar
with her performance, all of whom were waiting for the payoff
moment they'd come to see, she focused all her attention on *him.*

She couldn't see much at that distance, both because of the mask she wore and the spotlights still shining in her face. But she saw enough to send her heart—already beating frantically due to her performance—into hyperdrive.

From here, he appeared black-haired and black-eyed and black-clothed. She could make out none of his features, just that tall, dark presence—broad of shoulder, slim-hipped. He might be dangerous, given his size and the shadowy darkness swallowing him from her view—but now, at this moment, she felt lured by him. Entranced. Captivated.

Their eyes locked. He knew he had her attention. And in that moment, she desperately wanted to walk off the stage, across the room, close enough to see if his face was as handsome as his shadowy form hinted. Then closer—to see what truths lay in the mysterious depths of those inky black eyes.

But suddenly someone whistled…someone else catcalled. She realized she'd lost track of the music and the dance and the audience and her reasons for being here.

Titillation. Seduction. Those were her reasons for being here. Which made it that much more strange that, right now, the Rose was the one who felt seduced.

Enough. Time to finish.

Sweeping her gaze across the crowd, she gave them all a wickedly sexy look, as if her pause had been entirely purposeful. And entirely for their personal delight. In it, she invited them to imagine just who had her breathing hard—licking her lips in anticipation. Who had her skin flushed and her sex damp and her nipples rock hard.

She only wished she knew the answer.

With one more sidelong glance through half-lowered lashes, she reached for the tiny petals—pink, to match the tender skin of her taut nipples—and plucked them off.

The crowd was roaring as she disappeared behind the

curtain. They cheered for several long minutes during which she regained her breath and tried to force her pulse to return to its normal, measured beat.

When it did, she took a chance and peeked through the curtain, her stare zoning in on that dark place by the bar.

But the shadowy stranger was gone.

1

FOR THE FIRST TWO WEEKS after he'd returned from the Middle East, Nick Santori genuinely didn't mind the way his family fussed over him. There were big welcome home barbecues in the tiny backyard of the row house where he'd been raised. There were even bigger dinners at the family-owned pizzeria that had been his second home growing up.

He'd been dragged to family weddings by his mother and into the kitchen of the restaurant by his father. He'd had wet, sticky babies plopped in his lap by his sisters-in-law, and had been plied with beer by his brothers, who wanted details on everything he'd seen and done overseas. And he'd had rounds of drinks raised in his honor by near-strangers who, having suitably praised him as a patriot, wanted to go further and argue the politics of the whole mess.

That was where he drew the line. He didn't want to talk about it. After twelve years in the Corps, several of them on active duty in Iraq, he'd had enough. He didn't want to relive battles or wounds or glory days with even his brothers and he sure as hell wouldn't justify his choice to join the military to people he'd never even met.

At age eighteen, fresh out of high school with no interest in college and even less in the family business, entering the Marines had seemed like a kick-ass way to spend a few years.

What a dumb punk he'd been. Stupid. Unprepared. Green.

He'd quickly learned...and he'd grown up. And while he didn't regret the years he'd spent serving his country, he sometimes wished he could go back in time to smack that eighteen year old around and wake him up to the realities he'd be facing.

Realities like this one: coming home to a world he didn't recognize. To a family that had long since moved on without him.

"So you hanging in?" asked his twin, Mark, who sat across from him in a booth nursing a beer. His brothers had all gotten into the habit of stopping by the family-owned restaurant after work a few times a week.

"I'm doing okay."

"Feeling that marinara running through your veins again?"

Nick chuckled. "Do you think Pop has ever even realized there's any other kind of food?"

Mark shook his head. Reaching into a basket, he helped himself to a breadstick. "Do *you* think Mama has ever even tried to cook him any?"

"Good point." Their parents were well matched in their certainty that any food other than Italian was unfit to eat.

"Is she still griping because you wouldn't move back home?"

Nodding, Nick grabbed a breadstick of his own. For all his grumbling, he wouldn't trade his Pop's cooking for anything...especially not the never-ending MRE's he'd had to endure in the military. "She seems to think I'd be happy living in our old room with the Demi Moore *Indecent Proposal* poster on the wall. It's like walking into a frigging time warp."

"You always did prefer *G.I. Jane.*"

Nick just sighed. Mark seldom took anything seriously. In that respect, he hadn't changed. But everything else sure had.

During the years he'd been gone, the infrequent visits home hadn't allowed Nick to mentally keep up with his loved ones. In his mind, when he'd lain on a cot wondering if there would ever come a day when sand wouldn't infiltrate every surface of his clothes again, the Santoris were the same big, loud bunch he'd grown up with: two hard-working parents and a brood of kids.

They weren't kids anymore, though. And Mama and Pop had slowed down greatly over the years. His father had turned over the day-to-day management of Santori's to Nick's oldest brother, Tony, and stayed in the kitchen drinking chianti and cooking.

One of his brothers was a prosecutor. Another a success-ful contractor. Their only sister was a newlywed. And, most shocking of all to Nick, Mark, his twin, was about to become a father.

Married, domesticated and reproducing...that described the happy lives of the five other Santori kids. And every single one of them seemed to think he should do exactly the same thing.

Nick agreed with them. At least, he *had* agreed with them when living day-to-day in a place where nothing was guaran-teed, not even his own life. It had seemed perfect. A dream he could strive for at the end of his service. Now it was within reach.

He just wasn't sure he still wanted it.

He didn't doubt his siblings were happy. Their conversa-tions were full of banter and houses and SUVs and baby talk that they all seemed to love but Nick just didn't get. And wasn't sure he ever would...despite how much he knew he *should*.

I will.

At least, he *hoped* he would.

The fact that he was bored out of his mind helping out at Santori's and hadn't yet met a single *appropriate* woman who made his heart beat faster—much less one he wanted to pick out baby names with—was merely a product of his own re-adjustment to civilian life. He'd come around. Soon. No doubt about it.

As long as he avoided going after the one woman he'd seen recently who not only made his heart beat fast but had also given him a near-sexual experience from across a crowded room. Because she was in *no way* appropriate. She was a stripper. One he'd be working with very soon now that he'd agreed to take a job doing security at a club called Leather and Lace.

Forcibly thrusting the vision of the sultry dancer out of his brain, he focused on the type of *normal* woman he'd someday meet who might inspire a similar reaction.

He'd have help locating her. Everyone, it seemed, wanted him to find the "perfect" woman and they all just happened to know her. The next one of his sisters-in-law who asked him to come over for dinner and *coincidentally* asked her single best friend to come, too, would be staring at Nick's empty chair.

"Do you know how glad I am that your wife's knocked up?"

"Yeah, me too," Mark replied, wearing the same sappy look he'd had on his face since he'd started telling everyone Noelle was expecting. "But do I want to know why *you're* so happy?"

"Because it means she doesn't have time to try to set me up with her latest single friend/hair stylist/next-door-neighbor or just the next breathing woman who walks by."

Mark had the audacity to grin.

"It's not funny."

"Yeah, it is. I've seen the ones they've thrown at you."

"You seen me throw them back, too, then."

Nodding, Mark sipped his beer.

"Doesn't matter if she's a blonde, brunette, redhead or bald. Any single woman with a pulse gets shoved at me."

"And Catholic," Mark pointed out.

"Mama's picks, yeah. But *none* of them are my type."

Deadpan, his brother asked, "Women?"

"F-you," he replied. "I mean, I do have a few preferences."

"Big—"

"Beyond that," Nick snapped.

Mark relented. "Okay, I'm kidding. What *do* you want?"

That was the question of the hour, wasn't it? Nick had no idea what he wanted. It was *supposed* to be someone who'd make him want *this*. This sedate, small-town-in-a-big-city lifestyle.

"I don't know if I'm cut out for what all of you have."

When Mark's brow rose, Nick added, "I wasn't criticizing. You all seem happy. The couples in *this* family don't seem as…"

"Boring?"

"I guess."

"Thanks," his brother replied dryly.

"No offense. But you're all the exception, not the rule."

Mark murmured, "That's a lot of exceptions."

It was. Which meant Nick was out of luck. How many great, happy marriages could one family contain?

But damned if he wasn't going to give it a try. He'd been telling himself for the last three years of his active enlistment that once he was free—once he was home—he was going to have the kind of life the rest of his family had. The dreams of that normal, happy lifestyle had sustained him through some of the wickedest fighting he'd ever seen. He would not give them up now. Not even if they suddenly seemed a little sedate.

"Face it, they won't rest until you're 'settled down.'"

"Like *you?*" he asked, raising a brow. His twin was a hard-ass Chicago detective who could hardly be described as "settled down." The man was as tough as they came, despite his occasionally goofy sense of humor.

"Yeah. Like me."

Nick rolled his eyes. "You are in no way *settled down*." He glanced at the cuts on his twin's knuckles.

Mark smiled, a twinkle in his eyes. "Guy resisted."

"Does Noelle know?"

The smile faded. "No, and if you tell her I'll pound you."

"I'd like to see you try."

Leaning back in the booth and crossing his arms across his chest, Mark nodded. "I guess you might be able to hold your own now that the Marines toughened you up and filled you out."

It had long been a friendly argument between them that Nick had inherited their mother's lean, tall build like Luke and Joe. Mark and Tony resembled their barrel-chested father. But after many tough, physical years in the military, Nick was no longer anybody's "little" brother. "I think I could take you on."

"I think you could take *anybody* on. So why don't you come down to the station and talk to my lieutenant?"

"Not interested in your job, bro. I've had enough of rules and regulations for a while." They'd talked about the possibility a few times since Nick had returned home, but he wasn't about to relent on that issue. He'd done his time on the battlefields of Iraq, he didn't want to add to them in Chicago.

"Yeah, okay," Mark said, glancing around the crowded restaurant. "I can see why *this* is so much more up your alley."

Nick followed his glance and smothered a sigh. Because Mark was right. Helping at the pizzeria was no problem in the short term, heck he'd helped run the place when he was in high school, putting in more time than any of his siblings. But did he really want to become a partner in the business with his brother Tony, as he used to talk about…and as the family was hoping?

Seemed impossible. But Mark was the only one who would understand that. "I'm getting into protection," he admitted.

"You gonna mass-produce rubbers?" Mark sounded completely innocent, though his eyes sparkled with his usual good humor.

"I can't *wait* to tell your kid what a juvenile delinquent you were. Like when you put the Playboy magazine in Father Michael's desk drawer in sixth grade."

"Believe me, my kid will know Dad's on the job from the time he's old enough to even *think* about swiping candy bars. Now, what's with this protection business?"

"I'm going to work part-time as a bodyguard."

"No kidding?" Mark said, sounding surprised.

"Joe did some renovation work on a nightclub uptown and got friendly with the owner. Turns out they need extra security, so he set up a meeting. I went in Sunday night to talk to them."

"Bet Meg *loved* big brother Joe working in a nightclub."

Like the rest, their older brother Joe was happily married. Nick knew he'd never even *look* at another woman.

"So," Mark asked, "why does a club need a bodyguard?"

Nick knew *exactly* why this club needed a bodyguard after watching the erotic performance by a dancer called the Crimson Rose. The sultry stranger had inhabited his dreams and more than a few of his fantasies ever since he'd seen her on stage, revealing her incredible body while still remaining, somehow, so *above* it all. He imagined men with less control might try to do more than fantasize about the woman.

"The performers attract a lot of unwanted attention," he said, not wanting to get into details. Not because he was embarrassed about his job, but because he didn't want to start talking about the rose-draped dancer and her effect on *him*.

Nick didn't need that kind of distraction in his life. A hot stripper definitely did not fit in with the nice Santori lifestyle he kept telling himself he wanted. Not one bit. Which meant working with her was going to be a trick.

But he'd handled bigger challenges. Besides, meeting

her—talking to her—would take the bloom off that rose. Intense fantasies were meant for women who were untouchable, mysterious, unknown. It was, he'd come to believe while living in the Middle East, part of the allure of veiled women living in that culture. The unknown always built high expectations.

The Crimson Rose soon would *not* be an unknown. He'd see the face that had been hidden behind the mask and her secrets would be revealed. Which would make her much less intriguing.

Wanting his mind off *her* until it had to be when he started work, he changed the subject. "This place is hopping."

"So why aren't you out there taking orders from women who'd like to order a side of *you* with their thick crust?"

"Even the help gets an occasional night off."

He cast a bored glance around the room. A line of patrons stood near the counter, waiting for carry-out orders. Every table was full. Waitresses buzzed around in constant motion, all of them overseen by Mama. Nothing caught his attention…until he spotted *her.* And then he couldn't look away.

She stopped his heart, the way the dancer had, though the women couldn't be móre dissimilar.

The stranger stood near the door, leaning against the wall. Looking at no one, her eyes remained focused on some spot outside the windows. Her posture spoke of weary disinterest, as if she'd zoned out on the chattering of customers all around her. She was separate, alone, lost in her own world of thought.

Not fitting in.

That, as much as her appearance, kept Nick's attention focused directly on her. Because he, too, knew what it was like to not fit in among this loud world of family and friends and neighbors who'd known one another for years.

She was solitary, self-contained, which interested him.

And her looks simply stole his breath.

From where he sat, he had a perfect view of her profile. Her thick, dark brown hair hung from a haphazard ponytail, emphasizing her high cheekbones and delicate jaw. Her face appeared soft, her skin creamy and smooth. Though her lips were parted, she didn't appear to be smiling. He suspected she was sighing from her open mouth every once in a while, though out of unhappiness or of boredom, he couldn't say.

Dressed casually in jeans and a T-shirt, she also wore a large baker's type apron over her clothes. That made it impossible to check out her figure. But judging by the length of those legs, shrunk-wrapped in tight, faded denim, he imagined it was spectacular. With a lightweight backpack slung over one shoulder, she looked like she'd stopped off to grab a pizza on her way home from work, like everyone else in line.

Only, she was so incredibly sexy in her aloof indifference, she didn't *look* like any other person in line.

Across from him, Mark said something, but Nick paid no attention. He continued to stare, wishing she'd turn toward him so he could make out the color of her eyes. Finally, as though she'd read his mental order, the brunette shifted, tilted her head in a delicate stretch that emphasized her slender neck, and turned. Sweeping a lazy gaze across the room, she breathed a nearly audible sigh that confirmed she was bored.

Then her eyes met his…and there they stopped.

Hers were brown, as dark as his. As their stares locked, he noted the flash of heated awareness in her stare. She made no effort to look away, watching him watch her. As if she knew he'd been checking her out, she returned the favor, looking him over, from his face down, her stare lingering a little long on his shoulders, and even longer on his chest. Nick shifted in his seat, his worn jeans growing tight across his groin, where heat slid and pulsed with seam-splitting intensity.

Though he was seated and there was no way she could see her effect on him, the stranger began to smile. One corner of her mouth tilted up, revealing a tiny dimple in her cheek. But it wasn't a cute, flirty one…nothing about this woman was cute and flirty, she was aggressive and seductive.

Needing to know her—now—he pushed his beer away and slid to the end of the bench seat without a word.

"Nick?" his brother asked, obviously startled.

"I have to meet her."

"Who?"

Nick didn't answer, he simply rose to his feet, never taking his eyes off the stranger.

Mark turned around. *"Her?"* his brother asked, sounding so surprised Nick wondered if marriage had made him entirely immune to the appeal of a hot, sexy stranger. "You have to *meet* her?"

Already walking away, Nick didn't answer. Instead, he strode across the restaurant, determined to not let her get away. He had to meet the first *real* woman—not a fantasy dressed in rose petals—who'd made his heart start beating hard again since the day he'd gotten home from the war.

IZZIE NATALE HAD A SECRET.

Well, she had *many* secrets. But the secret she was trying to disguise right now was one that would get her thrown out of the windy city for life.

She preferred New York style pizza to Chicago deep dish.

Shocking, but true. In the years she'd been living in New York during her dancing career, she'd fallen in love with everything there, including the food. But she'd be taking her life in her hands if she admitted it. Because, man, they took their pizza *very* seriously here. Her grandfather would turn over in his grave if he found out she'd gone to the dark—thin-crust—

side. Her father, at whose request she'd made this stop at Santori's, would disown her. And her sister, whose husband ran this place, would never speak to her again.

Hmm. That might be a blessing. Considering her sister Gloria never had mastered the art of shutting up when the occasion demanded it, Izzie felt tempted to tell her that not only did she like her crust thin, but she also preferred the Mets over the Cubbies. That would get her stoned in the street.

How am I going to get through this?

It wasn't the first time she'd wondered that in the two months she'd been home, taking care of her family-owned bakery while her father recovered from his stroke. If her friends in Manhattan could see her—covered in flour, wearing an apron, working behind a counter—they'd think she'd been kidnapped.

This could not be Izzie Natale, the former long-legged Rockette who'd had men at her fingertips. Nor could it be the Izzie who'd gone on to land a spot with one of the premiere modern dance companies in New York, short-lived though that spot may have been after her ACL injury had required major surgery seven months ago.

But it was. *She* was. And it was driving her *mad*.

It wasn't that she didn't love her family. But oh, did she wish one of *them* could run the bakery. Because she was not happy being once again under the microscope, living in this big-geographically, but small-town-at-heart area of Little Italy.

Before she could groan about it, however, something caught her eye in the crowded pizzeria. Make that some*one* caught her eye. As she cast another bored look around, half-wishing she'd see someone she'd recognize from her *other* life here in Chicago—the one nobody else knew about—she spotted *him*.

A dark-haired, dark-eyed man was staring at her from

across the place. Even from twenty feet away she felt the heat rolling off him. An answering sultry, hungry fire curled from the tips of her curly dark hair down to the bottoms of her feet.

God, the man was hot. Fiery hot. Global warming hot.

His jet black hair was cut short, spiky. *A military man.*

His dark eyes matched the hair. They were deep set, heavily lashed…bedroom eyes, she'd have to say. His lean face was more rugged than handsome. The strong jaw jutted out the tiniest bit, and his unsmiling mouth was tightly set, as if intentionally trying to disguise the fullness of a pair of amazing male lips.

His shoulders were Mack-truck wide and his chest was football-field broad. And his attitude was all, one-hundred-percent Santori male.

Because Izzie knew it was Nick Santori who'd met her stare from across the room. Nick Santori who'd risen from his seat and was winding his way across the room toward her. Nick Santori who was making the earth shake a little under her feet, just as he always had when she was a teenager.

She told herself to breathe and not let him get under her skin. He sure had once…like at Gloria and Tony's wedding, when she'd been a bridesmaid of fourteen and Nick had been a groomsman. He'd had to escort her down the aisle, and his big, bad, going-into-the-Marines-eighteen-year-old self hadn't liked it. And that day was one she would *never* live down.

Somehow, though, that memory didn't steady the floor. Nor did it cool her off as he came closer. Those dark eyes of his were locked on her face as he effortlessly cleared his way through the crowd with a look here or glance there. Everyone made way for him. The men out of respect. The women… well, the women looked like Izzie imagined she did: dumb-struck. All because of the simmering sensuality of this one sexy man.

The one she'd wanted since the first time she'd felt heat between her legs and understood what it meant.

"Hi," he said when he finally reached her.

"Hey." She felt almost triumphant at having achieved that note of casual aloofness. She even managed to keep slouching against the wall, probably because she needed the support. She might have learned to handle men but she'd never gotten over feeling like Izzie-the-geek around this one.

"Is there something I can do for you?"

Oh, yeah. She could think of several somethings. Starting with her getting some payback for him ignoring her when she was a chubby, lovesick kid. And ending with him naked in her bed.

But getting naked in bed with Nick Santori would involve serious complications. Her sister was married to his brother. The families were old friends. If she so much as looked at the guy with interest the neighborhood would have them married off with her popping out brown-haired Italian babies within a year.

Uh-uh. No thanks. Not for Izzie. Sex with Nick would be delightful. But it came with *way* too many strings.

"I don't think so," she finally answered.

He didn't back off. "I'm sure there's something."

"What, are you a waiter now?" she asked, amused at the thought of him waiting tables. Especially since that chest of his could probably double as one.

Nick had, like all the Santori kids, worked in the restaurant in high school. Just as Izzie had worked in the bakery—often eating her paycheck to sweeten her teenage angst.

But he'd been in the Marines for years. She didn't see him slinging pizzas now that he was back in Chicago. Not after he'd been slinging Uzis or whatever those macho soldier guys carried.

"Maybe. Why don't you tell me what you want and I'll let you know if I can get it for you?"

Thin and cheesy New York style pizza was the first thing that came to mind, but Izzie didn't want to get strung up at the corner of Taylor and Racine. "I already placed my order."

He smiled slightly. "I wasn't just talking about pizza."

God, was that…it *was*. There was a flirtatious twinkle in those blackish-brown eyes of his. He'd been throwing some subtle innuendo at her and it had gone clear over her head.

"Oh," was all she could manage.

Cake flour must have clogged her femme-fatale genes in the past two months. It was the only way someone with her experience with men could have missed his double meaning.

"Want to sit while you wait for your order?" he asked, gesturing toward a few chairs in the waiting area.

"No, thanks." She fell silent. If she opened her mouth again, she might do something stupid like throw out a dumb, "Wow, what I wouldn't have given for you to look at me like that when I was a teenager," line, which she so didn't want to do.

She zipped her lips. She'd be Izzie the uninterested mute. Which was better than Izzie the lovesick mutant.

"How about at a table?"

"At a table…what?"

He smiled again, that sexy, self-confident smile that had probably had woman on five continents dropping their panties within sixty seconds of meeting him. "We can sit at a table while you wait for your order."

God, she was an idiot. "No, I'm fine here, thank you."

She had to give herself a break for being so slow. After all, Nick Santori had been scrambling her brains since she was ten—right around the time her sister Gloria had started dating his brother Tony. And though he'd always had a way with females, he'd never looked twice at *her* that way.

Especially not since Gloria and Tony's wedding. The one

where she'd tripped on her ugly puce gown—which hugged her tubby hips and butt—while they were dancing the obligatory wedding party waltz. She, the kid who'd been in dance lessons since the age of three, had tripped.

Maybe it wasn't so shocking. She'd been worried about what he'd think of her sweaty palms. She'd been *terrified* that her makeup was smearing off her face and revealing that she'd had the mother of all break-outs that morning.

Nervous plus terrified times the pitter-patter of her heart and the achy tingle in her small breasts from where they brushed against the lapels of Nick's tux had left her dizzy. So dizzy she'd stepped off the edge of the slightly raised dance floor and crashed both of them onto a table full of cookies and pastries made especially by her parents for the wedding.

It hadn't been pretty.

Colorful candy-covered almonds had flown in all directions. Her butt had landed on a platter of cream puffs, her elbows in two stacks of pizelles. Her dress had flown up to her waist to reveal the panty girdle she'd worn in an effort to hide her after-school-cookie-binging bulge.

The icing on the five-tiered Italian cream wedding cake—which she'd *somehow* managed to not destroy—had been Nick. He'd gotten tangled up in her dress, and had landed on top of her, sprawled across her chest.

And right between her legs.

It was the first—and last—time she'd figured Nick Santori would be between her legs, which both broke her heart and fueled some intense fantasies throughout her high-school years. Shocked by the unexpectedness and the *pleasure* of it, she'd been slow to part those legs and let him up. Slow enough for the moment to go from embarrassingly long to indecently shocking.

She'd thought her mother was going to kill her afterward. But that wasn't all. Because Izzie had the luck of someone who broke mirrors for a living, the incident had also been the money shot of the whole day. The videographer caught the whole thing on film, creating a masterpiece that would taunt her throughout eternity.

She'd been a laughingstock. Everyone in the crowd had whooped and clapped and teased her about it for months afterward. She might as well have worn a banner proclaiming herself, "Lovesick pubescent girl who crushed the cookies and dry-humped the groomsman at the Santori-Natale wedding."

"I haven't seen you in here before," he said, finally breaking the silence that had fallen between them.

"I come here a couple of times a week," she replied.

He shrugged. "I've been gone a long time."

"In the military."

"Right. Things have definitely changed around here in the past twelve years."

"Maybe in some ways," she said. Then she glanced around and saw a minimum of five people she knew—all watching intently as she talked to Nick. Frowning, she muttered, "In some ways it's still the same small town hell it always was."

She surprised a laugh out of him. "I somehow think we have a lot in common."

His laughter softened his tanned face, bringing out tiny lines beside his eyes. It also made him utterly irresistible, as several women sitting nearby undoubtedly noticed.

Nick had been incredibly hot as a teenager. Lean and wiry, dark and intense. As a thirty-year-old-man he was absolutely drool-worthy. Not that he'd changed a lot—he'd just matured. Where he'd been a sexy guy, he was now a tough, heart-stopping male, big and broad, powerful and intimidating.

She didn't suspect he'd changed on the inside, though. Once a Santori male, always a Santori male. The men of that family had always been good-hearted.

Honestly, looking back, if Nick had been a jerk about what had happened at the wedding, she might have gotten over her crush a lot sooner and this moment might be a lot simpler. She could tell him to f-off, remind him he'd once laughed at her and added to her humiliation. Only…he hadn't. Curse the man.

He'd been very sweet, carefully helping her up—once she'd released her thunder-thigh death grip from around his hips. He'd gently wiped powdered sugar and cream off her cheek. He'd helped her pull her dress back down into place without making one crack about her chubby thighs or her panty girdle. He'd pretended she hadn't practically assaulted him. And he'd helped her back up onto the dance floor and continued their dance. Absolutely the only annoying thing he'd done was to start calling her Cookie.

As her mother often said, he'd been raised right. Just like his brothers. He was every bit a gentleman—a protector—and he'd never given her a sideways glance that hadn't been merely friendly. In his eyes, she'd always been Gloria's baby sister—the chubby ballerina who looked like a little stuffed sausage in her pink tutu and tights and he'd treated her with nothing but big-brotherly kindness.

Until now.

Fortunately, though, she wasn't sweet Izzie the cookie-gobbling machine anymore. He hadn't seen her for almost a decade…she no longer blushed and stammered when a hot guy teased her. And she no longer even tried to imagine she could have been a ballerina with her less-than-willowy figure.

Once she'd stopped eating pastries and hit brick-shithouse stature at age eighteen, she'd known her future as a dancer would come from another direction than the ballet.

She'd also learned how to handle men.

Now, *she* was in the driver's seat when it came to seduction. She'd been running the show with men for years. And it was high time to let Nick Santori know it.

"So, when you offered to serve me…what *were* you talking about?" she asked, swiping her tongue across her lips. It was a move she'd perfected in her Rockettes dressing room. Men used to come backstage, trying to pick up the dancers and they all went for the lip-licking. God, males were so predictable. She held her breath, hoping for more from this one.

And she got it.

"I'm talking about me serving you with a line and you tipping me with your number. But since it's crowded and I'm rusty at that stuff, why don't you just give me the number?"

Izzie had to laugh. If he'd come back with a smooth line, the laugh would have been at his expense—because she doubted there was one he hadn't heard. But Nick had been completely honest, which she found incredibly attractive.

She also laughed to hide the nervous thrill she'd gotten when she realized Nick Santori really did want her number. That he really was trying to pick her up.

Her…the girl he'd once complained about having to dance with at a wedding. What were the odds?

"I think I've got *your* number." She'd had it for years.

He didn't give up. "Use it. Please."

He meant it. He wasn't teasing, wasn't trying to make her blush, wasn't treating her the way he treated his kid sister, Lottie, who'd been one of her classmates.

Nick Santori was trying to pick her up. Which shouldn't have been a big deal, but, for some reason, had her heart fluttering around in her chest like a bird trapped in a cage.

"My name's Nick, by the way."

No *duh.* She was about to say that, then she saw the look in his eyes—that serious, intense look. He wasn't kidding. He wasn't pretending they were just meeting.

She sagged back against the wall, not sure whether to laugh or punch him in the face.

Because the rotten son of a bitch had no idea who she was.

2

THE WOMAN HAD FLOUR in her hair. She smelled like almonds. Her apron was smeared with icing and whipped cream. Food coloring stained the tips of two of her fingers.

And she was utterly delicious.

The hints of flavor wafting off her couldn't compete with the innate, warm feminine scent of her body, which assaulted Nick's senses the way no full frontal attack ever had. Though they were in a crowded restaurant, surrounded by customers and members of his own family, hers was the only presence he felt. He'd been drawn to her, captured in an intimate world they'd created the moment their eyes had locked.

"You're name's Nick," she said, as if making sure. Her voice was a little hard, her dark eyes narrowing.

Worried she had an ex with the same name, he replied, "I'll answer to anything you want to call me."

"Anything?"

He nodded, unable to take his attention from that bit of flour in her hair. He wanted to lift his hand and brush it away. Then sink his fingers in that thick, brown hair of hers, tugging it free of its ponytail to fall in a loose curtain around her shoulders. His fingers clenched into fists at his sides with the need to tangle those thick tresses in his hands and tug her face toward his for a brain-zapping kiss.

She had the kind of mouth that begged for kissing. One that

promised pleasure. God, it had been a long time since he'd really kissed a woman the way he *liked* to kiss a woman. Slowly. Deeply. With a thorough exploration of every curve and crevice.

Recently, his sex life had been limited by proximity and his active status. He hadn't had any kind of relationship in years. And the sex he had was usually of the quick, one-night variety, where slow, indulgent kissing wasn't on the agenda.

He could kiss this woman's mouth for *hours*.

Nick didn't understand why he was so drawn to her. All he knew was that he was attracted to her in a way he hadn't been attracted to anyone for a long time. Not just because she was beautiful under the apron and that messy ponytail. But because of the wistful, lonely look she'd worn earlier that said she didn't quite belong here and she knew it. Just like the one he'd had on his face lately.

"You're single?" he asked, wanting that confirmed.

She nodded, the movement setting her ponytail swinging. It caught the reflection of a candle on the closest table, the strands glimmering in a veil of browns and golds that made his heart clang against his lungs.

"What's your name?" he finally asked.

She arched one fine eyebrow. "We haven't settled on what we're going to call *you* yet."

He turned, edging closer to her as a group came into the restaurant. The brunette slid along the wall, farther away from anyone else. Nick followed, irresistibly drawn by her scent and the mystery in her eyes. "I guess you have a Nick in your past?"

"Uh-huh."

"It didn't go well?"

"I'd have to say that's a no."

"Bad breakup?"

"No. We never even dated." One side of her mouth tilted

up in a half-smile. It held no happiness, merely jaded amusement. "He barely even noticed my existence."

"Then he was an idiot."

The other side of her mouth came up; this time her genuine amusement shone clearly. "Oh, undoubtedly."

"He didn't deserve you."

"Absolutely not."

"You're better off without him."

"Nobody knows that better than me." She sounded more amused now, as if her guard was coming down.

"Enough about him," Nick said. "If you don't like my first name, call me by my last one. It's Santori."

He watched for a flare of surprise, a darting of the eyes to the sign in the window, proclaiming the name of the place.

Strangely, she didn't react at all. "I think we've already determined what I should call you. You said it yourself."

Puzzled, Nick just waited.

"Idiot," she said, tapping the tip of her finger on her cheek, as if thinking about it. "Though, honestly, it doesn't quite capture you now. It might have sufficed years ago, but for today, I think we'll have to go with…complete shithead."

Nick's jaw fell open. But the sexy brunette wasn't finished. "By the way, that number you wanted? Here it is, you might want to write it down…1-800-nevergonnahappen."

And without another word, she shoved at his chest, pushing him out of the way, then strode out the door. Leaving Nick standing there, staring after her in complete shock.

"I'd say *that* didn't go well." Mark stood right behind him, watching—as was Nick—as the brunette marched off down the street like she'd just kicked somebody's ass.

Well, she had. Namely his. He just didn't know *why*.

"No kidding."

"I see you haven't lost your touch with women."

"Shut up." Shaking his head in bemusement, he lifted a hand and rubbed his jaw. "I don't know how I blew that so badly."

"But you sure managed to do it."

Hearing his twin chuckle, Nick glared. "At least I'm not wearing a ring. I can still *try* to pick up a hot stranger."

Mark just laughed harder. Which made Nick consider punching him. Only, Mama was standing behind the counter, glancing curiously at them as she waited on the customers. If Nick went after his twin, she'd come around and whack them both in the heads with a soup ladle.

"Hot stranger…oh, man, you are going to hate yourself when you figure out what you just did."

His eyes narrowing, Nick waited for his twin to continue.

"You really didn't recognize her, did you?"

Oh, hell. He should have recognized her? He *knew* her?

"Still not getting it?"

"Tell me how much trouble I'm in," he muttered, praying he hadn't just come on to a cousin he hadn't seen in years. If they were related—and he *couldn't* have her—that would be a crime worthy of a military tribunal. So he prayed even harder that she'd been some girl he'd known in high school.

"Pretty big trouble."

He waited, knowing Mark was enjoying watching him sweat.

"She *is* family, you know."

Damn. All the blood in his body fell to his feet out of embarrassment…and disappointment. "Why didn't you stop me?"

"You shot out of the booth like your ass was on fire."

Rubbing a hand over his eyes and shaking his head, Nick mumbled, "Who is she? Mama's side or Pop's? Please tell me she's not one of Great Uncle Vincenza's thirty granddaughters. Otherwise I just might have to re-up and hide from him and his mafia buddies for the next decade."

Mark's eyes glittered in amusement. The guy was enjoying this. "Not Great Uncle Vincenza. Think closer."

Closer. Christ. "There's no way she's a first cousin...."

"Not a cousin."

Oh, thank heaven. "So who?"

"I'll give you a hint. Did you happen to notice the icing and flour all over her apron?"

Had he ever. He didn't know if he'd ever smelled anything as good as all that messy, sugary stuff combined with the brunette's earthy essence. "Yeah. So?"

"You're not usually this dense."

"You're not usually this close to death."

"Think...the bakery...."

"Natale's? Gloria's folks?" And suddenly it hit him. "No."

"Oh, yes."

No. Impossible. It was out of the question. "Not Gloria's baby sister. *Tell* me that wasn't chubby little Cookie."

"She ain't chubby and I think if you called her Cookie to her face she'd slug you." Mark threw a consoling arm across Nick's shoulders, his chest shaking with laughter. "To answer your question, yes, my brother, that was Isabella Natale."

Nick couldn't speak. He was too stunned, thinking of how she'd changed. It had been at least nine—ten years, perhaps—since he'd seen her. She'd still been in high school and he'd run into her at a Christmas party at Gloria and Tony's when he was home on leave. She'd still blushed and stammered around him. And she'd still been girlishly round—pretty but with such a baby-face he'd never taken her crush on him seriously.

Oh, he knew about the crush. *Everybody* knew about the crush. His brother Tony had threatened to break his legs if he so much as looked at her the wrong way at the wedding.

Huh. He hadn't looked at her the wrong way. He'd just landed on top of her in a pile of cookies. And had been unable to get up because she'd wrapped her limbs around him like she was drowning and he was a lifeguard trying to save her.

He started to smile. "Izzie."

"Izzie. Formerly chubby sister of our sister-in-law, turned sexy-as-hell woman, now back in town working at the bakery."

"Her parents' bakery up the block?"

"That's the one."

"Is she here for good?" he asked, already wondering how things could have turned out this perfectly.

"I don't know. She's been home for a couple of months, since Gloria's father had a stroke. With the new baby, Gloria couldn't help much, and the middle sister's a lawyer."

"So the youngest one came home to take over." Not surprising. The Natales were much like the Santoris—family meant everything.

It almost seemed too good to be true. He'd finally come across someone who not only made his nerves spark and his jeans grow a size too tight, but who also came with a pre-made stamp of approval from the neighborhood. She was gorgeous. She was feisty. Her smile nearly stopped his heart. She'd had a crush on him forever—and was obviously still affected by him, judging by the way she'd taken off in a huff.

And she was *not* a faceless stripper behind a mask.

Enough of that. The Crimson Rose was every other man's fantasy. At this point in his life, Nick wanted *reality.* He was ready for what his brothers and sister had. And he had just stumbled across a *real* woman who he sensed could both drive him absolutely wild with want and be someone he could truly like.

"I think I'm feeling a need for some fresh cannoli," he murmured, smiling as he looked out the window at the sky, streaked orange by the setting sun. Izzie was no longer in sight…she obviously wasn't too desperate for pizza.

Maybe he'd deliver it to her.

"Judging by the way she bolted, you'd better think again."

Nick shrugged. He wasn't worried. After all, Izzie had had a thing for him once upon a time…she had practically chased him down. He just needed to remind her of that.

And to let her know he was ready to let her catch him.

"I SWEAR, BRIDGET, you should have seen his expression. It was as if it was the first time in his life a woman has ever turned him down," Izzie didn't even look at her cousin as she spoke. She was too busy punching into a huge ball of dough, picturing Nick Santori's face while she did it.

Though it had been nearly twenty-four hours since she'd run into him, she hadn't stopped thinking about him. Drat the man for invading her brain again, when she'd managed to forget him over the past several years. Ever since she skipped out of Chicago to follow her dancing dreams, she'd been convincing herself her crush on him had been a silly, girlish thing.

Seeing him had reminded her of the truth: she'd wanted Nick before she'd even understood what it was she wanted. Now that she *knew* what the tingle between her legs and the heaviness in her breasts meant, the want was almost painful.

"Didn't Nana always say the secret to a flaky crust was not to overwork it?" her cousin said, sounding quietly amused.

Izzie shot her cousin—who sat on the other side of the bakery kitchen—a glare. "You want to do this?"

Bridget, who was pretty and soft-looking, slid a strand of long, light-brown hair behind her ear. "You're the baker. I'm the bookkeeper." She sipped from her huge coffee mug. "So why did you walk away? You've wanted him forever."

"Maybe. But I don't want *forever* in general," she reminded her cousin as she floured the countertop and began to work the dough with a rolling pin. "You know I don't want *this* for any longer than I'm forced to have it." She glanced around the kitchen, where she was working alone to finish up the dessert orders for their restaurant clients. Including Santori's.

Not that she'd be the one delivering their order...no way. Her delivery guy would be in to take on that task shortly.

"I know. You'll be gone again once Uncle Gus is well enough to come back to work." Bridget didn't sound too happy about that, which Izzie understood. Her sweet, gentle-natured cousin was an only child, and she'd practically been adopted by Izzie and her own sisters. They'd been very close growing up.

Izzie missed her too. But not enough to stay here. As soon as her father recovered, and her mother no longer had to nurse him at home full time, Izzie would be out of here for good. Whether she'd go back to New York and try to reclaim some kind of dancing career she didn't yet know. But her future did not include a long-term stint as the Flour Girl of Taylor Street.

It also didn't include becoming the lover of any guy who her parents would see as the perfect reason for Izzie to stick around and pop out babies. Even a lover as tempting as Nick.

"So how's your life going?" she asked her cousin, wanting the subject changed. "How's the job?"

Bridget leaned forward, dropping her elbows onto the counter. "I guess I'm not very good. My boss obviously doesn't trust me, there are some files he won't even let me look at."

"Weren't you hired to keep the books at that place?"

Bridget, who'd gone to work three months ago for a local used car dealership right here in the neighborhood, nodded. "They're a mess. But every time I ask him for access to older records, he practically pats me on the head and sends me back to my desk like a good little girl."

Izzie assumed her cousin meant her boss *figuratively* patted her on the head. Because, though Bridget was in no way a fireball like Izzie and her two sisters—she wasn't a pushover, either. It might take her awhile to get her steam up, but Izzie had seen glimpses of temper in her sweet-as-sugar Irish-Italian cousin. That boss of hers obviously hadn't gotten to know the *real* Bridget yet. Because she was about the most quietly stubborn person Izzie had ever met…as anyone who'd ever tried to beat her in a game of Monopoly could attest.

"Why don't you quit?"

Her cousin lifted her mug, leaning her head over it so that her long bangs fell over her pretty amber eyes. She looked as if she had something to hide. And if Izzie wasn't mistaken, that was a blush rising in her cheeks.

A blush. Cripes, Izzie didn't even know if she *remembered* how to blush. The last time her cheeks had been pinkened by anything other than makeup was when she'd burned herself while lying out too long on the deck of a cruise ship a year ago.

Trying to hide a smile, she murmured, "Who is he?"

Her cousin almost dropped the mug. "Huh?"

"Oh, come on, I know there's a guy."

"Um…well…"

"For heaven's sake, you're looking at a woman who used to schedule two dates a night, just come out with it."

Chuckling, her cousin did. "There's this new salesman."

"A used car salesman?" Izzie asked skeptically.

Frowning, Bridget asked, "Do you want to hear this or not?"

Izzie made a "lips-zipped" motion over her mouth.

"His name's Dean," Bridget continued. "Dean Willis. And Marty hired him about a month ago. He's got cute, shaggy blond hair and big blue eyes—well, I assume they're big. They could look bigger because of the thick glasses he wears."

She watched Izzie, as if waiting for a comment. Izzie somehow managed to refrain from making one.

"He's sold more cars than anyone else because he's just so…quiet. Easy to talk to. Unassuming." Sighing a little, Bridget added, "And he has the nicest smile."

Izzie had never heard her cousin go on like this about a man. Must be serious. "So, have you gone out with him?"

Bridget shook her head and sighed again—only, much louder. "He's never even noticed I'm alive."

Snorting, Izzie replied, "I doubt that. You're adorable."

Bridget's bottom lip came out in a tiny pout. "Fluffy teddy bears are adorable. I want to be…something else."

Sexy. It was obviously what Bridget had in mind. Izzie eyed her cousin, considering making her over. Bridget had the basics—she just needed to bring them out a little. But she didn't think Bridget needed much. She was so quietly pretty, so gentle and feminine…any guy would be an idiot to want to change her.

Then again, she'd known a ton of guys, few of whom were Einstein material. "So ask *him* out. *Make* him notice you."

"I couldn't."

"Just for a cup of coffee."

Her cousin snagged her lip between her teeth.

"What?"

"Well, he *did* ask me to go for coffee once, but I was so flustered and nervous, I told him I didn't drink it."

Raising a brow and staring pointedly at the industrial-sized mug in front of her cousin's face, Izzie grunted.

"But it wasn't a date," Bridget added. "At least, I don't think so." Sounding frustrated, she added, "Maybe I should get a collagen injection. I've heard men like big lips."

Ridiculous. Bridget's beauty was the natural kind that needed no false crap like the stuff Izzie had seen other dancers do to themselves. But before she could say that—or threaten to lob a handful of ricotta cheesecake filling at Bridget if she did something so dumb—she heard the bell over the front door.

Glancing at the clock, she bit back a curse. It was nearly five—an hour after closing time. She must have forgotten to lock the door after her part-time lunch workers had left for the day and some customer had wandered in for a snack.

She doubted there was much left to serve. Mornings were their busiest time, with regulars and passers-by coming in for pastries and muffins. During the lunch hour, when Natale's served light sandwiches and salads along with decadent deserts, they were busy, too. Since Izzie had come up with the idea to offer free wireless Internet access to anyone with a laptop, some customers parked themselves at one of the small, café tables and remained there until closing time. They drank a lot of coffee…and ate a lot of sweets. By 4:00 p.m., Natale's display counter was generally wiped out, as this late customer would soon discover.

"Hello?" a voice called.

Grabbing a towel, Izzie wiped her hands on it and tossed it over her shoulder. "Be right back," she told her cousin as she walked down the short hallway to the café. "Sorry, we're closed for the…." The words died on her lips when she saw who stood on the other side of the glass display case, looking so hot she almost shielded her eyes from the glory of him.

"I know." He shrugged slightly. "But the door was unlocked, so I thought I'd take a chance and see if you were here."

Nick stood inside the shadowy café, illuminated by the late afternoon sunlight streaming in through the front window. The light reflected in his dark eyes, lending them a golden glow that seemed to radiate warmth. She felt it from here.

"You found me," she murmured.

"You didn't exactly need to leave a trail of crumbs, Cookie…this place has been here forever."

"*Don't* call me Cookie," she snapped.

He held up his hands, palms out. "Sorry."

Ordering her heart to continue beating normally, Izzie tossed the towel onto the counter, then crossed her arms over her chest to stare at him. "Are you trying to tell me you *knew* I'd be here because you *knew* who I was? Try again."

Nick cleared his throat, averting his gaze. Wincing in a cutely sheepish way, he said, "No, I didn't know you at first."

So, he'd recognized her after she had left?

"Mark told me who you were."

The jerk.

"I'm sorry I didn't recognize you. It's been a long time."

Not long enough to erase *him* from *her* mind, that was for sure. She'd recognize Nick Santori if she bumped into him blindfolded during a blackout. Because his scent was imprinted in her brain. And her body reacted in one instinctive way whenever he was near—a way it didn't react with anyone else, even men with whom she'd been intimate.

He made her shaky and achy and weak and ravenous all at the same time. Always had, for some unknown reason.

"Yeah. A long time," she mumbled, walking over to wash her hands in the small sink behind the counter.

Damn, she hated that he flustered her. She had known more handsome men. She'd been to bed with more handsome men. Maybe none who were as rugged and masculine, or so sensual. But she had dated drop-dead gorgeous actors and millionaires who wanted to notch their bedposts with a professional dancer who could kick her leg straight up above her head. None of them had ever affected her the way this one— who she'd never even kissed—did.

"I have to run, Izzie," a voice said. "I don't want to be…in the way."

Izzie had almost forgotten Bridget was in the kitchen. Seeing the grin on her cousin's face, she blew out a deep, frustrated breath. She'd intended to use Bridget as an excuse—or at the very least as a five-foot-five chastity belt, to keep Izzie from doing something stupid. Like smearing rich cheesecake filling all over Nick's body, then slowly licking it off.

But her cousin was bailing on her, already heading toward the exit. "Nice to see you, Nick," she said.

"How's your family?"

They fell into a brief, easy conversation, like most people who'd grown up in the neighborhood usually did. Except Izzie—who hadn't yet rediscovered that easy camaraderie with all the people she'd grown up with. While the two of them chatted, Izzie tried to regain her cool, forcing herself to look at this guy like she looked at every other guy. As nothing special.

Fat chance. She couldn't do it. He *was* special.

It had to be because he was the first man she'd ever wanted. Never having had him made the intensity of her attraction build. With no culmination—no explosion when she finally had him and got him out of her system—she'd remained on a slow, roiling boil of want for Nick for years.

So take him and get it out of your system.

Oh, the thought was tempting. Very tempting. Part of her desperately wanted to ask him to go with her to the nearest hotel and *do* her until she couldn't even bring her legs together. If she thought he would, and that he'd then forget about it, never expecting a repeat and never—*ever*—breathing a word about it to anyone, she'd seriously consider it.

But he wouldn't. Not in a million years. She knew that just as surely as she knew he'd never have even *kissed* her when she was underage, not even if she'd leapt on him and held him captive. Which, to be fair, she had…at the wedding.

He was a Santori. With everything that went with the name. His upbringing, his family, his own moral code meant he would never have a meaningless sexual encounter with his sister-in-law's younger sister. The daughter of his father's friend. The girl up the block. No way in hell.

He was the kind of guy who would have to *date* a woman he slept with. Dating—neighborhood style—as in hand-holding and miniature golf and pizza at his family's place and cannolis at her family's place. The whole deal. *Gag*.

Not that he'd actually asked her on a date. If he did? Well… that might have thrilled her once—years ago when she had actually thought the bakery and her family and Little Italy were all the world she'd ever need. Now, however, it just made her sad, because as she'd already realized, dating Nick equaled strings. Strings could very well choke her.

"Well, see you tomorrow," Bridget said as she walked out.

Izzie hadn't even noticed Bridget and Nick were finished talking. Cursing her cousin for bailing on her, Izzie cleared her throat, about to tell him she had to get back to work.

He spoke first. "So, do you forgive me?"

"Yeah, sure, no big deal," she replied, forcing a shrug.

A tiny smile tugged at those amazing lips of his and the dark eyes glowed. "No big deal? You seemed pretty mad."

Damn. He'd noticed.

"I wasn't mad. More…amused."

"Sure. That's why my chest is bruised where you shoved me."

Her jaw dropped and she immediately began sputtering denials. Then she saw his wide grin. "You're an ass."

"And a shithead," he replied, his grin fading though the twinkle remained in his eye. "I really mean it, Iz, I'm sorry I didn't recognize you." Stepping around the counter to see her better, he cast a slow, leisurely look at her. From bottom to top. Then down again. "But you have to give me a little bit of a break. You don't look much like you did."

"I'm not addicted to Twinkies anymore," she snapped.

"You weren't chubby."

"I was the Michelin Man in pink tights."

He shook his head. "You were just baby-faced the last time I saw you. A kid. Now you're…not."

"Damn right."

He didn't say anything for a moment, still watching her as he leaned against the counter. The pose tugged his gray T-shirt tight against his shoulders and chest, emphasizing the man's size. Lord, he was broad. But still so trim at the waist and lean at the hips. It was the hips that caught her attention—the way his faded, unbelted jeans hung low on them, the soft fabric hugging the angles and planes of his body.

It really wasn't fair for a man to be so perfect.

"So…about our conversation last night."

When staring at him—overwhelmed by his heat—she could barely remember her own name. Much less any conversation. "Huh?"

"What do you say? Will you give me your number?"

Oh, what she wouldn't have given to hear those words from him ten years ago. Or hell, even two *months* ago—if she'd happened to run into him in Times Square and he'd proposed a sexy one-night-stand for old time's sake. One nobody in Chicago would ever have to know about. She would have leapt on the offer like a gambler on a free lottery ticket.

"I don't think so."

"Come on, you know you can trust me. I'm not some stranger stalking you. We've known each other since we were kids."

Well, he'd known *her* since she was a kid. From the time

she'd met him, Izzie had only ever seen the glorious, hot, sexy *man*. Even if he had been no more than fourteen.

"Just a night out for old time's sake?"

He was so tempting. Because the only old times she recalled were the heated ones of her fantasies. And the incident at the wedding. He'd ended up between her legs during both.

"Well...."

He moved again, coming closer, as if realizing she was wavering. Dropping his hand onto the counter near hers, he murmured, "No pressure. We could just go grab a pizza."

She stiffened, any potential wavering done with. The last thing she would consider doing is having a public meal with Nick Santori at his own family's restaurant. Not when her sister would hear about it and tell their parents, who'd then get their hopes up about Izzie remaining safely in the nest, as they'd so desperately wanted her to do when she was eighteen.

Leaving home after high school had been a struggle. She'd been an adult, legally free, but she'd still had to practically run away in order to pursue her dream of dancing professionally. Especially because she was the only one of the Natale daughters who'd inherited their father's gift in the kitchen.

Probably because she loved food so much. As evidenced by every one of her porky-faced school pictures from kindergarten through tenth grade.

Her father had been crushed that she didn't want to work with him. But she had known she had to escape—had to take her shot while she could or risk regretting it the rest of her life.

So she'd gone. She'd hopped a train, determined to stay away until she'd given her dream of being a professional dancer everything she had to give.

Making it at Radio City hadn't eased her parents fears of

her being "out there all alone." It had actually increased them once they'd realized she was unlikely now to *ever* come back.

If they knew just how wild her life had been for the first few years she'd been on her own, they'd have felt justified in their fears. Like any good girl kept on a tight leash, she'd taken great pleasure in breaking every rule in the book once she was free and able to make her own decisions. Especially once she had men surrounding her and money to do whatever she wanted.

It had been wild. It had also been reckless—so in the past couple of years, she'd settled down. Stopped partying, stopped hooking up, stopped blowing every dime. She now had a nice nest egg…which she hoped to use to re-establish her life in New York. She'd been approached about going back to work at Radio City, as a choreographer this time. And she knew she'd probably get the same offer from her other modern dance company.

Or she could teach. She could open her own school…she had the money to at least give it a shot. That was among the things she'd been considering doing when she got back to reality.

Her parents, however, would give anything for her to stay here and never go back to that other life, the one that didn't include them beyond the weekly phone call and twice-yearly visit. Openly dating a local guy—a friend of the family—would raise their hopes unfairly and hurtfully. So she couldn't do it.

Before she could say so, however, he stepped closer. Close enough to stop her heart. "You're a mess," he murmured. He lifted a hand, touching a strand of hair that had fallen across her cheek. Closing his fingers over it, he slowly pulled, wiping away flour or cream or whatever had happened to be there.

The brush of his fingertips against her cheekbone almost made her cry. Almost made her whimper. Almost made her lean forward to press her mouth onto his.

"A sweet, delectable mess," he added, his fingers still

tangled in her hair. He touched her face, rubbing her skin as if he'd never felt anything so smooth, so soft.

Every muscle in her body went warm and pliant, until Izzie wondered how she could still be standing upright. As if sensing her weakness, he moved closer, sliding one foot between her legs, slipping one hand into her tangled hair to cup her head.

"I have to see how sweet you taste," he muttered, sounding as helpless as she felt. "If only once…I have to taste you."

Drawing her forward, he bent closer. Even knowing it was crazy and could go nowhere, Izzie prepared for a kiss she'd wanted for more than a decade. She'd cried over that mouth, had fantasized over those lips for more nights than she could count.

And she wanted it, God how she *wanted* it. Even if it was all she was ever going to get to have of him.

But rather than a simple kiss—the soft brush of his mouth on hers—he shocked her by immediately sampling her lips with his tongue, tasting her, as he'd said he must.

She whimpered, low and helpless.

"Oh, very sweet," he whispered, licking at the seam of her lips again, boldly demanding entrance rather than asking for it with a more typical, closed-mouthed first kiss.

Izzie couldn't deny him *or* herself. With a hungry groan, she opened to him, welcoming his tongue in a deep, sensual exchange that she felt from her head to the tips of her toes.

He'd thought she tasted sweet. She thought he tasted like irresistible sin. He was warm and spicy, his mouth just moist enough to whet her appetite. Just hot enough to send her temperature rocketing higher.

He sunk his other hand in her hair and held her close. Sagging against him, Izzie gave herself over to pleasure, wondering how it was possible for something to be as good as a dozen years of dreaming had promised it would be. It was a kiss more intimate than any she'd had even when making love. Because it was like making love. It was hot and sexy and powerful.

Their tongues found a common rhythm and tangled to it as their bodies melted together. Her nipples ached with need as they pressed against his broad chest. She arched harder against him, easing her legs apart to cup him intimately, whimpering again when she felt his huge erection.

He wanted her. Badly. As much as she wanted him.

The realization was almost enough to shock her into doing something stupid like ending the kiss. This was Nick—the guy she'd always wanted—hot and hard and hungry for *her.*

"Don't say no to me, sweetheart," he whispered as he finally—regretfully—drew his mouth from hers. He moved it to press kisses along her jaw, then down to the throbbing pulse point below her ear. "Say yes."

Yes, say yes! a voice screamed.

Oh, he was so tempting. And she wanted him desperately—wanted him to pull off her clothes, back her up against the counter and make love to her right on top of it. It would be incredible, the culmination of all her dreams and secret fantasies. She could finally put an end to all the years of restless, hopeless wanting.

But it wouldn't be the end. It would be the *start* of something, rather than the end of it. He'd make incredible love to her, make her come with a few more touches of his hands and a few more of those incredible kisses and she'd be alive and happy and completely fulfilled for the first time in her life.

But then he'd want to take her out for a pizza. Or get together with friends. And she'd be caught so deep in a quagmire of family and home that she'd *never* be able to get free of it.

"Say yes, Izzie," he ordered, sucking her earlobe into his

mouth and nibbling it—a tiny bite that she felt clear to the floor. "Give me your number and let's finally get this started."

Get this started. Get *everything* started.

She just couldn't do it. Izzie had always been strong and determined and had taken what she wanted. But she couldn't take *him*. Not now. It was much too late.

Yanking away, she winced as her tangled hair got caught in his fingertips. Her breathing ragged, her body crying out at the injustice, she shook her head, hard. Then she backed away, wrapping her arms around her waist in self protection. "No."

He started to follow, his dark eyes glittering…predatory. "You don't mean it."

She held a hand up. "Yes. I do," she said with a firm shake of her head. "Now, if you'll excuse me, we're closed and I have work to do in the kitchen." Taking a deep breath and striving to keep her voice steady, she added, "I want you to leave."

3

ON HIS FIRST NIGHT working at Leather and Lace, Nick showed up in a bad mood. He'd *been* in a bad mood for two days—since Izzie Natale had shot down his efforts to get closer to her.

The woman was unbelievable. Ten years ago, she might as well have taken out an ad in the Trib declaring her devotion to him. Now she wouldn't throw dog drool on him if he was on fire.

Damn, she was feisty. Had she always been that way? He figured with Gloria for a sister she had been. But considering he'd never seen her as a woman—just as a cute, lovesick kid—he'd never noticed. *Until now.*

Oh, yeah, now he'd noticed. He'd noticed everything about her. And he was not going to give up on her yet. Not when she'd become the first thing he thought of every morning and the star of his dreams every night.

Especially since that incredible kiss they'd shared.

Who would ever have guessed that the cute, pesky girl with the obvious crush on him would prove to be the most sensual, kissable woman he'd ever known? He'd suspected he could kiss her for hours. Now he knew better. He could kiss her for *ever.*

After she'd ordered him out of the bakery the other evening, he'd decided to play dirty, going right to Gloria to ask her for her sister's phone number. His sister-in-law had been glad to oblige. She'd also been more than candid about how Izzie had felt about him in the old days.

Not that Nick had needed her to tell him about it. He'd been well aware—as had everyone else.

"Not anymore," he muttered as he parked his truck—which he'd purchased right after getting home a couple of weeks ago—behind the club. He frowned, wondering how much of a jerk it made him now to be disappointed that a girl who'd had a wild crush on him as a kid didn't give a damn about him anymore. Probably a pretty big one. But he couldn't help it.

Knowing little Izzie had been crazy about him had been a constant during his teenage years. A given. Just another part of his reality. Certainly nothing he'd ever taken advantage of or embarrassed her about. It had just been…kinda cute, thinking there was a girl out there doodling his name in her school notebook. Innocent. Simple.

Man, he hated that that girl wouldn't even look at him now. Especially because he didn't think he'd done anything to deserve her coldness. No, he hadn't recognized her. But he also hadn't recognized the kid who had delivered the newspaper and now ran a newsstand on the corner. Or a couple of guys he'd played basketball with at St. Raphael's.

Mark thought he *did* deserve it. Not because he hadn't recognized her, but because he'd counted on her childhood feelings to give him an edge with Izzie the adult.

Hell, maybe he was right. Maybe he shouldn't have teased her, been so sure of her. He'd known enough women to know how they felt about being taken for granted. He should have taken her out to dinner before kissing her like he needed the air in her lungs to keep on living.

So he needed to start over with Izzie. Start slow, like he would with any other woman he'd just met.

It might not be easy. Because she already affected him more than any woman he'd ever met. He'd dreamed about her this week, thought about her, gone out of his way to walk past the bakery in the hope of bumping into her.

"Tables have definitely turned," he muttered aloud when he walked through the private, employees entrance into the back of the club. "Which is probably just the way she wants it."

Yeah, she could be stringing him along out of revenge. But somehow, Nick didn't think that was the case.

She hadn't been able to hide her feelings behind those incredibly expressive brown eyes. Though she'd sent him away after their kiss, she still wanted him. But something was preventing her from doing anything about it.

He just had to find out what.

"Nick, you're right on time!" The club owner, a beefy, good-natured guy with a Santa Claus-like belly laugh, emerged from his office and extended his hand.

Nick shook it. "Mr. Black."

"Call me Harry."

"Harry, then. Thanks again for the opportunity."

The other man waved a hand in unconcern. "Your big brother, he's one of the few honest contractors I've met in this city. Did beautiful work at a fair price. And if he says you're up to the job, I trust him completely."

Nick had already bought his brother, Joe, a beer in thanks for setting up his interview. He wished he'd made it a pitcher.

"All the paperwork's done, you check out exactly like Joe said you would," Harry said as he gestured Nick toward a seat in his office. "Now, you're clear on what I need from you?"

Nick nodded. "Have there been problems recently?"

Harry tapped his fingers on the desk and nodded. "The Rose has made a stir. Men want to see her and there have been a few *incidents*."

Nick stiffened reflexively, even though he hadn't met the woman yet. "Incidents?"

"Nothing too serious, thank God. But a couple of grabs, dressing room prowlers. A few disturbing notes." Harry shook his head, looking disgusted. "Can't imagine any man saying stuff that crude to any woman. But she was a sport about it, laughed it off." Staring pointedly, he added, "That's one reason I hired you—she tends to not take it seriously. And I want someone else to."

"I will," Nick replied, confident of his own words.

Harry nodded, obviously convinced. "Other than that, there's not too much trouble on a nightly basis. A guy'd have to be drunk as a skunk or just plain stupid to think he could go after one of the girls at the risk of taking one of the bouncers on. But we don't let anybody get drunk as a skunk in my joint." He chuckled. "And stupid people can't afford it."

That wasn't a surprise. When Nick had come in last weekend, he'd noticed the upscale feel of the club. Far from being seedy or shadowy, like most strip joints, this place was elegantly comfortable, from the earth-toned leather furniture to the framed pieces of classy-looking art on the walls. The prices reflected the ambiance; this was no after-work beer joint.

"I wanted to introduce you to the Rose, but she called and said she's running a little late tonight. I don't imagine there'll be time before her first number."

Nick stiffened, realizing he'd soon be seeing the woman behind the mask. Somehow, during the past few days when he'd been so focused on Izzie, he hadn't let the thought of the sultry stripper drift into his mind. Now, however, knowing he was about to see her again, he couldn't help but remember the way she'd made him feel last weekend.

Hot. Hungry. Needy.

So would any sexy, naked woman after such a long dry spell.

"She's something else."

"I noticed last weekend."

Harry Black shrugged. "Yeah, she's a looker, but there's something special about her even when she's not on stage. Got her head on right—a smart one. But that doesn't mean I'm not worried about her. She could get herself in trouble."

Nick could certainly understand that. Considering how attracted he'd been to her, he could see how a much more desperate man might react to her sultry performance.

"She's not going to like me hiring someone to mainly look out for her," Harry cautioned. "So we'll leave that part between us, okay? As far as she knows, you're just another bouncer."

"Fine." In fact, it was more than fine. He wanted as little interaction with the woman he was supposed to be protecting as possible. Not that he was truly worried about her effect on him—it had been a one time thing, that was all.

He'd been telling himself that for days. He'd also been ignoring the fact that none of the other strippers he'd seen that night had so much as caused his heart rate to increase its regular, lazy rhythm. Only *her.*

Meeting her would take care of that, he was sure of it. She wore a mask, meaning her looks were all from the neck down. She'd have muddy eyes or crooked teeth or a hooked nose. Or a voice like a truck driver. Or she'd snort when she laughed. Something would be wrong. Something would break the spell.

That would be the end of his interest. No doubt about it.

THE CRIMSON ROSE spotted the dark-haired man in black the moment she peeked through the curtains on the stage. And the moment she saw him—immediately recognizing him by his height and the power of his shadowed body—her heart began to beat harder.

He'd come back. For *her.*

This was the first night she'd been back to the club since last Sunday night, when she'd first seen him during her last performance on this stage. Inexplicably, she suspected this was his first night back, too. When she'd asked the other dancers about him, all had denied seeing such a man in the club during the past five nights.

She had drawn him back. Just as he—the very thought that he might be in the crowd again tonight—had worked to draw her here as well.

Not that she needed much of a draw. She loved what she did. She positively came alive while moving under a spotlight. The fact that her clothes were falling off her body as she did so was completely incidental.

She honestly didn't care.

"He came back," she whispered, almost bouncing on her toes, so excited she could hardly stand it.

Not just excited. *Relieved.*

Because though she'd only seen him from a distance, she already felt incredibly attracted to him. He'd be a marvelous distraction from the *other* man who'd been occupying her thoughts lately.

The one she couldn't have.

She began to smile, feeling, for the first time in days, a little upbeat. Working at the club was her one outlet, her only escape from the life she had so wanted to avoid coming back to here in Chicago. She loved these secret, wicked weekends.

And now that she'd realized there was another man— someone else—who could cause an instant, aching sort of want deep inside her, Izzie Natale sensed those weekends simply wouldn't come fast enough.

"You're not the only man in Chicago, Nick Santori," she whispered while the stage crew finished stripping the stage for her signature solo number.

When she'd first seen the ad in the paper for dancers for a Chicago gentleman's club, Izzie had had no illusions about what the job would entail. She wasn't some young dance ingénue who'd turned up for an audition only to be shocked at the very idea of taking off her clothes for a bunch of men.

Izzie had taken off her clothes for plenty of men. Sometimes even groups of them.

It wasn't as if the Rockettes danced in a whole lot of clothes. And during the three months she'd performed with the Modern Dance Company of Manhattan, she'd done two nude artistic performances.

The dancing she did at Leather and Lace wasn't *exactly* artistic. But, then again, she wasn't *exactly* nude, either. After all, she never took off her G-string.

Yes, her audience in Chicago was after sexual titillation rather than cultural stimulation. But, honestly, judging by the way some of the modern dance aficionados had come backstage and tried to pick up the dancers, she figured the motivations were, at heart, exactly the same.

Dancing was dancing. After the dire prognosis she'd received when having her torn ACL repaired several months ago, she didn't care where she was performing, or what she was wearing when she did it.

Honestly, now, having had a taste of it, she realized she couldn't have chosen a better venue. Because here, hidden behind a red velvet mask, she was free to be everything Izzie Natale of the famous Taylor Street Natale's Bakery was not.

Sexual. Uninhibited.

Free.

Before she'd even dragged her mind into readiness, she was introduced and her music had begun. Izzie moved onto the stage, dancing for herself and herself alone, as she always did, letting the petals fall where they may. She remained above everything, even oblivious to the money being tossed onto the stage—the crew would pick it up when she was finished. She also ignored the gasps and avid stares of the crowd.

Except one man's avid stare. His, she wanted to see, though it would prove difficult with him standing in the most shadowy area of the place and her nearly blinded by the spot-light. But when the choreography moved her downstage right—closest to the bar, and *him*—she risked it and looked.

And nearly fell off the stage.

Oh my God, oh my God, oh my God.

She lost the beat of the song and got a little tangled on her own feet. She also had to throw down an extra couple of petals a few measures too soon to try to cover her misstep.

Because in that quick flash when the light had hit him just right, she'd recognized the face, those shoulders, that hair.

It was Nick Santori who stood near the bar. Nick was the same dark, shadowy stranger who'd had her blood pumping through her veins, throbbing between her legs both last week when she'd first seen him here and a few moments ago when she'd glimpsed him again.

The bastard. Was she never going to be free of him? Would no man ever make her feel that crazy/excited/hungry feeling she got whenever he was in the vicinity? And what in the hell was he doing here, anyway?

Worse—what was he going to do about it if he realized she, the woman who'd shot him down in the bakery two days ago, was the Crimson Rose?

Her mind awash with the ramifications of Nick's presence,

Izzie finished her number. As soon as it was over, she darted behind the curtains and stuck her arms into a short, silky robe hanging right backstage. Barely noticing the crew members, who immediately got to work re-setting the stage for the more typical dancers, she hurried down the back stairs toward her private dressing room.

Normally, all the dancers would share one and Izzie was no prima donna who required her own space. But the owner of Leather and Lace had insisted on giving her a private, coat-closet sized room because of how serious Izzie was about protecting her identity. Once he'd realized just how much the "mystery" of the Crimson Rose enhanced the club's reputation—and brought in more customers—he'd upgraded her to one the size of a small bathroom.

Before she could duck into it, she heard his voice. "There you are! Hold up a second, I want you to meet someone."

She was in no condition to meet anyone—especially not another one of Harry's cousins or old fishing buddies. There was always someone ready to play on old friendships or family connection to meet the dancers.

On the positive side, Harry was as protective as a papa bear and the introductions never went further than a quick hand-shake or a signed autograph. Despite how much some of the men he brought around seemed to want it otherwise.

Pasting on an impersonal smile behind the mask she hadn't yet removed, she turned around.

"This is Nick Santori. I've just hired him to beef up our security."

Izzie sagged against the wall. If it hadn't been there, she might have just fallen sideways onto the tile floor, but thankfully, her shoulder instead landed on some hard wood paneling and it kept her vertical.

More than she could say for her heart. It had gone rolling

down and had landed somewhere in the vicinity of her stomach, which was now churning with anxiety.

"This is…"

"Rose," she quickly interjected, cutting Harry off before he could say her real name. She cleared her throat, seeking the sultry, husky tones she'd always used when greeting fans backstage at Radio City. The one that was quite different from the voice Nick had heard at the bakery just a couple of days before. "Nice to meet you."

He held out his hand. She took it. Time didn't stop or anything, and the floor didn't buckle beneath her feet. But, damn, his touch did feel *fine.*

He had big hands. Strong hands. A soldier's competent hands. They were capable of brute force. Yet equally capable, she knew, of tender care. Like when those hands had helped her pull her ugly bridesmaid dress into place, then gently lifted her back onto the dance platform and back into their waltz so many years ago.

"Nick's brother Joey Santori sent him in. You remember him, don't you? He did all the work upstairs. You met him last month."

Yes, she had…and it had been a closer call than this meeting with Nick, who could see almost nothing of her face because of the mask. She'd barely had time to duck behind a changing screen before coming face to face with Nick's older brother.

Now she had to wonder…had Joe seen her? Recognized her? And was he now playing Mr. Neighborhood Protector by sending his baby brother in to watch out for the girl up the block?

Possible.

God save her from Italian men.

One plus—he hadn't told Tony. Because no way would her overprotective brother-in-law have let Izzie's new job go undiscussed. He'd have come down on her with some big brother lecture about how she simply had to quit now, immediately, if not sooner. Either that or he'd have told Gloria, who would have had a shrieking meltdown over what the neighbors and her sweet, impressionable boys—wild little maniacs, in Izzie's opinion—would think.

"Harry, help! Some CEO's at the door saying he had reservations for ten," a frantic voice called from the top of the stairs. The hostess who worked the front desk came clattering down three stairs and spotted him, relief evident in her face. "You need to get up here."

Muttering under his breath, Harry offered Nick an apologetic shrug. "Sorry. Never fails. Tell you what, why don't you talk to…Rose…get an idea of what her routine and schedule are like and then meet me upstairs in thirty minutes?"

Nick nodded and they both watched Harry walk away. Well, Nick watched Harry. Izzie watched Nick.

She hadn't noticed at first—she'd been too frazzled herself—but Nick appeared tense. The muscles in his neck were rock hard, his jaw jutted out stiffly. Beneath his wickedly tight black T-shirt, his broad shoulders were squared in his military posture and his hands were fisted at his sides.

Interesting.

If she had to guess, she'd say he wasn't particularly happy to meet her. It was as if he actively disliked her…which didn't make much sense.

The only reason he could have for *already* disliking her was that he had somehow recognized her. That he'd looked into her eyes, revealed behind the mask, and seen something familiar. Or heard a note in her voice that he'd heard before. He certainly hadn't seemed very happy with Izzie-the-baker when she'd practically pushed him out of the bakery the other evening and imagined he'd convinced himself she was at best a pain in the ass and at worst a complete tease.

But if he looked at her and saw only a complete stranger…

what could he dislike about her after knowing her for all of two minutes? Nick wasn't the judgmental type. She couldn't see him working here if he had some kind of problem with women stripping.

Besides, his dislike seemed personal, directed only at her. He'd been perfectly fine with Harry.

"So, is tonight your first night?" she asked, keeping her tone low and thick. She sounded sultry—wicked—but that couldn't be helped. She needed to disguise her voice, at least until she knew for sure whether Nick had recognized her. Or if he'd been tipped off by his big brother.

"Yes."

"How do you like the club?"

He shrugged, noncommittal.

"Come now, you're not shocked are you? I imagine you've been in places like this all over the world."

His dark eyes narrowed. "How would you know I've been all over the world?"

Oh, man, that was stupid. She'd just tipped her hand. "I mean…you look like the military type, with the hair and the all-black commando look you have going on. Am I right?"

He nodded once, still not unbending one iota.

Izzie had to force herself not to react to all that simmering, intense male heat. Nick had been adorably sexy when flirting with her and trying to pick her up. And incredibly sensual when seducing her with his kiss.

Now…when he was all dark, intense business, he was absolutely devastating. Dangerous, almost, and though she'd never feared him, she couldn't contain a tiny shiver.

If he decided to kiss her now, it wouldn't be with sweet, sultry persuasion. It would be with raw, overpowering hunger.

She wanted that kind of kiss from him.

"I saw you here last weekend," she said, not even realizing she was going to admit such a thing until the words had left her mouth. That probably wasn't smart. She needed to keep the upper hand here—letting Nick know she'd been aware of him from first glance wasn't a good way to do that.

"I came in to talk to Harry about the job."

"And you watched me dance." She dared him to deny it.

He nodded once. The jaw flexed.

"Did you like it?"

"You're talented."

Oh, if only he knew.

"You're not...uncomfortable around me, are you?" she asked, trying not to laugh. "I mean, having seen so *much* of me?"

He shook his head. The shoulders tensed. "This is a job, Miss..."

"Rose will do."

"As you wish. The point is, I want to keep you...all of you...safe. Meaning we need to implement some new security procedures." He sounded impersonal, but every movement or flex of his body screamed that his tone was a lie. He was definitely reacting to her and Izzie would lay money it had nothing to do with him knowing her real identity.

If he knew who she was, he'd never remain stiff and un-yielding, trying to keep up this professional act. He'd be either seducing her—finishing what he'd started the other day—or else he'd be lecturing her for doing something so out of character for a nice Italian girl from the neighborhood.

Nope. He didn't know who she was. No way in hell. So why he was being so stiff and gruff, she really didn't know.

"Would you like to come in while I change?" she asked, gesturing to the closed door behind her. It had a cheesy little tinfoil star on it—a joke from one of the other dancers, who'd been remarkably welcoming after the first week or two. Considering their clientele had increased significantly since she'd been performing at the club, she figured they were all benefiting from the "mystery" of the Crimson Rose.

He hesitated for only a moment. Then nodded. "Sure."

Opening the door, she walked in and ushered him in behind her. "Sorry for the mess."

The space was crowded—one mirror, surrounded by bright lights, covered an entire wall. A long, sturdy vanity, connected to the wall, ran the width of the room, reducing the floor space to about a three-foot wide aisle. The vanity was covered with makeup and hair products. Not to mention G-strings and pasties.

He saw those and blanched, quickly looking away. Shifting uncomfortably, he moved back the tiniest bit, but was stopped from going far by the door, which Izzie had closed behind him.

A muscle worked in his cheek and he crossed his massive arms tightly across his chest. His feet spreading a little apart, he looked like a sturdy, unmovable sea captain standing on the deck of a ship. Unapproachable, unweatherable, unflappable.

Only, he *wasn't* unreachable. Because she'd seen that look at her sexy, glittery underthings. And his reaction to them.

Which was when Izzie started to get an inkling of what was bothering him. It wasn't a matter of him liking her or disliking her. Of him recognizing her or not recognizing her.

He wanted her. She just *knew* it.

Nick wanted to have sex with a stranger—a stripper—and he didn't like that about himself. He didn't like that weakness. She could practically hear his thoughts now, since she'd been raised exactly the way he had.

It wasn't good. It wasn't nice. It didn't quite fit the wholesome neighborhood-kid image.

It was, however, very honest. And despite how *he* felt about it, Izzie liked that very much. As a matter of fact, she *loved* that he wanted her. Not quite as much as she'd loved that he'd wanted Izzie—the invisible girl—but pretty darn close.

Trying to hide her smile, she walked around behind a changing screen and slipped the silky robe off her shoulders. Tossing it over the top of the screen, she murmured, "You're not…uncomfortable in here with me, are you?"

He didn't reply at first. Glancing at the mirror, she saw his reflection—saw him shake his head. Then he cleared his throat, answering aloud. "I'm fine."

He was turned toward the wall—away from the screen, away from the mirror. Which was probably a good thing, considering the reflection ran all the way to the far wall…even on her side of the changing screen.

If he looked in that mirror, the screen would prove to be completely superfluous. He'd see every bit of her…except her still-masked face.

She took her time getting dressed.

"That's good. If you're going to be working here, I suppose you're going to have to get used to seeing a *lot* of your co-workers." She licked her lips and almost purred as she added, "Much more than you'd see in a normal job."

"I'm not easily shocked," he muttered.

Turn around and we'll see.

But he didn't. Curse the luck.

"Can we talk about your routine, how you drive to work, what time you usually arrive?"

Bending over, she slipped out of the tiny G-string, then straightened and draped it over the top of the screen, answering his questions as she undressed. She never took her eyes off him, waiting for him to turn around, imagining how his eyes would widen and his mouth would drop when he realized he could see every move she made in the mirror.

He remained in the same position; however, the flash of movement must have caught his eye. Because his gaze shifted over—quickly, almost imperceptibly—but he definitely glanced.

She watched his reflection, seeing the way his body grew harder. His black trousers highlighted the clench of his muscular thighs and that tight butt. Though he made no sound at all, he dropped his head forward and slowly shook it, desperation rolling off him though he remained entirely silent.

Triumph surged through her as she realized what was happening. He was dying for her. And desperate to resist her.

Izzie continued to take her sweet time as she pulled on a pair of tiny panties—not much bigger than the G-string she'd just discarded. Then she added a matching lacy bra, cut low, almost to her nipples. Not the type of underclothes one would expect of a baker…they were the types of silky things she wore beneath her clothes to remind herself that she was *not* a sweet Betty Crocker wannabe.

Through it all, Izzie was careful not to dislodge the mask. She was also careful of her clip-in hair extensions. They took her shoulder-length dark brown hair down to the middle of her back, and added reddish highlights that worked well in her act. If he recognized her, the game would be over. And right now, Izzie was enjoying the game too much to let it end.

Particularly because she'd begun to see exactly how it could be played.

With no rules. No restrictions. Complete anonymity.

As the Crimson Rose, she could have him—take him—completely free of the repercussions that would surround her if she dared to do such a thing as Izzie Natale. She could have incredible sex with him, enough to get her deep-rooted need for him out of her system for good, then walk away, without anyone ever knowing the truth.

Including, if she was very lucky, *him*.

The question was—could she pull it off?

Catching sight of movement, Izzie realized Nick had finally turned around. He was reaching for the doorknob of the dressing room, his mouth open as if he was about to tell her he was leaving. Then he glanced toward the mirror and caught sight of her.

Nick's defenses dropped. He looked utterly helpless as he completely devoured her with his eyes. Visible hunger—primal and urgent—rolled off him in nearly tangible waves.

And in that moment, Izzie knew she could, indeed, pull it off. She was finally going to have the man she'd wanted for half her life.

4

HE SHOULD NEVER have come in here. Should never have walked into a small room with a woman who already had his head recling and his body taut with anticipation. One he was *supposed* to be protecting from guys who'd already threatened her.

Nick had been handling things okay up to now. Even while watching the dancers perform—while watching *her* perform—he'd felt in control of the situation. Yeah, she'd affected him. Any man not affected by the Crimson Rose had to have been castrated or born with no libido. But her effect was purely physical—not mental, not emotional. In his head, he still only saw one woman. Wanted one woman. And that was Izzie Natale.

He'd been feeling cool and confident when Harry had brought him downstairs to meet her. A little of that confidence had disappeared when he'd gotten close enough to her to smell the light, delicate perfume she wore—so at odds with her surroundings and her profession. His coolness had gone right out the window when she'd ushered him into her small dressing room where he'd felt like a bear trapped in a telephone booth.

And now…this…seeing her in the mirror?

Madness.

He'd seen her almost naked on stage and she'd stunned him. Now, close up, she blew his mind. Even wearing something that might pass for clothing on a sun-drenched beach, she was every bit as seductive as she'd been during her naked dance.

She was tall and she was curvy and she was soft and she was breathtaking. Her full breasts were contained by a bra that cupped the bottoms but left the tops nearly bare. Her cleavage spilled over the seam and the dark, pointed tips of her nipples thrust against the white lace, demanding attention.

Every man in the room had seen her breasts upstairs minutes ago, but now, up close, Nick was able to truly appreciate their perfection. How perfectly they'd fit in his hands, how delightful her nipples would taste against his tongue.

Nick drew in a deep breath, letting his attention drift lower. His gaze skimmed over the midriff, the slim waist. It lingered on the generous hips highlighted by the strips of white—the strings of her panties—slung over each one. The elastic top of her panties skated across the pale, vulnerable-looking skin below her hipbones. A tiny tuft of pretty brown curls peeked out from the top of them, the dark shadow behind the white silk was all he could see of the rest.

This was *more* than she revealed in her dance, and every male cell in his body reacted to the glorious sight. His heart rate slowed, the way it did when the world around him became dead serious. He swallowed—his mouth flooding with hunger. And his cock leapt, raging for release against his zipper.

The vanity interfered with the rest of his view, leaving him ripped with curiosity as his mind filled in the blanks of what he was not seeing. Those long legs. She had legs that could wrap around him twice, he knew that much from her dance.

It was all too easy to imagine lifting her onto that strong, flat surface, spreading her legs, then pulling up a chair to sit between them. He'd push her back, then loop her knees over his shoulders. Dipping his head in close for a thorough exploration, he'd sample those pretty curls and the shiny folds that they concealed. He'd pleasure her completely, devour her until his face was wet with the slickness of her arousal. He'd take the edge off his hunger, then focus only on her, giving himself a long time before he'd look up to watch the pleasure on her face as her orgasm rolled through her.

But in the vision, it wasn't the masked face of a stranger he saw. It was *Izzie's* face. This stranger had aroused him. Izzie was the one he wanted to fulfill him.

He needed to get out of here. Now. Because even if Izzie *had* shot him down—if there was absolutely nothing between them—she was still the one he really wanted. The one he'd dream about tonight, whether he got his rocks off right now or not.

He could do this stranger…and it might even be good. But it wouldn't get rid of his hunger. And it sure as hell would complicate things here in his new job.

Logically, he knew all that. The good Santori son who couldn't imagine bringing a woman like this around his traditional family should have been gone long before now.

Something made him stay. Maybe it was the *other* Nick. The one who'd grown predatory on the battlefield and bored in the real world. The one who'd been shot down by the reluctant woman he craved and was face-to-face with a willing one he desired.

They just locked eyes, hers mostly hidden behind that mask she still wore. Her lips slowly curled up into a sensuous smile and her chin came up in pure visual challenge.

Nick couldn't help it. He started to smile, too, a tight, dangerous smile that few would have recognized on the face of one of the affable Santori boys. "I don't think that screen works very well," Nick managed to say, his voice throaty.

"I'd say that depends on what I want it to do."

Knowing better, he asked, "If not giving you privacy to change, what is it you want it to do?"

The smile widened, a glitter of pleasure appearing in those shaded eyes. "Perhaps just heighten the anticipation. It's amazing how much more arousing it is to see some…but not all."

"You show almost all on stage."

"Almost," she conceded. "But if you noticed, it's mostly flash and petals, and only a tiny glimpse at the end."

His jaw clenched. "I noticed."

"Did it make you want more? Did a glimpse make you hunger for a look…which in turn made you ravenous for a touch?"

Which would make him insane for a taste.

He didn't answer, he didn't need to. She saw the answer in his face. As if tired of the game, she stepped out from behind the screen, still wearing only three things: the minuscule panties, the skimpy bra and the red velvet mask which was bigger than either of the other two.

"Why don't you take that off?" he asked, needing to see her face. He needed to find something about her that turned him off so he could get upstairs where his boss was waiting. So he could put her out of his head and get his libido back under control.

Quirking a questioning brow, she pointed to her bra, which startled a small laugh out of him. Because hell, yes, he'd like to see her without the bra—up close—but he knew he couldn't let that happen. Not if he wanted to keep his job. Not if he wanted to have the kind of life his brothers had.

Not if he wanted to work things out with Izzie.

"No. I mean that." He nodded toward the mask.

"I don't think so."

"You really take this anonymity seriously?"

"More than you know."

She moved closer and Nick honestly didn't know which pleased him more—feeling her warmth as she approached, or seeing her both in the flesh and reflected in the mirror. The woman's panties were not only tiny, they were thong-style and he could see the succulent curves of her ass in the mirror. His hands clenched with the need to fill them with those curves.

She reached for his left hand and lifted it. "No ring."

He shook his head.

"So there's no one…special?"

He hesitated a second before answering. A week ago the answer would have been an unequivocal no. Right now he wasn't so sure. He hedged. "That one's in the air right now."

Her bottom lip edged out in a tiny pout, glistening and wet against the red velvet cupping her mouth.

He wanted to bite it. Suck it into his mouth and lick the plumpness of it, then pull her down on his lap and explore all those curves and soft angles of her body.

"I'm unattached, too," she murmured, licking her lips as if she'd read his thoughts. "And frankly, in my line of work, I don't have much use for dating and get-to-know-you chats."

He suspected he knew where she was going. With some other woman—just about any other woman—he'd watch for signals, wonder if she was trying to pick him up. With this one, he knew she'd be very frank about what she wanted.

Her hand came up, she trailed the tips of her fingers across his shoulder, her nails scraping the cotton of his shirt. He felt the touch *everywhere.* Her scent overwhelmed him. Her heat screamed to him in pure sexual invitation.

She made it even more clear. "I want to have sex with you."

His heart skipped a beat. His pants shrunk across his groin and if the woman looked down, she'd know he could quite easily accommodate her. Several times, if she'd let him.

Before he could say a word, she quickly continued, "Despite what you might think since we just met, I'm not making this suggestion lightly. As Harry could confirm…I'm not in the habit of letting men in my dressing room. You are, in fact, the first one I've been alone with since I started working here."

Interesting. She sounded as if she was worried he'd question her morals or think she was trashy. He'd known trashy women. But in his experience, they were women with low self-confidence and lower self-esteem who grasped at sex with anyone in an effort to feed their egos and fill their empty hearts.

He could already tell Rose wasn't like that. She was *incredibly* self-confident. She could lift a finger and have any man upstairs ready to give her anything she wanted…and she knew it. She didn't need physical devotion to feed her self-esteem. In fact, he suspected it was her unshakeable self-esteem that enabled her to take off her clothes in front of a room full of men and yet remain so completely out of reach of all of them.

She could strip for them, entice them, seduce them…but never lower herself to a level that said she'd *ever* give them what they wanted.

But now, that's exactly what she was doing. Offering herself…to him. "I'm flattered," he said, his tone husky.

She reached for him, scraping the tips of her fingers along the waistband of his pants, tugging a little at his shirt.

"But it's not going to happen."

Her hand stilled. "You said you weren't attached."

"That's not the only issue."

"You're attracted to me."

He couldn't deny something so obvious. "We work together."

Shrugging in unconcern, she stepped closer, sliding one bare foot between his so that her leg scraped against his thigh. "Working together is what makes it so very…convenient."

She tilted her head, glancing toward the sturdy-looking vanity, and Nick knew she was picturing a very similar scenario to the one that had filled his mind earlier.

It would be shockingly easy to lift her onto that surface, step between her legs and drive into her body. Or to turn her around, lay her over it and come into her from behind. Their eyes would meet in the mirror…but he wouldn't see the passion in their depths. He could barely make out their color behind the fabric of her mask. And he knew one thing for sure—he would never make love to the woman as long as she wore the thing.

"I'm sorry, Rose. You're very attractive and sexy, but you're just not who I'm looking for right now," he said. "I've done the one night-stand-thing and I've had enough of it."

"Who said anything about one night?" Her words were flippant. Her husky tone was not.

The idea of having more than one night appealed to him. But it didn't change the basics: she was not the kind of woman he needed to get involved with right now. Not even on a purely sexual basis. "I'm sure there are a hundred guys upstairs who'd take you up on this in a heartbeat."

"I don't want any of them," she murmured. "I want you."

"You don't even know me."

"I don't have to know you to want to have sex with you."

"I'm not wired that way."

She made a sound of disbelief. "You've never had raw, wild, uninhibited sex with someone just for the sake of feeling good?"

"Just to get off, yeah," he muttered, making no effort to be delicate. "But only because time and expediency demanded it. I don't operate that way anymore."

"I could make it so good for you." She lifted his hand again, this time putting it on her bare hip.

Nick couldn't help squeezing it. "I don't doubt it."

"*Let* me," she ordered. "Let's see how good it can be."

His jaw stiff, he pulled his hand away. "I *know* how good it could be. I don't doubt we could screw ourselves senseless and make each other come a dozen times in an hour."

Her eyes closed behind the mask. He could see her pulse fluttering in her neck. Still talking in that throaty, sultry whisper, she asked, "And what would be so bad about that?"

Nothing would be so bad about that. In fact, it would be incredible. But he'd feel like shit afterward. He knew it as sure as he knew his brother Mark was never going to let him forget he'd been born twelve minutes before Nick had.

Some things were inarguable.

Like the fact that he couldn't have sex with this woman tonight and still look Izzie—the woman he sensed could be right for him for all the *right* reasons—in the eye tomorrow. So glancing at his watch, he found some nugget of resolve and said, "Harry's waiting for me upstairs. I'll see you later."

Without giving her a chance to try to stop him, he turned around and walked out of her dressing room. Judging by the way something went flying in that tiny room once the door was closed behind him, he knew he'd left a very angry woman in his wake.

"So HOW YOU DOIN', little brother?" Nick heard a woman's voice ask as he sat in a booth at Santori's the next day. It was early Sunday afternoon and the church crowd hadn't yet shown up for their traditional Sunday big mid-day meal, so he'd taken advantage of the lull to grab some lunch. Glancing up, he saw his sister-in-law, Gloria, Izzie's older sister.

They didn't look much alike. Gloria was pretty—especially for a thirty-something mother of three—but she didn't have Izzie's flamboyant looks. Her face was sweet, not dramatic. Her mouth soft, not sensual. She didn't have Izzie's amazing figure. Nor had she inherited her sister's desire to escape from here.

Gloria personified the world in which he'd grown up. She'd worked in her parents' business, gone to high school right here in the neighborhood. Married an Italian boy up the block. Gone to work in *his* family's business. And proceeded to produce lots of little Italian babies who looked just like her husband.

Though they were both hard-headed and volatile, and had been known to shout the street down when they got going, Tony and Gloria were absolutely crazy about each other. They had the kind of marriage anyone would want to have. The kind he would be lucky to have…once he figured out if he really wanted it.

Not knowing what he wanted was proving to be a real pain in the ass. Made more painful by the very sexy distraction called the Crimson Rose. He'd been able to avoid her for the rest of last night while working at the club, but every time their eyes met, she reminded him that she knew he was attracted to her.

"Nick?" Gloria prompted. "Everything okay?"

"I'm good, where are the boys?" he asked, looking past her for his two older nephews, or the carriage holding the baby one.

"I came in through the back…Tony Jr. and Mikey are in the kitchen with their father." She raised her voice, never shifting her eyes toward the swinging door leading into the kitchen. "Who had *better* not be giving them candy outta Pop's candy jar if he wants to *live* another day."

From the back room came the sound of Tony's deep

laughter. Nick would lay money the boys were already high on Pop's secret stash of gummy bears. "What about the baby?"

Gloria frowned, glancing toward the door of the restaurant. "He should be here any second. It's hard enough bringing the boys to mass without Tony there to help me. No way could I handle three of them. So he stayed with Auntie Izzie." Smiling in relief, Gloria nodded. "Here they are now."

Something about seeing Izzie pushing a baby carriage into the restaurant made Nick's stomach twist. Not because she looked like an absolute natural doing it…but because she looked miserable. Uncomfortable as hell.

He had to laugh. The woman was *so* unlike anyone else around here. Maybe that was why he couldn't get her off his mind.

"Hey, Iz, how'd you do with my little prince?"

"He puked in my hair. Twice."

Gloria swooped in and lifted the three-month-old out of the stroller, cuddling him close. "Aww, what'd you do to him?"

"I told him if he puked on me again I'd take him to the zoo and drop him in the bear cage," Izzie muttered. "What do you think I did to him?"

Gloria patted the baby on his back. "It's okay, Auntie Izzie's just grumpy because she doesn't have a sweet man to cuddle up with…much less four like Mommy's got."

Nick almost choked on his water at that one. If Gloria had been facing her sister, she would have seen the death ray that had come from Izzie's eyes. Apparently she heard him… because suddenly that death ray was sent in his direction.

Nick held up his hands, palms out, in a universal peace gesture. "I'm with you. Don't drop me in a bear cage."

Her glare faded and she half-smiled. "Don't tempt me."

"Careful, Nick," Gloria cautioned, still focused on the

baby, "our Izzie's not quite the sweet young thing you re-member. You don't want to tangle with her."

Oh, yeah, he did want to tangle with her. Tangle his hands in her hair and his tongue in her mouth and his arms around her body and his legs between her thighs. Mostly he wanted to tangle in her life…and tangle her in his. At least enough so she'd give him a chance to win back some of that interest she'd once felt toward him.

Before Izzie could say anything, the door opened and more family members poured in. His parents and his brother Joe—with wife and baby in tow—led the way. Folks from the neighborhood followed. Next came lots of cousins and aunts and uncles, all of whom came to the restaurant every Sunday for a big family meal.

Izzie's whole body went tense. He could see it from five feet away. She didn't want to be part of this—didn't *feel* a part of this. And Nick, more than anyone else in the room, under-stood. So without saying a word, he got up, took her hand, and tugged her toward his table.

She resisted. "What…"

"Come on, it'll be okay," he whispered as he pulled her down to sit beside him. "I'll tell you who I recognize, you tell me who you recognize and we'll get through this together."

She stared at him, her eyes wide, her mouth trembling. Looking for a moment like a trapped deer, she seemed on the verge of fleeing. She appeared unable to deal with something as innocuous—yet painful—as a neighborhood gathering.

"It's okay," he repeated. "You can do it."

It took a few more seconds, but that panicked look slowly began to fade from her eyes. As family friends and neighbors greeted her, he felt her begin to relax beside him. She even chatted a little, smiling at people she hadn't seen in years.

Everything went fine. Right up until the minute some old

lady from the block clapped her hands together, then pinched Izzie's cheek. "Oh, you're a beautiful couple!" she exclaimed. "At *last* you've got your man, Isabella Natale. All those years and you've finally landed him!"

Everyone fell silent, immediately turning in their direction. Especially Gloria. And Nick's parents.

"Shit," Izzie mumbled under her breath. Her face turned as red as a glass of the chianti Pop loved so much.

Nick put a hand on her leg under the table. But she pushed it off. And with a quick goodbye to her sister and the family— and a glare at Nick—she strode across the restaurant and stalked out the front door, not looking back. Not even once.

OVER THE NEXT couple of days, Izzie gradually began to lose her mind. Began? Heck, she'd been losing her mind since the night she'd toppled onto a table full of cookies and Nick Santori had landed on top of her. The man had been consuming her for *years*. This week, however, he was on track to win the gold medal in the Let's Drive Izzie Crazy games.

After her failed seduction attempt at Leather and Lace, he'd avoided her as much as he could when on the job. They hadn't been alone at all the rest of Saturday night, or when they'd both worked again Sunday. Just as well. She was still ticked about what had happened at the restaurant that afternoon.

He did take his job seriously, making sure she went nowhere alone. But *he* hadn't been alone with her for one minute. It was as if he feared "Rose" would make another move on him the first chance she got, and was making sure she didn't get the chance.

Grr…men. So untrusting.

But if Nick was frustrating her with his aloofness at the club by night, he was absolutely killing her by day. He'd come by several times in the past few days, popping into the bakery for a muffin and a coffee. Every time he was all cute and sweet and sexy. So different from the dark, brooding guy at the club that she'd have thought they were two different people.

She honestly didn't know which man appealed to her more. Probably whichever one she happened to be with at the time. Funny…he knew her as two different women. And while his name was Nick either way, she knew him as two different men, too.

Both of them were messing with her head. She'd been making all kinds of stupid mistakes at the bakery today—like using peppermint extract instead of almond in a batch of cookies.

Giving up in the kitchen since she had several hours before the restaurant orders had to be delivered, she decided to do some paperwork before closing. It was well after lunch, she was working alone but could hear the bell if anyone came in.

But even that didn't go well. She'd added up a column on a deposit slip four times and still hadn't gotten it right. She was tempted to call Bridget to ask her cousin to straighten out her books. But judging by the conversation they'd had earlier in the day, Bridget had finally worked up the nerve to ask her shaggy-haired used car salesman out. And Izzie didn't want to do anything to distract her.

Izzie just wished *she* had a distraction. Because she couldn't get Nick out of her head. He'd invaded her life. No, *both* her lives. When he stared at her across the club and devoured her with his eyes at night while physically spurning her, she felt ready to howl in fury.

Showing up here by day—the handsome guy next door who wanted to lick the cream out of her cannoli—and her having to refuse him? It was pure hell.

She wanted Nick the bodyguard at night. Not Nick the sexy guy up the block by day.

She wanted sex. Not romance.

Wanted temporary. Not ever after.

Wanted to *do* him. Not date him.

It was simply a matter of wills to determine which of them got what they wanted first. God, she hoped it was her.

"Izzie?"

Startled, Izzie yelped and spun toward the front of the shop, seeing a customer at the counter. So much for thinking she'd hear the bell—she'd been deafened by her own thoughts.

Recognizing the woman, a weary smile curled her lips. Lilith was a regular, who could supposedly read the future. A bit out there, but a good customer, and a nice one. "I'm sorry." She wiped her hands on her apron. "My head was in the clouds."

"If the clouds all smell like this bakery, that's not a bad place to be."

Maybe for the customers. But after practically living in this place for two months, Izzie was *over* the nauseatingly sweet smells that invaded her nostrils from morning till night. "Believe me, it's not so great going home from work with hair scented like anisette and clothes that reek of ginger."

"On the positive side, they say the scent of licorice is great for dieters because it controls your appetite."

Didn't seem to her that the sexy, short-haired brunette had anything to worry about in that regard. Frankly, neither did Izzie. She'd long since lost her taste for sweets…no more cookie-induced panty girdles for her. "Twizzlers can keep it. I try to ignore the smells unless someone burns something."

"Oh, come on, no one at Natale's ever burns anything."

Quickly washing her hands, Izzie had barely dried them before Lilith pointed with impatience at the lone cannoli remaining in the front display case.

When Lilith told her she'd be eating in, rather than taking the cannoli to go, Izzie asked, "Got a reading?"

While she didn't entirely believe in that stuff, Izzie knew a lot of regulars swore by Lilith's spiritual readings. Though she'd never considered it before, Izzie half-wondered if the other woman could help her figure out the quagmire that was her life. Especially the Nick part of that quagmire.

"Nah, I'm taking a break from the medium world right now."

"Just my luck. For the first time in my life I think I'd actually *pay* to have someone tell me who the heck I'm going to be next week."

Izzie the baker? Izzie the stripper? Izzie the New Yorker? Izzie the Chicagoan? *Izzie the horny?*

That was the one she really wanted an answer to. Was she ever going to get laid again, and oh, please, please, please, would it actually be Nick Santori who did the laying?

She didn't ask Lilith any of those things, though the medium promised she'd try to help her as soon as she was "back in business"—whatever that meant. But that might be too late. She might already have done something stupid—like having sex with Nick the bouncer as the Crimson Rose. Which would be fabulous but would make him hate her if he found out the truth.

Or something *more* stupid, like going out on a date with Nick, the guy up the block, which would have her parents planning their wedding. Then she'd hate *herself.*

Ordering a cappuccino to go with her treat, the mysterious brunette made herself at home at a front table, firing up a laptop. After making the frothy cappuccino, Izzie carried it over. "Doing some surfing?"

"I'm going to try. The most I've ever used the Web for is updating my Web site and answering e-mail."

"Don't forget shopping. Or maybe you're going to start haunting chat rooms?"

"No, I'm doing research."

Leaving the woman to it, Izzie went back to work. Concentrating on cleaning out the display cabinet, she was surprised to hear the bell jangle as another late-day customer came in. This one she didn't recognize—and she definitely would have, if she'd seen her before. The leggy brunette was dressed entirely in sleek, black leather and she looked like a predatory cat. The sexy little motorcycle parked outside the door suggested the woman was a risk-taker and a rule-breaker.

Izzie liked her on sight.

"Hey, Izzie," Lilith called, "what do you know about computers?"

Offering the new customer a quick smile, she answered, "Well, I don't know how to find any naked pictures of Heath Ledger, and I haven't figured out how to send a death ray to spammers, but I do the Web site for the bakery." It was a basic one, but Izzie was pretty proud of it.

"I hear ya. So you know how to enlarge pictures? Other than ones of naked movie stars?"

Izzie grinned. "Yeah, give me a sec." She looked at the newcomer. "What can I get you?"

"Espresso and a cannoli."

"Sorry, Lilith took the last."

Settling for just the espresso, the woman paid her and waited for her drink. After making it, Izzie went over to Lilith to see what help she could offer.

It wasn't much. It turned out the medium needed to enlarge a grainy newspaper picture in order to see a ring on some guy's finger. And Izzie just didn't have the know-how to do it.

The newcomer in black leather, however, did. Joining them, she asked a few questions, then bent over Lilith's computer and went to work. Watching her type, her fingers flying on the keys, Izzie figured she was experienced at this. But when the woman acknowledged that she was hacking into the newspaper Web site to try to find the original photo, she suspected there was a lot more than simple ballsiness to the woman.

She was mysterious. Maybe even a little dangerous.

They *both* seemed that way, really. Lilith with her supposed psychic abilities. This woman with her risky, who-gives-a-damn attitude. So unlike little Izzie of the bakery.

Maybe, however, not too unlike the Crimson Rose. She wondered what these two would think if they knew she wasn't quite the sweet, simple bakery worker she appeared to be.

"Who is this guy, anyway?" the stranger asked. "Don't tell me you're trying to figure out if that ring is a wedding band and he's the asshole you've been dating for the last three months."

"Ew."

"So he's not your lover."

"Say that again and I'll dump the dregs on you. He's a jerk I'm investigating."

"A jerk?" The stranger snorted. "What makes him different from every other man on this planet?"

"Good question," Izzie muttered, though her heart wasn't really in it. Nick had always been one incredibly good guy. The fact that he wouldn't have sex with her as a stripper didn't mean he was a jerk.

Even though he was.

She wandered away from the other two, cleaning off the empty tables in preparation for closing. As she worked, she kept up with the other women's conversation, trying to stay out of it, but unable to when she heard who Lilith was currently dating. Hearing that the sexy medium had hooked up with Mac Mancuso, a nice boy-next-door type turned Chicago cop, she had to put her two cents in. Mainly because their situations—whether Lilith would believe it or not—were very similar.

"Mac's not a jerk. He grew up just a few blocks from here. Our families know each other. I'd think any woman would love to catch a good, honest cop like him."

The stranger in black immediately stopped typing. "You're sleeping with a cop." Somehow, Izzie suspected the woman was allergic to anyone official—especially the police.

"I'm sleeping with him, not married to him," Lilith insisted. "Trust me when I say that my definition of right and wrong varies from his by huge degrees."

Huh. Sounding more and more like Izzie's situation. She almost wished she and Lilith were alone so they could talk.

"Keep working and your next ten espressos are on me," Lilith told the other woman.

"I won't be around that long, but thanks for the offer."

"Add her to my tab," Lilith told Izzie. "Any time she stops in, coffee's on me." Glancing at the stranger, she asked, "What's your name?"

"Seline."

Amused since Lilith's tab currently took up two pages in her accounts book, Izzie asked, "Does that mean you're actually going to pay it someday?"

Lilith shrugged in unconcern, watching as Seline kept working. When she finally struck pay dirt and got Lilith the information she wanted, they both seemed triumphant.

Izzie only wished her problems with Nick could be solved with an Internet search. Unfortunately, if she searched for the stuff she wanted to do with Nick Santori on the Internet, she'd probably get inundated with spam from sites like bigpenises.com from now till eternity.

Finishing up her cappuccino and shutting down her

computer, Lilith thanked Seline for helping her out, then turned to Izzie. "Thanks for the sugar boost and the wi-fi."

"Anytime." Unable to help it, Izzie called out, "Lilith, don't be so quick to write off a great guy like Mac. Maybe you and he can find a way to make it work, even if you think there's no way it ever could."

And maybe she was a sucker who should still be reading fairy tales. But hey, it didn't hurt to dream, did it? Even if she was dreaming on behalf of someone else.

Once Lilith was gone, the other woman, Seline, approached the counter. Even her walk was feline—sultry—and Izzie wondered if she'd ever danced before.

"Here," Seline said. She put a one-hundred-dollar bill on the counter. "For her tab. I sense that she needs the money more than I do. And I don't have to be psychic to figure that out."

Stunned, Izzie murmured, "Thanks." She opened her mouth to say more—to offer the money back—but the mysterious woman in black had already turned toward the door, her coffee in hand. She walked out into the bright sunshine without another word, got onto her sleek motorcycle and roared away down the street.

BRIDGET DONAHUE had always known she would never be wildly sexy and self-confident like her cousin Izzie. But there were times when she allowed herself to think that, maybe, since they were related, Bridget had a tiny bit of Izzie-power trapped deep inside her. So ever since she was a kid, she'd played a game. WWID, aka *What Would Izzie Do?* And then she'd try to do that.

Asking Dean Willis to go out with her one day at lunchtime had definitely been a WWID moment. And Bridget still couldn't believe she'd gone through with it. But if she hadn't, she wouldn't now be sitting at a coffee shop, looking across the table at his handsome face. Make that staring at his face.

Staring. Izzie wouldn't stare. Bridget ducked her head down, focused on her cup of Earl Grey tea. Not the double shot espresso she probably needed—because of her "I don't drink coffee" fib—but okay…mainly because of the company.

"You ready for a refill?" Dean asked.

Bridget shook her head. "I'm fine, thanks."

They weren't at her uncle's bakery, but at a big chain place not far from her apartment. Bridget had chosen the spot, which seemed safe, neutral and impersonal. Not the kind of place that said she thought they were on a date. Not the kind of place where a date would be absolutely out of the question.

God, she sucked at this. Izzie would have met him at a hotel bar.

Small steps, she reminded herself. Asking a man out was a first for her. It wasn't that she'd never dated—or that she was completely inexperienced. But if Izzie was on the top rung when it came to dealing with men, Bridget was still pulling the ladder out of the cellar.

They sat in an alcove by the front window. Bridget had her chair pushed back from the table, to accommodate the length of his legs beneath it. He looked crowded—bunched up in the small chair and the small corner—but he hadn't complained.

"You must be tired of hearing me rattle on about my land-lord problems," she said as the conversation lagged. "I haven't seemed to shut up."

He shook his head. "You're easy to talk to."

"You haven't been doing much talking…just listening."

"You're easy to listen to," he replied with a small smile.

Nice answer. And it was mutual, because he was also very easy—easy to like. But she still didn't feel like she knew anything about him. "So how do you like working for Marty? You've sold more cars in the month you've been there than any other salesman has sold in the past three."

He shrugged. "It's not hard when you have good products to sell." Lowering his gaze, he reached for his cup. "I guess you'd know that since you've worked for Marty longer than I have."

Sighing, Bridget shook her head. "Not much longer."

"Really?"

"I started just a couple of months before you did so I don't know much of anything, either."

He frowned. "But you keep the books, surely you know how things are going. I bet the place is raking in the bucks, huh?"

Grunting in annoyance, she admitted, "I have no idea. I see just enough to keep the books balanced and not much else."

Dean stopped stirring his tea and lifted his eyes to hers. Leaning forward over the table, he asked, "You don't know *anything* about what's going on at Honest Marty's Used Cars?"

"I know Marty's a bit of a con artist," she said tartly. "Honesty is just one of his…embellishments."

She suspected her boss also embellished some other things—like stuff he told the IRS. But she didn't have proof and was not about to say such a thing to anyone else.

He persisted. "But you must make the deposits, pay the invoices, keep an eye on the accounts receivable."

"I take what he gives me and do what I can." Shrugging, she added, "Honestly, I don't know much of anything about the business, it's all I can do to keep the checkbook balanced."

He held her stare, his blue eyes looking searchingly into her face, as if he was trying to find the answer to some question. She couldn't imagine what. She had no idea why he was so interested in the financial dealings of their employer.

Then she thought of something. It *could* be a matter of job security. Dean was personable and a good salesman, but he didn't exactly dress like someone who had a lot of money.

The sports coats he wore to work usually didn't fit well across his broad shoulders, and his pants were sometimes a little shabby.

Dean hadn't said a lot about what he'd done before coming to Honest Marty's. For all she knew, he'd been put out of work by poor management at his last job. That would certainly be enough to make anybody ask questions, especially somebody who lived paycheck to paycheck, as she suspected he did.

Not wanting to embarrass him, she carefully tried to set his mind at ease. "Look, I don't know specifics, but I know the dealership's doing well. I see the number of cars coming onto the lot and the number leaving it. You don't have to worry."

He frowned, as if not understanding what she meant. Some impulse made Bridget reach across the table and put her hand on his. She almost pulled her hand back right away, surprised to feel a warm tingle where skin met skin. But, swallowing for courage, she left it there. *Like Izzie would.*

If this was a date, he'd interpret her touch as a signal that she wanted more. If it was *not* a date, he'd interpret it as concerned friendship. Bridget considered it a little of both. "Your job is secure."

He was staring at their hands, still touching. "My job?"

He sounded—distracted. As if he was as affected by their touch as she was, which gave her a little thrill. "Marty would be a fool to let you go. You're the best salesman he's got."

He said nothing at first, he just slowly twined his fingers in hers, rubbing at the fleshy pad of her palm with the tip of his thumb. Her pulse raced and she wondered if he could feel it throbbing right there below her skin.

She somehow managed to concentrate on getting a positive message across, ignoring the tingling in her fingers and the flip-flopping of her heart. "It's okay, I know what it's like to worry about making ends meet, but please don't worry about the company. I'm sure you're not going to lose your job."

He looked up at her, his jaw dropping. "Lose my…."

"I thought that's why you were curious."

Dean's mouth snapped and he mumbled, "It's okay." He pulled the hand she'd been touching away and dropped it onto his lap. "Well, they probably want this table for other customers. I guess we should go."

Oh, God, she felt like a fool. She'd ruined this, he probably thought she had been pitying him or something. "Dean, I really didn't mean anything…"

"Hey, don't worry about it. I just wasn't sure what you meant at first. It's good to know the company's doing so well," he said, still sounding distracted. "Thanks again for meeting me. I'm glad we got the chance to get to know each other better, since we'll be working together."

Bridget managed to suck her trembling lip into her mouth, recognizing a brush-off when she heard one. Either he'd never intended this as a get-to-know-you date at all, or he *had* and she'd blown it. But whatever the case, it was finished now. He was not interested in seeing her again.

WWID…Izzie wouldn't cry. So she blinked. Hard.

"Bye, Bridget," he said as he escorted her outside.

She somehow managed to sound perfectly normal when she said goodbye too. But deep inside, she felt anything but normal.

In fact, Bridget felt a little bit broken.

5

OVER THE NEXT WEEK, Nick went out of his way to change Izzie's mind about going out with him. He stopped by the bakery, phoned in orders for stuff he didn't really want and made sure he was the one to sign for any deliveries at the restaurant, just in case she happened to be the delivery person.

She never was.

But he wasn't giving up. While at first she'd been a sexy stranger who'd caught his eye, she'd now become something of a challenge to him. He wanted to work his way around her protective wall and see if the smiling, funny girl was still there behind that to-die-for woman exterior.

Maybe it was just as well that Izzie consumed his thoughts by day. Because it made it easier to resist temptation by night. It definitely had on Saturday and Sunday night.

He'd worked at Leather and Lace for a second weekend. This time, knowing what he was in for, he'd been careful to avoid being alone with Rose, the club's sultry star performer, and hadn't even exchanged a word with her. Even still, it had been impossible to keep his eyes off her.

Especially when she danced.

Especially when she watched *him* while she danced.

If she'd made another move on him, he honestly didn't know that he'd have been able to refuse. So ensuring he was alone with her was probably a good thing.

Hell, he honestly wasn't sure why he was resisting. As long as he kept the woman safe, he didn't see Harry Black being the kind of man who'd have a problem with it. After all, he was married to one of his own former star performers.

And letting off a little sexual steam didn't have to have anything to do with Nick's normal, daytime life. In fact, nobody in his family ever needed to know about it. There was no law that said an unattached man couldn't have sex with a willing woman, just because he was interested in another woman.

One who wasn't interested in him.

Damn. That's why he hadn't done it. Because it was driving him crazy that Izzie wasn't interested in him.

Frankly, he'd never worked so hard to get a woman's attention in his life. The fact that Izzie was the woman in question made the whole situation that much more challenging.

She'd been crazy about him once. He'd get her to see him that way again if it was the last thing he did. Even if it meant doing stupid, sappy shit like showing up at her bakery with a handful of flowers.

Like he was right now.

God, how the guys in his unit would laugh to see him, standing on a street corner on a hot August day, holding a brightly colored bouquet he'd bought off a guy on the corner.

"What are you doing?" she mouthed through the glass late Thursday afternoon when he knocked on the locked front door.

"I'm bringing you flowers," he yelled back. "Open up."

"Don't bring me flowers."

Shrugging, he flashed her a grin. "Too late."

"I mean it."

"Like I said, too late. Come on, let me in. They're thirsty."

She glared at him. Seeing pedestrians stopping to watch the show, she went a step further and bared her teeth.

Man the woman was *hot* when she was hot.

"Go away!"

Tsking, he shook his head. Then he looked at the closest woman who'd paused mid-step to see what was going on. "Can you believe she doesn't want my flowers?"

A teenager and her girlfriend, who'd also stopped nearby, piped in together, "We'll take them!"

The older woman, an iron-gray haired grandmother, frowned. "What did you do?"

Good question. He wasn't *entirely* sure. "I didn't recognize her after not having seen her for ten years."

The grandmother's eyebrow shot up. Pushing Nick out of the way, she marched up to the glass, stuck her index finger out and pointed at Izzie. "Take the flowers you foolish girl." Rolling her eyes and huffing about youth being wasted on the young, she stalked down the street.

Izzie, still practically growling, unlocked the door, yanked it open and grabbed his arm. "Get in here and stop making a fool of yourself."

"I wasn't making a fool of myself," he pointed out. "You were making a fool of me."

"You don't require much help."

Shaking his head and smiling, he murmured, "What happened to the sweet, friendly, eager-to-please Izzie?"

"She grew up."

She yanked the bouquet out of his hand, stalking behind the counter and grabbing a glass to put it in. Watching her, he noticed the surreptitious sniff she gave the blooms, and the way she squared her shoulders, as if annoyed at her own weakness.

Nick didn't follow her, tempted as he was. Instead, he ⸮aned across the glass counter, dropping his elbows onto it.

　flowers are a peace offering."

　⸮ve at war?"

"It's felt that way to me ever since I was stupid enough to not recognize you that night at Santori's."

Ignoring him, she finished filling the glass with water, turned off the tap and plopped the flowers in.

"I still can't believe you're punishing me over that."

"Don't flatter yourself. I'm not punishing you over anything. I'm just not interested in you, Nick."

"Yeah, I got it." Only he didn't. He was in no way ready to concede that. Something had caused Izzie to put a wall up between them...and he was going to find out what it was. "But there's no reason we can't go back to being friends, is there? We were once."

"No. We weren't. You were the stud of the known universe and I was the puppy dog with the big, humiliating crush. You can't seriously think I'd go back to that."

"I tell ya, Izzie," he said, hearing the frustration in his voice, "I don't know for sure *what* I want from you. I just know I can't stand that you won't even look at me."

She finally did just that. Looked at him, met his direct stare. In those dark brown eyes he saw stormy confusion. It was matched by the quiver of her lush lips and the wild beating of the pulse in her throat.

"You liked me once," he said softly. "And we did pretty well helping each other out at the neighborhood-prying-session disguised as lunch last Sunday. Can we at least try being friends?"

She opened her mouth to reply. Closed it. Then, sighing as she pushed the vase of flowers to the center of the counter, slowly nodded. "I *guess*."

It was a start. Maybe not the start he wanted to make with her...but at least the start of something.

"Do you want some coffee?" She didn't sound particularly enthusiastic about the invitation.

He glanced at the industrial coffeemaker, scrubbed clean

for the night, and shook his head, not wanting to put her to the trouble.

"I have a small coffeemaker in the back."

"Sounds good."

Nick followed her down a short hallway between the café and the kitchen, trying to remember that it wasn't very polite to stare long and hard at the ass of someone who was just a friend. It didn't work. Because though she wore loose-fitting khakis and an oversized apron, the woman had a figure to die for. Every step pulled the fabric a little tighter across her curves, and the natural sway in her hips made him dizzy.

Friends. That's it. And *not* friends with benefits.

"How do you like being back in Chicago?" he asked as he sat at a tall stool beside a butcher block work counter.

Izzie ground fresh beans. At last—a woman who knew how to make coffee. One more thing to like about her, aside from the cute way her ponytail wagged when she moved and the way she smelled of sugar and butter and everything nice. "About as much as I like getting a root canal."

"That bad? You don't like being back in the family business?"

She glanced around the kitchen, immaculately clean and stocked with every baking supply ever invented. "My prison smells like anisette."

"Mine smells like marinara," he muttered, meaning it.

She nodded, not asking him to elaborate. She obviously knew exactly what he meant. "Not easy to come home, is it?"

He shook his head. "Not easy at all. My parents still haven't forgiven me for moving into an apartment, not back into my old room. It still has my high-school posters on the walls."

She snickered. "Mine, too. Though I don't suppose yours re of ballerinas and Ricky Martin."

"h…definitely not." A grin tickling his lips, he admitted, "ore and Lethal Weapon 3."

Izzie laughed softly. There was a twinkle in those dark brown eyes of hers and a flash of a dimple he remembered in one cheek. At last.

"Are you…"

"What?" he asked.

"I'm sorry," she said, "it's none of my business."

"What's none of your business?"

"I guess I was just wondering if you felt…a little…out of place with your family."

"I feel like I belong with the Santoris about as much as that kid in the Jungle Book belonged with the dancing bear."

She nodded, as if in complete agreement. "But if I recall correctly, I think he *wanted* to belong with the dancing bear and couldn't understand why he didn't quite fit in."

Nick said nothing. She'd made his point for him.

Izzie seemed to realize it. "Yeah. Me too."

"Something else we have in common," he said.

"Don't get too excited about it," she muttered, "I'm still not giving you my phone number."

"You must know I already have it."

She rolled her eyes but didn't frown. "Gloria. Dead sister walking." The coffee had finished brewing, so she poured two big cups. "Cream or sugar?"

"Neither." Taking the cup from her, he inhaled the steam. "My mother makes lousy coffee. So does your sister, who seems to have decided even the *smell* of caffeine can make our hooligan nephews bounce off the walls."

"Decaf's for quitters," she muttered.

Startled, Nick barked a laugh. This was no sweet little Izzie, the girl he remembered.

"I lived on coffee in Manhattan," she admitted. "It was the only way I could maintain my schedule."

He sniffed appreciatively, allowing the rich aroma to fil

his head. When combined with all the other scents permeating this room, it was making him weak with physical hunger.

Or *she* was. He honestly wasn't sure which.

"I think I would have killed for something this good even when it was one-hundred-twenty degrees in the desert."

Izzie sat on one of the other stools across from him, her cup on the counter between them. Watching him intently, with a bit of trepidation, she forecast her curiosity before the words left her mouth. "How did you make it through every day?"

What a good question—and one nobody had asked him yet. Oh, he'd been asked about the action and the things he'd seen. Asked if he'd shot anyone, killed anyone, saved anyone. Asked what he'd done to relieve the boredom, to accomplish his mission.

But nobody had asked him what it was that had held him together every single day. Not until now.

"I'm sorry, that's probably none of my business."

"It's okay. If you want to know the truth, it was *this* that held me together." He gestured around the room.

She frowned skeptically.

"I don't mean the bakery. I mean this lifestyle. Home, family, all the safe, secure stuff I grew up with that I thought would be exactly the same when I got back. Only, it wasn't."

Staring at him, Izzie revealed her thoughts in her expressive brown eyes. She understood what he meant—got it, exactly. Nick didn't look away, liking the connection even though they were separated by several feet of sweet-smelling air. Mentally, though, they were touching. Bonding. Sharing the unique brand of estrangement they had each been feeling the world they'd grown up in.

nally shook her head. "Well, obviously you have to figure out, man-cub."

He grinned, remembering what he'd said about the Jungle Book. "Yeah, well, so do you, right? You didn't get what you bargained for when you came home, did you?"

She shook her head.

"What'd you do in New York, anyway?" he asked, never having gotten the whole story. He knew she'd had a good job but had given it up to come home and help her family.

"I was…in the arts," she murmured, lifting her cup to her mouth. She blew across the surface of the coffee, sending steam curling up into the air. It colored her cheeks, already flushed a delicate pink from the heat of the yeasty kitchen. "On the stage."

An actress. The idea stunned him for a second, though it made sense. Izzie had looks and personality and a lot of self-confidence. He suspected she was amazing on stage.

"But I got hurt last winter and haven't worked since."

He lowered his cup, waiting.

A tiny frown line appeared between her eyes as she explained. "I tore my ACL in my left knee and had to have surgery. It required a lot of rehab."

"And you're on your feet working in a kitchen all day?" he asked, appalled at the idea of how much pain she had to have experienced. He knew guys who'd had those injuries during his high-school sports days. They were not fun.

"I'm better." She pointed down to the stool on which she sat. "And I work sitting down a lot."

Nick wanted to know more. Lots of things. Like what kind of life she'd led in New York and whether anyone had shared it. And what her neck tasted like. And what she planned to do once her father was well enough to come back to the bakery. And what she'd eaten today that had left her lips so ruby red. And why she was resisting something happening between them.

And when she was going to be in his bed.

But the phone interrupted before he could ask, much less get any answers. Excusing herself to answer it, she revealed her frustration with the caller with every word exchanged. Nick heard enough to understand what was going on—her part-time delivery person was calling in sick.

"I can't believe this," she muttered after she hung up the phone. "All these orders and he bails on me." Almost growling, she added, "Are the Cubs playing today? It sounded like the little bastard was at the ball park."

Fierce. He liked it.

"Don't sweat it, Iz. I'll help you out."

Blinking, she replied, "Huh?"

"I'll help you make the deliveries." Hopping off the bench, he walked over to a tall cart, laden with cardboard boxes labeled with the names of several local restaurants. "After all," he said, offering her a boyish smile over his shoulder, "what are friends for?"

FRIENDS WERE FOR going to the movies with. Sharing bad date stories with. Getting through boring reunions with. Crying over breakups with. Dieting with. Drinking with. Clubbing with.

Friends were *not* for having sex with. Or lusting over. Or inspiring lust simply by the way they handled a few heavy boxes and filled out their soft, broken-in jeans.

Nick Santori was no friend of hers. Because oh, God, she had already broken every "friend" rule in the book and she'd only agreed to his terms a few hours ago.

When they'd talked in the kitchen, he'd been friendly and that boyish smile he'd flashed her when he'd offered with the deliveries had made him seem so charm-ing. Completely the *opposite* of the brooding,

simmering hunk of male heat she'd watched through covetous
eyes at the club last weekend. It was like he was two people
in one body.

And she wanted both of them desperately.

She couldn't believe she'd thought she could handle being
merely his friend. Now, having been closed up in a delivery
van with him for the past couple of hours, she was definitely
having second thoughts.

He was being so damned *wonderful*. Not just offering to
help her, he had refused to let her lift a single box. They'd gone
to a dozen shops and restaurants, delivering cakes, pies and
pastries to some places for their dinner customers tonight, and
muffins and coffee cake to others for their breakfast crowds
tomorrow. He'd charmed her customers, and *her*. He'd even
driven, since Izzie hated dealing with the traffic. She'd sat in the
passenger seat of the bakery van, reading off the list of stops,
trying not to notice how big he was and how small the van felt
with him in it.

She also tried not to notice how wonderful he smelled.
How the sound of his low laughter rolled over her, more
warm and sultry than a summer breeze. How his short hair
curled a little behind his ear. How strong his lightly stubbled
jaw was and how thick his body was beneath his tight T-shirt.
How he warmed her from two feet away.

And how very, very much she wanted him.

Especially after the cannoli. It was the damn cannoli that
put the nail in her coffin…and the wetness in her panties.

They had an extra box. Izzie had been so wiped out from
working so many hours, both at the bakery Tuesday through
Saturday, and at the club Saturday and Sunday nights, that
she'd miscounted. She'd boxed up an extra two dozen of the
decadent ricotta-and-cream filled treats. Once they'd finished
all the deliveries, thanks mostly to Nick's strong back—oh,

heavens, that strong back—she'd noticed the extra box and realized her mistake.

So, when they'd gotten back to the bakery and parked in the small private lot behind it, she'd offered him one. He'd immediately taken her up on it, not even getting out of the van before digging in. And seeing him eat it with such visceral, sensual appreciation, was making her a quivering, shaking mess.

"God, these are amazing. No wonder they sell out every day at Santori's," he said as he licked at the creamy center of the tube-shaped pastry.

Izzie shifted in the seat. Licking. It was not a good thing to watch a man do if you wanted to have sex with him but couldn't.

He nibbled some of the flaky crust.

Nibbling. Also bad. She added it to her mental list of no-nos to watch.

Then he bit in and closed his eyes in rapturous delight. Oh, Lord. Biting—anything that put that look of intense pleasure on his face—was absolutely out of the question.

Thankfully, he finished the thing so quickly—devouring it in three bites—that she didn't have time to do something foolish, like, say, offering him her tongue to lick and her breast to nibble and her inner thigh to bite.

"You are going to let me have another one, aren't you?" he asked. Not waiting for an answer, he got out of the driver's seat and bent over to step into the back of the van. Metal racks were attached to each side of it, with an aisle down the middle. Opening the lone box remaining on one shelf, he held it toward her. "Come on, have one."

She hadn't voluntarily eaten a cannoli since tenth grade, the day after she'd split her pants while trying to do a sit-up in gym class. They'd torn with a resounding flatulent sound and she'd almost dropped out of school then and there. "Uh-uh."

He smiled, his eyes glittering in the near darkness. Dusk had fallen while they were out making the rounds, and it was now after eight o'clock. The book shop next door was also closed, their private parking spots empty, and the small lot was entirely quiet and deserted. Very private.

She really should hop out of the vehicle and go inside. Being out here, in the near-dark, alone with Nick, was not a very good idea. Of course, being inside the closed shop, in the light, alone with Nick, probably wouldn't be much safer.

"One little taste. How can you tell how good you are at doing it if you never give it a try?"

Nearly choking, she repeated, "How good I am at *doing* it?"

"You know. Making them."

Yeah. Sure. That's what she'd thought he meant.

A small smile continued to play on those incredible lips of his as he watched her, as if he knew what she'd been thinking. And had intentionally put those thoughts into her head.

Get out. Now.

But she didn't reach for the door handle. Instead, like a kid lured by the ice cream man, she ducked into the back of the van with him. There wasn't room to stand, but Nick had already sat down on the carpeted floor. One leg was sprawled out in front of him, the other bent and upraised. He was carefully picking his way through the open box of pastries, as if searching for just the right one to satisfy his craving.

Izzie sat down across from him, cross-legged, wondering whether the temperature in the van had just gone up forty degrees or if it was her imagination. Considering it was a breezy summer evening and the front windows were open, she somehow doubted the air had gotten hotter...only *she* had. In fact, being this close to Nick was setting her on fire.

"You going to let me tempt you with one?" he asked, still looking down at the box, not at her.

They did look good. *So* good. "I really shouldn't."

"Just a taste," he whispered. Not waiting for her to answer, he lifted one out, then put the box back on the shelf. He scooted forward...close, so close she felt his heat wash over her and his warm, masculine scent fill her lungs. He lifted one of his legs over her crossed ones, until her right knee brushed his hot, jean-covered butt.

She didn't move. Not one inch.

"Won't you have one little lick?" he murmured, lifting the cannoli to her lips.

Staring at it in his hands—the flesh-colored cookie, the pale creamy cheese oozing from the end—she suddenly realized just how phallic the thing looked. Her mouth flooded with hunger—she wanted to lick, to taste, to devour.

Not the pastry. *Him.*

Almost whimpering, she lowered her mouth to it, scraping her tongue along the flaky crust, brushing his finger as she did. He shifted a little in response, as if no longer comfortable sitting the way he had been. The way they were sitting, she quickly realized why.

He was rock hard, his erection thick and long against her leg. She almost drew her legs together, the pressure in her sex demanding relief.

Izzie could hardly think or breathe. Unable to resist, she moved her leg a little, rubbing it against him, and got a low groan in response.

"Taste, Izzie."

She tasted. Imagining it was him she was sampling, she nibbled at the filling, brushing her lips against it.

She didn't need to invite Nick to share it. He was already there, kissing the corner of her mouth, his tongue flicking out to clean some of the sweetness off her lips. "Good," he whispered.

Oh, *very* good.

She licked again, dipping her tongue inside the cookie shell for a deeper taste. Nick tasted deeper, too. He covered her lips with his, stealing some of the cream right out of her mouth, their tongues tangling over it for a long, delicious moment.

"Get your own," she whispered with a soft laugh when he pulled away to offer her another lick.

"I'd rather have yours," he murmured, moving his mouth to her cheek, then lower. He nibbled her jaw, scraping his lips along it until he could nuzzle the sensitive spot just below her ear. "Actually, I'd rather have *you*."

His words washed over her, echoing in her head. With his warm breaths on her neck, his mouth on her skin, his hard body radiating heat just inches from her own, she couldn't remember a single reason why she shouldn't have him.

"I noticed." She shifted back far enough to uncross her legs. Without thinking or considering, she draped them over his thighs, scooting close—so close—that that thick ridge in his jeans pressed against the damp seam of hers.

He arched forward reflexively, grinding against her, and Izzie gasped. Moisture flooded her and her sex swelled almost painfully against her clothes. Her clit felt as if it had doubled in size and she bucked into him, needing to come so badly she could almost taste it.

"More?" he asked.

She arched harder. She definitely wanted more.

He lifted the cannoli. She shook her head, then let it fall back. She wanted to *be* the dessert now. Right or wrong, stupid or not, she wanted Nick Santori too much to resist him again.

When they stepped out of the van, the real world would return. He'd still be the great neighborhood guy she couldn't publicly date. But for now—oh, for now—she wanted him desperately, with a longing that had built in her for more than a decade. "Have me, Nick," she whispered, saying yes to the question he hadn't quite asked.

He made a low sound that might have been unrestrained—want or might have been triumph. Honestly, Izzie didn't care. Especially when he nibbled her earlobe, then worked his way down her neck. "Mmm, you taste like sugar and almonds." He kissed his way down to her collarbone, lightly biting her nape, and she shivered.

Never taking his mouth off her, he reached up and pulled her ponytail holder off. Her thick hair fell around his hand and he twined it through his fingers. Cupping her head and supporting her, he pushed her back a little so he could have better access to her neck.

When she felt the cool wetness touch the hollow of her throat, she gasped. The ricotta filling felt good against her heated skin. When Nick licked it off, it felt amazing.

Dropping back to support herself on her elbows, she watched through heavy-lidded eyes as Nick began slipping open the buttons of her sleeveless blouse. After every button was freed and another bit of skin revealed, he dabbed filling on her. Soon there was a trail of dots from her throat, down her chest, in the middle of her cleavage, and all the way down to her belly.

He wasn't tasting them. Not yet. She twisted and arched up, desperate for him to, but he ignored her silent plea.

Once he tugged the top free of her jeans, it gaped open. Shrugging, she let it fall off her shoulders, then watched him devour her with his eyes. His breaths grew audibly choppy as he saw the way her breasts overflowed her skimpy bra. Bent back as she was, she could barely keep the thing in place, and one nipple was actually peeping freely above the lace.

"Beautiful," he muttered hoarsely. He lifted the pastry and dabbed some of the filling on her nipple.

This time he didn't move on. He stopped for a taste.

"Oh, God," she groaned as Nick bent over and covered her nipple with his mouth, licking and sucking at the cheesy filling. He lapped up every bit, pushing her bra all the way down so he'd have complete access to her breast.

"You are glorious," he said as he lifted a hand to cup her. His fingers were dark and strong against her pale skin, and she literally overflowed his hand. "You hide a lot behind that apron you usually wear."

She hid a lot more behind the mask she sometimes wore. The thought flashed through her head, but she thrust it aside. This was not the time to be thinking about her alter-ego…or what Nick might do if he ever found out they were one and the same.

Now was for savoring. Indulging.

Reaching for the clasp of her bra, he unfastened it and pulled it off, catching her other breast as it spilled free. Scooping out a large fingerful of filling, complete with tiny chocolate chips, he smeared it all over the taut tip, then devoured it as completely as he had the other side.

Her legs clenched, heat shooting from her wet nipples down her body, straight between her legs. She jerked up, dying to be freed of her jeans. "I need…"

"I know," he whispered. He dropped his mouth to hers for a deep kiss that shut her up and zapped her brain. He tasted sweet and hot and decadent.

Izzie worked at Nick's shirt as they kissed, pulling away so she could tug it up and off him. Then she sagged back, staring in disbelief at the perfection that was his body.

In his clothes, he was an incredibly well-built man.

Out of them he almost defied description.

He was rock hard, not an ounce of excess on him, with a massive chest and thickly muscled shoulders. His huge arms rippled as he moved, highlighting a sizeable tattoo—a Marine Corps logo. Just the perfect amount of dark, curly hair emphasized the breadth of him before narrowing down to his waist and hips, where he was incredibly lean.

"I'm not finished my dessert yet," he muttered when she reached for his waistband.

He tossed the tiny bit of cannoli away and grabbed another one out of the box. Taking her hand, he pushed her arm over her head until she had to lie flat on the floor. Then he worked his way down her body, kissing, nibbling and licking off all those spots of cream he'd deposited on her earlier.

"It tastes sweeter now," he said when he dipped his tongue into her belly button and swirled it there. "It just needed one more ingredient to make it absolutely addictive."

Her. It needed her.

And she needed *him*.

His hands. His mouth—oh, heavens, his mouth. His amazing body. And that big, hard erection she could feel pressing against her leg as he slid farther down her body.

He didn't even move his mouth off her as he undid her pants and pushed them down her hips. Izzie lifted up to help him…and unintentionally offered herself to him *much* more intimately.

He was *on* her immediately.

"Nick!" She gasped and panted when he covered the front of her tiny panties with his mouth, breathing through the fabric, sending warm tendrils of pleasure right where she needed them most. "Please."

"I bet this will taste even sweeter," he whispered as he tugged the satin away.

Izzie barely breathed as he pushed her clothes down and off, until she lay naked beneath him. And she absolutely flew out of her skin when he took the new tube-shaped pastry and smeared one creamy end of it through her curls and across her sex.

"Oh," she groaned.

He pushed at her inner thighs and Izzie parted her legs, giving him the access he'd silently demanded. When he took a first, slow lick at the filling, thick and heavy in her curls, she came up off the floor.

"Oh, definitely sweeter," he said. He moved farther down, sliding his tongue over every inch of her, eating every drop of sticky cream as if it was the best thing he'd ever tasted.

Izzie was a quivering mess, shaking, panting, bucking. Desperate for more, she didn't know whether to beg or remain still for fear he'd get distracted from what he was doing.

He didn't get distracted. And before she knew what he was up to, she felt the flaky shell of the cookie scraping across her clit. She cried out again, feeling the climax build inside her. When he licked at her again, working her clit with his tongue and his lips—lathing, then sucking—she finally got what she'd been waiting for. Pleasure erupted through her, rocking her hips, sending a pulse of heat through her.

Nick didn't even pause, beyond muttering a soft "Yes," in acknowledgement of her orgasm. He just kept going, sliding the cannoli further…following it with his tongue. Until finally he began working the delicacy between her drenched lips.

"You're not…you can't…" she gasped.

But he did and he was. He slid the tip of it into her wet crevice—sending a cacophony of sensations rushing through her. The roughness of the delicate shell, the smoothness of the filling, she'd never felt anything like it. It was wicked—erotic. A little outrageous.

And she loved it. "Nick…"

"I'm not quite finished with dessert. Though I'm just about full," he murmured.

She only wished she were.

She didn't get too impatient, however, because she was too anxious to see what this supposedly "nice neighborhood guy" would dare next.

He wanted to keep playing, obviously. He slowly sunk the treat deeper, as far as he could, then gently tugged it out. He did it again, leaving Izzie to wonder how long it would take before the shell broke and the oozy cream filled her.

Finally, when she thought she'd die of the wild wantonness of it, he started working it out with his teeth, rather than his fingers. He nibbled off little pieces as it came out of her, whispering sweet words about how good it tasted…how good *she* tasted. How juicy and creamy she was.

His words were almost as arousing as his touch.

"Gotta make sure I got every drop," he whispered once the last of the cookie was gone. And he did, plunging his tongue into her and stroking—in and out—until she lost her mind and came again.

She threw her head back, closing her eyes, giving herself over to the rocking of her body, which seemed to go on forever. When it had finally eased up, and she opened her eyes again, it was to find Nick over her.

She lifted her legs, realizing his were bare. His lean hips brushed her inner thighs, and his thick cock lay heavy on her pelvis.

Whimpering, she looked down. "Let me see you."

"Feel me," he whispered, burying his face in her neck. He slid up and down, his cock separating the slick lips of her sex, hitting her clit at the perfect angle.

"See *and* feel," she insisted, sliding her arm between their bodies to reach for him.

She caught his erection in her hand, shocked at how big and hot it was. He'd already sheathed himself with a condom, but she could feel his pounding pulse through the rubber.

"You're bigger than that cookie," she said, nibbling on her lip as she acknowledged just how much Nick Santori had been hiding beneath his clothes.

He groaned and dipped closer, sliding in her a little at a time. "You're sweeter than that cookie." He pushed a bit more, easing into her with incredible restraint. "And you are definitely creamy enough to handle me."

She didn't doubt it. He'd aroused her half out of her mind and right now, she wanted him plunging to the hilt inside her. Grabbing his hips, she dug her nails into his butt and arched up for him. "Take me, Nick. Fill me up."

He seemed to forget about restraint because he did exactly what she asked, plunging hard and deep until Izzie howled at how good it felt.

He stretched her, embedded himself in her, then drew out and plunged again. "Oh, my God," she groaned. "This is amazing."

Better than amazing. It was absolute perfection. Worth every one of the years she'd waited for it.

Thrusting up, Izzie took what he gave and demanded even more. When she became too frenzied, he slowed the pace, showing so much control she wanted to sob in frustration. But he wouldn't relent, taunting her with slow, deep strokes and teasing half-ones. He kissed her so often and so deeply she wasn't sure she'd remember how to breathe when she wasn't sharing the breath from his lungs.

Finally, though, she heard the tiny groans he couldn't contain. His hips thrust harder, more frantically, and she wrung as much as she could out of every stroke.

"I can't…oh, Izzie…"

"Do it," she ordered, feeling another climax building in her from the friction of their locked bodies. "I'll come with you."

That seemed to satisfy him—that he had her permission—and he finally lost his head and gave her the deep, pounding thrusts they both needed. Again. And again. Until he threw his head back and shouted as he reached his climax.

She found hers a second later and wrapped her legs tightly around him to ride it out.

As if knowing the floor was hard against her back, Nick scooped her in his arms and lay down, dragging her on top of him. They were both panting, gasping for air, and he kissed her temple, smoothing her hair away from her sweaty face.

"Izzie? I have to tell you something." His words were rushed. Choppy.

"Yes?"

Closing his eyes, he dropped his head back onto the floor. "I'm going to call you Cookie until the day I die."

6

FUNNY. Nick had once thought that having absolutely mind-blowing sex with a woman would make her friendlier. At least more approachable.

No. Uh-uh. Not Izzie Natale. Because within *minutes* of their incredible lovemaking in the back of the delivery van, she was back to freezing him out, trying to act like nothing had changed between them.

After sex like that, he'd kind of expected to be invited in for a cup of coffee…if not dessert. Oh, man, he was *never* going to look at a cannoli the same way again.

But she hadn't invited him in. Hadn't answered him when he'd asked if she wanted to go get a bite to eat somewhere. And over the next couple of days, hadn't returned his calls. Hadn't even met his eye in the past couple of days.

The woman was killing him, she really was.

When he'd finally confronted her on the sidewalk in front of the bakery Friday afternoon, she'd erupted. "It was a one time thing, Nick. It was fabulous, I loved it, but it's not going to happen again. Because if it does, then you're going to be *more* of a pain about wanting me to go get a pizza with you, or go visit the folks, and then the whole neighborhood will be congratulating poor little Izzie for finally landing her man."

She'd stalked inside without saying another word. She hadn't needed to. He got the message, loud and clear. She'd loved the sex, she just didn't want all the stuff that went with having a sexual relationship. Or any relationship whatsoever.

He thought about proposing that they just set up a weekly sex-buddy meeting in the parked van behind her shop, suspecting he could have her on those terms if he wanted her.

He didn't want her on those terms.

"Hell, admit it, you want her on any terms," he muttered aloud as he walked out the back door of Santori's that night. He hadn't even realized anyone else was there until he saw his brother, Joe, who'd just parked his pickup in one of the empty spots in the alley. Fortunately, Joe hadn't heard Nick talking to himself and so wasn't dialing for the rubber-walled wagon.

"Hey, where you off to?" Joe asked as he hopped out and pocketed his keys. "I was going to take you up on that pitcher you owe me."

"I'm not very good company right now," he admitted.

Joe, who was the best-natured of all of the Santori kids, threw his arm around Nick's shoulders. "Then what better time to share a beer with your brother?"

He had a point.

"Okay. But not here," he said, looking back at the closed door to the kitchen. "I really need someplace quiet."

Joe's smile faded and he immediately appeared concerned. "Everything okay? Is there a problem?"

"No problem. Just a case of family overdose."

"I hear ya. Come on, let's go across the street."

Following Joe into a neighborhood bar on the corner, Nick ordered a couple of beers and paid the tab. If Mark had been sitting across from him, Nick knew he'd be getting one-liners aimed at making him say what was on his mind. Lucas would be doing his prosecutor inquisition. Tony would throw his oldest-brother weight around and try to browbeat him into talking. Lottie would jabber so much Nick would say anything to get her to shut up.

Joe just watched. Listened. Waited.

"Thanks again for pointing me toward the job," Nick finally said, filling the silence. The bar was pretty empty—it was too early for the weekend regulars, who'd be drifting in for a long night of drinking and darts before too long.

"How's that going?"

"Pretty well. I've only worked the past two weekends but the money's good."

"You still haven't told the rest of the family?"

Nick shook his head. "Just Mark."

Joe nodded. "Probably just as well. I know Pop and Tony are talking nonstop about you coming in on the business."

Yeah, they had been to him, too. Nick couldn't prevent a quick frown. Because managing a pizzeria was not the way he saw himself spending the next six months, much less the rest of his life.

"It's okay, Nick. Nobody can force you to do anything you don't want to do."

"Guilt goes a long way," he muttered.

"Don't I know it. But guilt didn't stop you from enlisting. It didn't stop me from picking up a hammer and learning construction. Didn't stop Mark from strapping on a gun or Lottie from…well, from doing whatever it is Lottie does."

"Like marrying a man who killed someone?" Nick asked dryly, still not having gotten used to the idea that his new brother-in-law, Simon, had killed a woman, even if in self-defense.

"Let's not go there," Joe said with a sigh. "She's happy, and he's crazy about her."

True. Lottie and Simon's recent marriage had contributed to the 95 percent marital success rate in the Santori family.

"The point is, you can live your life the way you want to live it, and nobody will try to stop you." As if realizing he'd left Nick with one major argument, he added, "Except for Mama's crying. Which we're all used to and you can get past. You just need to figure out what you want to do, and go after it."

Good idea. And lately, Nick *had* been figuring out what he wanted to do, especially since he'd been working at the club. "An old buddy of mine from the service is putting something together with a couple of the other guys. They're talking about opening up a protection business."

"Professional bodyguard?" Joe asked, looking surprised.

"I have the military background for it and I like what I'm doing at the club."

Joe smiled. "Especially when the people you're guarding are very easy on the eyes."

"Like you'd *ever* look at another woman."

The twinkle in his brother's eyes confirmed that. "Hey, I'm not *you*. You're the single one. Have you met anybody, uh… interesting?"

Nick felt heat rise up his neck. Because that was a loaded question. He had definitely felt interest in the Crimson Rose. But now that he'd had Izzie—tasted her, consumed her, made love to her—he knew he didn't want any other woman. But he couldn't very well explain that to Joe…without hinting about what had happened with Izzie. She'd never forgive him if that little tidbit became common knowledge. "I guess."

"Their star performer?" Joe sipped his beer. "I hear she's one-of-a-kind."

Clearing his throat, Nick sprawled back in the booth. "She is that."

"Have there been any more problems with her?" Joe sounded only casually interested, but Nick's guard immediately went up.

"Problems?"

"Threats, freaks trying to grab her?"

Nick sat up straight. "No. What are you talking about?"

"Didn't Harry even tell you why he hired you?"

He had, but only in the most general terms. Nick didn't realize Rose had actually been threatened. "What do you know?"

"Just what the guys were whispering about when we were working at the club. That there had been a few incidents that had disturbed Harry and scared the dancers. Especially the featured one."

Harry Black had said almost nothing about any specific threats. Rose had said even less. Why would they hire him and then tie his hands by not giving him all the information he needed to do his job? He just didn't understand it. "Maybe whoever was causing the problems got caught and the threat has been eliminated," he murmured, speculating out loud. "Because I haven't gotten any kind of specific heads up."

Joe kept his eyes on his beer, for some reason not looking Nick in the eye. Which made him wonder about his brother's interest in the stripper.

He immediately discounted any suspicion that Joe was interested in the woman for himself. He was married to the sexiest kindergarten teacher ever born, and he adored her and their baby daughter. Besides, of all the Santoris—who'd been raised to equate cheating with a mortal sin—Joe was the very last one who'd ever stray.

"Well, if I were you, I'd stick close to the featured attraction at Leather and Lace. I think she might be more of a target than she or Harry would like to admit." Shaking his head, Joe added, "There are some really sick guys out there who like stalking vulnerable women."

Suddenly feeling on edge, Nick nodded, anxious to get to the club and question Harry Black. He didn't particularly

want to confront Rose—not alone, anyway—but one thing
was sure. He had been hired to do a job: protect her. It was
about time he stop letting his physical response to the woman
interfere with doing that job.

And it was well past time for him to stop letting his feelings
for Izzie Natale consume so much of his attention that he
didn't even *realize* a stalker might be threatening someone
he'd been hired to protect.

That had to end. Starting right now.

So it looked like Izzie was finally going to get what she
wanted. Him…out of her life.

"HEY, SOMEBODY SENT you flowers."

Izzie hesitated, her hand on the doorknob of her dressing
room. One of the other dancers, a young blonde with a sweet
smile and a killer body, approached her. "They were waiting
on the stoop at the back entrance when I got here. Had your
name on the envelope. I put them in your dressing room."

Izzie's first reaction was a tiny little thrill as the image of
Nick's handsome face filled her mind. But it quickly dissi-
pated. Nick had no idea she worked with him every Saturday
and Sunday night.

Damn good thing. Because if he found out now, after she'd
had such incredible sex with him, he was going be mad. More
than mad—irate. Especially because of how insistent she'd
been that it was a one-shot deal.

Boy did she wish it didn't have to be a one-shot deal. She
still got shaky and shivery and weak and wet thinking of that
amazing interlude in the van. It had been the most intensely
sensual experience of her life.

But not to be repeated. Never.

Not as Izzie. Not even as the Crimson Rose. Because now
that he'd had her naked in his arms, it was all too possible that

he'd recognize her as Rose. Dancing and interacting with him at work was going to be difficult enough. If she let him get close—the way she'd invited him to that night in her dressing room—there was no way she'd be able to keep her secret.

So tell him the truth.

The idea had merit and Izzie knew it. Part of her truly wanted to—it wasn't easy maintaining a double life with no one to talk to about it. He'd listen—she knew he would. And she even suspected he wouldn't judge her about what she was doing. Given the things he'd said about feeling so hemmed in by his own family and their expectations, she thought he might even understand. A little.

But telling him—bringing him in to her alternate life—would mean involving him deeper in her real one. Each secret shared would be another rope tied to her body, holding her down, dragging her back into the world she'd fought so hard to escape.

If he knew she was Rose, there would be no reason they couldn't get more involved, at least at work. That, however—a secret, sordid affair conducted in dressing rooms and closets at Leather and Lace—wouldn't be enough for him. She knew it down to her very soul. He'd insinuate himself in her daily life, start tangling her in the ropes of a relationship, make her fall for him even harder...so he would be even harder to leave.

No. She could not tell him.

"Rose? Didja hear me?"

Realizing the other dancer was waiting expectantly for her reaction to the flowers, Izzie nodded. "Yes, thanks Leah."

"Not a problem. It was pick 'em up or trip over 'em," she said with a cheery smile. Without the stage makeup and the sequins, the young woman looked so fresh-faced and wholesome an average set of parents would have asked her to babysit.

She'd been the first of the dancers to befriend Izzie when she'd first taken the job at Leather and Lace. The others had been slower to warm up, especially Harry's wife, Delilah, who'd been the featured dancer up until a couple of years ago when she married her boss. Now she served as a sort of warden to the others…and hadn't liked that Izzie wasn't interested in her rules and regulations. She *especially* hadn't liked that she couldn't get her husband to order Izzie to listen to her…and that the Crimson Rose had become hugely popular.

The rest of them had all come around, though, especially since they had all started bringing home more money every weekend that she performed.

"How did you get into this, Leah?" she asked.

The girl shrugged. "Typical story. My parents divorced, father split out west somewhere. Mom remarried an asshole who tried to touch me after she'd passed out on their wedding night."

Izzie instinctively reached out and put her hand on the other woman's shoulder. "I'm sorry."

"Hey, I survived. Stabbed him in the wrist with a fork and took off. Never looked back."

"Do you…" she didn't know how to proceed without seeming judgmental. It just seemed so sad to think of this young woman making this, dancing at Leather and Lace, her only career goal. For Izzie, it was a part-time thrill to stay in shape and save her sanity. Some of the women here, however, saw no other future for themselves.

"What?"

"Do you think you'll do something else when you get tired of this?"

Leah nodded, her blond curls bouncing around her pretty, heart-shaped face. "I got my GED last year and I'm taking college classes. I'm planning to be a nurse."

"Good for you."

Hearing footsteps upstairs, Izzie glanced at her watch. It was only six—a couple of hours before her first number. Usually Nick showed up later than this. But hearing the deep, male voice from upstairs, she immediately stiffened.

"That's our sex-on-a-stick bodyguard I hear up there."

"Damn," Izzie muttered, immediately whirling around. "Stall him if he comes down the stairs, okay?"

"You still playing the 'nobody can see me' game with him?"

Izzie nodded. "I *don't* want him to see me. Please help me."

The woman offered her a big smile. "You got it…in exchange for one of those flowers your secret admirer sent you."

"I'll do you one better," Izzie said as she pushed open her dressing room door. She grabbed the vase and thrust the bouquet at the young woman. "You can have all of them. Just don't let him near my door."

Either Leah was true to her word, or else Nick hadn't yet ventured downstairs. Whatever the case Izzie had privacy for the next twenty minutes. Long enough to get her hair extensions clipped in place and put her mask on. Only after she'd yanked it into position did she realize she'd forgotten her false eyelashes.

"Damn Harry for not giving me a lock," she muttered, glancing at the closed door. If she took the mask off to put her lashes on, she risked Nick walking in on her. No, he hadn't exactly gone out of his way to be alone with her as the Crimson Rose, but she couldn't count on her luck lasting forever.

Frowning at her reflection, she did a quick evaluation, wondering if she really needed the lashes. Her eyes had disappeared. She looked like the Marquis de Sade.

"Need the lashes," she muttered.

She'd been putting false lashes on her eyelids for years, she could probably do it…well, not blindfolded, but *masked*.

"Sure," she whispered as she bent toward the mirror. Grabbing one lash, she dabbed special glue on it, then carefully reached into the eyehole of her mask and applied it.

"One down," she said as she blinked rapidly, pretty proud of herself.

The second one was a little trickier, mainly because it was hard to see out of the first heavily lashed eye. But she managed it. And a moment later, when she heard voices in the hall, she was very glad she hadn't taken the chance and removed the mask.

"Hey, Nick, how's it shakin' baby?" a woman's voice said. Loudly.

Bless you, Leah.

"I need to talk to Rose." He cleared his throat. "I mean, I need to talk to all of you, *and* Rose."

Huh. Still too chicken to see her alone.

She quickly squelched the thought. That man had the most incredible, powerful body she'd ever seen in her life. He was afraid of nothing.

Besides, refusing to see her alone was exactly what she needed him to do. Even if it wasn't what she *wanted* him to do.

Tightening the sash on her robe, she reached for the doorknob and opened the door. Nick's immediately looked over, stiffening when he saw her there.

He *so* didn't want to be attracted to her, his expression said it all. Knowing he didn't want anyone else made Izzie, the baker he'd made such incredible love to a few days ago, amazingly happy.

"I need to talk to you, and all the other girls, in the green-room for a few minutes," he said. Without waiting to see if she was coming, he spun around and walked toward it.

Shrugging, Leah followed. So did Izzie. Once they were

inside, Izzie realized all the other dancers—nine or ten of them—were already present, including Delilah with her two-foot-tall pile of red hair on top of her head and three inches of makeup on her face.

In varying states of undress, all the other dancers practically licked their lips when Nick walked into the room. She couldn't blame them. In his tough/bodyguard mode, he looked incredibly hot. Gone was any trace of the sweetheart who'd helped her deliver baked goods. Or the sensual lover who'd given her more orgasms in one lovemaking session than she'd had in entire previous relationships.

In their place was a frowning—scowling almost—man, dressed all in black, looking not only menacing but dangerous. And absolutely delicious.

"I asked you all in here to discuss your security."

"Let's discuss your ass," one of the dancers cracked.

"I'd rather talk about his shoulders."

"I vote for his co…"

"Ladies," another voice said as Harry entered the room. Rolling his eyes, he gave Nick an apologetic look. "Please go ahead, Nick."

Nick got right back on track, hitting them all over the head with the need for tighter security around the place. Though he was talking to everyone, he looked at Izzie so often, she knew she was the one on his mind.

There wasn't any reason to single her out. Well, not *much* reason. Yes, she'd had a few persistent customers. One guy had lunged at her on the stage a few weeks back. Another had burst into her dressing room. And there'd been a few parking-lot lurkers who'd been chased away by one of the bouncers, Bernie, who'd been watching out for her since her first night. Long before Nick had come on the scene.

In this job, she'd expect nothing else. But Nick was relentless in his lecturing. He kept on about how they all needed to look out for one another, report anything suspicious. Yadda yadda. Izzie zoned out somewhere between "drive a different route home from work every night" and "have a buddy when you go to the restroom."

That one did spark an "I'll be your bathroom buddy, Nick," from one of the girls, a glare from Delilah and another long-suffering sigh from Harry.

Finally, though, the meeting broke up and the other dancers raced to finish getting ready. Izzie quickly ducked out of the room, hoping Nick wouldn't see her. She'd gotten about ten steps from her dressing room when she realized he'd followed.

"Rose, wait a minute."

She froze, but didn't turn around.

"I'm particularly concerned about you. The 'who's behind the mask' element puts you at higher risk. Some whackjob might decide to try to find out for himself."

She glanced over her shoulder. "Thanks for the warning."
Now go away.

Before she could look away again, she saw a dark frown pull at Nick's handsome face. "What in the hell?" he muttered, staring at her face.

Fearing he'd recognized her, she quickly lifted her hands to ensure her mask was still in place. It felt okay—but Nick was still staring at her, blinking in confusion.

"What?" she snapped. Remembering at the last minute that she needed to lower her voice to the sultry whisper he'd grown familiar with, she rephrased. "Is something wrong?"

He reached for her. Izzie immediately lurched back, almost tripping over her own feet. If she hadn't backed herself up against the wall, she would have.

"Careful," he muttered, still frowning. "It wouldn't look

good on my résumé if somebody I'm supposed to be guarding trips and breaks her neck."

Right. He needed to guard her.

Not look at her. Not watch her. Not batter at her defenses with every flex of that body, every whiff of his spicy scent that filled her head whenever he was near.

God, this was hard. So much harder than it had been last weekend, when she hadn't *had* him. When she didn't know what he was capable of.

"You have something on your..., it's ..."

Shrugging uncomfortably, he reached for her again. This time, she stayed still. At least until he yanked at her eyelashes hard enough to jerk her eyelid off her face. "Ouch!" she yelped, slapping his hand away.

His hand was still stuck to the lashes so when she smacked him, she only ended up hurting herself more. As his hand flew away, he took the lashes with him, ripping them off her lid.

"I thought it was a bug," he said with an uncomfortable grimace.

She yanked her false eyelashes out of his fingers. "A *bug?* You thought I had a bug on my face?"

"It's not like you'd be able to tell if you did with that stupid mask on. Why do you wear it when you're not on stage, anyway?"

Oh, boy. A question she definitely couldn't answer.

"You don't have to keep up this mysterious woman act for the staff, do you? So why not take it off and take a deep breath?" Swiping a frustrated hand through his short, spiky hair, he added, "Or at least put your damn false eyelashes on more securely?"

She almost growled in annoyance. *He* was the reason she'd had to put the lashes on through the eyehole in the mask. "I want a lock on my dressing room door," she whispered harshly.

He glanced at the knob. "You don't have one?"

"No." Thinking quickly, she added, "And that's one reason I keep the mask on all the time. I have no place to go for complete privacy. A reporter who did an article on the club a few weeks ago came creeping around down here one day, trying to get a picture of the real me."

Nick moved in close, towering over her, burning her with his heat. Putting his hands on the wall on either side of her, he trapped her in. "Who is he?"

Izzie nibbled her lip, trying with every ounce of her strength not to throw her arms around his shoulders and her legs around his waist. Or to shove him away so he'd stop looking searchingly at her, seeing her eyes…how could he not recognize her eyes? How could he be this close and not know the smell of her body?

It was good that he didn't, she knew that. But it was also starting to tick her off.

"Just some reporter," she murmured.

"Have you had any problems with him since?"

"No, he hasn't been around since the story came out. Would you relax?"

"You tell me if you see him." Then, staring hard at her, he slowly pulled back, releasing her from the prison of his arms. An odd look appeared on his face, as if he'd suddenly realized just how close they'd been and wasn't happy at himself for it. Clearing his throat, he added, "I'm sorry I hurt your eye."

"It's all right." Slipping away from him, she headed again to her door, relieved to have escaped his scrutiny. Good thing he'd let her go, because the longer he stayed so close to her, the more angry she was going to get that he didn't know her.

Especially because a mask would never prevent *her* from knowing *him*.

Huh. Men. So painfully unobservant.

"I hope you're taking me seriously," he said, that gruff, no-nonsense tone returning to his voice, his apology obviously done.

"I am, I am." She practically bit the words out from between her clenched teeth, ready to smack him if he didn't shut up and let her go get herself back under control. And fix her eyelashes.

"No more running out to your car alone to get something you forgot."

"Yes, your majesty."

"No more coming back upstairs and mingling close to closing time."

She seldom did that, anyway. Whirling around, she offered him a sharp salute, and snapped, "Got it, chief." Then, determined not to listen to another word, spun on her heel and strode into her dressing room, slamming the door shut behind her.

It was only after she'd shut him out that Izzie realized how *stupid* she'd just been. Nick had annoyed her so much— —both because of his overbearing protective bodyguard schtick and his inability to see what was right in front of his face—that she'd completely forgotten her role in this. The role she played as the Crimson Rose.

Because during those last three words, when anger had overtaken common sense, she'd forgotten to speak in her sexy, husky voice.

She'd been pure, 100 percent Izzie.

7

Leather and Lace employed a few burly bouncers to watch the doors and to stand in the back of the crowd during the show. Their presence was mainly to inspire intimidation to keep the audience on its best behavior. And they did their job well, especially the tallest one, Bernie, whose beefy build concealed a guy with a deep belly laugh and a good sense of humor.

Nick, however, wasn't technically one of them. His job involved more than rousting out rowdy drinkers or breaking up any fights. He was there to make sure nobody touched the dancers. Especially Rose. And the bouncers were his backup.

He typically moved around during the performances—sometimes in the audience, sometimes backstage, sometimes downstairs. He kept a low profile, his eyes always scanning the crowd, looking for the first sign of trouble.

Tonight, he was standing close to the dance floor, in a shadowy corner just left of the stage. He couldn't say why. It wasn't as if he expected anyone in the front row to leap up and try to grab Rose or one of the others. Yes, it'd happened. But usually not until at least the second set, late in the night, when the patrons had consumed more than a few fifteen dollar shots of top-shelf whiskey. And when they'd forgotten how big the bouncers were or how stupid they were going to feel having to call their wives to get bailed out of jail.

Tonight, Nick was close to the stage because he wanted to watch *her*.

Something had happened earlier, something that was still driving him crazy. Oh, she drove him crazy in any number of ways, already—mainly because of that blatant sexuality oozing off the woman. But this didn't have anything to do with her attractiveness, or Nick's reaction to it.

It was something else. Something he couldn't define. Ever since he and Rose had exchanged words outside her dressing room, a voice had been whispering in his head that there was something he wasn't seeing. Some truth he had overlooked.

He had replayed their entire conversation, thinking about every word, wondering what had seemed so *off* with it. Aside from her being such a smart-ass about the self-protection tips he'd asked her to follow, they hadn't been confrontational. Hadn't been unpleasant in any way, other than when he'd accidentally almost ripped her eyelid off.

So why are you so tense?

Good question. He was wound as tight as a ball of rubber bands, his jaw flexing, his hands clenching. His heart wasn't maintaining its usual pace, it was rushed, as if adrenaline had flooded his body.

When they introduced her, something *did* flood his body. Heated awareness. Maybe adrenaline, too.

She didn't spot him when she started, and from here Nick had a perfect view of every move she made. She was using the pole tonight, taking advantage of it to showcase her strength and flexibility. Not to mention inviting every man in the audience to imagine being the one she was writhing against, the one cupped between her incredibly long legs.

He tensed, then thrust away the flash of jealousy. It was none of his business what Rose did—in her professional life or in her personal one.

She'd begun removing her petals now, they fluttered onto the stage, one even wafting so close it was only about a foot away from Nick's corner position. Something made him step closer, to reach for it. Whether to give it back to her, or to save it as a souvenir, he couldn't say. Fingering it lightly, he stuck it in his pocket and kept watching.

When this close, he had a very good view of the Crimson Rose…a view of a trim waist made for his hands. Of supple legs he could almost feel wrapped around his hips. Of slender fingers that had tangled easily in his hair. A delicate throat for nibbling. Lush round breasts for cupping. And when she removed the petals covering those breasts, his mouth flooded at the image of sucking on those dark, pebbled nipples.

Every bit of her was familiar…to his eyes, and to the rest of his body. He knew what it would be like to taste her, to touch her, to hear her soft little moans of pleasure.

To hear her….

Her voice. That *voice.* That body.

"Oh, my God," he whispered, certain he'd lost his mind but unable to chase the thought away. Because as he watched the performer disappear behind the curtain after her dance, he saw a face behind that mask. A face he saw in his dreams every night.

Izzie's face.

"It can't be," he mumbled, staggering back into the shadow. He hit the wall in the corner and slid down it, bending over so his hands landed on his knees. Sucking in a few deep breaths, he kept his head down, thinking over everything he knew about Izzie Natale. And about the Crimson Rose.

She'd taken dance lessons throughout her childhood, he remembered that. She'd gone to New York to become a performer. On the stage. She hadn't exactly said she'd been an actress.

My God, had she been a stripper at some high end Manhattan club? And when she'd been forced to return to Chicago after her father's stroke, had she taken up the same profession here—wearing a mask so she wouldn't possibly be recognized?

Their bodies were so alike— how could he not have seen it before? Then again, he had never seen Izzie naked before, until two nights ago, so he couldn't possibly have known that her legs were as long and supple as a dancer's. That her hips were full enough to make a man hard just at the thought of getting his hands on them. That her breasts were big, high and inviting.

She'd hidden a lot behind the apron. So much that he hadn't registered that Izzie and Rose were the same height, had the same builds. Or that their hair was close in color—the length of Rose's obviously caused by some kind of hairpiece or wig.

Now it registered. But it still seemed impossible. Absolutely unbelievable that cute little Izzie, Gloria's baby sister...the girl who'd crushed the cookies for God's sake...was the woman driving men all over Chicago insane with lust.

Including him. *Especially* him.

At that moment, he knew it was true. He'd been reacting to Rose and to Izzie the very same way from the moment he'd seen each of them. With pure, undiluted want based on absolutely nothing but instinct and chemistry.

They were the same. His body had known that immediately. His brain had finally caught up.

Somehow, he managed to stay on the sidelines and finish doing his job throughout the long night until the club closed at 2:00 a.m. He stayed upstairs, sending one of the other guys down every so often to do a sweep outside the dressing rooms. He didn't trust himself to go down there and confront her yet.

If he did, it might get loud. And neither one of them might be ready to go back to work after they had the blowout fight Nick suspected they were going to have.

It was definitely going to be a blowout, and probably not for the reasons Izzie would suspect. Yeah, it bothered him that his sister-in-law's kid sister was working as a stripper. But he was no prude, nor was he judgmental. He'd seen her act…she was not only good, she was damn good.

As someone who was—and might again be—Izzie's lover, he was not happy. Couldn't deny that. But again, not so much because of other men looking at her, but more because she was working in a very risky field. Putting herself in danger.

The real reason he was fuming was because she'd lied to him. She'd been deceitful, letting him chase after Izzie by day while Rose pursued *him* by night. The woman had nearly sent him out of his mind—for what? Some twisted game? A power trip?

He didn't know. He just knew he wanted answers. And when the club finally shut down and everyone began to drift away, he walked downstairs, determined to get them.

Nick knew she hadn't left yet, he'd been watching her car in the parking lot, which was emptying as everyone departed for the night. She usually left much earlier—since her last number took place around midnight. And it didn't take her long to get ready since she didn't bother taking her mask off before getting into her car and roaring away. Obviously for his benefit.

But she was still here. So he could only assume one thing: she was waiting in her dressing room, either hiding in the hopes that he'd leave first. Or preparing herself for his arrival.

Because she had to know he'd figured her out. All she'd have had to do was look out at him in the audience during her second set and see the steam pouring out of his head. And the fire burning out of his eyeballs.

Reaching her closed door, he remembering she'd said it had no lock. He gave her a one-knock warning, then entered without waiting for an invitation. It wasn't like she had anything to hide…he'd seen her body, both as Izzie and as Rose.

"What do you think you're doing?" she asked, staring at him from across the room, where she'd been slipping a jacket on. She was dressed casually, in a loose, comfortable-looking pair of baggy pants and a tank top. If she hadn't been wearing the mask, she'd have looked just like the girl next door.

Like Izzie.

God, what a blind idiot he was not to have seen it before. The eyes were the same—though "Rose's" were shadowed by the mask. Those lips couldn't be denied. The shape of her jaw, the length of her neck. Everything about the Crimson Rose was Izzie under a sexy microscope. Everything about Izzie was the Crimson Rose in nice girl trappings.

"What do you want, Nick?"

"You're here late," he murmured, stepping inside and shutting the door behind him.

"Um, yes, I guess so," she replied.

"You don't usually stay until closing time."

She tilted her head back, her chin up, displaying outright bravado. She was going to try to bluff her way through this, since she couldn't be certain she'd been busted. "One of the other dancers got sick and had to leave. I wasn't sure if Harry would need me to cover for her."

He hadn't. Nick knew that much. If he'd had to watch "Rose" in a third performance on the stage, he would have lost it. He didn't know that he'd have been able to keep himself from going up there and confronting her right in front of the audience.

She fell silent, just watching him. Waiting. Nick said nothing, not giving himself away yet. He wanted to see what she'd do. How far Izzie would go to maintain her secret.

God, it killed him that she didn't trust him. He had no il-lusions about why she'd put that mask on her face in the beginning. Her parents would be upset if they found out. He could even see why she'd kept quiet the first couple of times he'd worked here—before she knew she could trust him.

But now he was her lover. She'd trusted him with her body. She *should* have trusted him with her secret.

"Well," she said, "I guess it's time to go."

"So soon?" he murmured, leaning back against the closed door, blocking her escape. He crossed his arms and stared. "But this is the first time we've been alone in quite a while."

She licked her lips nervously. Nick almost felt that moist tongue on his own mouth and had to force himself to stay cool.

"It's late."

"I know. It's also nearly deserted. You and I might be the very last ones here," he said. Watching her closely, he saw the way she gulped as that truth dawned on her. They were practically alone in this big building. No one would hear if she decided to shout for help.

As if Nick would ever *hurt* her. He'd sooner cut off his own arm. That didn't mean, however, that he didn't intend to torment her just as much as he possibly could.

She was nervous, quivering, her whole body in miniscule motion. And he knew why. He *could* just put her out of her misery and confront her on her deception, but something made him string her along a little more. Maybe it was the way she'd been stringing him along. Maybe it was just because he liked seeing the wild flutter of her pulse in her neck. Plus hearing the choppy, audible breaths she couldn't contain.

He liked having her at a disadvantage for once. He also knew how to put her at more of one.

"So, Rose," he said, finally straightening and stepping closer, "about our very first conversation?"

She slid back, trying to increase the space between them

again, but couldn't go far before hitting the folding screen. Nick pressed closer, relentless in his silent, stalking approach. "I've been giving it a lot of thought."

"You have?" she whispered. "I haven't been, not at all."

What a liar. "Really? Because I think by the way you watch me, you've been thinking about it a lot." Lifting an arm, he put it on the top of the screen, blocking her with his body. They were close enough for him to feel the brush of her pants.

"I need to go."

"I need you to stay." Tracing the soft line of her neck with the tip of one finger, he added, "I've changed my mind about your invitation."

Her mouth opened. "You don't mean…"

He tipped her mouth closed, sliding his thumb across her bottom lip. That juicy, full lip he had tasted the other night and wanted to lightly bite now. "You're very attractive, Rose."

"But…"

"I can't take my eyes off you."

Though she sighed at his touch, her soft body also stiffened. Her fists curled. She obviously didn't know whether to melt or erupt. It was all he could do not to laugh.

"You were so dead-set against it," she said in that hot whisper. "Why now?"

"Men can change their minds, too. You're all I've been thinking about for weeks."

The fists rose to her hips. The sultriness disappeared. She looked indignant, verging on angry. "Oh, yeah?"

"Most definitely." He dropped a hand onto her shoulder, feeling the flexing of her muscles. He kneaded it softly, easing away the angry tension, knowing he was only going to build it back up again. "I want to touch you, everywhere."

She shook under his hand.

"Want to taste you." Knowing how to make the top of her

head blow off, both with lust and with fury, he leaned close. Moving his mouth to the side of her neck, he placed an open-mouthed kiss at her nape, licking lightly at her skin, flavored the tiniest bit with salt from her energetic dancing. "Aww, Rose, do you know what I want to do to you?"

She just whimpered, not saying a word.

"I'd like to smear something luscious and sticky all over you, then lick it from every sweet crevice of your body."

That did it. Izzie/Rose shook off her half-hungry, half-worried daze and reacted with gut fury. She lifted one of those fists and whammed it toward his face. If Nick hadn't been prepared for it, he might have been caught in the jaw. As it was, he deflected the blow by grabbing her hand in mid-air.

He didn't let go, holding her tightly as she struggled to pull away. "Damn you, Nick Santori," she spat out, completely forgetting her sultry whisper.

"What's the matter, sweetheart," he snapped back, "you afraid to get a little oral?" Sliding an arm around her shoulders, still gripping her first, he added, "Or do you just like to *give* it rather than *get* it?"

"Put *anything* in my mouth and I'll bite it off."

"Oooh, rough. I like it." Tracing the opening in the velvety fabric with his finger, he added, "I couldn't *fit* anything in your mouth with that thing on your face. Especially not my cock, *as you well know.*" He pressed hard against her, pushing her back against the wall, grinding into her. Because while her actions and her continued deceptions drove him crazy with anger, her nearness was driving him crazy with lust.

He was rock hard for her, raging with need.

She whimpered and stopped wriggling for a second, her hips bucking toward his in response—once, then again. She lifted one leg slightly, tilting her pelvis so his bulge hit her in the spot she most needed it to. "Oh, God," she mumbled, "I get the point, you've got a lot to offer."

She'd whispered that, calming herself down, and Nick almost groaned at her determination.

She *still* hadn't quite let herself believe it had already gone too far, that her masquerade was over. Izzie had lost her temper at the thought that he'd play the same sexy, wicked games with another woman that he'd played with her the other night in the van. And she'd reacted with honest—if mo mentary—fury.

Now, having realized it, she was almost desperate to convince herself she could salvage the situation. She was hoping he *hadn't* been talking to Izzie, who knew firsthand what he had to give her since she'd taken him into her body the other night. And that he was instead talking to Rose, who was right now feeling the size of his cock as it pressed against her.

Bending to the side, he grasped her bent leg, gripping her thigh to tug her up for a better fit. She groaned as their bodies came together more intimately. He could feel the heat of her—her moisture—through her thin pants and his own. She was wet and aroused, flushed and ready.

Yet still too damn stubborn to whip off the mask and take him on open, honest terms.

"So you ready to play those kinds of games?" he muttered as he rocked against her, inhaling her little cries of pleasure.

"I don't like to be manhandled," she muttered through hoarse breaths. The excited pulse in her throat and the desperate tone in her voice made a lie of that statement. She liked it. A lot.

He bit lightly on her bottom lip. "Yes, you do."

She started to shake her head, but he kissed her, thrusting his tongue against hers, loving the silky feel of her mouth almost as much as he hated the scrape of the mask against his cheek. That mask was what finally brought him back to his senses. He didn't want the masked woman, he wanted the real one. The one who trusted him and exhibited honesty. And guts.

He'd had enough. Enough of the lying, enough of the deception. Even enough of tormenting her.

So he dropped her leg. "I think we're done."

She sagged back against the wall. Even with the mask he could see the way her eyes widened with shock. And hurt. *"What?"*

It wasn't easy to stay back, keep his hands off her, ignore the heat in small room and the overwhelming smell of sexual want filling his head. But he did it. "I changed my mind."

Turning his back to her, he took one step toward the door. Then he heard her whisper, "You son of a bitch, you *do* know."

He put his hand on the knob. Glancing over his shoulder to meet her stare, he frowned and sighed. "Yeah, Izzie. I do."

Then he walked out.

FOR THE FIRST TIME in the nearly three months that she'd worked at Leather and Lace, Izzie called in sick Sunday night. She told herself she was a coward ten times over. But that didn't change the way she felt.

She couldn't face him. Not after what had happened in her dressing room Saturday night.

His anger had been undeniable. His revenge understandable.

But it was his *hurt*—that glimpse of sadness on his face as he'd looked at her over his shoulder before walking out the door—that had been the real punch in the gut.

He'd been pursuing her relentlessly for weeks and had finally caught her that night in the van. He'd been nothing but honest about what he was going through—with his family, his life, his attraction to her.

And she'd been lying to him from the first moment. Lying about her secret job, lying about her feelings for him. Lying about what she really wanted.

Hell, she'd even been lying to *herself* about those last two. She'd been denying her feelings for him though they had existed for as long as she could remember. And she'd pretended she wasn't dying for him physically when the thought consumed her every waking moment.

Even her parents had zoned right in on her mood when she'd gone to visit them Sunday. She'd tried so hard to paste on a smile, especially around her father, who was just now starting to seem like his old self. But her mother had immediately noticed something was wrong and had questioned her about it.

She'd covered…promising everything was fine.

One more lie to add to her list. She was becoming quite adept at it. And frankly, she hated herself for that.

"You deserve to feel this way," she told herself as she sat in the closed bakery a few evenings later. It was her quiet time again, when the café staff had left for the day but the evening kitchen and delivery help hadn't arrived. She was sipping a big, fattening cappuccino laden not only with whipped cream but a swirl of caramel. Feeling like absolute scum.

"Iz?" a voice called. A female one.

Turning on her stool, she saw her cousin, Bridget, enter through the employees' entrance in the back.

"Hey," Izzie mumbled.

"I've been calling."

"I don't usually answer the phone after hours."

Bridget frowned. "I mean your cell phone."

"Turned off." Izzie blew on the steaming coffee drink. "There's more if you want to make yourself one."

Bridget looked longingly at the mug and fresh whipped cream and got to work. She remained quiet as she did it, but Izzie saw the worried sidelong glances her cousin cast her way.

When Bridget had finished—topping her hot drink with a sprinkle of cinnamon—she took a seat on the opposite side of the counter. "You look like hell. You haven't been sleeping."

"Thanks. And you're right. I haven't been."

Bridget sighed. "Me, neither."

Finally looking seriously at her cousin, she saw the dark circles under her pretty eyes and the droop of her normally smiling mouth. It was an unusual combination. Bridget was not the cheerful, constantly giddy sort, but she was always quietly happy. And her face reflected that.

Not today, though. "What's wrong?"

"I hate men."

"I hear ya," Izzie mumbled, though her heart wasn't in it. She didn't hate Nick, not at all. She just hated that look of disappointment on his face. Hated how it made her feel.

Low. Rotten.

Yes, she'd had a reason to keep her identity hidden from most of the world. But once she'd let Nick lay her down in the back of that van and do things to her that would cause a real good little Catholic girl to faint of shock, all masks should have been torn away.

"I don't understand them."

Sensing her cousin was talking about one man in particular, Izzie set aside her own emotional misery. "What's going on?"

"It's that guy at work I mentioned a few weeks ago. Dean."

"The new salesman?"

Bridget nodded. "I finally met him for coffee one day, kind of figuring it was our first date. But obviously I totally misread him. He made it clear he was just interested in getting to know a coworker. And he hasn't asked me out again."

Izzie frowned, disliking the look of unhappiness on Bridget's face. "Have you made it clear you're interested?"

"I went out with him, didn't I?"

"Yes, but did you make it *clear* that you were looking at him as more than just a coworker?"

"How was I supposed to do that?"

"I don't know—flirting, smiling, brushing up against him. All the typical weapons of the female romantic arsenal."

"I…don't suppose I did. We talked mostly about business…at least when I wasn't griping about my landlord."

"So, he might not even know you're interested in him *that* way. Which means, you need to let him know, then figure out if he gave you the brush or retreated out of self-preservation."

Bridget blinked. "Self-preservation?"

"Some men won't make a move on a woman unless they're sure she's interested. It takes a lot of self-confidence."

Self-confidence like Nick's. It had taken a boatload of it for him to keep pursuing her when she'd kept turning him down.

"Is that what *you* would do? Make it more obvious?"

"Yeah. I would."

Her cousin mumbled something, then cleared her throat. "You know, I'd think you're right. But there's something about Dean that makes me think he's not quite as nice and shy as he seems."

Izzie instantly stiffened. "Has he done anything to you?"

"*Done?* Oh, goodness, no. He's barely looked at me since the day we went out. But there have been one or two times when I've caught him staring at me—with this, oh, God, it sounds so stupid, but I'd swear he looks almost *hungrily* at me when he thinks I'm not looking."

"Hungry's good. If it's coming from someone you *want* to want you." Not just a room full of horny men turned on by a naked dancer. Her audience sometimes annoyed the hell out of her. Sometimes it seemed like dancing naked alone would be better than dancing naked in front of a crowd. Of course, she wouldn't get *paid* for that. A definite drawback.

"Not if he constantly hides it. And there's more, he sometimes just comes across so much harder—tougher—than this nice, quiet, soft-spoken salesman. It's almost like he's trying really hard to be on his best behavior."

Izzie didn't like the sound of that. Guys who tried that hard to be on their *best* behavior had to be pretty *bad* during their not-quite-best behavior. She said as much to her cousin, but Bridget waved away her concerns.

Though they talked a little while longer, Izzie couldn't keep her mind on anything. Her cousin noticed her distraction and tried to get her to talk about it, but she wasn't ready to.

It wasn't that she didn't trust Bridget to keep her secret. Or that she feared her cousin would be shocked by it. But the truth was, it didn't seem right for Bridget to be the one she talked to about this. Not when Nick was the first one who'd realized what she was doing on Saturday and Sunday nights.

She wanted to talk to him.

She wanted him. Period.

She just didn't know if it was too late to get him. Judging by the way he'd slammed out of her dressing room Saturday night, she greatly feared it was.

IT TOOK EVERY OUNCE of willpower Nick possessed to avoid going into Natale's Bakery that week. Something inside him insisted that he go up there and confront Izzie now that he felt at least moderately calm. Unlike the way he'd felt Saturday night at the club.

Something else demanded that he stay away, let her figure

out what the hell it was she wanted from him and clue him in when she was ready. Maybe he'd accommodate her. Maybe he wouldn't. It depended entirely upon what she wanted: him in her life, him out of her life? A secret affair, or a public one? A lover...a friend?

There were a lot of different possibilities. He honestly wasn't sure which he was most hoping for. The only thing he knew he wanted was for Izzie to come clean with him about everything. Then they could figure out the rest.

He assumed it would take a while. Considering she'd called in sick from work Sunday night, he had the feeling she was going to avoid the confrontation for as long as possible. But, unless she quit working at the club, she wasn't going to be able to avoid him forever.

Quit working at the club. He couldn't deny that his first reaction had been to want her to.

He didn't want other men looking at Izzie. He didn't want other men fantasizing about her. And he most certainly didn't want anyone getting fixated on her...fixated enough to stalk her, threaten her or hurt her.

Once he'd calmed down, though, he realized he understood exactly why she'd gone to work at Leather and Lace. It was probably for the same reasons *he'd* gone to work there.

She was every bit as out of her element in this old-new environment as he was. Fitting in about as well as he did.

Fitting in...hell, what he was doing right now was proof he didn't fit in. It was Thursday night and he was holding a brown paper bag clutched to his side. Walking to his building, his eyes scanned side to side in the hope that he didn't bump into his parents or another elderly relative who'd rat him out.

Chinese carry-out was probably grounds for his mother to call for an exorcism. Especially since he'd refused yet another doggy bag full of calzones and Pop's lasagna tonight. If he bit another piece of pasta, he was going to explode like the giant marshmallow man in *Ghost Busters*.

"Tough," he muttered, his mouth watering for the Kung Pao Chicken he could smell from the bag. Not to mention the eggrolls, fried rice…he'd bought enough to feed an army.

Nick knew a little something about clandestine missions. Enough to know that when you were on one, you accomplished as much as you could the first time, in the hopes that you could delay going back. And a big bag of food meant leftovers. Enough to last a week or so, meaning no more dangerous, secret excursions to Mr. Wu's for a while.

Unless, of course, he had unexpected company for dinner. Female company. Like the female standing right outside his apartment door, her hand lifted to knock.

"Izzie?" he mumbled as soon as he stepped off the elevator, wondering not only how she'd gotten into the building, but also how she'd found out where he lived.

She whirled around, her eyes wide and bright. She hadn't knocked yet, which meant she hadn't quite prepared herself to face him. He'd caught her off guard.

Nick tried not to wonder what this meant, tried to remain casual. Tried not to notice how curvy and inviting her body looked in her tight tank top and sexy short skirt.

It would be like not noticing an earthquake shaking your house down around you. She was just too beautiful to ignore.

As they continued to stare, he finally murmured, "Hi."

"Hi."

They said nothing else for a moment. Long enough for him to notice the smudges of shadow beneath her pretty brown eyes and the paleness in her cheeks. She was practically biting a hole in her bottom lip as she tried to figure out what to say.

He couldn't help taking pity on her…at least taking pity on that gorgeous lip before she bit a hole right through it.

Shifting his bag to his other hip, he walked to the door and lifted his keys to the lock. "You hungry?"

She glanced at the bag. "No pizza?"

"Nope. I've got egg foo young, lo mein, couple of different chicken dishes, you name it."

"Oh, God, feed me," she exclaimed, following him into the apartment with a smile on her face.

Once inside, she tossed her purse onto his couch, a large one that dominated the small living area of the very small apartment. He didn't mind—compared to sharing a barracks with twenty other guys, this was pure luxury. He'd picked the place because it was clean and high, with a great view of the college a few blocks away. And he'd barely started furnishing it, figuring he'd get the most important things first.

Big, comfortable reclining leather couch. Big TV for watching football. He could live for a while on that…plus the huge, comfortable bed dominating his bedroom.

A flow of warmth washed through him at the thought of that bed. He'd imagined Izzie in it many times. He'd *dreamed* of her in it many times.

Now, here she was. So close he could smell her perfume and hear her breaths. Like a fantasy come to life.

"Minimalist, huh?" she asked as she stared pointedly at the couch and the big screen TV.

"I'm working on it."

He couldn't believe how normal they sounded. Like two old friends getting together for dinner. Considering the last two times they'd been alone they'd been either fighting or practically ripping each other's clothes off, he figured that was a pretty good trick.

"I, uh, wanted to…"

"Save it," he muttered, not wanting to start their discussion yet. "I'm hungry. Let's eat first."

Relief washed over her pretty face as she followed him into the kitchen. When she lifted something up onto the counter, he realized she hadn't come empty handed.

"Peace offering." She pointed toward a six-pack of beer.

"Are we at war?" he asked, repeating a question she'd once asked him.

"We've been doing a lot of battling."

Yes, they had. And he, for one, was tired of it.

Getting some bowls, plates and silverware, he spread all the food out on his small kitchen table, and they each loaded up, smorgasbord style. "Where…"

"Do you mind the floor?" he asked.

Shrugging, she followed him into the living room, watching as he sat down in front of the sofa, stretching his legs out in front of him, with his plate on his lap. It wasn't quite as easy for her, since she wore a skirt.

Nick forced himself to focus on his food, not on her long, sexy legs so close to his on the floor. Picking up the TV remote, he flicked the power button, then channeled up to a station playing soft music. It was background noise, filling the silence that grew thicker as they ate…as they drew closer to the conversation they both knew they were about to have.

When they'd finished, he took their plates into the kitchen. She followed, working on putting away the food. Within a few moments, there was nothing left to do—no dinner to eat, no dishes to clean—nothing to do but face each other.

"I don't want to do this," he said, surprising them both.

"Do what?"

"Fight with you. Do battle. Whatever you want to call it."

She shook her head. "I don't want to either. But I need to tell you…I need to get this out."

Crossing his arms, he leaned back against the kitchen counter and waited. "Okay."

She closed her eyes, then spoke in a rush. "I'm sorry I was dishonest with you about being the Crimson Rose. At first, I didn't trust you—didn't trust *anyone.* I'm sure you know that my parents wouldn't be happy about what I'm doing, and I don't want to do anything to add to my father's health problems."

"I understand that." He did. It made perfect sense for her to go incognito at her risqué job. "But once you and I..."

"I know." She raked a hand through her brown hair, which was loose around her shoulders tonight, rather than up in its usual ponytail. "I should have told you immediately. Instead I panicked and pushed you away."

"Yeah. I gotta say, I felt pretty damn humiliated when I figured it out. I should have known you."

"I *am* a performer. I know about portraying someone else."

"About that...when did you start in this line of work?"

"Stripping's not my line of work. Dancing is. I was with the Rockettes until a year ago."

"You were one of those kick-line chicks?"

She glared at him. "It's harder than it looks."

"Right. Tough life dancing with giant nutcrackers and Santa Claus." He quickly put his hand up. "I'm joking. You must have been damn good to make it."

"I was," she said, with complete confidence. "But I got bored with it and went with a modern dance company in Manhattan. Then came the injury. Then came Dad's stroke. Now I'm here."

Her life in a nutshell.

"And now what?" he asked, knowing that was the question he really wanted answered. Where was she going from here? Where did she see him fitting into that?

"I don't know. Right now I'm biding time, trying to figure out what I want." Her jaw tightening, she continued. "But it's not the bakery, and it's not the neighborhood. It's not Gloria's life—a repeat of my mother's. And it's not my sister Mia's life as a hard-ass lawyer with tons of drive and no happiness."

"I understand," he murmured.

Nodding, she said, "I'm sure you do. If anyone would, it's you." The tension easing from her shoulders, Izzie walked across the small kitchen, covering the distance between them in a few short steps. Putting her hand on his chest, she looked up at him, her eyes bright. "Which is why I have to repeat this: I am sorry, Nick. Please say you'll forgive me."

He hesitated, then offered her a short nod. Appearing relieved, she began to pull her hand away, but he covered it with his, not letting her go. "Where do *we* go from here?"

She hesitated, so he pressed her. "We can't be just friends."

"We can't be a couple."

Their eyes locked, they both said the same four words at exactly the same moment. "We can be lovers."

Nick chuckled as Izzie smiled. Tightening her fingers in his shirt, she scraped the tips of them along the base of his neck. "Where I'd *like* to go right now is into your bedroom to see if it's furnished any better than your living room is."

Lifting her hand to his mouth, he pressed a warm kiss on the inside of her palm. "Oh, it is, angel. You bet it is."

8

MAKING LOVE TO NICK in the back of the van had been erotic and spontaneous and incredibly hot. It had also been a week ago and in that week, Izzie had begun to wonder whether it had really been as amazing as she remembered.

As soon as Nick led her into his bedroom, turned her to face the mirrored door of his closet, and slowly began to kiss her neck, she knew it had been. He was so slow—so patient—so deliberate. The man had incredible control and he had used it to drive her absolutely wild.

Izzie had flipped the light switch on as soon as they entered the room, determined to see all, savor all, enjoy every minute of this experience. When Nick studied her in the mirror, consuming her with his eyes, she was very glad she had. She liked watching him watch her. Liked having his eyes on her. And she wanted to watch everything he did to her.

"You've been driving me absolutely insane since I saw you that night in the restaurant," he whispered, his lips hovering just above the sensitive skin below her ear.

"You've been driving me insane since you landed on top of me on the cookie table."

He turned her to face him. "Izzie, I'm sorry I didn't..."

"I was a kid. You needed to wait until I caught up a little," she said with a smile.

He glanced down at her, his stare lingering on the scooped

neck of her shirt and the clingy fabric hugging her breasts. "You caught up a lot."

She reached up and unfastened the top button of his shirt, then moved to the next. "Oh, more than you know," she whispered, feeling incredibly free. A sensual woman capable of knocking him back on his heels the way he'd knocked her back last week.

Their first time together had been about him overwhelming her senses. Tonight it was Izzie's turn.

She was not going to lie back and *take* the pleasure he wanted to give her, she intended to *give* with every lustful molecule in her body. He'd offered her an experience she would remember until the day she died. Now she planned to do the same.

Using the one thing she did best.

She quickly scanned the room, thinking ahead. "Where'd that come from?" she asked, pointing to an old-fashioned, straight backed chair in the corner. It, a simple, immaculately clean dresser and an enormous four-poster bed were the only things in the room. The chair didn't look at all new like the rest.

"My parents insisted on giving me stuff...I had to take *something* and there's no room for it in the living room."

"It won't fit with that TV that's more suited for the Jolly Green Giant's living room," she said with a low laugh. Licking her lips, she pointed to the chair. "Go sit down."

One of his eyebrows rose, but he obeyed, watching with interest to see what she was up to. Izzie glanced around the room, looking for a radio, a boombox, something.

No luck. Nick's bedroom was nearly empty, with just the furniture and a smaller TV on the dresser. There wasn't a piece of clothing on the floor, or a speck of dust anywhere. It was nearly Spartan...military, she assumed. And it lacked the warmth she knew Nick possessed.

She hoped that someday he allowed that warmth to spill free and become part of his home as well as a part of his life.

"You got me where you wanted me," he drawled from the chair. He put his hands behind his head, his fingers laced, and leaned back against the wall. His sleeves were rolled up to his elbows and his forearms bulged and flexed. His big, strong legs were sprawled out in front of him and for a second, Izzie was tempted to climb right onto his lap.

She could unzip his jeans, tug them out of the way, release that big erection she could see from here. It would be delicious to slip her panties off, lift her skirt, then slide down onto him to ride him to her heart's content.

Not yet. First she needed to delight his senses the way he'd delighted hers last week. He'd focused on her sense of touch and smell—she could still inhale and remember that sweet, cheesy filling he'd smeared all over her. And her body tingled at the memory of his lips and tongue removing that filling.

They'd played games with food. She intended to whet his taste buds with something else.

The sight of her body.

Suddenly remembering what he'd done with the TV in the other room, she grabbed the remote control and turned on the bedroom one. Punching in a few numbers—familiar, since she liked listening to the same station at her own apartment—she landed on a channel that played sultry Latina music.

Because luck was a woman, the song was a slower one with a sultry back-beat and a sensuous rhythm. Easy to dance to.

"What are you…"

"Watch me," she whispered. *Watch me and I'll make you burn.*

She began to move, closing her eyes and letting the music roll through her. Since childhood Izzie had had an affinity for music—all types of music. It had always made her want to move. To sway or to spin, to leap or to bend. She just had a dancing gene that demanded release whenever the right beat hit her ears and rolled on down through her body.

This one was perfect for seduction.

Keeping focused on her own instincts—giving herself pleasure by the simple act of moving—she knew Nick would gain pleasure, too. At first she simply danced. Her eyes still closed, she threw her head back and tangled her hand in her hair. Rocking her hips, she gyrated against an imaginary partner, sliding down and up against an invisible thigh, quivering under the touch of a hand that wasn't there.

She heard Nick groan softly. Licking her lips, she slid her hand down her own body. Her hips still rocking, she touched her stomach, then slid her hand lower, resting her fingertips on her pelvis. Her other hand she moved across her chest, scraping her nipples, already rock hard in anticipation and excitement.

"Izzie…"

"Shh."

She didn't look at him, didn't let him distract her. Instead, she tugged her top free of her waistband. Flicking at the snap and pushing down the zipper of her skirt, she rocked until the thing fell to the floor. She kicked it out of the way, never losing the beat, her body in constant, sensual motion.

Her top came next. She dragged it up—slowly, so slowly— letting the fabric fall back an inch for every two she raised it. She could hear Nick's ragged breathing over the music. Could hear her own heart pounding in her chest, too. Every move she made was an invitation and a promise.

She pulled the top off, sensual even when untangling her hair from the material. Clad in nothing but a skimpy bra and thong panties, and her high heeled sandals, she bent over and swung her head, letting her hair fly free.

"You're killing me here," he whispered.

"So take care of yourself. Get ready for me," she replied, coming closer—but not too close. "Do what you *want* to do when you watch me dance."

"I want to *have* you when I watch you dance."

Tsking, she shook her head in disbelief, still swaying like a woman being sexually aroused by the touch of the musical notes on her body. "Pretend you don't know you're going to have me, Nick. Let me see what you'd do then."

She turned around, her back to him, returning her attention to her dance. Bending at the waist, she put her hands on her thighs and did a booty rock that she knew would drive him out of his ever-loving mind.

His low groan told her it had worked. But Izzie ignored it,

Grabbing the end post of Nick's bed, she used it, hooking one leg around it and bending back. The wood was hard against her swollen sex, but she needed it—got off on it—rubbing up and down in a way she never rode the pole at the club.

"Izzie," he whispered hoarsely.

She glanced over and almost smiled in triumph. He'd finished unbuttoning his shirt and it hung from his shoulders.

Even better, his jeans were open, his briefs pushed down. And his hand encircled his huge erection.

"Yes. Imagine it's *me* touching you," she told him.

He never took his eyes off her, beginning to stroke, up and down, his movements timed to match her strokes against the bedpost. But when she let go of it, he didn't stop.

"The bra," he ordered.

"Just as the customer desires," she whispered, taunting him with every bit of her sexuality.

She unfastened the bra, dragging out the moment before it fell away to reveal her breasts. This usually marked the end of one of her numbers, but tonight, Izzie was just getting started. She touched herself, showing him the way she wanted to be touched. Crossing her arms—her hips still rocking—she cupped each breast. Capturing her nipples between her fingers, she tweaked and rolled. The pleasure she gave herself—and the way Nick reacted to it—sent pure liquid want rushing to her sex, already dripping with readiness.

Hearing Nick clear his throat, she glanced over and saw he held a twenty dollar bill in his hand. He was enjoying this game. Getting into the fantasy.

"You have something for me, mister?" she asked, almost purring the words as she danced closer, wearing nothing but her skimpy panties and shoes.

"Uh-huh. But you have to work for it."

She moved again, closer, stepping over one of his legs to straddle it. She lowered herself closer to his thigh, rocking a few inches above it. Her breasts swayed close to his face. "What'd you have in mind?"

He leaned up, his mouth moving toward her breast.

"Uh-uh, no touching," she said, easing back a little. "I can touch you…you can't touch me."

"Those the rules?"

"Uh-huh."

"Not sure how long I'll be able to obey them."

"You'll just have to keep your hands busy *elsewhere* until I say you can break them."

He flexed his hand again, lazily working the erection that still jutted out of his unfastened pants. "That means the rules *will* eventually be broken?"

She bent down again, low, brushing her silky panties over his strong thigh. "If you're very, very good." Her mouth watering, she inched closer, so her leg could brush against all that male heat. He instinctively arched toward her, branding her with that ridge of flesh that had given her such intense pleasure last week.

She wanted it. Badly. In every way it was possible for a woman to take it.

"You want a lap dance, mister?" she asked in her heavy, Crimson Rose whisper.

His eyes narrowed. "I didn't know you gave them."

"I don't. But you're an extra *special* customer."

Izzie had never done this particular type of dance, but she figured she could fake it. Frankly, she didn't think Nick would care if she didn't get it exactly right.

So she went with her instincts. With both hands on the back of the chair, she swayed over him, brushing her breasts against his cheeks, shivering at the delicious roughness of his skin. She danced above him, writhing just above one leg, then the other, then straddling both. He watched with glittering eyes, groaning with need as she taunted him—coming close, so close—then pulling away.

"Gonna have to break that rule soon, lady," he growled.

"We'll see."

Driving them both closer to the brink of insanity, she dipped lower than she'd ever gone, until the silky wet fabric between her thighs met his arousal and set them both completely on fire. He grabbed her hips, helping her rock up and down on him until they both moaned with the pleasure of it.

"You're touching," she said.

He thrust up harder, the hot tip of his erection easing into her, bringing her silky panties along. "I'm going to be touching you a lot more in a minute."

Oh, she liked playing these wicked, sexy games with Nick. It was unlike anything she'd ever done with anyone before, and Izzie sensed she could be happy playing bedroom games with him and *only* him for a very long time.

"But you still haven't paid me." She licked the side of his neck, biting lightly on his nape. Feeling the scrape of the bill against her skin, she pulled away just enough to watch him slip it into her panties. "Big tipper."

"You're worth every penny."

"I think maybe you should get a little bonus for being such a good customer."

She needed a little bonus herself. Needed to do something she'd been aching to do since she'd first seen him take off his pants in the back of the van.

Sliding back, she lowered herself to the floor, then moved between his thighs. She reached for his hand, covering it with hers, mimicking his slow, easy movements up and down his erection. Eventually she pushed his hand away, pleasuring him with her fingers and her palm. Encircling him as best she could, she slid down to the base of his shaft, then eased back up. She trailed her fingers across the thick, bulbous head to moisten them with his body's juices, then repeated the motion.

But it wasn't *quite* enough. Izzie inched forward, wetting her lips with her tongue.

"Iz…"

"Let me," she murmured.

She didn't wait for permission. Kneeling between his spread thighs, she drew closer, flicking out her tongue for a quick taste of the sac pulled up tight beneath his erection.

He jerked up, thrusting harder into her hand, which still encircled him. Izzie didn't stop. Parting her fingers to make way for her mouth, she licked her way from the base of his shaft all the way up to its tip. "You taste so good, Nick," she whispered before flicking her tongue out to catch more of that fluid dripping out of him.

"So do you." Still sprawled out before her, he tangled his hands in her hair. "But I'm hungry. I want some, too."

Mmm…mutual oral pleasure. She'd love to savor that experience with Nick. But for right now, she wanted to concentrate on him. So, ignoring his comment, she moved over the thick, pulsing head of his cock and took it into her mouth. As she sucked, he hissed. The deeper she went—taking as much as she could—the louder his groans.

Shifting around for better access, Izzie began to slowly make love to him with her mouth, getting off on hearing *him* get off. She slid up and down, taking more with every stroke, wanting to swallow him all the way down, though he was, of course, much too big for that. But she gave it her all, focused on his sounds of pleasure, the smell of sex rolling off his body, the feel of his hands delicately stroking her hair and the back of her head.

"Ride me, Izzie," he whispered, not demanding but pleading. "Come up here and take me."

Take him. Izzie had never had a man beg her using those words, though she, herself, had spoken them. She found herself liking the sensuous power of it. He didn't just want her, he *needed* her. Was desperate for her.

With one last little suck, she pulled her mouth away and looked up at him. He was staring down at her, his dark brown eyes gleaming with want. Reaching for her shoulders, he began to tug her up and repeated his plea. "Take me, Izzie."

Offering him a half-smile, she rose to her knees. She was nearly naked, but Nick was still half-wearing his clothes. So she reached for his waistband and pulled his pants and briefs down. He lifted up to help her, kicking his shoes off and his clothes with them. His shirt fell off his shoulders with a simple shrug, and now the tables were turned—she was the only one wearing a stitch of clothes.

It was, of course, a tiny stitch. And as she rose to her feet, Nick didn't take his eyes off it. Reaching for her hips, he tugged her closer until he caught the elastic seam of her panties with his teeth. Nudging them down, he tasted her with two quick, heart-stopping flicks of his tongue. Her clit swelled against his lips. "Please," she whispered, not knowing what she needed more—for him to lick her into an orgasm, or to tear her panties off and plunge down onto him.

"Since you asked so nicely," he murmured, returning his mouth to her most sensitive spot. Taking her hips in his hands, he pushed the panties down and nuzzled in deep in her curls.

Feeling a climax rocket through her, Izzie threw her head back and groaned. She was still groaning when Nick tugged her down over him. He glanced at his jeans. "My pocket..."

"We're safe," she assured him since she was on the pill. "As long as you're comfortable with that."

"Oh, I am so comfortable with that," he muttered hoarsely. "I cannot wait to feel you wrapped around me, skin to skin."

Straddling him, her toes on the floor, Izzie rubbed against him, loving the tangle of his chest hair on her rock-hard nipples. Nick dipped his head down to suck one of them, hard and demanding. "Ride me," he ordered, his mouth still at her breast.

She eased onto him, taking the hot tip into her wet channel a little at a time. He was right—skin to skin was incredible. She could feel every beat of his pulse through his velvety smooth erection.

"Can't...take much..." he said through choppy breaths.

As if he'd reached his breaking point, he squeezed her hips and thrust up, impaling her hard and deep. "Oh, Nick," she groaned, shocked at the full intensity of it.

It took her a second to catch her breath, he filled her so deeply. But when she did, she had to move. Had to slide up and then ease back down. She rode with slow strokes, her arms on his shoulders, looking down into his face as he stared up into hers.

Nick lifted one hand and cupped her cheek, drawing her toward him. Covering her lips with his, he kissed her deeply, sliding his tongue in and out of her mouth in strokes matched by the ones deep inside her core.

The kiss went on and on, slowing or growing frenzied in mirror reactions to the movements of their bodies. Izzie rode him, took him as he'd demanded, using muscles she didn't even remember she had to stretch out their pleasure.

Their position was perfect for pleasing her both inside and out. And within moments, the friction on her clit provided her with another mind-blowing orgasm.

Finally, though, her legs began to weaken. She wasn't sure how much more she could take. As if he knew, Nick wrapped his arms around her, cupping her backside, and rose from the chair.

The strength of the man defied description.

Still buried deep within her, he continued kissing her as he walked the few steps to the bed. He dropped her on her back, coming down with her, and took over control.

"Yes, Nick," she gasped, her legs around his lean hips.

He didn't reply. He was gone now, mentally just *gone*, at the mercy of his wildly plunging body. Izzie held on for the ride, whispering frantic words of pleasure, telling him how much he pleased her.

Until she, too, was incapable of words. Together they lost themselves to the power of it until Nick shouted and came deep inside her, sending Izzie spiraling over the edge again, too.

BRIDGET HAD BEEN thinking about her cousin's words nearly all night Thursday. So much so that she barely slept and climbed out of bed long before her alarm went off Friday morning.

If there was one thing Izzie knew, it was men. And if she thought Bridget hadn't been sending out strong enough signals to Dean, she was probably right.

Izzie would make her interest more obvious.

So that's what Bridget would do.

That morning, she dressed for work a bit more carefully than usual. Her regular workday attire was typically a pair of pastel capris or a pair of slacks and a blouse. Today, she shimmied into a yellow skirt that cupped her butt like she'd sat in a tub of butter. Pulling a tight white tank top on with it, she glanced in the mirror and was surprised at what she saw.

She didn't look much like Bridget, the nice, smiling book-keeper. In fact, she looked sexy. She had curves…nice ones. Her breasts were high and shapely, highlighted by the scooped neck of the tank top. And while she didn't have es-pecially long legs, they looked pretty good in the skirt.

Feeling almost armored for battle, she donned a light-weight sweater—which she intended to remove as soon as she saw her quarry—and headed to work. She wanted to get there early so she could get used to walking around the office in the minuscule skirt and high-heeled sandals without tripping and making a fool of herself.

Usually, she was the first one at the dealership, anyway. The lot didn't open to customers until ten o'clock, with most of the sales staff showing up around nine…a half hour or so after her regular starting time. By the time she got to the lot, it was only seven-thirty, an hour early even for her.

The inside was dark, as expected, and as she entered, she reached for the switch to turn on the bank of overhead lights. But before she did it, something caught her eye…a sliver of light coming from beneath the door to the business office. Where *she* usually worked.

She supposed she could have forgotten to turn the light

off last night when she left. But she was still cautious as she approached. This was a pretty safe area, but occasional robberies certainly weren't unheard of. She wasn't about to open the door and surprise some junkie looking for a petty cash box.

When she got to within a few feet of the nearly closed door, she heard a voice from inside. She tensed for the briefest second, then recognized the voice and relaxed.

It was Dean. He'd obviously shown up early for work. Though she didn't hear whoever he was talking to, she figured someone else must have come in early, too.

Too bad. Had he been alone, she might have been able to put her "send stronger signals" plan into action. If, of course, she had the nerve, which was questionable.

Reaching for the knob, she paused when she heard Dean speak again, answering a question she hadn't heard asked. That was when she realized the conversation was one-sided. He was talking on the phone to someone.

Not wanting to eavesdrop, she stepped away, catching only the snippet of a comment Dean made. Something about a deal going down. Sounded like their star salesman had landed another buyer—one who liked to close deals very early in the morning.

When she heard his voice stop, she figured she'd see if he was done, and knocked once on the door. Feeling a little foolish—since she was, in essence, knocking on her own office door—she pushed the door open and stepped inside.

"Good morning, early-bird," she said.

He jerked his head up, so surprised he dropped his cell phone right onto the floor near her feet.

"Sorry, didn't mean to startle you," she said. Normally, she'd wait quietly and let him pick up the phone himself. But Izzie's words kept ringing in her ears. So instead, she carefully bent at the knees, reaching down to pick it up for him.

She kept one hand on her skirt, to hold it in place, but Bridget couldn't deny that it slid up several inches, high on her thighs, despite that.

Still appearing shocked, Dean didn't say a word. His narrowed eyes were locked on her thighs. His jaw was visibly clenched and he breathed over parted lips.

He looked…hungry. Just as she'd seen him look at her once or twice in the past. More than that, he seemed dangerous. Not nice Dean looking at a pair of woman's legs, but wickedly sexy Dean looking at a pair of woman's legs and imagining them wrapped around his waist.

She could do that. She could definitely do that. Whether it was what Izzie would do or not.

It is.

"Here you go," she said, handing him the cell phone.

He took it from her, their fingers brushing lightly. Standing, he stuffed the phone in his pocket. His lean face looked weary, as if he hadn't slept well.

"So, was it worth your early trip in?" she asked, knowing she sounded coy. She couldn't help channeling Izzie a little bit. "Everything…satisfactory?"

His pale blue eyes narrowed. "What do you mean?"

"I mean, did you get whatever deal you're working on taken care of this morning?"

He nodded slowly. "The deal. Yeah. It's all good."

"Good. You might set another sales record this month."

With a casual manner she had never suspected she could pull off, she tossed her purse onto her desk, which was laden with files, legal paperwork and financial stuff. Holding onto her courage, she slipped her sweater off her shoulders. She had to move close to Dean—very close—to reach the coat rack on the wall. Her arm brushed against his as she lifted the sweater onto one of the hooks.

"Bridget…"

Smiling, she turned and glanced up at him. "Yes?"

He wasn't looking at her face, his attention was focused lower. On the scooped neck of her tight, spandex tank top. The heat in his stare warmed her all over and she felt her body reacting to it. A lazy river of want flowed through her veins. She clenched her thighs in response to it. But there was no way to disguise the way her breasts grew heavier, her nipples hardening to twin points that poked against her shirt.

He noticed. Most definitely.

Swallowing hard, he growled, "Why are you dressed like that?"

"Like what?"

"Like you're trolling for men at a club rather than working with a bunch of used car salesmen and wrench jockeys at an auto shop?" he asked, his tone harsh.

Bridget instinctively stepped back. A little hurt. A little confused. "I just…." *Channel Izzie. WWID?* Taking a deep breath, she tilted her head back and jutted her chin out. "What business is it of yours what I wear to work?"

He reached for her, grabbing her arm as if he couldn't help himself. "Put your sweater back on."

"*Make* me."

His whole body tense with frustration, he lifted his other hand and grabbed her other arm. Bridget wasn't sure what he was going to do—shake her or haul her into his arms and kiss her.

She was most definitely hoping for option two.

She should have been intimidated, maybe even scared given his size. But she already knew he wouldn't do anything to hurt her. He was attracted to her, she was sure of it now, and he just didn't know what to do about that attraction since they were coworkers.

"Either take your hands off me or do something with them," she snapped, still thinking the way her cousin would.

"Damn it, Bridget."

But before he could do either one, they heard the sound of voices coming from right outside the door. They weren't, it appeared, the only two who'd arrived to work early.

Dean instantly released her and stepped away. He shook his head, as if to clear it, and eyed her warily. Finally he said, "I really think you should put your sweater on."

Bridget hid a smile, liking the tiny thrill of power she felt at having this big, handsome man react so strongly to *her*. Crossing her arms in front of her chest—which pressed her breasts even higher and harder against her top—she shook her head. "I don't think so, Dean. If you don't like the way I'm dressed…I suggest you don't look at me."

Knowing her bravado wasn't going to last for much longer, she sashayed past him, out onto the showroom floor to greet the other salesmen who'd arrived. Leaving Dean watching her with eyes that blazed like the sun.

IZZIE HAD SPENT the night in Nick's arms, but she'd slipped away early—around dawn. Knowing the bakery would open soon, he didn't protest.

He wanted to, of course, but he kept his mouth shut.

Izzie's whole reason for being here in Chicago was her devotion to her family's business. He wouldn't even think of interfering with that. Because he *liked* her working at the bakery. Right here close by.

As for her other job, at the club? Well, that, Nick had to admit, might be a tougher proposition. He hadn't yet been tested, but he didn't imagine it would be easy watching the woman he was absolutely crazy about take her clothes off for a roomful of other men. Especially since he'd almost certainly be picturing what had happened last night, when she'd taken her clothes off only for him.

It had been the most unbelievable night of his life. And he had to wonder how she'd had the strength to get up and walk this morning considering he'd spent so much of the night between her legs.

Izzie wasn't the only one who had to go to work. Nick had promised Tony he'd help him handle the delivery of a new wall oven at Santori's. So after showering, he got dressed and walked the few blocks up to Taylor. He passed right by Natale's on the way, but, mindful of Izzie's feelings, he didn't pop in. It felt strange as hell to walk on by and not say hello to the woman he'd made love to in so many wild, different ways the night before.

But she wanted their relationship to remain entirely between them. Meaning he couldn't single her out, couldn't grab her hand in public, couldn't ask her to do so much as walk across the street with him.

"This is gonna suck," he muttered aloud as he reached the restaurant. He had no idea how long he'd be able to maintain this secret, nighttime-only relationship with Izzie.

He only hoped she'd change her mind. That she'd realize she didn't have to give up *herself* to become part of a relationship with him.

A relationship. Yeah. He wanted one. He was falling for her in a big way, just as he'd suspected he could when he'd seen her looking so bored and aloof on the other side of Santori's all those weeks ago.

It was pretty ironic, really. He was starting to think he really could have found the perfect woman. He was already falling in love with her. And a union between them would absolutely delight everyone in both their families.

But Izzie didn't want one.

"Women," he muttered as he pushed into the restaurant.

His brother Tony, who'd been standing right inside the door, greeted him with a clap on the back. "Can't live with 'em...but they're sure as hell better than living alone."

As usual, his larger-than-life older brother coaxed a smile out of him.

Fridays were usually busy at Santori's, so the day flew by quickly. And, as usual, the rest of his family started drifting in after their workdays had ended. By eight o'clock, all of his brothers were here with their wives and kids, as was his sister, along with her new husband. Those two were cuddling like the newlyweds they were. Though he'd been skeptical, given what he knew about Simon Lebeaux's shady past, even Nick had to admit the two of them were obviously crazy about each other.

Besides, if Lebeaux could put up with his mouthy little sister, he had to be one hell of a strong man.

"Come on, take a load off," Mark said to Nick as he emerged from the kitchen, where he'd been helping his father.

"Yeah, I guess my slave-driver boss will let me knock off now," he replied, glancing over his shoulder at Tony, who stood in the swinging doorway.

"Not boss...partner," his brother reminded him with a grin.

Uh, no. Not in Nick's opinion. But he still hadn't wanted to have that conversation.

His siblings and their families took up several tables in the restaurant—tables that would probably have been appreciated by the paying customers lining up near the front counter. But Mama would never dream of shooing them out to free up the space. She clucked around, ordering them all to eat, cooing over the grandbabies and beaming when Noelle, Mark's wife, offered to let her feel the baby kicking in her stomach.

In Nick's opinion, that was Twilight Zone stuff. But *all* the women got into it, and Mark looked like he thought it was the coolest thing since Optimus Prime and the Transformers. Nick, however, was freaked by the very idea. The only thing he wanted to feel moving around inside a woman was his own cock. A baby? Forget it.

Unless the woman was Izzie.

The thought was crazy—bothersome, even. But it wouldn't leave his head.

"Hey, look who's here," Gloria called, waving toward the front door. "My baby sister! How you doin', Iz?"

Nick immediately swung around, seeing Izzie at the counter.

"Ah, Isabella, you haven't been to see me too much. What's wrong with you, eh?" Mama said as she bustled over. She cupped Izzie's face in her hands, pressing a kiss on her forehead, then grabbed her arm and dragged her over.

Smacking Lucas on the shoulder, she said, "Move over and make room for Gloria's little sister."

"Yes, ma'am," his older brother said with a grin. Luke was the next oldest above Nick and Mark and, as a prosecutor, was used to ordering other people around. But, like all of them, he couldn't refuse a command from their bossy mother.

"How's everything, Iz?" he asked as he stood and moved his chair out of the way. "You remember Rachel, right?"

Izzie nodded, smiling at Luke's pretty blond wife, the only fair-haired one of the bunch. A die-hard southerner, she'd somehow made herself fit in so well that Nick couldn't imagine what the family would be like without her.

Fortunately, the room Mama had forced Luke to make was between his chair and Nick's. Rosa Santori stole an unused chair from a nearby table and slid it in place, nearly pushing Izzie down onto it. Which had Nick ready to kiss his mother's hand, even though Izzie looked less than happy.

"I was just picking something up for dinner on the way home from work," she said, sounding almost dazed at how quickly she'd been shanghaied into a family dinner.

He understood the feeling. His mother was a powerhouse.

"Such a silly girl," Mama said. "You will eat here, with the family. You're one of us!" Trying to squeeze past her to get back to the kitchen, Mama said, "Scooch over a bit, eh?" and she pushed on Izzie's chair until it was so close to Nick's their thighs touched under the table.

Nick would lay money that his mother had done it on purpose. When he saw the smirk on her face as she left to check on dinner, he knew it was true.

Everyone wanted them to hook up. *If only they knew....*

"Hey *Isabella*," he whispered from the side of his mouth. She kicked him under the table.

"So, how do you like being back in Chi-town, Izzie?" his brother Joe asked. "Guess it's pretty tame and unexciting after your life in New York. You must really need a creative outlet."

There was a surprising twinkle in Joe's eye. As he and Izzie exchanged a long stare, Nick began to have a suspicion that Joe knew a little more than he'd let on about Izzie's nighttime life. Remembering the way Joe had steered him toward the job, and had been so adamant about Nick taking care of the "featured dancer" at Leather and Lace, he had to wonder if Joe had seen Izzie there during the renovations.

"It's okay," Izzie replied. Smiling, she added, "I'm just busy trying to avoid resuming my cannoli addiction. They're my absolute weakness."

Everyone at the table laughed. Except Nick. Because there'd been a sultry purr in her voice and he believed she'd been speaking only to him.

When he felt her hand—concealed by the red-and-white checked tablecloth—drop onto his leg, he was sure of it.

There was something really hot about having a woman you were supposed to just be casually friends with feel you up under a dinner table. Especially when that table was filled with curious family members who would love to see any sign of interest between the only two singles there.

Izzie was careful. So they definitely didn't see her hand creep up his leg to trace the outline of his dick. That, he assumed, would be taken as a definite sign of interest.

He was going to make the woman pay for her sensual torment. Right now, however, he was enjoying it too much to try slipping his hand down to beat her at her own game.

The conversation soon resumed, Izzie falling into it as if she'd never been away. She traded barbs with his brothers, reminisced with his sister Lottie about their school days.

She fit. She just fit. Like a normal neighborhood girl.

But no normal neighborhood girl he knew would be working Nick's zipper down, reaching in and pulling him free of his trousers. She definitely wouldn't be brushing the tips of her wicked fingers across his cock, arousing him until he hardened into her hand.

This was incredibly dangerous. If someone dropped a fork and bent over to get it, they'd get an eyeful.

But Nick didn't give a damn. Maybe he and Izzie couldn't be the "normal" couple the neighborhood would like to see. Somehow, though, this was *better.* Having an erotic secret… and acting on that secret in public where they could be exposed, it was mind-blowing.

It made him hot. It made him desperate.

It made him finish his dinner quickly and declare himself so tired he had to call it a night.

And thankfully, Izzie found an excuse of her own, followed him out the door, and led him to her place for another long night of the wildest sex he'd ever had.

9

"HOW ARE YOU FEELING, Rose? All better?" Holding the back door of Leather and Lace open for her early Saturday evening, Harry watched her closely, as if worried she wasn't up to dancing tonight.

Izzie had to stop for a moment to wonder why. Then she remembered. *Crap.* She'd called in sick the previous Sunday night. Probably really leaving him in the lurch.

"I'm fine, Harry," she said as she walked past him into the building, watching him shut and lock the door behind her. Security had improved around here ever since Nick had been hired. "I am so sorry about last Sunday night."

Harry waved an unconcerned hand. "Hey, don't worry about it, something wicked had to be going around for three of you to get knocked on your butts."

"*Three* of us?"

Harry nodded. "Leah got sick Saturday night."

"I remember."

"She came back in Sunday evening, was here for two hours, got sick all over again and had to leave. So did Jackie."

Jackie was Leah's dressing roommate. Whatever was going around had obviously nailed both of them.

Izzie was about to open her mouth to confess that she really had not been sick—just cowardly. But before she could do it, the back door was unlocked from the outside and opened again. She knew before she even saw him that Nick had arrived.

She recognized his warm, masculine scent. And her nipples got hard. Oh, yeah, it was definitely Nick.

His gaze immediately went to her, hot and appreciative. She'd had to leave his bed early this morning to go to work at the bakery. But right before she'd gone, he'd whispered how much he looked forward to seeing her tonight in her dressing room…which now, he'd made sure last weekend, had a lock.

She'd shivered all day, thinking of that first night he'd been in there, when he'd seen her naked reflection. *Mmm.*

"Nick," Harry said with a nod. He looked back and forth between the two of them. "No more mask, Rose?"

Smiling, she shook her head. "I've decided I trust him."

Nick returned the smile, the two of them sharing a silent intimacy that excluded Harry, though he stood right beside them. Finally, though, Nick broke the stare and addressed their boss. "Everything looking okay so far?"

Harry nodded. "Been kind of a quiet week. Last night was the slowest Friday we've had in a while." Glancing at Izzie, he added, "But I bet the crowd will be roaring back to see you."

"Are you short-staffed again?" she asked, wondering if Harry would need her to dance an extra set.

He shook his head. "Everybody's here, sound and healthy."

"What do you mean?" Nick asked, a frown furrowing his brow.

Harry began to explain about the sick dancers, which made Izzie feel guilty again. Especially when he groaned over how hard it had been to tell Delilah, his "retired" wife that she wasn't in shape to go on in their place. Oy. She wouldn't have wanted to see the redhead's expression during that conversation.

Something else she didn't want to do was have to look Nick in the eye and admit she'd called in sick rather than face him last weekend. She figured he knew that much, but didn't particularly feel the need to confirm it.

Excusing herself, she headed to her dressing room. The door wasn't locked, but she immediately noticed the deadbolt, which had not been there the previous weekend.

"You sneaky man," she whispered with a smile as she dropped her purse and keys on the vanity. She could think of several wicked ways Nick could help her kill time between her numbers.

Of course, being the hard-ass guy he was when on the job, she suspected he might resist her. That was okay. Izzie had found she was pretty good at working around his resistance.

Having stood most of the day at work, she wanted to relax before going onstage. Kicking her shoes off her feet, she pulled her chair out from under the makeup vanity and sat down at it.

She immediately heard a cracking sound, but didn't register what it was until the chair broke apart beneath her, sending her crashing to the floor. "Son of a bitch," she snapped as she lay still on the tile. The back of her head had scraped the concrete block wall on the other side as she'd fallen. She rubbed at it, shocked to see a few flecks of fresh blood on her fingertips.

"Izzie? Are you all right? What was that noise?" Nick asked as he burst into the room.

He swung the door open so hard he almost hit her with it. An inch closer and she would have taken a flat piece of oak square in the face.

"Oh, my God." He immediately dropped into a squat beside her. "You're hurt."

"It's okay," she insisted, slowly sitting up.

He put his hand under her arm to help her. "What happened?"

"My chair broke," she admitted, almost embarrassed about it. She'd never fully gotten over that chubby girl terror of breaking a chair in public.

"Is that blood on your fingers?" he asked, his voice so taut it almost snapped.

She lifted it to the back of her head again. "Yeah, I scraped my head on the wall when I fell."

"You need to go to the hospital." He rose and tugged her up, too. "Come on, I'll take you right now."

"No, Nick, I don't. I didn't bang my head, I promise. I just scratched it on the way down."

He frowned, obviously not believing her.

"Check and see for yourself. I swear, it's nothing but a scratch." She turned around, tilting her head back so he could see the spot where the blood had come from.

Nick gently pushed her hair out of the way. Izzie watched him in the mirror, seeing the frantic expression on his handsome face. And the way his jaw clenched as he tenderly examined her.

He was worried about her. Truly afraid for her.

"See?" she asked softly.

"Looks like a scratch," he admitted.

"Good."

"But that doesn't mean you're not hurt anywhere else. God, Izzie, what the hell happened?"

She gestured toward the remains of the chair, in pieces at her feet. "It fell apart as soon as I sat on it." Glaring at him, she added, "No big butt jokes."

He rolled his eyes. "As if." Stepping away, he ran his hands up and down her arms. "You're sure you're not hurt anywhere else?"

She was hurt elsewhere. Her hip was killing her from where she'd banged on the floor. But thankfully, she hadn't landed on her bum knee. "I'm okay."

Nick shook his head, muttering something, then bent down to examine the pieces of the chair. It was a sturdy rolling one that easily slid around when Izzie needed to reach something on the vanity. But it had fallen apart into several pieces.

"This doesn't make any damn sense." His tone was curt, all business now. "How could it just fall apart like that?"

"I have no clue. Maybe it was just defective."

Nick didn't even look up. He was poking around in the pile, picking up a couple of screws and staring at them hard.

"Rose? Nick? Is everything okay? Somebody heard a crash."

Glancing at the door, she saw Harry Black, and, right behind him, one of the bouncers. They both stared wide-eyed from her, down to Nick and the broken chair.

"Are you okay, honey?" Harry asked.

"Can I help you up?" the bouncer, Bernie, her self-appointed watchdog, asked.

"I'm fine. Just a little mishap."

"She could have been badly hurt," Nick barked.

"But I wasn't," she murmured, trying to calm all three down. If Nick was like a protective lion, Harry was like a fatherly teddy bear. And Bernie was like a big grizzly somebody had poked with a stick. They all looked equally upset.

"It's okay, I swear. Just an accident. Now, if you don't mind, Harry, could you find me another chair? I need to get ready to go on." The older man nodded and backed out of the door, taking Bernie with him.

Glancing at Nick, she added, "You need to get to work, too, making sure everything is safe and secure for me to perform."

He slowly rose, his eyes locked on hers. "Are you really worried about something, or are you trying to get rid of me?"

Izzie offered him a cocky grin, put her hand on his chest, and pushed him toward the door. "I'm trying to get rid of you. I have to be onstage in an hour, and with you in here oozing all that hot man stuff, I'm going to be tempted to test that lock and seduce you."

His eyes twinkled. But his frown remained. "You're not going to seduce me into forgetting you could have been hurt."

"And you're not going to bully me into forgetting I have a job to do."

He reached up and cupped her cheek. Izzie couldn't help curling into his hand, loving the roughness of his skin against her own. "I would never bully you into doing anything, Izzie."

They hadn't yet talked about her job. They'd officially been secret lovers for two wild, passion-filled nights, and she hadn't had a chance to even ask him if he was going to have some kind of macho problem with her dancing. Now he'd opened the door for the question.

"Are you going to be all right upstairs, watching me?"

He brushed his thumb over her jaw. "I love watching you."

Nibbling on his finger, she murmured, "I meant, will you be okay watching everyone else watch me?"

His jaw stiffened and his dark eyes flashed. But he didn't pull away. Instead, he drew closer, tipping her head back so sweetly, so tenderly, she knew he was still worried she could be hurt. "Izzie, I can't promise anything because I haven't experienced it yet. But I can tell you this…I know and want the real you…both sides of you. The Rose and the woman you become when you walk out of this place every Sunday night. I'm in this with *both* of you."

Without saying anything more, he bent down and covered her mouth with his, kissing her sweetly and tenderly. Then, with one more brush of his hand on her face, he turned and walked out.

As IT TURNED OUT, Nick did not have to test himself to see how he'd handle watching Izzie strip for other men. Because before she ever went onstage, Nick was forced to deal with a couple of punks who didn't understand the rules of a place as upscale as this one. One of them had made a move on a waitress, another had lunged at a dancer. Nick and Bernie plucked the guys up and dragged them out the front door, where, high on liquid courage, they'd both tried to put up a fight.

Maybe it was the residual anger he'd felt at seeing the blood on Izzie's fingertips. Or maybe it was the rage that flooded his head at the thought that it could have been Izzie the prick had grabbed, but as soon as the guy threw the first punch, Nick reacted harshly.

He'd had a few fights in his day, both before his military days and during them. And it was painfully easy to take down a drunk. The fight was over almost immediately after it had begun. Bernie dispatched of the drunk's friend just as quickly and the two of them nodded to each other in appreciation for the backup.

"Thanks, man," Bernie said.

"Not a problem."

Bernie shook the bleary patron. "I think this is the same prick who grabbed Rose a month ago."

Nick's jaw went rock-hard. If the man hadn't already been in Bernie's firm grip, he might have found a reason to throw another punch. But he was a fair fighter and wouldn't do something so out of bounds.

Unless the guy got free…then all was fair.

The guy didn't get free, Bernie had a tight grip and had begun chewing him out for harassing Rose. That incident had obviously been a more serious one than Nick had been led to believe, because Bernie hadn't forgotten a moment of it.

Because things had gotten physical, Nick decided to cover

his own ass, as well as the bouncer's and the club's, and called the police. He wanted this thing on record, now, when there were plenty of witnesses who'd seen both the assault on the female workers inside, and the provocation in the parking lot.

It was just his bad luck that Mark heard the call to Leather and Lace and decided to respond. Nick saw his brother get out of his unmarked car and saunter over, smiling widely. "Get in a fight without me?"

"Just doing my job," Nick replied, trying to figure out a way to get Mark to leave without going inside the club. If he was on duty, it wouldn't have been an issue—his brother was too good a cop to go inside a strip club while on duty. But he knew Mark's hours. No way was he working this late on a Saturday. "What are you doing here, anyway?"

"I heard it on the scanner. Noelle was already in bed—that woman goes to sleep by eight every night now. So I thought I'd head on over and see if you were okay."

"You know this guy?" one of the officers asked.

"My baby brother," Mark replied, his dimples flashing.

"By ten minutes," Nick said, shaking his head.

It took about an hour to clear up matters outside. Nick had stayed near the entrance, far from the stage, but he'd gotten reports from the bouncers about what was going on inside. So he knew when Izzie had performed...and when she was finished.

She'd done her first number and wouldn't be back on for at least an hour or two. Long enough to get rid of his brother.

"Come on, let me buy you a beer," Mark said once the last of the police cars pulled away.

"I'm working."

"Okay, then you buy me a beer." Not taking no for an answer, he threw his arm across Nick's shoulder and tugged him into the club. "Come on, I've never been in this place."

"Noelle probably wouldn't like it."

"I'm visiting my twin at work. No harm in that, is there?"

"Depends on whether you visited me blindfolded."

"I'll keep my back to the stage," Mark said. "Seriously, we haven't talked in weeks. I know something's going on with you."

His twin was right. They had been…disconnected. Not just because of what had been going on with Nick and Izzie, but also because his brother was about to become a father. Mark had changed. He had different priorities, talked a different language, looked at the world a different way.

Noelle and their baby were his family now. Oh, sure, he loved the rest of the Santoris, but he'd crossed that threshold from son and brother to husband and father.

Nick was the only one of the Santori siblings who had not.

"Let's sit out here," Mark said, nodding toward a couple of low, round tables in an outer chamber between the lobby and the main lounge area. They were out of view of the stage.

Nick wasn't surprised. Mark was a good husband. Like the rest of their brothers.

"All right." Gesturing to one of the waitresses, he ordered a club soda for himself and a beer for his brother. Returning to the table, he sat down across from his twin. "Can't be away for too long, though."

Mark settled back into the leather chair. "Nice."

"Yeah, it is."

"Good fringe benefits?"

Holding back a smile, Nick just shook his head.

"Hey, I'm married, these days are long gone. Throw me a bone."

"Throw me one," Nick replied before thinking better of it. "Tell me what it's like."

Mark frowned, obviously confused by the question. "It?"

"Marriage. What's it like being tied down, committed?"

Those deep dimples that had charmed girls from the time he was two years old flashed in Mark's cheeks. "It's the best. Noelle's everything I ever wanted."

"Yeah, but how'd you know what you wanted?" Nick muttered as he lifted his drink and downed half of it.

Chuckling, Mark admitted, "I didn't. I think it was more of a case of meeting her, and *knowing* that whatever I eventually did figure out I wanted for my life, she'd be part of it. It was always her. Everything else fell into place around her."

Somehow, that made a lot of sense to Nick. Because even though he'd been thinking of dozens of reasons why he and Izzie couldn't make it work—the primary one being that she didn't *want* it to—he couldn't help hoping it would. Because, as Mark had said, he suspected she was the one. That whatever else happened in his life, whatever direction he went in, whatever he chose, he'd want her to be a part of it.

Surprisingly, his brother didn't press him about why he was asking so many questions. Probably not because he didn't care—or didn't suspect there was a reason behind them. But because he knew Nick well enough to know that pushing for answers usually only made him clam up tighter.

Nick appreciated the courtesy. And realized yet again just how much he'd missed his twin.

"Hey Nick, we got a live one at the bar," a woman said.

Glancing over, Nick saw one of the waitresses, who was rolling her eyes. "Serious?"

"Not yet. But he could be if he's not handled right."

"I'll be there in a minute." Addressing his brother, he added, "Is there a full moon out tonight? The crazies are out."

Mark stood. "Yeah, including me. I must be crazy to be out here with you instead of home in bed with my wife."

Feeling better than he had in the hours since Izzie's accident with the chair, Nick reached out and grabbed his brother for a quick hug. Mark's eyes widened. He was the demonstrative one, not Nick. "What's that for?"

Nick shook his head. "I don't know. Give it to your wife."

"I've got plenty of my own to give," Mark said with a grin. "But thanks just the same."

The rest of the evening went by quickly, with more of the same insanity to deal with. Nick hadn't been kidding—the crazies were out tonight, and a lot of them had decided to show up at the club. The bouncers had had to forcibly eject more guys in this one evening than he'd seen them eject in the past month.

The only positive thing about keeping so busy was that Nick missed the Crimson Rose's final performance of the evening, too. He hadn't even realized she was on until he heard the thunderous applause, whoops and whistles of her audience. But at that point, he'd been outside, doing a sweep of parking lot to make sure none of their uninvited patrons had decided to come back.

Fortunately, they hadn't. But there were still other issues to deal with, like his conversation with Harry about Izzie's broken chair. She had called it an accident…and it might have been one. But he wasn't taking any chances. He and Harry had talked about adding security cameras to the basement area of the club, to hook into the system already covering the upstairs. Izzie's accident had confirmed the idea for both of them.

Just in case.

Saying goodbye to Harry, he headed downstairs, glancing at his watch. It was after two, the club was closed, everyone drifting out. But he knew she'd have waited. She wouldn't have left without seeing him. Partly because she'd want to see his reaction to her act. Partly because she knew he'd kill her if she'd walked out to her car alone.

"Iz?" he asked, knocking lightly on her dressing room door.

She opened it immediately. "Hi." She was nibbling on her bottom lip and her hands were clenched in front of her. Rather than being dressed to go home, she wore just a slinky robe. Thankfully, though, the mask and hairpieces were gone.

"You doing okay?"

She nodded, then looked at him through half-lowered eyelids. "Um, so? What'd you think?"

He reached for her and drew her into his arms. "I didn't see you dance."

"What?"

"Sorry, other stuff was going on."

"I heard there were some problems."

"Yep."

She fisted her hands and put them on her hips. The pose did really nice things, like pulling her short pink robe apart at the neck to reveal the lush, upper curves of her breasts.

"You're telling me you just happened to have to deal with various crises during the exact times I was on stage? And that was simply coincidence?"

She might not believe it, but it was true. At least, he *thought* it was. He guessed he could have done the parking lot sweep a few minutes earlier or later. He hadn't evaluated his decision before. But now, looking back…well, maybe something inside him had made sure he didn't have to see other men looking at the beautiful body of the woman he considered his.

"You're *sure* you're going to be all right with this?" Her chin went up. "I won't be able to handle it if you go all Cro-

Magnon man and try to drag me by the hair back to your cave."

"You woman. Me man," he said, slipping his hands down and parting her robe further. He nuzzled into her neck, breathing in her essence, realizing twenty-four hours had been far too long to go without making love to her. "Me got heap big appetite."

She swatted at his shoulder. But she didn't back up. "You're such a dork."

Nick had *never* been called that, or anything like it, in his entire life. Ass maybe. Jerk. Cold-hearted pig, on one occasion. But never a dork. And it surprised a laugh out of him.

She delighted him. Simply brought every good feeling that existed inside him out into the open.

"God, I love being with you," he muttered, unable to help revealing a little bit of what he was feeling.

"I know, I feel the same way."

She didn't admit that easily, the words had come haltingly out of her mouth. Which made Nick value them that much more.

He moved his mouth down, sampling her collarbone.

"Did you put that lock on my door yourself?" she whispered as she tilted her head farther, silently begging for more.

He nodded, continue to kiss and lick, lower now, to the curves of her breasts, beautifully bare under the robe.

"Let's use it."

"My thoughts exactly," he murmured.

He didn't let her go, he simply reached back and flipped the lock, then dipped down lower to lick his way down her to her pert nipple. Flicking it with his tongue, he waited until she was quivering to cover it with his mouth and suckle her.

"Mmm…more."

Nick stroked her sides, his thumbs meeting near her belly button and scraping lower to tease the top edge of her pretty pink panties. With one last sweet suck on her breast he moved down her, following the path his hands had taken.

Izzie moaned softly, swaying on her feet. Nick kept her steady as he kissed his way down the front of her body. The soft robe brushed his face. So did her soft skin.

"Do you know what I wanted to do to you the first time I came into this room?"

She tangled her hands in his hair as he dropped lower, kneeling on the floor in front of her. "I think I have an idea."

He pressed his face in her belly, licking at that tender bit of skin right above her pelvic bone, slowly pushing her panties down as he dipped lower.

"Did it involve that nice, big, flat surface in front of the mirror?" she asked.

Smart girl. "Uh-huh." Gently holding her hips, he flicked at the panties, watching appreciatively as she shimmied out of them. The robe fell, too. Under the bright light bulbs ringing the mirror, he was able to see every glorious inch of her. But he wanted to see more—didn't want his view blocked even by her pretty brown curls. So he turned her and edged her back until her bottom brushed the edge of the vanity top.

"Wait," he said, suddenly remembering her accident. Wrapping his hand around the edge of the vanity counter, he tugged at it sharply, testing the shelf's sturdiness. It remained firmly in place, well secured into the wall.

"Good," she murmured. Rising on her tiptoes, she slid onto the vanity, parting her legs just the way he wanted her to.

Someone had brought her another chair, and Nick grabbed it, sitting on it directly in front of her. Reaching for her knees, he slowly pushed them apart, watching a pink flush rise through her entire body.

She made no effort to resist. Confident. Sensual. Incredibly seductive. She knew what he wanted and she wanted it, too.

He pushed her legs further, until he could see the glisten of moisture on the sensitive slit between her legs. "Do you have any idea how beautiful you are?" he asked.

It was a rhetorical question. She couldn't possibly know how beautiful she looked to him, wanton and aroused, opening herself up so he could pleasure them both.

He couldn't wait any longer. With a low groan of need, Nick dropped his face to that sweet, warm spot. He lapped at her in one slow, long lick, feeling her thighs quiver beside his face.

Izzie tilted up for him, inviting him further, and he sampled her again. "You taste just as good without the cannoli, Cookie," he mumbled.

She managed a choppy laugh. "Don't call me Cookie."

"Can't help it." He nibbled his way up to catch her erect clit between his lips. He played with it even as he scraped his fingers across her swollen sex. She was drenched and ready to take whatever he wanted to give her. Wanting that warm, wet flesh wrapped around part of him while he continued to savor her with his mouth, he slipped a finger inside her.

"Mmm," she groaned. "More. More of everything."

He complied. Licking harder and sucking deeper, he slid another finger into her, then slowly moved them in and out, timing his strokes to her helpless moans.

With one more swirl of his tongue on her most sensitive spot, Izzie cried out and climaxed. He wanted to be part of that climax, to experience the spasms of her body as she clenched and shook. Standing, he tugged his shirt up and off, then unfastened his belt and pants and pushed them down, out of the way.

When he looked up again, Izzie had slid down to stand before him. He frowned. "I wasn't *nearly* done."

Her eyes sparkled. "Neither was I." Then, with an Eve-like smile on her face, she turned around, facing away from him, until they were both looking in the mirror. She slowly bent forward, putting her hands flat on the vanity, curving that sweet ass back in pure, unspoken invitation.

His pulse roared. "You're sure…"

"Oh, I'm *very* sure," she promised him. She was still smiling, her eyes still glittered in avarice and hunger. "It's *your* turn to take *me,* Nick."

Remembering the way he'd begged her to take him the other night at his place, he nodded in lazy agreement. "Oh, honey, you can't imagine how much I want to take you like this."

Making love to her face to face—watching her incredible eyes widen with pleasure, and her sweet mouth fall open on every long sigh—was amazing. He knew he'd never tire of doing it.

But the idea of taking her like *this*— with raw, hot passion—excited him beyond reason. He'd be able to see her expressions in the mirror, be able to plunge deeper than ever before until he imprinted himself somewhere deep inside her. Deep enough that, perhaps, she might never want to let him go.

"Nick," she begged, "please." She arched again, those long, dancer's legs putting her curvy butt directly in line with his cock. She backed into him, as he moved forward to her.

He held her full hips in both hands, bending a little so he could see her sweet entrance and ease his way into it. She hissed and arched, trying to take him deeper, but powerless. His hands held her firmly, he was setting the pace.

And he planned to go slowly, wanting to savor every second of the experience.

"Give it to me," she begged, watching him with desperation.

He smiled at her in the mirror and thrust forward a tiny bit. Rewarded by her gasp and the flare of her eyes, he pulled out again. This time, she didn't beg for more, she simply licked her lips and watched, trusting him to make it good.

He didn't make it good. He made it amazing. By the time he finally sunk all the way into her tight heat, Izzie was whimpering. And by the time he began to lose his mind and thrust wildly, in and out, over and over, she was practically sobbing.

He thought they were alone in the building. But he couldn't be sure. "Izzie…," he said, slowing to ease out of her, to calm them both a little, "…wait."

"Don't stop."

"I'm not stopping, sweetheart," he said. Then he stopped. She whimpered, watching him, then realized he was turning her around. "I have to kiss you, Iz," he murmured.

She twisted in his arms to face him, twining her arms around his neck and one leg around his waist. Plunging his tongue in her mouth, he tangled it with hers keeping his eyes open so he could stare into her beautiful face. Lifting her back up onto the vanity, he went right back into her, deep and fast, knowing this last stretch would be a quick, pulsing one.

"Sweet heaven, you amaze me," she whispered against his mouth as he filled her again.

"Amazing. Yeah."

Those were the only words he could manage. Wanting to be connected with her everywhere, he kissed her again, wrapped his arms tightly around her body and drew her up against him.

Stroking and thrusting, he rocked into her with every bit of himself, her cries of pleasure echoing sweetly in his ears. And when he finally heard those cries turned into desperate gasps as she climaxed, he let himself go, too, erupting inside her until he was completely empty.

"HEY HOT STUFF, you're looking delicious again today."

Bridget jerked her head up, blinking the columns of numbers out of her brain as someone stepped into her office

Sunday afternoon. She knew it wasn't Dean…he didn't speak to her like that, which was good. She wanted him to notice her, wanted him to realize she was interested in him. But she definitely didn't want a man who'd speak to her so coarsely.

"Oh, hi," she said, seeing one of the salesmen standing in the doorway. The guy, Ted, was a middle-aged divorcé with a phlegmy chuckle. He also had what she and her friends in middle school used to call Roman hands and Russian fingers.

He was grabby. Touchy. But he'd never gone too far beyond pats on her shoulder. She hoped that wasn't about to change.

Ted wore his usual ugly striped sports coat over a dingy dress shirt and a red tie. In other words, he looked a mess. Usually, she saw him as a kind of sad guy whose wife had dumped him. He was smarmy and coarse, but had never given her any reason to be wary of him personally. Now, however, goosebumps had prickled her body and tension throbbed in her temple.

She didn't like the look in his eye.

"You dressing like that just for me, hot stuff?" he asked as he sauntered into the office.

"I think that question would be called sexual harassment," she said as she stared hard at him, hoping he'd take the warning as a threat and get out now, before he'd gone too far.

When he smiled and pushed the door shut behind him, she had a sinking feeling he'd *already* gone too far.

Damn. She should have left an hour ago. It was four o'clock, an hour after the dealership closed on Sundays. And she had to assume everyone else had gone home. Ted hadn't been around since this morning. Judging by the whiff of alcohol she caught wafting off him, she figured he'd gone for a long lunch at a local bar.

Dean, why didn't you show up? She'd thought for sure he'd

be here. He'd worked every weekend since he started. That was the only reason Bridget had come in herself today…to see him!

It had been for nothing. She'd worn another short, sexy skirt that she'd bought at a cute local clothing store last night. That, with the silky sleeveless shell that draped across her curves invitingly would have been enough to get the man's temperature rising. And he hadn't even been here to see it.

Instead, Ted was. *Ick.*

"Girl, you have been hiding your light under a bushel." He stepped closer. "It's closing time. Let's go have some fun."

"No, thank you," she said, her tone icy. She stuffed her paperwork into a drawer. Normally, she'd be more tidy. Today, she was in a hurry. She wanted out of here.

"Aww, come on, sweetie, I know there's no man in your life. You must be lonely. Why don't you let me keep you company?"

She'd rather keep company with a dead skunk. "No, Ted."

Hopefully that firm tone would get the message across and he'd get out of her way and let her leave. But as she stood, Ted stepped between her desk and the door, right in her path. "You know you really want to stay."

"No. I *really* don't."

Trying once again to be like Izzie, she fisted one hand, retrieved her purse, and tried to walk past him.

He grabbed her arm. "Not even a few minutes conversation?"

"Not even that," she insisted, jerking her arm away.

Her angry tone and the heat in her eyes must have finally gotten through. Because Ted went from stupid drunk trying to *score* to angry drunk trying to *control* in one blink of her eyes. Without warning, he put both his hands on her shoulders and pushed her back. Bridget stumbled over her own high-heeled sandals, landing on her butt on the edge of her desk.

"Perfect." Dropping his hands onto her thighs, he crudely pushed her legs apart and forced his way between them.

"Let me go!"

"Not yet, hot stuff."

She reached around on the desk behind her, hoping she'd left her scissors or stapler out, but all she managed to grab was a small desk clock. Wrapping her fingers tightly around it, she swung, but only managed a glancing blow to Ted's shoulder.

His nostrils flared even as his eyes narrowed in anger. "Playing hard to get?"

"Let me go or I'll scream."

"Nobody to hear you, pretty thing," he said, any hint of charm gone from his voice as his true nature emerged.

Before she could say a thing—or think what to say—Bridget heard something that sounded like an angel. But it was no angel.

It was Dean Willis. *Roaring.*

"Get the hell off her you son of a bitch."

Suddenly he was. Ted was lifted off her and tossed to the side of the room. Bridget saw him land hard against the wall and crumple to the floor. He yelped in either fear or pain. Or both.

He had reason to be afraid. Dean was already reaching for him, his face red, his body emanating danger. "You're dead."

Ted's bravado when facing her disappeared under this new threat. Before Dean could even grab him, he'd launched himself to his feet and run out the door, leaving the two of them alone. The whole thing—from Ted's entrance to his speedy departure—had taken place in under three minutes.

Her head was spinning. Breathing hard and shaking a little, she mumbled, "Thank you so much."

Dean swung around to look at her, that blood rage still evident on his face. His blue eyes were like matching chips of ice. He looked as much like a cute, nice-guy car salesman as she looked like Xena the Warrior Princess.

No. This was not gentle, good-natured Dean. This was a dangerous man in a high fury. And her shivers of fear turned to shivers of excitement.

"What the hell happened?"

Still sitting on the desk, she could only shake her head. "He obviously had been drinking. He came back and caught me alone. It's the first time he's ever…I mean, he's a creep, but I never thought he'd…"

"Maybe if you'd wear clothes that didn't scream 'do me' men wouldn't try."

Bridget's jaw dropped and she stared at him in shock. "What did you say to me?"

"Look at you," he snapped, stepping closer. He pointed to her legs, still splayed open on the desk.

Bridget tried to jerk them back together, but Dean stepped between them before she could do it. With absolutely no warning, he plunged his hands into her hair and bent to cover her lips with his. He thrust his tongue in her mouth, tasting her, devouring her. His body was hard against hers, his hips between her thighs, and Bridget couldn't even try to deny the absolute flood of heat that roared through her in response.

She wrapped her arms around his neck, tilting her head to kiss him back just as deeply. And for a long, heady moment, they made crazy, wild love with their mouths.

Then the moment ended. Dean let her go and staggered back a few steps. "Bridget, I'm…"

She put her hand up, palm out, to stop him. Sliding off the desk, she straightened her skirt and said, "Don't. Okay? Just don't say anything. I wanted that. Maybe I *needed* it just so I could wash Ted out of my memory. I didn't exactly jump up there and part my legs—he pushed me."

Dean instinctively swung his head to look at the door, that tense rage returning.

"He's long gone. Thank you for coming in when you did."

He ran both hands through his hair, his anger finally draining away. "I'll take care of him, Bridget."

"Marty will deal with him." She stepped closer, offering him a tremulous smile. Because now there was no doubt that Dean's interest in her was one of more than friendship. That kiss—and his body's hard, instinctive reaction to it—told her he wanted more. Maybe as much as she did. "I guess that makes you my hero, huh?"

Dean stared at her, his eyes softening, the tension easing. Reaching for her, he pulled her into his arms. But this time, he didn't attempt to kiss her. His embrace was pure, sweet comfort. He held her tightly, running his hand up and down her back. "I'm sorry. Sorry for what he did…sorry for what I said."

"It's all right. You were angry." Tilting her head back, she smiled up at him. "I thought it was kinda sexy."

For a second—a brief one—she thought he was going to smile back. To laugh, then lower his mouth to hers and kiss her again, gently this time.

But it didn't happen. Instead, Dean sighed heavily and his mouth drew tight. "I'm also sorry for kissing you. I should never have done that."

"I've been wanting you to…"

He put his hand up to stop her. "Don't. It was a mistake, Bridget. A big one. And it won't be repeated."

She gasped, unable to believe he was rejecting her. *Again.*

"What is your *problem?*" she asked, completely indignant.

He just shook his head. "I don't have a problem. I just

can't…don't want…hell, Bridget, this just can't happen." As if needing to convince himself, as much as her, he reiterated. "It *won't* happen."

10

WHEN NICK MANAGED to get through another evening at Leather and Lace *without* watching her dance, Izzie got a little nervous. She didn't want to ask him about it over the next few nights since they were having such an amazing time doing wildly sensual things to one another. But she couldn't help wondering.

On Sunday night, he'd been too *busy* to watch her dance. Or so he'd claimed. He'd conveniently had to go put out another fire in the club every time she was scheduled to go on.

Suspicious. She didn't want to be, but she was.

He'd said he could handle it…but he wasn't acting like he even wanted to try.

It wasn't that she didn't understand. In fact, putting herself in his shoes, she'd have to say she'd probably have a major problem with other women looking at *her* naked man with covetous eyes, thinking of ways they could have that incredible body and handsome face.

Her man. Her man? Oh, God, had he somehow become *her* man?

Sitting in her apartment, she realized that yes, at some point in recent weeks, Nick *had* become her man.

Maybe it had been when he'd made love to her in the back of the van. Or when he'd cared for her after she'd fallen in her dressing room. Maybe it was because of his sexy smile and the intimate way he watched her when he thought no one was looking.

Maybe it was even because of the way she'd felt every single time she'd woken up in his arms.

Those pre-dawn moments. Yeah. They'd probably done it.

Because each time it had happened—whether at his apartment, or hers, she'd had to lie there and watch him sleep. Study the line of his jaw and the curve of his cheek. Wonder how a man could have such a sensuous mouth and still be so damned tough. Note the small scars on his body, and his tattoo, and grieve for the things he must have gone through as a soldier.

Yes. In those moments, her heart had opened up. And she'd let him in just as surely as she'd let him in her body.

There were moments when she allowed herself not to care. To even consider whether they could make this crazy relationship of theirs work. *Maybe a masked wedding…the Crimson Rose and the sexy night watchman.*

That was *so* lame.

But it was no more crazy to think about than the idea of an official union between Izzie Natale and Nick Santori of Taylor Street.

"Would that really be so bad?" she whispered. She'd been telling herself it would, but at moments like this, she had a hard time remembering why.

"I need sugar," she mumbled as she headed for her kitchen, dying for something sweet. She'd been so good at the bakery and tried to resist temptation, so she never brought any of that stuff home. At moments like these, though, she regretted it.

Nick had called a while ago, saying he'd be leaving the pizzeria in an hour and would come by. She glanced at her watch, wondering if she had time to run to the corner market. She was so desperate she'd go for a packet of Ho Hos at this point.

Before she could grab her shoes and dash for something to binge on, her cell phone rang. Glancing at the caller ID and recognizing the New York City number, she immediately began to smile, now knowing another sure-fire way to escape—at least mentally—from her troubles.

"V!" she exclaimed as she answered.

"Girl-*friend!*" was the reply. "It has been for-*evah*, where have you been?"

Plopping down on the sofa, Izzie kicked her feet up and leaned back, so happy to hear a voice from her old life, she wondered if fate had sent Vanessa's call as some kind of mental gift. Vanessa was a good friend from her Rockette days. The striking, long-legged African American woman had been Izzie's roommate on the road and the two of them had hit it off from their very first hotel stay, when they'd both decided to call for room service French fries at two in the morning, despite the matron's orders to go to sleep by eleven o'clock.

"I'm still in Chicago."

"Still doing that bakery thing?" Vanessa asked, sounding completely shocked. "I can't believe you've lasted this long."

"Join the club. I sometimes forget I haven't spent the past seven years with my arms in cookie dough up to my elbows."

"How's your father?

"Getting better every day, already pestering my mother to let him go back to work."

"That's great. And as soon as he does you can quit."

Yes, she could. Why that idea would send a shot of sadness through her, Izzie didn't know. It wasn't as if she liked working at the bakery. Even if she *had* made friends with all the staff, gotten on a first-name basis with their restaurant clients and the regulars who stopped in every day for break-fast.

Well, maybe she did like it. A little. But certainly not enough to want to stay there permanently.

Vanessa laughed softly. "And then you can come home. You still thinking of choreographing, or teaching?"

She had been, though, not as much lately. But she didn't tell Vanessa that.

Fortunately, her friend quickly moved on. "You've got to come back soon. You are so missing out." Launching into an explanation of all the things that had been going on—with the Rockettes, and in her personal life, Vanessa soon had Izzie laughing so hard she had to wipe tears from her eyes. The other woman was a wild one, and the ballsiest female she'd ever known.

The stories were entertaining, particularly when told with Vanessa's flair. But even as she laughed, Izzie couldn't help wondering whether her friend was truly happy. She sounded a little…empty. Lonely. Bored.

Which made Izzie suddenly remember the way she'd been feeling right before she'd hurt her leg.

Very much the same way.

All the things Vanessa had been describing were things Izzie had been doing the past few years in New York. She missed none of them. Honestly, all she really missed were her friends and her apartment. The lifestyle she'd already begun to outgrow even before she'd been forced to leave it.

Going back to it didn't sound very palatable.

She shook off that crazy thought—not go back to her life? Insane. Like she had anything better going on *here?* "So which guy did you shove in the fountain?"

"The French dude. Pierre from Paris. Only, I think his name was probably really Petey from Poughkepsie or something. He wasn't French any more than my dry wheat toast was French this morning." Sighing, her friend added, "Why do men suck so bad?"

"Not all of them," she said before thinking better of it.

Vanessa caught the tone in her voice and leapt on it. "Talk. Who is he? What's he do? When did you start doing him?"

Having had no one to truly confide in since she'd been here...about her feelings, her relationship with Nick, even a bit about her sexy weekend job, she found herself spilling all of it to Vanessa. She must have talked for a solid five minutes without letting her friend get a word in. Finally realizing that, she whispered, "You still there?"

Vanessa murmured, "Oh, honey. This is serious."

Yes. It was. Very serious.

"This Nick, I remember you talking about him."

Izzie was afraid of that. Nick had always been—for her—the dream guy she'd never landed.

Now she'd landed him. She just didn't know if she was going to get to keep him. Or if he even *wanted* her to, considering he hadn't been able to bring himself to watch her dance again at the club.

"He might be a man worth settling down for, Izzie. Giving up your dancing...wait, what the hell did you say is the name of this place you're dancing at?"

She should have known that would interest her friend more than any potential romance. "It's called Leather and Lace."

"Holy shit, girl, you're strippin'."

"Yeah. I'm stripping. And I'm having the time of my life." Well, the stripping wasn't giving her the time of her life. Nick was. But she'd already talked enough about Nick.

Vanessa demanded all the details on Izzie's secret life, not sounding the least judgmental, and asking a bunch of questions. "That sounds like *fun*. You know, I've thought about taking a strip-dance exercise class they offer at my health club, but there's a waiting list."

"You're joking."

"No, honey, I'm not. It is the hottest thing going—there's a three-month long list to get in this class and everybody I know is putting their name on it. If you come back, you need to teach me how and maybe I'll retire and we can start a school somewhere. Teach housewives how to shake their booties."

Izzie laughed softly at that silly idea. Then she thought of the word Vanessa had used. *If.* "What do you mean, *if* I come back? Why wouldn't I come back?"

Vanessa grew very quiet, as if working out what to say. Knowing her friend was street-wise in a way Izzie never had been, she very much wanted to hear it. Anything Vanessa put this much thought into had to be worth hearing.

Finally, her friend murmured, "Why would you come back here when the life you really want is there?"

"You think I want to be a *baker* for the rest of my life?" Izzie protested, shocked that her friend would even suggest it.

"I don't know whether you want to be a baker or a stripper. A pizza-delivery gal or a ballerina. All I know is that whatever you end up wanting to do, it'll be tied up with that man you've loved for half your life."

Izzie's jaw dropped. She flinched so hard the phone fell onto her lap. Scrambling to get it, she heard Vanessa's words echoing in her head. Especially because they'd come so quickly—mere minutes—after Izzie had been tearing herself apart to try to figure out just what she felt for Nick.

She really shouldn't have had to think about it so hard. She knew what she felt for Nick. It was the same thing she'd always felt for him, only deeper now, adult. Sensual. Mature.

Forever.

Vanessa was right. She loved him. Part of her knew she should resent that, since it had been what she'd feared—and why she'd thrown up walls between them when he'd first pursued her. But she already knew she didn't regret it. How could she regret feeling so emotionally alive for the first time in years?

"You still there?" her friend asked when Izzie finally brought the phone back up to her ear.

"I'm still here."

Vanessa chuckled. Then, in a very low voice, she added, "I better be in the wedding."

Then all Izzie heard was the dial tone.

"HEY, LITTLE BROTHER, when are you gonna come talk to the business lawyer with me and Pop?"

Nick stared at Tony, who'd followed him out the front door of Santori's Friday afternoon. He'd been planning to head up the block to Natale's. He had a real taste for cannoli. The fresh kind that could only be found in Izzie's kitchen.

Or in Izzie. But that was another kind of decadent dessert altogether.

"I dunno, Tony, I really haven't thought about it."

His brother frowned. "I don't get it. I thought it was all set. You know how much Pop wants to retire completely."

"Bullshit."

Chuckling, his brother nodded in agreement. "Okay. We know he won't ever get outta that kitchen until they pry his wooden spoon out of his hand for his own funeral. But I know he's hoping to get you settled."

Get Nick settled. It sounded so archaic. And constricting.

"If you're worried about coming in as a financial partner rather than just a working one, I am sure willing to let you buy in with some of that money you said you saved while you were in the service."

Honestly, that had been one of Nick's big concerns. He didn't want anyone covering his way, he liked to pay his fair share. And if he were seriously considering going into business with Tony, he would absolutely insist on those terms. He did have the money, he did have the desire to get involved in a successful business and help it grow.

But that business was not a pizzeria. He knew it in his heart. He just hadn't figured out how to tell the family that yet. "I haven't made any decisions."

Tony met his stare, obviously trying to figure out what was going on in Nick's head. Nick thought about how best to put into words that he didn't want the life his family had mapped out for him. But before either of them could say anything, Nick spotted Izzie walking up the street, coming up behind Tony. Considering his big brother was a mountain of a man, she probably hadn't even seen Nick yet.

The sight of her face brought a stupid smile to his. But he didn't give a damn. At least, not until his brother turned to look over his shoulder at whatever had made him so happy.

"Whoa-ho," Tony said, when he looked back at Nick. "Izzie? It's *Izzie?* Holy shit, Gloria's gonna love this."

"Gloria's not going to know about this," Nick muttered. Izzie was not twenty steps away and if she heard what they were talking about, she'd probably bolt. Then ignore him for the next week until he could work his way around her defenses again.

Damn, but the woman was prickly.

"Why not? Cripes, the family's been wanting you two to hook up forever."

"That's the problem. Izzie isn't the kind of woman who likes to do what's expected of her."

Maybe that's one reason they got along so well. Because

Nick felt exactly the same way about his family. He just hadn't been able to make that clear to them yet.

"Okay, I won't do anything to jinx it. But I don't know how long I'll be able to keep it from Gloria." Tony grinned, shaking his head back and forth. "The woman can get anything out of me with her sexy…"

"Don't want to hear it," Nick smoothly interjected. He continued to watch Izzie, realizing the exact moment when she spotted him. A quick grin flashed across her face. But when she saw who was with him, the grin disappeared.

"Hi, Tony. Nick," she murmured, reaching them. She sounded so cool and calm. As if she hadn't been in a huge tub of warm bubbles and cold champagne with him twelve hours ago, loving each other until the water got cold and the champagne got flat.

God, what a night. Another amazing one in Izzie's arms. He didn't know what he'd ever do without them.

"How's it going, little sister?" Tony asked, giving her a one-armed hug. "Sorry I couldn't make it to lunch at the folks' house Sunday. Work—it kills me." He glanced at Nick and wagged his eyebrows. "If only I had a partner to take up the slack."

Nick managed to suppress a sigh. Then he turned his attention to Izzie. "I was just on my way to the bakery. I'm jonesing for something sweet."

She chuckled. "I was last night, too. I almost dashed out and got a Ho Ho to tide me over until you…" She quickly snapped her mouth shut, remembering Tony was there.

His oldest brother had never been the king of tact. In fact, his wife affectionately called him Lunkhead. Well, *usually* affectionately. Right now, however, Tony managed to pull it off. "Well, it was great seeing you, Iz, but I have to get back to work. Nick, you're gonna swing by the bank after you go up to the bakery and grab us some of Izzie's fabulous cannolis?"

They had plenty of cannolis left in the restaurant, but, he

assumed, it was the best Tony could do on such short notice. "Sure, Tony. You bet."

They both watched Tony go back into the restaurant, with breezy hellos and good wishes to every customer he passed on the way back to the kitchen. When they were alone on the sidewalk, Izzie continued to stare at the glass restaurant door. Finally, she murmured, "He knows, doesn't he?"

Nick nodded. "Yeah."

"How?"

With a helpless shrug, he told her the truth. "He saw the look on my face when I saw you walking toward me just now."

She finally tore her gaze off the door and directed it toward him. Staring into his eyes, she searched for the meaning of what he'd said.

He didn't try to hide it. He was in love with Izzie and his eyes affirmed that, even if his mouth didn't.

He just didn't know if she'd *want* to see the truth there.

He understood why she wouldn't. Putting the reality of their feelings out there meant they had to deal with them. It meant she could accuse him of breaking their "secret lovers" deal and freeze him out of her life again.

It could also mean she'd acknowledge that she was falling for him, too. And that maybe they could make something work between them. Something good. Right.

Permanent.

"I can't handle this, Nick," she whispered, appearing stricken. "He'll tell Gloria."

"Not intentionally."

"And she'll blab to the known universe and the neighborhood will have me married and fat before winter and my parents will be eyeing a perfect little row house for us right up from theirs, getting our future kids on the waiting lists to go to Sacred Heart and St. Raphael's."

She sounded pained, as if the very idea of living that life devastated her. He understood why. Because he didn't want it, either. Any of it. Oh, he wanted Izzie, no doubt about it. But as for how they lived? Well, it wouldn't be like anything anybody on Taylor Street would understand.

But before he could reassure her, Izzie shook her head and started walking. "I can't talk about this now. Not here."

He fell into step beside her. "Tonight."

"I'm going to my parents tonight. My sister Mia's coming into town for the weekend and I had to promise to come for dinner—which I can't do tomorrow or Sunday."

In a normal relationship, she'd ask him to come with her. In a normal relationship, he'd do it.

They weren't normal, of course.

"Call me when you're done and I'll meet you at your place."

She hesitated, glancing at him from the corner of her eye. "I need a little time, Nick. Just a little time. Can we…maybe take a break until tomorrow?"

One night. She wasn't asking for much. But the thought of going without her tonight nearly killed him.

"All right, Izzie." He caught her arm, holding her elbow before she could stalk away. She looked frantically from side to side, as if to see if anyone was watching, but Nick didn't release her. "Don't panic," he ordered her. "Don't see trouble where there is none."

She flashed him a grateful smile, murmured, "I'm mentally kissing you goodbye," then tugged her arm free and walked away.

He mentally kissed her goodbye, too, until she disappeared into the bakery.

SPENDING FRIDAY NIGHT with her family actually turned out to be a very good experience. Izzie had been half-dreading it, since she'd felt like an alien among all of them since the day she'd gotten home. But something about this gathering was different. Maybe because Mia was home and therefore got a lot of the attention. Or because Gloria's boys were there—the grandsons always caused everything else to cease to exist for her parents.

Or maybe it was just because Izzie forced herself to relax. Not having to talk a lot meant she didn't have to watch every word she said. Didn't have to worry about letting something slip regarding her dancing—which they all assumed she'd given up entirely because of her knee.

Not being so on edge actually allowed her to relax and, to her shock, even enjoy herself.

She was still mulling it over the next day, remembering the smile on her father's face as he talked about returning to work soon. When he told her he'd been talking to his brother—who was about to retire—about coming to work with him at the bakery, Izzie began to see a silver lining in the cloud of her life. With another member of the family coming in to the business, the pressure would be off Izzie to stay involved. Maybe she could get back to something like a real life of her own.

Whatever she did—staying in Chicago or going back to New York, continuing to strip or giving it up—loving Nick or letting him get away—she knew she did not want to be a baker for much longer.

Nick tried reaching her a couple of times Saturday but she'd missed his calls. Not intentionally—the first time she'd been in the shower and the second she'd been waiting on customers at the bakery. By the time she had a minute to call him back, he'd been the one who hadn't answered.

Still, not having spoken to him for more than a day—since that tense moment on the street when she'd realized Tony had stumbled onto the truth of their relationship—she was a little nervous. Heading to work at Leather and Lace, she immediately scanned the parking lot for his car, but didn't see it. She was early— probably two hours earlier than she needed to be, and she knew it was because she was hoping he'd be here.

"Hi, Rose," someone said as she came in the back door.

"Hi, Bernie. How's the week been?"

The bouncer shrugged, offering her one of his big, boyish grins. "Knocked a few heads together, wiped up the ground with a drunk or two. You know, the usual."

Laughing, she began to walk past him

But he stopped her with a hand on her shoulder. He glanced at the big canvas bag she carried, which was filled with some street clothes and supplies. "Can I help you in any way, Rose? Carry that? Get you some dinner?"

She shook her head. "You are so sweet, but no, honestly, I've got it." The guy had been tripping over himself to take care of her since her first night at work. If he'd ever made a move on her, she'd suspect it was because he was interested. But he'd never been anything but a nice—if overprotective— friend.

Still smiling as she walked toward her dressing room, Izzie acknowledged just how comfortable she felt here. The club staff was like a second family already. Bernie and Harry. Leah and Jackie and the other dancers. They were all people she cared about, who seemed to care about her.

She didn't *want* to give this up. Which was another reason she didn't quite know how to deal with Nick's seeming inability to watch her perform. It was as if ever since he'd become her lover, he no longer liked her doing her job.

That was how it *seemed*. But she couldn't be sure. "Maybe he really is just busy," she mumbled, trying to convince herself.

When she reached her dressing room, she put her new key in the new lock and twisted it. Before going inside, however,

Leah stopped her. "Hey, I feel like I'm always picking up your presents!" the grinning girl said. She held up a gold foil wrapped box. "Yum. Have I told you how much I love chocolate?"

Izzie glanced at the box, looked down at her own full hips—at least an inch bigger than they'd been when she moved back from New York—and sighed. "Have I told you how much chocolate sticks to my hips and butt?"

The one plus was that the candies were chocolate-covered cherries. And she wasn't too crazy about them. If they'd been caramels, she'd probably be much more tempted to grab a fistful. As it was, she easily waved them away. "Take them out of my sight, would you?"

Leah clutched the box to her chest. "Woo-hoo! Remind me to watch for the next jewelry box heading your way."

Entering her dressing room, Izzie slowly slipped out of her clothes and put her robe on. She took her time—there was lots of it. Over the next hour, she got ready for her night. The chatter of women's voices from the greenroom couldn't drown out the sound of lots of footsteps walking in the lounge above her head. Customers were already pouring in, performers already on stage judging by the low bass beat she could almost feel reverberating in her chest.

The whole place felt alive and vibrant. Exactly the way *she* felt when she was here. The only other time she felt as good was when she was with Nick. What on earth was she going to do if he couldn't take her working here anymore?

"Don't think about it," she reminded herself as she glanced at her watch. She'd been here over an hour and he still hadn't come in. Which was making her very jittery.

Izzie forced everything else out of her head and finished putting on her makeup. Her audience might not see much of her face, but that didn't mean she didn't cover the stage makeup basics. She was puffing anti-shine powder on her

cheeks when she heard a knock on her door. "Come in."
Almost holding her breath, she let it out with a pleased sigh
when she saw Nick. "Hi."

"Hi yourself," he said. He pushed the door shut behind him,
bent down and kissed her on the mouth. Quick, hard…hot and
sexy. "Been needing that," he said when he finally straightened.

"Me, too."

"Want more later."

She grinned. "Me, too."

"Things are already heating up upstairs, but I wanted to see
you before it got too crazy."

Izzie turned away, slowly lifting the powder puff to her
face again. "Do you think it'll be too *busy* again for you to
be there during my numbers?"

Nick met her eyes in the mirror. "I don't know," he muttered. "I can't promise anything."

He was still hesitant, she heard it in his voice. Nick was
avoiding having to acknowledge how he really felt—was
going to feel—about her stripping. Izzie wanted to cry,
sensing she knew what that answer would be.

He'd hate it. Sure, he'd been fine with her taking her
clothes off when she was a stranger. But now that they were
lovers? Well, if he was like every other male of the species,
he was going to turn into the caveman he'd once jokingly pretended to be and get all overbearing. He'd want her to quit,
he'd be surly and pouty until she did.

There weren't many men who'd be able to take having
their girlfriend strip down to a G-string in front of a bunch of
strangers…why should she expect Nick to be any different?

"I'm doing my best, Iz."

"Okay," she murmured, blinking rapidly against unexpected moisture in her eyes, welling up not because she didn't

understand, she *did.* But because she so feared what this was going to mean when it finally came to a head between them.

"Oh, God, somebody get a bucket!"

Hearing the loud shout from the corridor outside her dressing room, Izzie immediately rose to her feet.

"Catch her!"

Nick flinched. "Wait here while I see what's going on."

She just rolled her eyes. "Yeah, right."

Following him out, she immediately saw a small crowd of a half-dozen dancers gathered around someone who was lying on the floor. Nick pushed through them, and immediately bent down. "Leah, what happened? Are you okay?"

"She's sick," someone said. "Like, all over the floor sick."

Poor Leah. She'd been ill last weekend, and now again. Izzie briefly wondered if the poor kid was hiding an unexpected pregnancy or something. Then, as the crowd parted and she saw Leah's face, she discounted that idea.

The pretty blonde looked like she was in misery. Her face was ghost white, slicked with sweat, and she appeared too weak to even stand on her own. She looked absolutely nothing like the pretty young thing Izzie had run into a little over an hour ago. She had to have been hit with some kind of fast-moving bug.

Nick didn't waste time asking questions. He bent to lift the dancer, easily cradling her in his arms as if she was a child, and carried her into the greenroom down the hall. "Somebody get her a cold cloth."

One of the dancers rushed off to do as Nick said, the rest of them crowded around. Izzie couldn't say whether their avid interest was more on Leah's behalf, or because of the incredible sight Nick made playing hero. His muscular arms bulged and flexed, but he spoke so softly—gently—to Leah as he gently laid her on the lumpy sofa in the greenroom. He even brushed her hair out of her face.

It was enough to make the hardest of women melt. Even the half-dozen strippers surrounding the sofa.

Izzie, of course, wasn't surprised. She knew the tenderness the man was capable of. She also knew the way he'd been raised and imagined he'd have done the same thing if his little sister, Lottie, had been the one lying on that floor.

"What happened?" he asked Leah.

Leah groaned. "It just came over me out of nowhere. I haven't been nauseous or anything, then all of a sudden, boom."

"Have you eaten shellfish today?" someone asked.

"Or some old lunch meat?" asked another.

Leah shook her head, gratefully accepting a wet clump of paper towels her dressing-roommate, Jackie, had brought her. She pressed it to her forehead and replied, "I had a salad for lunch, then nothing until I binged on Rose's chocolates."

Seven heads swung around to stare at Izzie, seven pairs of eyes wide and curious. Maybe even a little accusing.

She opened her mouth to reply, wondering if they thought she'd done something to make Leah ill, but didn't have to. The sick dancer herself spoke up again. "I found them lying on the stoop when I got to work today, with Rose's name on them. She never even opened the box, she just gave them to me."

That seemed to calm everyone down. Everyone except Nick. Because while all the others turned their attention back to Leah, offering to get her some ice or to drive her home, he frowned and stiffened his jaw so much it looked ready to break. "Where are these chocolates?"

"My dressing room."

He looked up and stared at Jackie. "I'll get them," she said, quickly rushing out of the room.

It seemed ridiculous and Izzie didn't for one second believe Leah had been brought down by some kind of poisoned candy…intended for *her*. That was strictly CSI stuff and she absolutely did not believe it. Judging by the look on Nick's face, however, she knew better than to say that. He was going to see for himself no matter *what* she thought.

"Nick, I just heard one of the girls is sick, what's going on?" Harry came rushing in the room, out of breath as if he'd just run down the stairs. The expression of worry on the older man's face had to make all his employees feel better—no one could accuse Harry Black of not appreciating and caring about his dancers. Which probably made him a rarity in this industry…and was probably why few dancers ever quit here for any reason other than to move on to a different career.

Seeing Leah, he hurried over. "Should we call 9-1-1?"

Leah shook her head. "I don't think so. But I do want to lie here for a little while, if that's okay."

"Oh, honey, don't you even think of getting up," another voice said. A woman's. Delilah had heard the news, too, and followed her husband to the green room. She sounded concerned—a rarity for her. "We can cover you tonight and someone can take you home if you want."

The room was getting crowded. But everybody made way for Jackie when she returned with the box of chocolates. "Here you go, Nick." Frowning, she put her hand on his arm and nodded toward the corner of the room.

Nick took the box and followed Jackie. They exchanged a few words, and whatever she said to him made his scowl deepen. He kept the box tightly clutched in his hand and Izzie wondered if he was going to crush it.

Harry joined them, murmuring, "What's wrong?"

Nick's reply was softly spoken, he obviously didn't want everyone else to hear. Jackie, having delivered whatever message it was that had gotten Nick even more fired up, called 9-1-1 after all, then went back to help take care of her friend. All the others hovered over Leah. Someone offered to get her a pillow for her feet, someone else offered a bucket for her head. That broke the ice a little and the group laughed.

Izzie didn't join them. Nick suspected someone had tried to slip her poisoned chocolates. Damned if she was going to stay out of that conversation.

Striding across to the two men, she asked, "Well? Satisfied that I'm not a mad poisoner's target?"

Nick didn't look at her at first. Neither did Harry. They were both staring intently at the open box of chocolates on the makeup table. One of the men had flipped over all the remaining individually slotted pieces in the package, so they were bottom-side up. And in the bottom of each, very easily visible, was a small hole.

Something that wouldn't have happened at the candy factory.

"Oh, hell," Izzie whispered.

It appeared someone had, indeed, tried to poison her.

And when Nick turned to her and said, "Tell me about the roses," she realized it might not have been the first time.

11

WHEN NICK REALIZED there were holes in the bottom of the candy, he saw red. And it wasn't the cherry cordial filling.

He needed to know more—especially after what Jackie had told him about some flowers Izzie had passed to Leah last weekend. But he didn't want to do it here.

"The police are on their way," he muttered to Harry. Then, without a word, he grabbed Izzie's elbow and pulled her out of the room, straight to her private dressing room.

She stumbled to keep up and he realized he might be holding her too tight. But he couldn't let go, couldn't release his grip. He wasn't letting her get more than six inches away from him…or letting anyone else getting within six feet of *her*.

"Nick, calm down," she muttered.

"I'm calm." *Deadly calm.*

"No, you're not. You're volcanic," she said as they walked into her dressing room.

Nick shut and locked the door. The last time he'd locked the door to this room had been at the start of one of the most amazing sexual experiences he'd ever enjoyed. He really wished he was doing it for the same reason now.

He wasn't. He was locking the door to keep Izzie—the woman he now knew he loved—safe from someone who'd tried to hurt her at least twice now. Maybe even more.

Looking down, he saw the new chair sitting in front of Izzie's vanity and the steam built again. He leaned over and smacked it with his palm, sending it crashing against the wall. It did not fall apart.

But that didn't ease his suspicion about the last one.

"Why did you do that?" she asked, her voice calm and even.

Good thing one of them was. "Just making sure our friend didn't sabotage another chair."

Izzie's pretty mouth opened into a perfect *O* as understanding washed over her. That, more than anything, seemed to finally make this situation sink in. She grabbed the edge of the table and sagged against it. "Someone really is trying to hurt me?"

He stepped close and wrapped his arms around her shoulders and tugged her against him. "I think so, babe."

"Why?"

"I have no idea. Why do stalkers do any of the crap they do?"

Tilting her head back to look up at him, she murmured, "*Stalker?* Why would someone wanting to get *close* to me only to do something as dumb as make me sick?"

He had a few ideas. There were a lot of men out there who liked to play hero. Maybe somebody was setting Izzie up to get sick or take a fall just so he could get near her by being the one who came to her aid. Who knew how some dark, twisted minds worked? "Maybe somebody was hoping you'd pass out on stage and he could say he was a doctor and come to your aid."

She blew out an impatient breath. "That's silly."

"But not impossible," he insisted. "Those flowers that came last week…Jackie said they were for you, but that you gave them to Leah?"

Narrowing her eyes, she nodded. "You think they have something to do with this?"

That seemed incredibly obvious to Nick. "You get a couple of anonymous gifts, and the person who ends up with them gets sick."

She quickly figured out where he was going. "Harry said Leah was sick Sunday night…."

"So was Jackie. They share a dressing room and both smelled and touched the flowers when they were putting them in a vase."

Izzie shook her head, obviously not wanting to believe it. He didn't blame her. It couldn't be easy for her to think someone out there had been targeting her.

Because it was absolutely *killing* him to think it.

"And you think there was something on the roses…."

"Could have been insecticide, roach powder, anything. They both got nauseous and dizzy, and went home with horrible headaches."

Nick didn't know a lot about common household pesticide exposure, but he sure knew about its military applications. He'd been trained in dealing with all kinds of chemical attacks and imagined the most basic symptoms would be similar.

Izzie finally slipped out of his arms, her lovely face taut and strained. Her mouth drooped and she shook her head, appearing almost…*hurt*…that someone would be after her.

But the hurt didn't last for long. As she stared toward the replacement chair, her frown deepened and her eyes narrowed. He saw the clenching of her jaw and knew she was working herself into a temper.

"The cowardly bastard." She smacked her hand flat against the tabletop, muttering a few more choice curses. "You find out who did this, Nick."

He liked the return of that fierceness. Izzie wouldn't let

anything keep her down for long—it was one of the things he loved about her. Which he planned to tell her, just as soon as they got around to having that whole "I love you," and "I love you, too," conversation. Which would be soon, if he had his way. Very soon.

"I intend to. We'll start by questioning everyone to see if anybody noticed your anonymous gift-giver hanging around."

Though he didn't say it to her, Nick also intended to carefully watch the staff when he talked to them. It wasn't impossible that someone who worked right here at Leather and Lace was behind the attacks. An obsessed bartender, a jealous dancer who wanted Izzie's headliner spot. Maybe even a bouncer wanting to be her hero. Hell, maybe even Harry wanting to stir up a big news story as publicity for the club. He could see the headline now: *Hottest mystery dancer in Chicago stalked by unknown assailant.*

It was possible. Anything was.

"I'll watch the crowd tonight and see if anybody acts suspiciously, or if I recognize some of the guys who come every night I'm on." Glancing at her watch, she added, "I have to hurry up."

That comment drove everything else out of his mind. Nick shook his head hard. "You're not going on tonight.

She lifted her mask, turning to the mirror. "Of course I am."

Nick met her reflected stare. "Like hell."

"It *can* be like hell in here if you force me to make it that way," she shot back. "Because if you say that again, we're going to be having a major fight."

Nick couldn't believe her. She'd just found out someone had likely tried to poison her and she still wanted to perform. "Izzie, you can't be serious."

"Oh, you bet I am. We're already down one girl with Leah being sick and I left Harry in the lurch last weekend." Her eyes flashing fire, she added, "Besides, *no one's* going to force me off the stage."

Her expression betrayed her sheer determination as much as her words did. And he had to wonder if they had a double meaning.

Because despite everything that had happened this evening, he hadn't forgotten what they had been talking about before Leah got sick. She'd basically asked him if he was going to watch her dance, and he'd hedged on his answer. He hadn't missed the shine in her eyes or the disappointment twisting at her mouth. But he hadn't been able to reassure her, because even Nick didn't know how he was going to react when that moment came.

"It's too dangerous."

"There are four big, burly bouncers upstairs to make sure nothing happens," she insisted. Piercing him with her stare, she added, "Besides, you'll be there to protect me. Or *won't* you? Maybe there'll be something more *important* to deal with."

Nick now knew for sure she was referring to their earlier conversation. And maybe she had a right to.

But being a little slow to want to watch the woman he loved get naked in front of a bunch of other guys had absolutely nothing to do with his concern for her now. "It's not about that."

"Oh, yes, it is." Izzie stalked around the privacy screen. Given that it offered no privacy whatsoever, considering the mirror, that was a statement in itself.

A frank one…that the walls were going up between them.

"And frankly, I'm tired of asking you about it. You can watch or not, but the Crimson Rose is performing tonight."

She yanked her robe off, then, watching him watch her, dropped her bra and panties to the floor.

"Damn it," he muttered, as always unable to take his ravenous eyes off her. She was just so incredibly beautiful. The woman stopped his heart every time he looked at her.

Izzie continued to ignore him, reaching for her G-string

and pulling it on. Then she covered her dark, puckered nipples with those two ridiculous pink petals.

"Don't do this," he ordered through a thick, tight throat. "Not until we know you're safe." When she stepped out from behind the screen and lifted her chin in challenge, he added, "You don't have to go out there."

"It's my job."

"It's something you do part-time for kicks and to rub it in your family and the world that you're not sweet little Isabella Natale anymore," he said, frustrated beyond belief at her stoic refusal to listen to reason.

She appeared stunned by his accusation. "How can you *say* that? My family doesn't even know I'm here."

"I know and that proves my point. You get your *secret* kicks out of it without ever having to face the consequences. You're not being honest to anyone—not even yourself—about why you're doing this and what you really want."

She jerked as if he'd slapped her. Closing his eyes and shaking his head, Nick wondered how he'd let this whole conversation spin so badly out of control so rapidly.

"You certainly are a fine one to talk," she finally said, her tone steely.

"What?"

"You accuse me of that, but you're doing exactly the same thing, Nick Santori. Stringing your family along with this idea that you're going to be singing *O Sole Mio* and slinging pizza dough with Tony and your father. Meanwhile, you hide your nights doing something exciting and dangerous at a place they would never approve of. I call that hypocritical."

He couldn't believe she'd turned things around on him like that. "That's ridiculous."

"So why haven't you told Tony you're not sticking around? Why haven't you told your father about this 'protection' business you're thinking of going into with your Marine buddies?"

Leave it to a woman to use something he'd told her less than a day ago in a fight against him. "That has nothing to do with whether you go out on stage and flaunt yourself in front of someone who wants to *hurt* you." But even as he said it, a small voice in his head whispered that she might be right. At least a little.

Not that he was going to admit that now…not when they still had the issue of her physical safety to work out. So he pushed on. "And I'm not on stage intentionally taking off my clothes to try to turn on a hundred strangers—one of whom might be trying to poison me."

She'd stiffened at the world flaunt. By the time he'd finished speaking, Izzie's face was as red as her mask. "Well, that's it, then, isn't it? We've finally gotten down to it."

"Izzie…."

She put a hand up to stop him. "I knew it would come to this, and now it has. You need to leave. I'm going on stage tonight. By the time I get back, I hope there will be a new lock on my door, for my own protection." Her chin quivered, her full lips shook. But she had one last thing to say. "And you most definitely will not have a key to it."

NICK WASN'T IN the audience. Izzie scanned the crowd for him throughout her performance, wondering if he'd be lurking in the shadows, watching out for her.

He wasn't.

It was over.

Somehow, she managed to not cry as she gyrated to the music. Managed to not show the hungry-looking men in the audience that her heart was broken.

It shouldn't feel this broken, after all, she'd known going

into this crazy, wild relationship with Nick that it would have to end badly. From day one, they'd wanted each other on opposite terms. He'd wanted the cute kid sister of his brother's wife, who worked at the bakery every day. She'd wanted the sultry, sexy bodyguard who guarded *her* naked body every night.

That he'd tried to put his foot down and forbid her from dancing the very *first* moment he had a convenient excuse emphasized that and more.

As she dipped and swayed and thrust and jumped on the stage, four words kept time with the music. They played over and over, keeping the 4:4 beat.

It can not work.

By the time she was finished dancing, Izzie was as much angry as she was heartbroken. Aside from being her lover, Nick was supposed to be the club's bodyguard. And yet when she'd been the most vulnerable—exposed—he'd been nowhere to be seen.

She'd have something to say about that the second she saw him. But that moment came almost immediately—he had been watching her back. Literally. He was standing, dark and predatory, in the wings just off stage. He'd been watching for her to come off…out of a direct line of sight to center stage. So he *hadn't* watched her dance. And he most certainly hadn't experienced watching her dance with the rest of a big, male audience.

Nothing had changed.

"I'll escort you to your dressing room," he said, his jaw as stiff as his shoulders. *"Rose."*

She didn't even respond as she slipped her robe on over her nearly naked body, then sailed past him toward the stairs. She didn't need his help, she didn't need his approval.

Yes, she needed him. But she'd learn to do without him,

just like she'd done without him all those long, lonely teenage years when she'd pined for the man.

Of course, never having had him might have aided her then. Now that she had?

Izzie feared she was never going to get over Nick.

"Ahem." As they reached the bottom of the stairs, Harry stepped out of the greenroom.

"Everything okay?" Nick asked, instantly on alert.

"It's fine," the older man said, but he didn't sound convinced. In fact, his voice was weak, his face a little pale.

Izzie reached out and put a hand on his shoulder. "Harry, what's wrong? Is Leah all right?"

He covered her hand with his. "Yes. Jackie called earlier. Leah's fine." He glanced over his shoulder into the quiet greenroom. He stepped out of the room and eased the door closed. "But I need to talk to both of you. Will you come with me, please?"

Hearing his urgency and seeing his very obvious concern, Izzie immediately went on alert. Something else had happened…maybe someone else was hurt.

"What is it?" Nick asked in a low voice, obviously realizing the same thing.

The man just shook his head, leading them back up the stairs to his small office which was on the other side of the lobby. They took a private, back hallway—a good thing since Izzie still wore just her long, silky robe. Whatever was bothering Harry, it had to be serious because he hadn't even offered to wait while she put some clothes on.

Harry's office was unpretentious and simple. Comfortable. Much like the self-deprecating man who occupied it.

But Harry Black did not look at all comfortable right now. As he gestured them toward the two armchairs across from his desk, his hand shook.

Izzie almost held her breath, watching him sit down behind the desk. Before he said a word, he dropped his head forward and put it in hands. "I can't even look at you when I say this."

Izzie had no idea what the man could be talking about, but beside her, Nick sucked in a sharp breath. "You…"

Their employer immediately looked up, shaking his head. "No. Not me." Moisture appearing in his eyes, he continued. "It was Delilah."

Izzie suddenly got it. Delilah had been the one after her. She'd poisoned the chocolates—and perhaps the roses.

Nick muttered a foul word, but Harry didn't leap to the defense of his wife. She deserved their scorn. No, she hadn't succeeded in hurting Izzie, her target, but she had certainly made Leah miserable.

"Tell us," Nick said, leaning back in the chair and crossing his arms over his chest.

His eyes were narrowed, his expression forbidding. Izzie recognized that tension in his rock-hard body. It was a good thing Delilah Black was not here for a personal confession. A very good thing. Because if Izzie didn't rip her apart, Nick just might have.

"I thought she *wanted* to retire," Harry said. He had a dazed expression, the same one many men wore when trying to understand their wives. Izzie had certainly seen it on her father's face. "She seemed happy helping me with management."

"How long ago did she stop?" Izzie asked, feeling a sharp sense of pity for the man. She sensed Harry needed to build up to telling them the worst of it.

"A few years ago when she turned forty. Right after we got married." Opening his desk drawer, Harry reached in and grabbed a silver flask and a shot glass. He poured himself a drink, raising a brow toward Nick and Izzie to see if they wanted one.

Neither took him up on it. Izzie because she was already feeling queasy at the story Harry was telling them. Nick… well, probably because he was already on a low simmer in the chair next to her. Throwing alcohol on a slow burn could make it erupt.

"And what, she thought if she could get rid of your headliner, you'd suddenly put her back on stage? That makes no sense," Nick said, disgust dripping from his words.

"Not to you. Not to me," Harry said with a sigh. "But to her." Growing slightly pink in the cheeks, he added, "I, uh, think there might have been a little more to it, though. I guess I talk a lot about you Rose…Izzie," he clarified, calling her by her real name for the first time since he'd hired her. "And I think Dee got a bit jealous, thinking my interest was something other than professional." Almost blushing to the roots of his balding head now, he quickly added, "That wasn't at all true. I'm as proud of you as if you were my own daughter…but Dee didn't get that."

The man had never even looked at her the wrong way. Izzie didn't doubt he was being truthful.

"Was she responsible for the roses?"

Harry nodded, taking another deep sip of his drink. "She put some kind of bug powder on them. And before you ask, yes, she did the chair too. I got her to admit to both of those things, as well as putting some kind of syrup—Ipecac—in the chocolates."

This time Izzie was the one to call the other woman a bitch under her breath. She simply couldn't help it. Again, Harry didn't make any effort to defend his wife.

"Why'd she come clean?" Izzie asked.

"I suspected as soon as I saw the box of candy. Dee loves that kind. And she came home with some of that syrup a couple of days ago, saying she wanted it on hand in case one of her nieces or nephews came over and swallowed something poisonous."

Nick shifted a little, his arms still cross, his body still rigid. "So you confronted her?"

Harry nodded. "And she confessed. When she saw how sick Leah was, she felt awful."

"Wonder if she'd have felt that way if it had been Izzie lying on the floor," Nick snapped.

He sounded very protective. Which made Izzie feel all warm and gooshy inside, even though she told herself that was stupid.

"I dunno," Harry admitted. "Maybe not."

Gee, it was nice to be liked.

Nick finally sat up and leaned toward the desk. Fixing a firm eye on Harry he said, "Have you called the police?"

The man slowly shook his head. But before Nick could confront him on it, he added, "I went to Leah first and told her everything. She and Jackie decided to press charges, and they made the call to the police themselves."

Nick relaxed. A little.

"I understand why that needed to happen." Tears rose in Harry's gray eyes and oozed a little onto his round cheeks. "But I couldn't be the one to turn my wife in."

Izzie reached over and put her hand on Nick's leg, sensing he was about to make another comment about Delilah. She squeezed his thigh, warning him not to. Harry was suffering enough. He didn't need to be told he was a fool for loving someone so hateful. "I understand," she murmured.

"I hope you do. And I hope you'll understand that I'm going to see her through this. She'll be facing assault charges."

"At the very least," Nick mumbled.

"I know this might make you want to leave, Ro...Izzie. But

I wish you wouldn't." The man smiled weakly. "You're family."

Huh. If poison was the way Delilah treated members of her *family,* Izzie would hate to see what she did to her enemies.

"I know that, too," Izzie said, slowly pulling her hand away from Nick's warm thigh, already missing the contact. Already missing *him.* "You love her. That's what people who love each other do…they support one another, even when they make what other people might see as bad or foolish decisions." Hearing a quiver in her voice as the subject touched much too close to home, Izzie offered Harry a tremulous smile.

Nick she didn't even look at.

"Thank you for telling me, Harry. I'm going to go get ready for my next number." Without another word to either of them, Izzie walked out and went back to work.

And Nick didn't come anywhere near her for the rest of the night.

WHEN BRIDGET WENT back to the dealership on Monday morning, she looked for Ted, wondering if he'd have the nerve to show up.

He didn't. That was good.

Neither did Dean. That wasn't good.

Hopefully Ted had been scared off, either by Dean, or by the ramifications of his own stupid actions.

Hopefully Dean had *not* been scared off and was just stuck in traffic.

Bridget had spent all Sunday night wondering what on earth she was going to say to him—how she was going to climb that wall he'd erected between them after he'd kissed her so passionately in the office. But for nothing. He wasn't there.

She trudged through her day, going through the same song and dance with Marty about the books. She found problems. He waved them off as unimportant. A typical day in the life.

"I am so gonna quit this job," she muttered that afternoon.

Soon. Maybe she'd even give her notice today. After all, she'd only stayed to see if something was going to happen between her and Dean Willis. Judging by yesterday, it seemed pretty clear nothing was.

She went so far as to open up a document on her computer to type her resignation letter. She'd give two weeks notice, even though she had no other job lined up. She had enough of a cushion to be unemployed for a while. And if she didn't come up with another bookkeeping job quickly, she'd lay money that Izzie would hire her on at the bakery, just to pay the rent.

But before she'd typed so much as the date, Bridget heard a commotion—shouts, coming from the sales floor. Her first thought was that Ted had come back and was making a scene. But there were several voices, all yelling at once.

She grabbed her purse and threw it under her desk, then wondered if she should crawl under after it…this could be a robbery. But when the door to the office flew open and she saw a uniformed police officer, she didn't.

"Is anyone in here with you?" the officer barked.

"N-no. Just me."

"You need to come with me, ma'am."

Dazed, Bridget followed the officer, seeing all the other employees being herded together by other policemen. All of them were gathered just inside the front door, and Marty was shouting loud enough to break the glass in the windows.

Everyone was talking—demanding answers. Everyone but Bridget. She didn't have to. Because the second she saw Dean Willis—dressed in a perfectly fitted dark blue suit—talking to other dark-suited men right outside the front door, she knew what was going on.

He was no car salesman.

"Sir, you'll have an opportunity to call your attorney soon," one of the officers said, trying to calm Marty down.

It worked for a brief second, until Dean walked through the door. When Marty saw him with the rest of the investigators, he started ranting and struggling against the officer trying to handcuff him. Another one jumped in to help and between them they got the livid man into custody.

Dean looked her way once. His nice blue eyes were frigid. His smile absent. His tousled blond hair was slicked down and parted on the side—conservative, professional. And his clothes were immaculate, right down to his shiny black wing-tip shoes.

He could have been a picture from an FBI agent's handbook come to life.

The rest of the day went by in a whirl. She was questioned endlessly—never by Dean, who stayed away from her—but by his fellow agents. Apparently there had been a reason Marty hadn't wanted Bridget to do a good job with the books. They were never *supposed* to balance out. Because, if the agents were to be believed, Honest Marty's Used Cars had been bringing in and cleaning up a whole lot of dirty money for some pretty bad guys.

And she'd fallen right in the middle of it.

By the end of the day, Bridget was utterly exhausted. Ready to collapse, her throat sore from answering so many questions. She hadn't asked for a lawyer—had cooperated fully, believing that's what an innocent person *should* do. And she'd spent the last four hours in the conference room, going over months' worth of seized bank statements and ledgers with some FBI accountant, watching step by step as they built a case against her boss.

At first, she felt a little sorry for Marty. But not too sorry. Especially when she caught snips of conversation about where the dirty money had come from. In her opinion, anybody who cleaned cash that had been earned off the sale of filthy drugs to kids deserved what he got. She was just sorry the creep had dragged her into the sordidness.

She'd seen Dean only briefly, when she'd been brought to tears by the relentless questions of the accountant. Dean had appeared out of nowhere, appearing behind the other officer's back, barking, "She's not a suspect, she's a witness. Treat her like one." Then, with one long, even look at Bridget, he'd left again to go back to work with the other investigators.

Finally, when it was nearly dark out, Bridget was told she could go home. She'd be called in to help again—and, likely, to testify—but for now, she was free.

Free. Great. She was free to go home, look back on this horrible day—on these past few horrible weeks—and think about what a damned *fool* she'd been.

Dean had *used* her. He'd feigned an interest in her so he could build his money laundering case against Marty. He'd played her like an instrument, obviously seeing the quiet, sweet-faced bookkeeper as an easy mark.

She hated the son of a bitch with a passion she'd never had toward anyone in her life.

That rage carried her down the block as she strode away from the dealership, heading toward her nearby apartment. Usually when she made the walk home, she kept her purse clutched tightly to her side, and constantly scanned for any possible danger. This wasn't a bad part of town—but as a young woman walking alone, she didn't take chances. Tonight, however, she practically *dared* anyone to mess with her. She felt capable of doing real violence.

"Bridget, wait, please!" a voice called.

Though she kept walking, she peered over her shoulder to see who'd called her. She almost tripped over her own feet when she realized it was Dean. "Stay away from me," she snapped, picking up her pace.

He picked up his, too, chasing her down until he reached her. "Would you stop? I've been calling you for two blocks."

"Not real quick on the uptake, are you?" she said. "I don't want to talk to you."

"You have to let me explain."

"I don't *have* to do anything," she said, though she did finally stop and face him. "And you don't have to explain, I got it, okay? You were working undercover. I was the easy mark. Of course you'd come after me by any means at your disposal."

"It wasn't like that."

"Like hell."

"Just…calm down and let me explain. I did not mean to hurt you, and I definitely never meant to get personally involved with you."

"You mean that wasn't in the manual?"

"No, it wasn't. But I was worried, I felt sure early on that you were caught in something you didn't know about." He put a hand on her arm. "I was worried about you."

She shrugged his hand of. "Sure you were. I'm sure your concern was the reason you asked me out. And your fears that I was being used by my boss to help hide money was the only reason you kissed the lips off my face yesterday."

He closed his eyes, breathed deeply—as if for control—and tried again. "I lost my detachment where you were concerned."

Those were the first words he'd said that actually made her pause. Because he'd whispered them hoarsely, as if against his will. Like he didn't want to admit to the weakness.

And she believed him.

Not that it made a damn bit of difference. "Well, that's too bad for you then," she said, lifting her chin, amazed that her voice didn't even quiver. "Because I never want to see you again." She began walking again.

"Bridget, I know you're upset now. But I want to make it up to you. Soon, when you've…"

"When I've what?" she asked, swinging around again. "When I've calmed down? Well, keep dreaming, buddy. Because it's not going to happen. *Ever.*"

Dean met her stare, but didn't try to stop her this time when she turned again to start walking. He did, however, have one more thing to say, low, as if making a vow,

"I'm not giving up."

"Well, too bad for you," she snapped back, feeling both proud of herself for being so strong…and sad at having lost something she suspected could have been very special.

"Bridget…."

This time, she didn't turn around. And she didn't have to wonder what Izzie would do.

Bridget knew what *she* wanted to do.

So without a pause, she lifted her hand, flipped him the bird over her shoulder, and kept on walking.

12

IZZIE DIDN'T SEE or hear from Nick for six long days. The longest of her life.

Since she'd walked out of Harry's office Sunday night, Nick had apparently taken her orders to leave her alone seriously, because that's exactly what he'd done. He hadn't tried calling, hadn't popped in to the bakery, hadn't even nonchalantly walked by the shop and pretended not to look in at her.

That's what *she'd* done, at Santori's, but she hadn't seen the man at all.

"Why didn't you fight for me?" she whispered as she drove to the other side of town Saturday evening on her way to work. "Why did you listen to me and leave me alone?"

Why did you tell him to?

Good question. And Izzie was already forgetting the answer, though it had seemed so important Sunday.

Yes, she was still upset that he'd suddenly gone from an approving coworker to a disapproving lover when it came to her dancing. But maybe they could have worked it out. Maybe he wouldn't have reacted so badly to watching her on stage.

Maybe...hell, maybe she loved him enough that she could have quit and never regretted it.

But he hadn't given her the chance.

In the six days since she'd seen him, Izzie was questioning a lot of the choices she'd made. After accusing Nick of living a lie, too, she'd realized that she was tired of living one all the time. So she'd actually begun to share her secret. Only with her sisters and her cousin so far, but it was a start.

And they'd been remarkably supportive. Even Gloria who had, to Izzie's utter shock, admitted that she'd love to see her perform. Honestly, it felt as if a weight had been lifted, and she'd decided then and there to start thinking of how to work her daytime life into her nighttime one. Slowly…a little at a time. But she might just have to find a way to do it.

Because if Nick ever *did* come back after her, she wanted to try to find a way to make all the pieces of both their lives fit.

Performing again…that caused more stress. Izzie couldn't deny a small amount of trepidation when she arrived at Leather and Lace Saturday night. This was her first time back since last Sunday, the night of Delilah's confession—and her arrest. She hadn't talked to Harry since and she was worried about what the older man was going through.

Bernie was waiting at the back door. "Hiya, Rose," he said without a smile. Obviously the mood around here was still dour.

"Hi. Harry around?"

He shook his head. "He hasn't been here much." Shaking his head, he added, "Wish he'd just ditch that witch and get back to work, this club ain't gonna run itself."

Izzie didn't say anything. She honestly didn't want to think about what she'd do in her boss's situation. He was a man who loved his wife…warts and all. Should he be faulted for that? Maybe. But it wasn't her place to judge.

The dressing rooms and greenroom were pretty quiet for a Saturday night, any chatter between the dancers was going on quietly. Just as well. Izzie didn't feel very social. There was only one person she wanted to see…only, she didn't know what on earth she'd say to him when she did.

I miss you. I love you. Please love me as I am and let's work it out.

All of the above.

He never appeared. She didn't see him downstairs, and he certainly didn't come to her dressing room. Izzie went through the motions getting ready, tense and anxious…but for nothing.

By the time she was ready to go on, she was seriously wondering if she'd made a mistake in coming in at all. Her heart was not in it. Not tonight. "The show must go on," she reminded herself as she walked upstairs and took her place backstage.

She'd like to think she gave her audience her all, but as she began removing her rose petals in time to the music, she knew her heart wasn't in it. Her heart was in little pieces, scattered around Nick Santori's feet. Wherever he may be.

Usually, Izzie ignored the audience as she performed—it was part of her "mysterious appeal" as Harry had described it right after she'd started working here. And he'd been right.

Tonight, however, something caught her attention. Rather, some*one*. Normally, all were still when she performed—including the waitresses. But now, someone was walking from the back of the room straight down the center aisle toward the stage.

It was a man. A dark-haired, dark-eyed man.

A *familiar* dark-haired, dark-eyed man.

"Oh, God," she whispered, stumbling a little.

Because it was Nick. A Nick like she'd never seen before.

Though he wore his typical on-the-job tough-guy uniform of black pants and tight black T-shirt, he was carrying a bouquet of roses. A huge bouquet of them. He was also smiling, his eyes locked on her, apparently not caring that she was dancing nearly naked on stage in front of a bunch of strange men.

And for the first time in her entire dancing career, Izzie did something entirely unprofessional. She committed the cardinal sin. She stopped right in the middle of her number.

"Nick," she whispered.

He had reached the edge of the low stage, which was about as high as his mid-thigh and was staring up at her. The look in his eyes...oh, God, that look. He was smiling broadly, adoring her with his gaze.

He not only looked approving, he looked absolutely enraptured. "Hi, Izzie," he said, his voice low, intimate, just for the two of them.

The music slowly faded away into silence. The audience began to murmur. One man yelled something like "Down in front," but he was shouted down by several others who obviously wanted to see what would happen next.

She'd like to know that herself.

"Hi," she whispered. "Uh...what are you doing?"

His smile widened. "Watching you."

"I noticed."

"You're wonderful."

She nibbled her bottom lip. "Thank you."

"I could watch you dance every night and be a happy man."

"Who couldn't?" someone from a nearby table called.

Nick never even glanced over, not distracted. Instead, he lifted the bouquet and offered it to her. Izzie took it, bringing the flowers up to her masked face and sniffing the heady fragrance permeating the red blooms. "They're beautiful."

"I figured roses were your flower."

"Good call." Laughing a little, she asked, "Is there some reason you gave them to me here? And right *now?*"

He nodded. "I wanted you to know how proud I am of you and how much I love seeing you dance. No matter who else is here."

He'd said it. He'd put it into words. Exactly what she needed to hear. "Oh, Nick, really?"

He nodded. "*Really.* I have more to say. But not here." He glanced over his shoulder at all the men leering at them. "Some things were not meant to do in front of an audience." Then he looked back up at her. "And the next thing I want to say to you can't be said when you're wearing that mask on your face."

She shivered, anticipation rolling through her. Oh, how she hoped she knew what it was he wanted to say to her. That it involved talk of a future. And a lot of uses of the word *love.*

"I'll meet you downstairs in two-and-a-half minutes," he said. "I've timed your song…that's how much you have left."

"You're on," she said with a broad smile as she clutched the flowers close to her body and slowly backed away from the edge of the stage. She put the flowers down right in front of the curtain, where she could easily retrieve them.

Nick turned around and walked back the way he'd come. From where Izzie stood, she could see every man in the place turn to watch him go. Most were regulars who had to have recognized him. And probably all of them wanted to know exactly what he'd said to her…and what he meant to her.

That was easy to explain. *Everything.*

Nodding toward the crew member on the side of the stage, Izzie waited for her song to resume. Now she danced joyfully, the way she hadn't in a very long time. And she smiled during every moment of it.

As soon as the last notes of the music played, Izzie grabbed her flowers and darted toward the wings, pausing only long enough to stick her arms in her robe before tearing toward the staircase. She took the cement stairs two at a time, almost stumbling. But even if she had, it would have been okay. Because Nick was waiting at the bottom of them, staring up at her.

He would have caught her. She knew that, from now on, he would be there to catch her.

"Come on," he murmured, taking her hand. He twined her fingers in his, then lifted them to his mouth to press a soft kiss on them. "Let's talk privately."

She followed him, easing against his body, her curves fitting perfectly in his angles, as if they were two pieces of a puzzle. When they reached her dressing room, Nick opened the door and held it for her, then followed her inside.

"Thank you again for the roses," she murmured as she put them on the makeup-strewn counter. They'd already begun filling the room with their heady perfume and she inhaled of it deeply.

"You're welcome." He immediately added, "You were right."

"About?"

"Everything," he admitted evenly, making no effort to hedge or share blame for what had happened between them. Even though Izzie knew she bore some of the responsibility. "We both…"

"No, Iz, let me finish, please. You were right to accuse me of living the same double life I'd accused you of. *You* had legitimate reasons, with your father's health and your, uh…"

"Being a stripper?"

He grinned. "Yeah. That."

"I told Gloria and Mia."

His eyes widened. "Really? How'd they react?"

"Better than I expected." Much better. But she'd fill him in on that later. "It's a first step, anyway."

"I know. I made that same step. I told my father and Tony that I wasn't interested in the business. And what I am interested in doing."

"Being a bodyguard?"

For the first time since he'd walked up to her during her dance, Nick looked a little hesitant. He glanced to the side, and scrunched his brow. "Well…not exactly."

Immediately on alert, Izzie crossed her arms. "What did you do? Tell me you're not going to be a cop like your brother!"

He shook his head, as if appalled at the idea. "Not a chance. As it turns out, Harry's going to need to take a step back from this place to deal with Delilah's legal situation."

Not a surprise.

"And he asked me if I'd manage it."

Izzie couldn't prevent a shocked gasp. *"What?"*

"There's more."

Still stunned at the very concept, she waited, mouth agape.

"He needs an infusion of cash…I think he anticipates a lot of legal bills. I have money I've been socking away during all the years I bunked with Uncle Sam. So I've just become a part owner of this club."

That was so unexpected, Izzie couldn't help sinking down to her chair in absolute shock. "You're serious?"

"Very serious."

"You're going to work *here*."

"Uh-huh. You okay with that? Working with your husband?"

"Oh, I'll love…." His words sunk in, banging around in her head. *"What* did you say?"

He smiled. "I thought diamonds would go well with roses."

Izzie remained still, in a stunned silence, as Nick reached into his pocket and pulled out a ring. A gold one. With a big fat diamond on top of it. "I'm going to slide this on your finger, but not until you take that mask off your face."

Dazed, she reached up and unfastened the clasps of her mask, one on each side of her head. The slow-motion feeling of the moment continued as she drew the red velvet away, letting it fall to the floor at her feet.

He reached for her hand, drawing her up to stand in front of him. "I love you, Izzie Natale. I love you, Crimson Rose. And I want you both in my life from this day on," he said, his voice serious and unwavering. His expression was every bit as serious—as proud and determined as she'd ever seen him—as if he placed more value on this moment than he had on any other.

She certainly did. Because this could be the moment when her life changed forever. When, as silly as it sounded, all her secret dreams—the ones she hadn't even acknowledged to herself—might actually start coming true.

"Whether we stay here, or go to New York, whether you work at the bakery or take off your clothes for a living…I'll follow you. I'll lead you. I'll stand beside you." He reached up and cupped her cheek, brushing his fingertips over her skin in a caress so tender it brought tears to her eyes.

"Be with me. Always."

Now the teardrops gushed. Izzie seldom cried, but, at this moment, it was absolutely the only reaction she could manage. "I will, Nick. I love you so much. I've loved you for so long, I can't remember what it felt like to *not* be in love with you."

Reaching for him, she twined her arms around his neck and drew him toward her. She rose on tiptoe, touching her lips to his in a gentle kiss that gradually deepened. Their tongues sliding together in delicate intimacy, their bodies melted together. They shared breaths and promises not yet made but never to be broken, making a bond in that deep, unending, heady kiss that would last forever.

It was the most beautiful kiss of Izzie's life. Because she was kissing a man she'd loved forever…and his amazing mouth had just given the same words to her.

When they finally paused, Nick smiled down at her. "Are you really going to wear my ring?"

She stuck out her hand. "Starting now. Lasting forever."

Once he'd slid it on, she stared at the beautiful, glittering stone and gasped at the beauty of it. "Oh, thank you for waiting for me," she whispered to him.

"Thanks for pulling me on top of you on that table of cookies to let me know how much you wanted me."

Izzie glared at her new fiancée. "I did not pull you on top of me."

"I'd have to say you pulled, Cookie."

Reaching for the sash to her bathrobe and slowly unfastening it, she smiled a wicked, sultry smile. "Nick? You want to see what's beneath this robe?"

His eyes glittered in hunger and need. "Oh, you know I do."

He reached for her, but Izzie put her hand over his, stopping him. "Then I have one piece of advice for you. *Don't* call me Cookie."

Epilogue

THOUGH THE COLD WINTER air outside buffeted the city with an early blast of winter, inside Leather and Lace, everything remained *hot*. As usual.

The club was packed this Saturday night, every table full, mostly with men, but a few daring women were in the audience, too. Leather and Lace had started earning a reputation as a "couples-friendly" club and more pairs were coming in. Laughing and partying as they entered…quite often whispering and cuddling seductively as they left.

Nick had thought that a fine idea…until tonight when he'd looked up and had seen his brothers Joe and Luke walk in, their wives on their arms. That had given him a momentary heart attack, but once he'd sat and had a drink with the quartet, he'd realized something: Rachel and Meg were excited beyond belief, not at all judgmental and certainly not jealous that their future sister-in-law was about to strip in front of a bunch of men…including their husbands.

He hadn't understood it at first, until his brothers had confessed that their wives—as well as Tony's wife, Gloria, and Nick's sister, Lottie—were all taking the pole-dancing classes Izzie was now teaching at a Chicago dance studio. Mark's pregnant wife was on a waiting list for a future class.

He had to grin every time he thought about it. Now that she'd stopped working at the bakery, Izzie had found herself a full-time job teaching the housewives and professional women of Chicago how to stay healthy while learning to be ultra-sexy.

"I can't wait to see her. I mean, she's done her routine for us at the gym, but to see her here, in front of an audience…oh, sugar, just you watch and see what I'm going to be doing in a couple of months." Rachel leaned close to Luke, curling her arm around his, and whispered something that made his brother cough into his fist.

Okay. This appeared to be a good thing. And obviously Izzie was aware they were coming, so he didn't have to go track down his fiancée—and star performer—and give her a heads-up.

Leaving his family to their drinks, he ran another sweep of the room, touching base with Bernie and the other bouncers. He'd had to hire another bartender to work on weekends and both guys were rushing around pouring shots of high-end liquor and now, making frou-frou drinks for their female patrons.

Harry would be proud, if he'd been here to see it. But the man had come in less and less, leaving the management to Nick.

"Hey, boss, somebody to see you," one of the bouncers said.

Glancing up, Nick saw four men approaching the bar. Even if he hadn't known them, their postures and bearing would have told them they were brothers in a way that only those who'd been *there* would understand.

"Semper fi, man." He nodded to the first, recognizing the black hair and even stare of an old friend…a good man to have at your back when the situation turned rough. Reaching for the extended hand, Nick shook it, saying, "Been a long time, Joel."

The man nodded. He'd gotten out four years ago, just

before Nick had been deployed to Iraq. "I figured I'd come in and see why this was so much better than coming to work with me."

As Nick greeted the rest, another of the men, also an old Marines friend, glanced toward the stage where one of the girls was doing her thing. "I think I'm catching the vision," he mumbled.

"What can I say?" Nick shrugged. "I've settled down, become respectable." His mouth widening in a grin, he added, "And the little woman didn't want me doing anything as risky as working security with you guys."

Joel's big shoulders moved as he chuckled. He had a pretty good sense of humor considering he was one tough son of a bitch.

Nick gestured to one of the hostesses, asking her to get his friends a good table. But before they walked away, he murmured, "Seriously, thanks for offering to let me in. But I'm pretty happy with what I'm doing."

Joel nodded. "Got it. Still, if you ever change your mind…" He reached into the pocket of his black leather jacket and pulled out a crisp, white business card.

Nick read it. Then he looked back at his friend, offering him a short nod. "I'll keep it in mind."

Reaching out with his elbow bent and arm up, Nick grasped the other man's hand again in a brothers-of-the-field handshake, then watched the group head to their table.

He could have been one of them. Hell, he and Joel even *looked* like they were in the same line of work since they were both dressed in black from head to toe. Old habits sure died hard.

But he didn't regret it. He hadn't been lying when he said he liked what he was doing. A lot. Maybe not forever, but for now, working with Izzie doing something nobody had ever expected either of them to do was suiting him just fine.

"What time you got, Bernie?" he asked the bouncer, who stood nearby, on constant, vigilant guard.

"Eight-twenty," the other man said.

Hmm…about forty minutes before the Crimson Rose's first performance of the night.

Forty minutes. That *might* be enough time to tell the woman again how crazy he was about her. And how very glad he was that she'd stayed in Chicago with him.

When he got downstairs, walked into her dressing room, and caught her standing behind her screen wearing nothing but her G-string, however, he reconsidered that idea.

Forty minutes wasn't going to be enough. Not nearly.

"Hey, lover." She smiled at him in the mirror.

He smiled back. "Hey, Cookie."

Never taking his eyes off her beautiful face, Nick reached behind him and closed the door, flipping the lock to keep the world *out*. And to shut them *in* the wild and sultry one he thrived on with the woman he loved more than life.

* * * * *

A note from Leslie:

Wait…you thought that was the end? Well, so did I, but I just can't say goodbye to the Santoris of Chicago! So for all you readers who've loved this family right along with me, I'm offering one more glimpse at this wonderful clan before it's goodbye forever.

Izzie and Nick are getting married, and five of Izzie's bridesmaids – Bridget, Leah, Vanessa, Mia and Gloria – are all going to have romantic adventures of their own.

It's five sexy stories in one sexy book…all written by me. And it'll be capped off by the one Santori story I never got to tell…Gloria and Tony's!

I hope you'll watch for One Wild Wedding Night, *launching the new Blaze®* ENCOUNTERS *mini-series in February 2009!*

COLD CASE,
HOT BODIES

BY
JULE McBRIDE

Dear Reader,

I admit to being a fan of stories about cold cases. The older the mystery and colder the trail, the more intrigued I get. A second thing I love is reading about sexy cops, so it was only natural that I'd eventually put these two things together for Blaze®.

Oh, and before I forget – a third thing I love is a super-hot romance! So, quite simply, the idea for *Cold Case, Hot Bodies* came to me when I put all my favourites into one steamy love story. When an old case involving a haunted property is reopened, a descendant of the harmed party finds herself wrapped in the strong arms of the law. And what could be better than that?

Enjoy!

And thank you so much for reading! It's what keeps me writing.

Very best wishes,

Jule McBride

JULE McBRIDE

is a native West Virginian. Her dream to write romances came true in the nineties with the publication of her debut novel *Wild Card Wedding*. It received the *Romantic Times BOOKreviews* Reviewer's Choice Award for Best First Series Romance. Since then, the author has been nominated for multiple awards, including two lifetime achievement awards. She has written for several series, and currently makes her happy home at Blaze®. A prolific writer, she has more than thirty titles to her credit.

For Kathryn Lye, editor extraordinaire,
for helping me mind my p's and q's,
and for knowing how to wrestle commas,
semicolons and everything else, too.

Prologue

December 1890

GEM O'SHEA GLIDED her hands beneath her lover's shirt, feeling his nipples contract. It was exactly the kind of well-made shirt she'd sewn in sweatshops when she'd first come from Ireland, and her lips curved into a smile against the linen. "Do you remember when you first...*bought me,* Nathaniel?"

He grinned, his eyes catching light through the carriage window, from one of the gas lamps lining the dark river road. "I don't believe I do."

But he couldn't have forgotten the night she'd presented herself at Angel's Cloud, in New York's notorious Five Points neighborhood, determined to sell herself to the highest bidder. "Should I remind you?"

"Of every detail." He urged her closer, between his legs, and the satin dress she'd worn to the wedding bunched between them, an unwanted barrier. She brought her mouth to his, and the taste of wedding cake invaded her senses.

"I had too much champagne," she whispered.

"You won't hear me complaining."

Heat surged through her limbs despite the cold. Everything but passion vanished as Nathaniel deepened the kiss—the pounding hooves on the cobbled road, the rushing of the

East River's wild currents, the crack of the driver's whip. Hungrily, her fingers opened the studs of his shirt. Just as quickly, his tongue swept inside her mouth. Heat exploded as she stroked his chest hair, and she felt it catch on the backs of her rings—beautiful rings that were gifts from him, just a few of the countless jewels he'd given her over the years.

As desire took her, Gem thought of another kiss, the one they'd just witnessed at the altar between her and Nathaniel's son, Mark, and his young bride, Lily Jordan. With the memory, her arms swept around Nathaniel's neck, and she wished with all her heart she could marry him. How many nights had she lain awake, knowing her heart's deepest desire would remain an impossible dream?

She dropped down, moaning against his chest, her tongue searing a nipple, his answer a sound of need as he grasped her hand, urging it into the folds of his trousers. Soon they'd be at Angel's Cloud, where countless warm beds waited—either in the hidden rooms, or in the bawdy house, or in the rear building where she'd lived—but she wanted Nathaniel now. Her body was burning all over, just as it had the night they met.

She'd been desperate then, still speaking with a brogue so thick that most American natives couldn't understand her. She'd rarely even kissed a man, but she'd heard other, less reputable girls talk at the sweatshop, claiming men paid them for sexual favors, and because she'd been determined to earn her mum's passage from Ireland, she'd soon found herself standing on the shell-strewn floor of a Five Points bawdy house.

"Two hundred dollars," a man had called.

She'd nearly fainted. When he'd stepped from the shadows, his sparkling blue eyes had captured hers, then she'd recognized Nathaniel Haswell. He'd gotten his start as a self-made, import-export man, a buyer and seller of whatever prospered, and he owned acres of real estate on Manhattan Island. His picture was always in the papers. Without ceremony, he'd grabbed her hand and hauled her toward the stairs, and she'd foolishly blurted the first thing that had come to mind, "You're married!"

He'd turned to stare, the set of his mouth incredulous. "Don't tell me that bothers you?"

"Of course not," she'd managed quickly. All the men in Angel's Cloud were probably married. "In fact," she'd added brazenly, "I do prefer it, sir."

He'd continued toward the room. "And why might that be?"

"No messy attachments. I'm a professional, you know."

"I see," he'd returned as they reached the bedroom. "Experienced at this sort of thing, are you?"

"Indeed," she'd enthused, the pulse at her throat ticking madly as he'd shrugged out of his jacket.

She'd been trembling all over, still scared of the rowdy men downstairs, her head pounding from cigar smoke. Her throat had tightened as Nathaniel undid his trousers, and she'd considered running, but she'd thought of circumstances in Ireland, and of her mum, then of the poor girls still working in the sweatshop, scarcely earning a wage to buy adequate food. Her stomach growling, she'd taken a deep breath, stared boldly in the general direction of Nathaniel's private parts, then she'd plunged on. "Why, I've been to Angel's Cloud many a time, sir."

With a yank, he'd brought her against his chest. "You're a virgin if I've ever seen one."

"No, sir!" she'd protested, tears stinging her eyes.

"What are you doing this for?"

She'd been so surprised at his demanding tone that she'd started crying, then the whole story had tumbled out. She'd lost her father in Ireland, and her mum had been left behind, trying to work land that could no longer grow potatoes, much less anything else.

Nathaniel had comforted her, and she'd cried harder, then his lips had settled on hers, nibbling at the beauty mark beside her mouth, and within the hour, they'd made love. Ever since, she'd been his mistress, and his alone. He'd arranged for her to keep accountancy books for Angelo Donato, at Angel's Cloud, earning far more than she had making shirts, and for her to live on the upper floor of a building behind the bawdy house, removed from the rowdy clientele. She'd benefitted from being Nathaniel's lover in other ways, too. He'd given her jewels, and most important, brought over her mum who'd died due to natural causes on American soil. He'd given her a son, too. Twenty-three years ago her reputation may have been lost, but she'd fallen in love.

"Can you stay tonight, darling?" she whispered.

When he didn't respond immediately, Gem imagined trouble was brewing on the home front. Long before she'd met him, he'd been carousing in Five Points, searching for the love his wife withheld. He was an honorable man, though, and did as Isme wished by maintaining separate bedrooms and attending public functions together. Isme had borne him one son, just like Gem, a boy the same age as Mark, named Dirk. The young man was reputed to be wild, even dangerous, and Gem suspected it was due to the loveless bond that had created him.

Suddenly feeling furious with herself, she shook her head in self-admonishment. "Never mind. I've no claim on you. I shouldn't ask—"

He tilted back her head, to look into her eyes. "We have a son…"

She craved more of him, though. He rarely shared a bed with Isme, but they did share a home. A real home. He could come and go in sunlight, not under a cloak of darkness. Why can't you let this be enough? she thought. Nathaniel escaped to her bed at every opportunity. He loved her. He adored their son. But she wanted times to be different! Codes of morality to change…wanted their passion to have full rein.

Something broken came into his voice. "How could you believe I'd leave you on our son's wedding night? Damn it, Gem. You're the one I love."

"Kiss me," she whispered, the depth of their passion drawing them together. Like the current of a river, it ran between them—reliable and unstoppable, so when his lips found hers once more, an arrow seemed to pierce her heart. He would leave in only a few hours! His tongue thrust deeper. She met the thrust, pushing back. The carriage was flying, bouncing on cobbles, throwing her into his arms. His hands raced down her sides, flesh seeking flesh. He moaned when his fingers stroked the smooth skin of her thighs. Grasping a garter, he opened it. As he pulled down the stocking, she gasped.

"Let's recreate the night we made our son," he murmured.

He was rocking her against his hips now, making her feverish. She shuddered from the heat in the wandering caresses of his hands. When he squeezed her thighs, she thought passion had seized him, but no…he was alarmed! Abruptly, he broke the kiss, and she craned to stare through the carriage window, but she saw only the black winter's night.

"What was that?" she whispered, hearing a rattle as she fumbled with her clothes, in case they needed to get out of the carriage.

"The wheel," Nathaniel returned hoarsely.

The carriage was wobbing, but the horses continued to run. If the carriage overturned, she hoped no reporters would find them…a town father with a woman associated with Angel's Cloud. Nathaniel drew back the curtain and leaned his head through the window to shout. "Something's wrong with—"

Before he could finish, the wheel spun away. The rear of the carriage dropped and the driver screamed. Gem thought he'd been thrown. The horses reared, rising on their hind legs, then hooves came down hard, clattering on cobbles as the animals galloped, dragging the carriage. Gem's head slammed into the seat. She could hear metal dragging on stone, then through the window, she saw sparks from the friction.

"Oh, God," Nathaniel muttered hoarsely. He was trying to grasp her waist, but his hands couldn't find purchase. Neither could hers. They were being tossed like weeds in wind. Pounding hooves raced on, and as the sound diminished, she realized the horses had broken free. The carriage was flying on its own momentum, careening toward the river.

Nathaniel reached past her for the door handle. "Somebody's tampered with the carriage. Jump!"

Had their carriage been sabotaged? If so, who had done it? And why? His words were in her ears as she realized the carriage was rushing down the riverbank. She tried to jump, as he'd commanded, but her dress caught, holding her back. Just as they plunged, she heard the fabric ripping, and as her dress gave away, Nathaniel pulled her through the open door, into the dark currents.

He was her hero. Her only love. He was trying to save

her, but the water was too cold, and she was sure they were going to die. *Not on our son's wedding day,* her mind shrieked in protest as her fingers laced with Nathaniel's. *Stay with me, my love,* she thought, but then she felt his fingers slip away.

1

Five Points, 2007

"Can you believe somebody called and complained about me and Sheila Carella?" Dario Donato asked as he strode through Police Plaza toward the courthouse, his long, jeans'-clad legs eating up the pavement. Realizing he was a half hour late for court, he uttered a soft curse. It was the wrong day to have to help his landlord dad straighten out legal matters about a rental property. Clapping a hand on his chest, over his heart, as if wounded, he said, "I mean, who would do something like this to me, Pat?"

"A taxpayer?" his partner suggested as he ran a hand over his buzz-cut red hair. "Or maybe you just pissed off the Fates. Anyway, the chief wants you to lay low until the complaint blows over. Pick up a couple cold cases."

"Budweiser or Rolling Rock?"

"You know those aren't the kind of cold cases he means."

No, Dario was supposed to rot behind a desk while an arsonist got away, and all because he hadn't kept his pants zipped. "You know we're going to wind up arresting a land developer on the arson case," he mused. Ever since plans had been underway to develop Manhattan's riverfront, properties near the water had started going up in smoke, then the land was sold for a relative pittance. Relative for Manhattan, anyway.

"I'm thinking Ralph Stone or Chuckie Haswell," said Pat.

They were the biggest players. Trump was too smart to get his hands dirty with arson. Dario nodded. "Seriously, are we on for a cold case later? Now I'm talking brewskies again."

"Tomorrow's good, but tonight I've got a date with Karen."

"Ah. The girl next door."

"Not every woman can live up to Sheila Carella."

"She does set a high bar."

Dario had met Sheila a month ago, when he'd busted her for unpaid parking tickets. She had big hair, bigger breasts, and always wore fishnet stockings with miniskirts and spike heels. She was kinky as hell, too, and liked to play all kinds of sex games, which meant things had been going extremely well. At least until Dario had taken her home to meet his folks. Not that he'd expected Sheila to blend seamlessly, but his mother, Bianca, had kept crossing herself and whispering, "When's my only boy going to grow up and meet a nice girl he can marry?" It didn't help that Dario knew she lit candles each morning at mass, in front of whatever saint presided over philandering sons. On the night of Sheila's visit, Dario's sister, Eliana, had kept rolling her eyes and mouthing, "It's her brains you like, right?" Fortunately, Sheila's main concern had been her lipstick, so she hadn't noticed. Or else Dario's dad's meatballs and red sauce had distracted her. Beppe Donato was one of the best cooks in Little Italy.

"I like Sheila," Dario defended as he and Pat started up the courthouse steps. When they reached the top, they flashed their badges at a security guard.

"The only kind of man who wouldn't like Sheila," said Pat as they headed inside, "is in the morgue."

"True," Dario agreed, now walking down a hallway. "But

I don't like Sheila enough to have to lay low for a couple weeks. Another ten buildings could burn. I just don't get it. Who could have complained about me dating somebody I arrested? Who cares?"

"Maybe Sheila called the boss. Did you two have a fight?"

"You have a devious mind."

"Of course. I'm a cop."

Dario thought back to his and Sheila's last date, when they'd skipped dinner and headed straight to bed, then he shook his head. "Last time I saw her, I put a smile on her face. She could have done a toothpaste commercial. She claimed multiples."

"Personalities?" Pat joked.

Dario shook his head. "Orgasms."

"Then I'm out of suspects. But don't worry. I've got the arson case covered, and I'll call if anything happens. Meantime, do what the boss ordered, and rustle up some cold-case files to keep yourself company."

"Will do." Dario splayed a hand on the courtroom door and prepared to push. "See you around, partner. And watch out for Karen. The glint in that girl's eyes says she's got diamonds and wedding cake on the brain."

There was a long pause. Then Pat said, "Uh…I have something to tell you. I proposed last week."

Dario's jaw slackened. "To Karen?"

"Yeah."

"Congratulations," Dario managed, but he felt hurt. Pat had been his partner for two years. They'd double-dated, played ball. "Why didn't you tell me?"

"I was going to…"

But he didn't think Dario would understand. Not Dario, who was still chasing women like Sheila Carella. "That's okay, partner," he said quickly. "I forgive you."

"Good. Because you're going to be my best man."

Even so, Dario was still reeling from the news as he entered the courtroom. Everyone was getting married. Even his sister, Eliana. She'd fallen for the nephew of a man reputed to have mob connections, but who was legitimate, according to Dario's sources at the precinct. Not that the information had calmed their mother's fraying nerves. For months, his parents' Mulberry Street apartment had been "wedding central," and in three weeks, Dario and Eliana's other six siblings—all sisters—would arrive from around the country for the wedding.

Now, Eliana's diamond engagement ring flashed as she waved from the front of the courtroom. With bright red lip-sticked lips she mouthed, "Where have you been? Ma's freaking out!" Before Dario could respond, his sister turned to face the judge again, her black hair swirling around her shoulders like a cape.

Great. They'd drawn Judge Zhang, one of the most ponderous deliberators in the history of New York courts, which meant this informal hearing might drag on. Judge Zhang was so small that his robes seemed to swallow him, and his hair and eyes were as shiny and black as the cloth itself.

As his family scooted to make room for him, Dario noticed Brice Jurgenson on the other side of the courtroom, flanked by Beppe's furious tenants. Skinny and bespeckled, Brice had only a few wisps of white blond hair left. An attorney, as well as a tenant, he'd convinced the others to put their rent into escrow until Beppe finished repairs to the building.

Luther Matthews, a museum curator, was present, as Dario had anticipated, and he was delivering a speech about preserving the property for historical reasons. But why was Chuckie Haswell here? Because he was a prime suspect in Dario's arson case, Dario did a double take. Chuckie was short, with sandy hair and assessing brown eyes, and his suit probably retailed for Dario's annual salary. Was the realty mogul present because Beppe's property was on the waterfront? Did he know Beppe was desperate to sell, and that Luther Matthews was determined to declare the property a historical landmark, which would sour their chances of selling?

"Mr. Matthews," Judge Zhang said. "Would you mind starting from the top? We've had a disruption."

"Sorry," Dario murmured.

"No problem," returned Judge Zhang. You've come before my court many times, so I know you're a busy man, Officer Donato."

"Busy giving Sheila Carella parking tickets," Eliana muttered.

"At least I'm not marrying the mob," Dario shot back, before turning his attention to Luther.

"I'm from the Centuries of Sex Museum," Luther began again, using a forefinger to push horn-rimmed glasses upward on his nose. "As we all know, the geographical area in question, not just Mr. Donato's building, is of significance."

"Go on," urged Judge Zhang.

"The intersection where Orange, Cross and Anthony Streets once met, and where Mr. Donato's building stands today, used to be called Five Points. It was synonymous with vice. Tap dancing originated there, as well as our city's most notorious gangs. Famous travelers such as Abraham Lincoln were given tours of the neighborhood's crowning jewel, Mr. Donato's property, which was a brothel called Angel's Cloud."

"After Angelo Donato," Beppe put in, losing his patience. "My ancestor. We all know this. It's why I own the property. And since it's mine, I don't see why other people are allowed to turn it into a historical landmark so I can't sell it."

Dario's mother, Bianca, crossed herself. She felt the family's long-time connection to a house of sin was tantamount to a curse. "If you don't sell, Beppe," Dario had heard her vow many times, "your only son is never going to settle down with a nice girl. Due to this legacy, he'll be a womanizer his whole life, just like Angelo." To whatever extent this was true, Dario hadn't minded.

Luther continued, "When Angel's Cloud was first built, nearly every house radiating from Five Points was a brothel. So-called panel games were invented at establishments such as Angel's Cloud, where women would remove panels in the walls and rob male clients while other women kept the men…" Luther smiled "…shall we say, *occupied.*

"These were powerful men, too. Lawyers, doctors and town fathers. Many wives, under the guise of temperance societies, tried to shut the places down. Because of morals, yes." Luther flashed another smile. "But also because their husbands were having such a good time." Stepping forward, Luther lifted some folders and began handing them out. "I've put together a package of pictures, to illustrate why Mr. Donato's property must be declared a landmark."

"Ridiculous," insisted Beppe.

"As curator of the Centuries of Sex Museum," Luther continued, "I've learned a great deal about life at Angel's Cloud. Of particular interest is the possible murder of a woman named Gem O'Shea. Recently, her ancestors have been in contact with me, but before I say more about that, I'd like to acquaint everyone with the O'Shea family tree…" After pausing to catch his breath, he rattled off names, then listed Angelo Donato's relatives, including Dario's great-grandfather, Enrico, and his grandfather, Salvador.

"My predecessor acquired many items from Angel's Cloud through the Donato family," Luther continued. "For years, the museum has owned all the original furniture, as well as portraits of the women who worked for Angelo. Replica rooms are roped off in our museum, preserving rooms exactly as they once were. I think this proves that our relationship with the Donato family has been excellent, but now that Mr. Donato has voiced intentions to sell, we have to try to save the building itself.

"While an old bawdy house may not seem a national treasure, Judge Zhang," he concluded, "Angel's Cloud is one of the only original Five Points buildings still standing today."

"I have to sell," Beppe muttered, twirling the end of his inky black mustache anxiously. "The taxes are through the roof! Besides, I've been renting to tenants for years!"

"But now the area's been rezoned, and if the property winds up in the hands of a developer—" Luther stared pointedly at Chuckie Haswell "—a high-rise will appear in its place."

"This is what the Donato family gets for being patrons of the arts," fumed Beppe.

"Patrons of the arts?" whispered Eliana. "By contributing to a sex museum?"

"Shush," commanded Bianca.

"Of course Mr. Donato wants to sell!" Brice Jurgenson burst out, rising to his feet and shaking his fist. "On behalf of the few remaining tenants, I'm here to say the place is unlivable! Overrun with mice! Every Donato slumlord has renovated it, breaking it into ever smaller rental units, and now it's full of architectural oddities and tenants can't—"

"I'm no slumlord!" said Beppe in shock. Noticing how his father's liver-spotted hands were starting to shake, Dario felt a surge of protectiveness. His folks had wanted a son desperately, so they hadn't quit having kids until Dario came along; he'd been a late baby, behind seven sisters. Now his dad was too old to keep up with a rental property full of disgruntled tenants.

"There are strange sounds in the hallways late at night," Brice pressed on. "Very strange sounds. Loud music. Foot-steps. Some tenants believe the place is haunted, and—"

"It may well be!" added Luther. "That's exactly my point. We must preserve this piece of history."

"This isn't about history!" protested Beppe. "Just mice. And that's why my son, *Officer Donato*," he emphasized, "has agreed to move in, starting tonight. He says he's going to take care of everything."

Inwardly, Dario groaned. "What?"

"I already told them," assured Beppe under his breath. "Before you came. You're a police officer, so you can fix anything."

He was hardly a miracle worker. "I'm on an arson case."

"Nope," countered Eliana. "I tried to call you earlier, and wound up talking to Pat. He said you got bumped down to desk duty because you were dating criminals, and I told Pop."

Chalk one up to sibling rivalry, but Sheila Carella wasn't exactly a felon. "She forgot to pay her parking tickets," Dario reminded in a hushed tone.

"A hundred of them?" returned Eliana.

Then Luther captured their attention. He was speaking again. "Gem O'Shea may have been the madam of Angel's Cloud, but no one's sure. We do know that her death in a carriage accident was rumored to have been a murder. She was believed to have a son, but he vanished, the father unknown. We have found a record of *his* son, however. He married a maidservant named Bridget in 1910. She had a daughter, Emma, who had Fiona, who had Erin, who—"

"Should be none of my business," Beppe finished.

"Not so," countered Luther. Erin is the mother of Cassidy Case." Approaching the bench, he showed a letter to Judge Zhang. "Cassidy forwarded a copy of this letter to the museum. As you can see, it indicates that a will existed, giving Cassidy's ancestor, Gem, all rights to the property in question."

Beppe gasped. "Who wrote the letter?"

"Clearly, the owner of the property," said Luther. "But it's signed only, 'your beloved.'"

"The property has been in the Donato family for over a century," countered Beppe.

"Cassidy will be in town next week, with part of the actual will, as well," Luther went on. "Legally, Mr. Donato may have only squatter's rights to this property, Judge Zhang."

"You say…" Judge Zhang stared down at his notes "…Mr. Case is going to be here next week, with the documents?"

"On Tuesday," Luther confirmed.

"We'll reconvene then," said Judge Zhang. "Ten o'clock."

"There's just one problem," said Chuckie Haswell, speaking for the first time. "Because my firm, Haswell Realty, had hoped to make Mr. Donato an offer on this property, we've been doing our own research." Heading to the bench, he put a folder in front of Judge Zhang. "As these documents prove, the property was owned by my ancestor, Nathaniel Haswell. Even if Angelo Donato had wished to will the property to Gem O'Shea, it wasn't his to give. He was a front man for Nathaniel Haswell. To protect his reputation, my ancestor only used Angelo Donato to conceal the true ownership of Angel's Cloud—"

"Used Angelo?" Beppe shook his head. "The first guy wants to declare my building a landmark, so I can't sell it, and now this one's saying I don't even own it." Hearing his father's disbelief, Dario winced. Beppe had hoped to use proceeds from a sale to pay for Eliana's elaborate wedding.

"As you'll see," continued Chuckie, "Nathaniel Haswell willed the property to his son, Dirk, and his wife, Isme. The original records, of which you now have copies, are still on file at the courthouse."

Judge Zhang said, "This is all the more reason to reconvene next week. Then we can take a look at whatever documentation Cassidy Case is bringing to town."

"Next week!" exploded Brice. "On behalf of the tenants, I have to protest! We've already had a cold snap, and the boiler didn't come on. And like I said, there's something fishy happening. We hear music late at night. Sounds of dancing. I'm a reasonable man, Judge Zhang, and I don't believe in ghosts, but—"

"Apparently, Officer Donato has promised to oversee the property during this upcoming week, as a favor to his father," Judge Zhang said. "That means you'll have on-site police protection until the matter is resolved." The judge's dark eyes landed on Dario. "Am I right?"

Dario bit back a sigh of annoyance. He hadn't anticipated the dovetailing cases to entail him moving into an old brothel. "Absolutely, sir."

"Then I'll see you next week. Mr. Matthews, you may inform Mr. Case."

A second later, Bianca said a quick goodbye and forced Beppe toward the door, clearly fearing he'd unleash his temper on Chuckie, Brice or Luther, and Dario took the opportunity to open the folder Luther had given him, feeling glad he wasn't going to have to hunt for a cold case to work on. He'd never heard of Gem O'Shea, much less her possibly unsolved murder, but now it looked as if he could both help his dad and appease his boss by delving into the matter.

He surveyed a picture of the bawdy house, then a photocopied daguerreotype of his own ancestor, Angelo. His hair was wild, and his piercing dark eyes held a devilish glint. Often, Dario had been told he was the spitting image of the man. When he moved on to the next picture, his heart missed a beat. Gem O'Shea, he thought, feeling a tug at his groin. God, she was hot. Untamed waves fell over her shoulders, and the ends of the curls looked like flaming tongues. They licked an ample chest that spilled from a laced-up dress that was sexy as hell. Lots of cleavage.

The picture was black-and-white, of course, but Dario would bet her hair was flame-red. Her eyes would be blue or green. But which?

Eliana chuckled. "And they say normal men only think about sex sixty times a day."

Dario blinked. "Huh?"

"What's this for you? Six hundred?" When he didn't immediately respond, she chuckled. "Since you're going to be staying in Dad's building, maybe you'll get lucky. Maybe Brice will introduce you to that woman's ghost. But be careful, little brother."

"Because?"

"Sheila Carella might get jealous."

"Who?" he teased, still staring at Gem O'Shea's picture. "I don't remember any woman named Sheila."

"You're incorrigible," his sister muttered, rising on her toes to peck-kiss his cheek. "But be forewarned. When guys like you fall, they fall hard."

Dario held up Gem's picture. "Let's just hope when I fall, that it's right on top of a woman who looks like this."

Eliana hooked her arm through his. "You really are impossible."

"But you love me," he guessed.

"In exactly the way all women love guys like you," she assured.

"How's that?"

"Completely against my will."

2

"GEM, YOU'RE A HOTTIE," Dario said late that night as he tossed back a shot of whiskey, drinking from the bottle. He'd showered in a cramped stall down an unlit hallway, deciding against using a tub in the empty apartments upstairs, then he'd put on briefs, gotten into bed and opened the file, mostly so he could look at Gem's picture again.

Her finger was crooked and her mouth was pulled into a sexy pout. She would have looked frivolous, but her eyes held too much awareness. Pain, maybe. Something that hinted at emotional depth. According to his information, she'd survived a famine and fled her country. She'd crossed the Atlantic, only to find herself in one of the world's worst slums, but she'd made a decent life, anyway.

Dario felt a magnetic pull, a sense of impending fate. Plain old lust, too. Or else maybe he'd just had too much to drink. Whatever the case, he was fantasizing about playing out the age-old cliché about hookers and cops. It had been a long night, and he was desperate for release. Pat had called about another arson case, and although Dario was supposed to be laying low, he'd visited the scene. Then, because Beppe's tenants had waylaid him to air their grievances as he was leaving court, Dario had wound up hauling in surveillance equipment to appease them.

Now cameras were arranged strategically around the

premises. At least, by the end of the week, Dario would be able to prove his pop's building wasn't haunted. When he glanced at the tripod-mounted camera placed discretely in a corner, his lips stretched into a slow grin.

With this camera, he was going to catch a woman, not a ghost. As soon as he'd called and told Sheila about the history of Angel's Cloud, apologizing since he'd be busy and unable to meet her this week, she'd said she'd never had sex in a haunted house and wanted in on the action.

"It's different," Dario had assured playfully. "And not something I can just tell you about. You'll have to come over and experience it yourself."

"See you at eight," she'd said.

But eight had come and gone. Typical Sheila. Punctuality wasn't her strong point. It was nearly midnight, and anticipation had left Dario as horny as the men who used to patronize the room where he was about to sleep.

To keep his mind occupied, he'd interviewed tenants. There was a middle-aged woman who ran an Italian ice stand, Carmella Liotella, and Chinese sisters, Zu and Ling, who shared an apartment on the otherwise vacant third floor. Brice, whose law office was around the corner, lived in the attic. Rosie, a liberal-looking single mom, was on the first floor, just beneath Carmella and opposite the apartment where Dario had set up camp. She had a crush on Brice, and an alarmingly flirtatious thirteen-year-old, Theresa, who'd been wearing skintight jeans, a midriff exposing a fake tattoo, and enough makeup that she could have been applying for a job as a madam herself.

Dario had moved in opposite them because everybody said that's where the noise was coming from. The previous tenant had left in a hurry—supposedly due to the haunting—which meant the apartment had ramshackle furnishings. Shirts were still in the closet. The tenant had been a big guy, almost Dario's size, so it was hard to believe he'd been scared off.

There were nine empty units, three per floor, discounting the attic where Brice lived—and that seemed weird, too, since Beppe was a soft touch and the rent was low. Ghost sightings increased whenever he made moves to sell, but Dario had always figured people would lodge complaints, no matter how absurd, to discourage the building's ownership from changing hands.

Still, people had left despite having rent-stabilized leases, when they'd have difficulty finding similar bargains, and the place was creepier than Dario remembered. While in the basement, putting out environmentally friendly mouse traps Eliana insisted he buy, he could have sworn the air temperature dropped abruptly. Shrugging off the event, he'd spent an hour trying to fix the boiler before realizing he'd have to buy a new one. The whole time, he'd felt as if somebody were watching him. Most disturbing, the tenants seemed genuinely scared.

"The sounds started about two weeks ago," Zu had reported. "We hadn't heard anything in a long time, about six months, but then all of a sudden…"

"Gem O'Shea is walking the halls at night again," Ling had added in a hushed tone. "Luther Matthews came by. He has a key to the place, you know. And he told us about Gem O'Shea. That she was murdered. I'm sure she's haunting us."

"Maybe trying to tell us who killed her," said Rosie.

"The music's, like, really loud," added Theresa.

"Here," Brice had added angrily, coming from the attic, and dumping a box of papers at Dario's feet. "This is everything I was able to find out about the place. Something fishy's going on. You should take a look."

And Dario had. Apparently, these old walls had absorbed plenty of lovers' whispered secrets, and many illicit back-room deals. The old news clippings collected by Brice jibed with records Dario had found in cold-case files at the pre-cinct, as well as family materials related to the property that Beppe had kept, and that Dario had brought with him. A sheet in the police file indicated Gem had stashed jewelry in the house; an inventory list had been submitted in case of theft.

Definitely, the tenants hadn't lied about the shoddy work-manship. It was Dario's grandfather's fault, since he'd hired bad contractors. The original bar, which had been about fifteen feet long, was still in Zu and Ling's apartment. Someone had renovated it as a kitchen island. Brice's shower stall was in his kitchen, and because his wiring was inadequate, he'd run an extension cord to an outlet in the hallway.

Outside, Dario had stood on the sidewalk, surveying the exterior, and something had niggled, but he didn't know why. The building was tall and skinny, with a sharply graded roof and louvered windows. The bricks crawled with ivy, and a downstairs back door led into unkept gardens. The rear building, where Gem had lived, had been torn down long ago.

His cell rang. He clicked on. "Yeah?"

"Sorry I'm late."

Sheila sounded tipsy, a good sign. "Are you coming now?"

"There's more than one way to take that."

"Not once you get here."

"On my way," she said, giggling. "Keep the bed warm."

"I'm getting sleepy," he returned with mock grouchi-ness. "Are you sure you're going to show?"

"Put a key under the mat, sailor, and let Gem O'Shea wake you up."

Not a bad idea. "Done. Two pots on the porch are planted

with ivy. The key to the lobby doors will be in the one on the right. I'm the first door on the left—I'll leave it ajar." Maybe that wasn't the brightest thing to do, but the neighborhood was relatively safe nowadays, and besides, he'd put his gun under the bed.

"Given what I'm going to do to you," she was saying, "you'll think you're dreaming."

"So you have plans for the bawdy house?"

"Just call me Gem O'Shea."

She ended the call, and he grinned. "My kind of girl."

Yawning, he thrust his legs into jeans, took the key to the planter and returned. Then he found a pen, scrawled "I'm in here, babe," and taped it to the door, drawing an arrow toward the bed. The tenants were tucked in for the night and wouldn't see it. Absently scratching his chest, he stared into the open folder before transferring it to the floor, suddenly glad Eliana had reminded him to bring sheets, a blanket and towels. Without a boiler, the steam heat hadn't come on.

Where the hell was Sheila? He could sure use some body heat. After taking another swig of whiskey, he set the bottle on the nightstand, along with his wallet and badge. Checking to make sure his gun was under the bed, he switched on the video recorder.

Sheila was going to love his surprise. Pat would get a kick out of the story, too. Suddenly frowning, he thought about Pat's engagement, then pushed aside the thought. Everybody he knew might be settling down, but Dario wasn't going to let it get in the way of his own lifestyle.

Rummaging in his jeans pockets, he put some open condom packages and a twenty-dollar bill on the nightstand. Since Sheila was intent on playing Gem O'Shea, he'd pay her. As soon as she got here, he'd turn on the light, then they could make the homemade movie while polishing off the rest of the whiskey.

He smiled. He was glad he'd met Sheila. All she cared about was sex. She was like a female version of him. His other half. Taking off his briefs, he tossed them to the floor. Might as well be ready when she gets here, he thought.

A second later, he was out like the light.

"WAKE UP, SAILOR."

Husky murmurings sounded beside Dario's ear. Hot breath tickled his earlobe. His head was pounding, and he groaned when he realized he must have had way too much to drink last night. The warm whiskey had tasted great going down, burning a path from his mouth to his belly, just as surely as a kiss, but now...

Fingernails raked upward on his bare chest, then stopped to trace circles around his nipples. He groaned again, arousal catching him unaware. Music was playing, sounding faraway. Probably coming from one of the other apartments, he thought, but who was up so late? Zu and Ling said they went to bed early. Brice and Carmella had to work. And Rosie had a kid. Maybe he'd just drifted, and it was still only a little after midnight.

Weight was bearing down on him. Sheila, he guessed. He'd tossed and turned, so the sheet had tangled around his legs, and now, even if she hadn't been on top of him, he couldn't have moved. Opening his eyes a fraction, he saw only vague shadows, enough to know he wasn't dreaming. A woman was definitely straddling him.

"Finally," he whispered. Shutting his eyes again, he lifted his hands, curving them over hips. Nice, plump womanly hips. Not too skinny—he hated women who starved themselves—but not too padded, either. Just right. It was one of the many things he liked about Sheila. After uttering a lusty sigh, he smiled. Her muscles flexed beneath his fingertips as she rocked against him, her inner thighs squeezing.

She was so responsive. That was another thing he liked. Now, if she'd only move upward a tiny inch. She was a hair's breadth from where he was aching for her. So close.

Please. He thought the word as soft hands curled around his shoulders, then dug deep—now exploring dips and crevices around his collarbone. After a moment, flattened palms pressed down hard on his pectorals, feeling like heaven.

"What time is it?" he whispered, his voice barely audible over all the racket. It was hard to believe somebody thought whatever was playing was music. He slitted his eyes open, but again, saw only inky darkness. The music sounded like show tunes, maybe something from Broadway.

"Three," she whispered.

"In the morning?"

"Yeah."

No wonder he felt like hell. "Better late than never."

"Do we still have time?"

He didn't have to be at work until nine. "We can get a lot done in six hours."

"Sorry I didn't make it earlier, the way I promised."

"Me, too."

"You *feel* sorry," she whispered, the brush of her belly making clear what she meant. He was as hard as a rock. Her voice sounded deeper than usual. So husky that she didn't even sound like Sheila. She must have felt as sex-crazed as he, waiting all day for this. That's why she was talking like a sex siren from an old movie. She sounded like Bette Davis, Lana Turner and Marilyn Monroe all rolled into one. All shivery and whispery, as if she'd had way too much to drink and had just smoked cartons of cigarettes, and was offering him something forbidden. He imagined her in a black-and-white picture, wearing a slinky gown, and holding a highball glass and a long black cigarette holder.

Then he remembered she was pretending to be Gem O'Shea. That's why she'd worn a wig, too. Long strands of hair were brushing his face, teasing his cheeks and shoulders.

He rubbed her thighs, stroking them with the backs of his hands and shifted his weight, straining unsuccessfully to feel the crushing pressure of her pelvic bone against his erection. When she just missed the magic spot, he uttered a frustrated sigh. She was still in outerwear, a jacket and tight leggings, no shoes. "That's the great thing about clothes…"

"What?"

"We can get rid of them."

"That's why I came over."

Cold insteps with high arches were molding his calves, warming themselves. Threading fingers into her hair, he explored the wig and chuckled. Sheila really was great. She'd do anything to please a guy. What an imagination. "Are you ready to make up for lost time?"

"If you can forgive me for being late."

"Kiss me and I'll think about it." Splaying his fingers, he dragged them through her hair, using the strands to pull her face down to his. Her mouth was open, and it melted against his as their tongues meshed, sparking electricity that began dancing wildly down his nerves, making them sizzle at the ends. Rushing between his fingers, tendrils of hair felt like palm fronds under water, softer than anything he'd ever felt, even softer than her mouth. His hands found her waist again, guiding the movements of her lower body, urging her closer, as he brushed his kiss-dampened mouth across hers.

When the friction turned maddening, he feathered, then nibbled. Judging by her soft whimper, it was working, really turning her on. She whispered, "What do I have to do to make *absolutely sure* you forgive me?"

"This." He arched his hips, his body surging.

She pushed back, her thighs quivering, the inner flesh shaking deliciously as she scooted into the cradle of his legs and settled on the hard ridge of his sex. He gasped, a shiver ripping through him. Something in the back of his throat caught, and he said, "I'm glad you made it."

She was panting softly, rolling her hips with the dexterity of a belly dancer and grinding herself against his groin. "I can tell."

As she undulated, waves of need lapped through him. Pliable, ready lips fit to his again. Wet and promising, they clung as if she didn't want to let go. His sentiments, exactly. Tonight, she didn't even taste like Sheila. Her usual mint flavor had been replaced by chocolate and coffee, and the lipstick he'd eaten off was raspberry. Not a hint of alcohol, which was what he'd expected, given how tipsy she'd sounded on the phone.

"I tried to hurry," she murmured.

"You're here now," he whispered back.

Against his, her cheek still felt cool from the night air, making the spear of her tongue seem even hotter. It was warm and runny—like hot honey or butter or molasses. It was like lazy sunshine on a Sunday morning, streaming through a window. And it was climbing, too, just like the sun, its radiance gaining intensity and heat.

Every time she licked the inner recesses of his mouth, renewed fire ignited in his abdomen. Warmth was pouring through her leggings, like jets of liquid joy, and when she started nuzzling the stubble of his beard, roughening her relatively tender skin, Dario tilted back his head, simply reveling in the feel of her—her long legs bracketing his, her ample breasts cushioning his chest.

"Don't stop."

"Does it seem like I'm stopping?"

"No," he murmured. "But you could."

"I could do a lot of things."

"Then do them."

As she swirled hot saliva down his neck, in sloppy, looping kisses, the scratchy fabric of her jacket further aroused his nipples, chaffing until they were raw and painfully aroused. Merciless, she languidly licked his skin as if they had eternity, not just a night, then she dipped until a taut nipple was firmly in her mouth. Quick suckles made his mind fog....

He was sure he'd drifted again. He didn't know for how long. He was floating in bliss. Sheila felt so good...impossibly good. Every time they got together, sex just got better. Tonight it was excellent. Better than ever before. Right now, the touch of her mouth was torture. Every fiber of his being was starting to sing for release. Slowly, he caressed her bottom, thrilled when she kept playing with his nipples...

Then, from somewhere far off, he heard another song start, and strained his ears. He heard piano music and stomping feet. Clapping hands. A hoot of merriment.

"Give me another pint of ale," someone yelled.

"A pint for the whole house," another hollered.

He must be dreaming. Or else someone was playing an old dance hall recording. He felt unbelievably hot. Sweat prickled his nape as he shook off sleep once more, and opened his eyes. Still, only darkness. What was happening? He felt almost as if he'd been drugged. "You feel so good," he whispered.

"You're not bad, yourself."

As he inhaled sharply, Sheila's scent settled in his lungs. It wasn't the musky perfume she usually wore, but something lighter that evoked coy flirtation. As the music climbed toward crescendo, she continued nibbling that one nipple, making the other yearn for the ministrations of her mouth. She was raking teeth against the sides until fever took him, and the fire raging beneath his naval turned more fluid. A coiled spring of swirling lava became more diffuse, prickling through his veins, lazily roping into all his extremities.

"Are you going to wake up for me, sailor?"

Yawning and stretching beneath her like a huge jungle cat, he lifted his hips, the muscles of his buttocks straining. Between his legs, his heavy erection felt more than bothersome, an irksome annoyance that needed to be dealt with soon. Frustration surfaced in his husky growl. "Where have you been, anyway?"

"I got tied up."

He imagined her naked, and strapped to a bed with long silk scarves. "I like the sound of that."

"You would," she teased.

"Damn right I would," he whispered.

His eyes had adjusted, but it was too dark to see her features. He imagined her high cheekbones, the long, straight patrician nose. He wanted to see her undressed, her breasts swinging free from the restrictive jacket and whatever she wore beneath. He could see them softly bouncing as she rode him. "Oh, yeah," he whispered, another swift pang claiming his groin.

He reached to turn on the lamp, but her hand glided over his, stopping him. It was just as well. He could tape them later. Maybe the camera was even picking up some of the action, anyway. After all, he could see shadows, and it was motion activated.

He grasped a lock of hair and chuckled. Had she really

rustled up this wig just for him? This was almost as good as the time she'd let him arrest her in the shower. Or when she'd handcuffed him to bed. Or when she'd come over, wearing nothing under a raincoat.

"It feels so real."

"Of course it's real."

He rubbed the strands between his fingers, his loins still firing. As he brought silky waves to his face, another series of jolts pulsed into his bloodstream. He breathed in, finding the scent was more like shampoo than the neutral scent he'd expected from a wig.

"You're good," he murmured in admiration. She must have brought a boom box, too. That's why the bawdy-house music was playing. It wasn't coming from another apartment, after all. It was all part of Sheila's act. Slowly untying the belt of her jacket, he flicked open buttons, then pushed the garment off her shoulders and down her arms, exposing what felt like a tight cotton blouse. "I almost believe you're Gem O'Shea."

"You had doubts?"

"In my line of work, we're not known for our trusting natures."

"Can you trust me to give you the ride of your life, sailor?"

"I think I can manage that."

She started unbuttoning her blouse. In the darkness, he sensed, rather than saw, the edges open.

"You didn't take the money from the table," he murmured, his voice low.

"Paying me, are you?"

"Oh, yeah."

Clasping his hands, she brought them to her chest and placed them on her breasts. Slowly, he traced the lace edges of the bra cups she swelled to fill. She was spilling out, and thrusting her chest, too, as if begging for his touch. Her quickening breath urged him on, making him want to touch between her legs to make her climax.

As he opened her bra's front clasp, his own chest constricted. Light-headed, he swallowed against the sudden dryness of his mouth and pushed aside the cups. After licking his own fingers, he trailed slippery swirls of saliva on the distended tips of her breasts. Capturing one with his mouth, he squirted wet heat until she muttered something senseless. Her hips suddenly wrenched. As he sponged her, he lifted his hips, rubbing her until she was bucking. Her hands flattened on his chest, as if to slow him down, and her long delicate fingers curled, tugging wildly at strands of his chest hair. He leaned back on the pillow.

Her voice was husky. "How much are you paying me?"

"Not nearly what you're worth."

"Is this your first time on Angel's Cloud?"

"Yeah."

"And did you request me? Or was this just luck of the draw?"

"Absolutely intentional."

"You heard good things about me?"

"I heard you're the best."

"Hearsay's of little matter. Am I the best?"

He was about to explode and he wasn't even inside her yet. "You're convincing me of it right now."

"I didn't expect to find you like this."

"Like what?"

"Naked. In bed. And…so hard." She shivered as if to emphasize her point.

"Is that a crime?"

"Do you want me to arrest you?"

"You can keep me locked up for a long time."

The music seemed to surge then, and he gasped in protest as the heat of her lower body left his, at least until he realized she was only stripping off leggings. As soon as her legs were bare, his hungry hands sought flesh. Disappointment filled him when he found her panties still on. By the feel of it, it was a tiny silk thong with a string waistband. She straddled him again, her knees on the mattress. Just her scent was enough to make him beg for mercy.

Overcome, he grasped her back, hugging her, then nuzzled her face. The music seemed to be coming right through the walls as his tongue stroked the scanty fabric. When she flung back her head to take the pleasure, long hair whipped behind her, and when her back arched for the intimate kiss, his rigid tongue dove for her clitoris, soaking it. Using a hand to steady her, he pressed his mouth to her, making her writhe.

Not even air passed between them as his tongue did its magic, vibrating. Under damp panties, her cleft opened all the way, and both her hands raked into his hair, digging into his scalp. She moaned, then shuddering cries came in a steady stream. She was wet, his kiss was wetter, and in a second, her panties were drenched, but he didn't think she'd come yet. She was holding back.

"Come." He murmured the word against the silk. "Now."

But she only cradled his head tighter. No wonder it had taken her so long to get here, he thought vaguely. Where had she found dance hall music on such short notice? And whatever equipment she'd brought, so she could play it? She'd done all this for him—the wig, the music, the late-night rendezvous. And now he was going to make the effort worth it for her.

Curling his fingers over the string waistband, he fisted

his hand, yanking her nearer. Then he ripped the waistband. He was still tearing the panties when his mouth fell to her flesh, covering her completely. She was creaming, hot and slick, and she gasped.

Thighs braced his sides, shaking uncontrollably, her knees threatening to buckle as he tongued her, but she was still holding back. This really wasn't at all like Sheila. What had gotten into her tonight?

"What do you want?" he whispered hoarsely. "What's going to make you come?"

"You…inside…" Her utterance was broken. "I want…I want…"

He couldn't wait for her to spell out the rest. He was too swollen. Painfully thick, his erection was pulsing, and just a hair-trigger touch would make him explode. Blindly reaching, he grabbed a condom and roughly kicked away the sheet. A moment later, he grunted softly, voicing the agony only she could relieve. Quickly wrapping his arms around her, he urged her to lie beside him. She was naked and quivering, burning up.

"What?" he whispered raggedly, dragging kisses across her cheeks, willing to give her anything.

"Fuck me," she whispered softly, the words barely audible.

It was the sexiest thing he'd ever heard. At first, he wasn't even sure he'd heard right, but now his heart hammered with increased desire. The words hadn't sounded dirty at all, not like a curse, just needy. Even sweet. He'd never heard so much frustrated desire in a woman's voice. Hell, the more he knew Sheila, the more he discovered vulnerability he'd never have guessed was there, and it was starting to get to him. She was like a difficult case that never seemed to add up. This really didn't seem like the same Sheila he'd had sex with before, and it was intriguing him.

Maybe he was falling in love with her after all.

Mutterings emanated from nowhere as she molded to his body. He whispered sweet nothings in return, then peppered kisses into the wig. Urging her onto her back, he kneeled, turning her so he could gain the deepest possible access. Silken thighs parted, and his heart stuttered. Burning and throbbing, he teased her, parting the cleft with his erection. Catching drops of her natural lubrication, he stroked, wishing his own sex wasn't sheathed.

When he could take no more, he placed his hands on her thighs, parting them farther still, wishing the light was on so he could see everything. Crooking a hand under her knee, he raised a shapely leg, then everything seemed silent. It was as if the music had stopped, although it hadn't, or as if their panting breaths had calmed, although they were both breathing harder than ever.

She arched, silently begging.

He thrust hard, and she parted like a river, much tighter than he remembered. He'd never felt so big, thrusting harder and filling her. She sobbed as she stretched to take him, flinging her arms around his neck. When he was in all the way, he rocked his hips, then he rested and just felt the bliss, sighing.

Her heart was hammering against his heart. Her breath mingled with his breath. After a long moment, he withdrew and thrust again, staying skin to skin.

"Oh, yes," she whispered as something primal grabbed hold of him. Her possessive nails were dragging down his back now, and her claiming lips, teeth and tongue were suckling his neck. She was pulsing all around him, and with her first orgasm, she cried out, a wrenching twist of her body coming in tandem with a sob that shook his emotions. Her second orgasm sent a shudder through him, then palpitations. By the third, he was putty in her hands. She was cooing like a dove as he went over the edge, gasping once, his mind losing itself to darkness.

He'd never know how many seconds had elapsed. But when consciousness came again, she was still there, wrapped tightly in his arms, making sweet, soft sounds. Slowly, their breathing evened. Multiples, he thought. Now *that* was like Sheila. After a long moment, a smile tugged at his lips. "I think my hangover's gone," he whispered.

But she was fast asleep.

He laid in the dark for a long time, only now realizing that the music she'd brought had switched off. He hadn't even noticed. As a cop, he was usually very alert. On the job, he had one of the highest arrest records at his precinct, but when it came to sexy women, he always lost his head. He might be a cop, but he was a man, too.

He glanced down, unable to see her in the dark. Hair had fallen over her face, obscuring it, and since the wig wasn't bothering her, he let it lay. Maybe it was time to fess up, he thought. After all, he had taken Sheila home to meet his folks, hadn't he? And he didn't do that with every woman. Oh, maybe he and Sheila hadn't seemed to have much in common at first, but if sex was this good, surely they'd find areas of compatibility, wouldn't they?

He couldn't believe how content he felt right now. As if all was right with the world, and he'd arrived exactly where he was supposed to be. As if he was home. He didn't remember Sheila fitting quite so perfectly into the crook of his shoulder. Why hadn't he noticed before?

His smile broadened, turning whimsical. Maybe Gem O'Shea's ghost had a hand in this. Maybe Sheila wasn't the brightest, maybe she didn't get most of his jokes, and she'd never be able to keep up with him in a verbal sparring match. But that didn't really matter, did it?

Of course it didn't, he thought now. It was amazing how only an hour of sex could change a man's thinking about a woman. Earlier tonight, before he'd gone to bed, he hadn't even been thinking of Sheila as a potential mate. But now...

With her, sex was hotter every time. Tonight had been the best by far. She'd gone to so much trouble to please him. She had to be crazy about him. In the morning, he'd make a huge move and tell her he felt the same way, he decided.

And then he slept.

3

DANCE HALL MUSIC was playing again. As soon as Dario registered it, he bolted upright. "What time is it?" he asked, glancing toward the beside clock. When he saw only a whiskey bottle, he realized he was at his pop's building, not in his apartment in Battery Park. As he registered that the sunlight from a front room looked bright, the events of the previous night came rushing back in a barrage of hot images, but the bed was empty. The doorway to the outer hall, which he'd left ajar for Sheila, was wide open. "Sheila?"

As he stared toward the shut bathroom door, he heard a soft whirring sound. The camera was working, which seemed impossible at first, then he recalled that it was motion-activated. This and the other cameras he'd borrowed from the precinct were used on stakeouts, so maybe it had recorded last night's activities, after all. He hoped so. Even shadows of what happened between him and Sheila would be worth watching this morning. His sitting up in bed must have activated the camera again. He'd never have heard the soft whir over the music.

"Sheila?"

No answer.

That strange bawdy-house music was still sounding. It was loud and coming from…

"Under the bed?" That was weird. And where was his cell, so he could check the time? Squinting, he reached a hand under the bed. His gun was beside the cell. As he lifted the phone, he smiled. So that was the source of the music. Sheila had changed his ringer.

"Cute," he whispered. No doubt, she'd expected him to hear it during the day, and recall the bawdy-house music she'd played while they'd made love. Not just had sex, he thought. Last night, they'd definitely taken things to a new level. Surely, she'd want to meet after work.

He looked for the boom box she must have brought, but he didn't see it. He didn't see her jacket or leggings, and he hoped she hadn't gotten dressed. If so, he was only going to remove her clothes again. Flipping open the cell, he saw that it was only eight, which meant they had time for a quickie.

Sobering, he swallowed hard, something resembling a lump forming in his throat. Was he really going to tell her how he was starting to feel about her? Did he really feel the same way this morning? "Yeah," he whispered. "I do."

If work was calling, he'd tell Pat he'd be a few minutes late, to buy some extra time with Sheila. "Donato here."

"We need to talk."

It was Sheila.

Inwardly, he groaned. That explained why the jacket and leggings weren't on the floor. "You're home."

"That's what I want to talk to you about."

Probably, she'd wanted to change for work, and while he didn't share her impulse, he admired her for wanting to be where she was supposed to be. Under the circumstances, that showed dedication. If she hadn't run off, they'd be having more great sex.

"Thanks for letting me sleep," he said, meaning it. After what she'd done to him last night, he'd needed the rest.

Suddenly, his heart was in his throat, and his mind was racing. He was trying to frame what he most wanted to say. "I have something to tell you—"

"No," she said quickly. "I have something to tell you."

Maybe. But he needed to tell her he enjoyed last night so much that he wanted them to become even more intimate. He figured he'd better do so before he lost his nerve. "Me first. I want you to know I think you're the best—"

"Best lay?" she burst out. "And it's always you first! Have you ever noticed that, Dario?"

He almost chuckled. Last night must have affected her as much as it had him. She was nervous now, trying to push him away, and he didn't blame her. "Go ahead," he said. "Say whatever you need. Get it out of your system. And then I'll say my piece. I've been thinking about us—"

"Me, too! For the past couple of weeks, ever since we've been—"

"Making love?"

When she made a snorting sound, he frowned. "I don't know that I'd dignify what we've been doing with that phrase."

"We are explosive together," he admitted, "but I don't think that means our emotions can't be involved."

"Well, I do."

Their lovemaking must have really shaken her. Probably, she was hoping he'd voice his feelings. She needed assurances. It was what all women wanted. At least, that's what his sisters told him. "What I'm trying to say, Sheila—"

"At first it seemed fun," she raced on, as if he hadn't spoken. "Especially since Bobby and I broke up, as you know. I was so sure he'd never want to make a commitment—"

His heart had missed a beat. "Bobby?"

"O'Hare?" she queried, sounding confused. "He sits two desks over from you?"

Bobby O'Hare was a rookie. "Bobby O'Hare? From vice?"

"Yeah."

"I didn't know you dated Bobby O'Hare."

"I told you. I just don't think you were listening to me, Dario. To be blunt, you always have sex on the brain. You don't pay attention."

He was sure she'd never told him about her past relationships. "What's Bobby got to do with—"

"Everything. And that's what I've been trying to tell you. We'd been dating six months, and I was falling for him. All my girlfriends said it was too much, too fast. Maybe it was. But I knew Bobby was the one. I had such a strong feeling. Like we were meant to be, so I couldn't stop myself from chasing him. When I see something I like, I go for it."

"I noticed."

There was a long pause.

"You were saying?" he prompted.

"Well, the day you brought me in," she plunged on. "You know, for the parking tickets. Well…" She inhaled sharply, then blew out a short sigh. "The night before, I'd seen Bobby out with somebody else, and I was pissed. So, when you brought me in, I tried to be cool. I didn't even look in his direction. It must have worked, because after that, he kept calling me. But I didn't return the calls. Besides, by then, well…even when you booked me, you were coming on strong, so I guess I…"

"Go on."

"…was using you to get him out of my system. Don't get me wrong," she added quickly. "You're cute. A megahunk. Calendar quality. But you're even less the committing type than Bobby. Or so I thought."

His recent moves must have convinced her otherwise. The smile returned. Admitting his feelings was going to be so much easier than he'd anticipated, he realized. Sheila was doing all the work. "But now?"

"Bobby heard about you and me through your partner, Pat. You must have made me sound incredibly hot, because Bobby got jealous. He started sending flowers. And then he called and told me his real feelings. And you know the girl I saw him with?"

Dario could only shake his head.

"It was his sister!"

"Imagine that."

"Funny, huh?" she enthused. "One thing led to another, and, well, now I—"

Her voice cut off abruptly. On his end, morbid curiosity had taken hold. "Now?"

"Well...I know you're going to be happy for me. Bobby proposed. Can you believe it?"

As near as Dario could tell, everyone on earth had proposed lately. "You don't say."

"He gave me a ring and everything. It's beautiful, and while the date isn't set in stone, we've pretty much agreed."

"You can spare me the details."

There was a long pause. "You're not upset, are you?"

After last night? "I'm furious."

"Dario, we're friends. C'mon."

"When did this happen?"

"Yesterday."

How could she have lain in his arms last night, cooing like a love bird, when she'd known she was marrying Bobby? "When, yesterday?"

"In the afternoon."

"He gave you the ring in the afternoon?"

"Quit interrogating me. I didn't do anything wrong."

Her scent was still on his skin. She'd gotten out of his bed maybe an hour ago. Suddenly, he glimpsed something. Fishing in the covers, he held up what looked to be a sparkling blue rhinestone. "Your earring's still in the bed," he said.

"Don't worry about anything I've left behind at your place." There was another long pause. "Look, Dario, I'm really sorry. I didn't think you'd care. I mean, you have a reputation for being great in bed, but uninterested in commitment."

"We don't even know the same people. How could you know about my reputation?"

She named countless tangential connections they had through the police force. It was more than he'd imagined. Then she said, "Anyway, it doesn't matter. The main thing is that I really can't see you anymore."

"You could have thought of that last night." Dammit, her legs had been like long silk ribbons stretching around his back, wrapping tightly around his waist and stealing his breath.

"I did. That's why I didn't show."

"Didn't show?"

"I know I called. I was out with the girls, and we were doing shooters, and I thought maybe I'd come over, personally, and break the news to you then."

"Which is why you were flirting? Implying you were going to give me the best sex of my life?" Sex that, in fact, she'd delivered.

"Forgive me," she murmured contritely.

It didn't help that she'd asked for his forgiveness last night, too, while they'd been making love.

"It was the booze talking," she continued. "I admit it. I'm not perfect. But I wanted to...well, let you down easy. Not that I figured you'd care. But I thought once I came over, it would be easier to tell you about my and Bobby's—"

"But you came over and slept with me?"

There was yet another interminable pause. And then she said, "I didn't come over, Dario."

He'd had it. She'd been all over him. Licking every inch of his skin, and doing that mind-bending thing with his nipples. "Sheila, we had sex all night."

She gasped. "What?"

"I left the key in the pot, remember? And you showed up around three…"

"I don't know what you're talking about."

"What?"

"I never showed. I swear."

"Dammit, Sheila," he cursed softly, realizing she must be teasing him, the way she always did. She was good at it, too. She sounded so honest. "Quit jerking my chain." Last night her playful nature had sent his senses soaring, but this morning, he wasn't in the mood.

"I wasn't there."

"You wore a wig," he reminded, his voice turning husky. "A jacket and leggings. A little cotton blouse."

"I don't know what you're talking about."

He heard a rustle. Then a male voice. "She was here. With me."

Dario shut his eyes, unable to believe any of this was happening. It had to be Bobby O'Hare. It was as if the two men were at work. Sheila had committed a crime, and they were discussing her alibi. "Bobby?"

"Yeah."

"I don't know what's going on here," Dario began, "but—"

"Sheila and I are getting married. I proposed. She ac-

cepted. That's what's going on. She was here all night."
There was a pregnant pause. "We were awake all night, if
you catch my drift."

"I think I do," Dario managed.

Before ending the call, Bobby rambled a few lines about
how he hoped the situation wouldn't be awkward at work.

Regarding that, Dario would do his best. Still…as talented as Sheila was, she couldn't be in two places at once,
which left Dario stuck with one of the more interesting
mysteries of his career.

"Who was in bed with me last night?"

The carting wasn't much to go on. Her hands had been all
over him, and while he knew he could get a good print off his
skin, he didn't really want to explain that to the guys at the
precinct. The money on the dresser was gone, when he checked
his wallet, his money was gone, too. His gaze landed on the
camera. Maybe it, or the others, had recorded something.

He was going to use all his detecting skills to find her.
He had no idea what he'd do when he found his mystery
woman.

Time would tell.

A HALF HOUR LATER, Dario was showered, dressed and getting ready to replay the tapes. Somebody pounded on the
front door, and it swung open.

"Rosie?"

The liberal-looking single mom from across the hallway
peeked inside. "So, you heard it?"

The last thing Dario wanted to do right now was chat with
neighbors. His mind was focused on what he might see on
the tapes. "Heard what?"

Rosie's voice was hushed. "The music."

"It was loud!" Zu and Ling crowded into the doorway

behind Rosie, although Dario wasn't sure which one of them had spoken.

"I didn't sleep a wink," added Carmella.

It was as if they'd been waiting in the hallway until they heard him rustling around inside the apartment.

"And you were looking at us yesterday as if we were crazy."

This time, it was Brice.

Rosie's daughter, Theresa, edged in, squeezing between her mother and Brice. She was wearing a multilayered outfit that involved leggings, two skirts and a few jackets, making her look like a homeless waif. He guessed it was the style for teens. "It was, like, so loud," she said. "And I couldn't sleep. And now I'm going to fail my math test." She glared at Dario. "It's going to be your dad's fault if I'm held back a grade. We could sue. I just want you to acknowledge that."

"Theresa," her mother admonished.

"Well, it's true," said Theresa.

"What are you going to do about this?" demanded Brice.

"Nothing, if you don't leave me alone, so I can watch these tapes," Dario returned calmly. He was thirty, and years of working on the force had taught him how to keep his cool in tense situations. Not that he always bothered. But he didn't like being railroaded. He sent the tenants a long look.

"So, you may have found something?" Brice didn't sound angry now, only relieved.

"I hope so."

"Then we'll get out of your hair," said Rosie.

"One minute," said Dario.

They stared expectantly. He said, "The music you heard last night—"

"Didn't you hear it?" asked Brice.

He didn't want to admit he'd heard what they believed

to be some supernatural event. "I'm not sure what I heard. But I want to know if it's what you've heard in the past."

"So, you did hear it," accused Theresa.

Her mother was more pragmatic. "That's exactly how it always sounds, Officer Donato. The hoots and catcalls. The foot stomping. All of it."

"But not lately," reiterated Carmella.

"It quit for six months," agreed Zu.

"For a couple days it was loud," clarified Brice. "And then nothing."

"Thank you for your help," Dario told them.

A second later, the tenants were gone, closing the door behind them. He was still thinking about the music. If he hadn't slept with Sheila last night, then she hadn't brought a boom box. Wondering where the music had come from, he selected the tape from the machine by the bed. Shadows flitted, and while he couldn't see everything perfectly, he felt a pang at his groin.

When he checked the machine in the hallway, the test image was very clear and in color. He stared at the empty hallway. Then he did a double take. Sudden movement activated the camera. A woman passed, but too quickly. Hair, which he'd thought was a wig, turned out to be red. Encased in tights, those looked to be the same long legs that had hugged his hips like a vise.

He rewound the tape and played it again, freezing the image when she turned toward the camera. Instead of Sheila's sharply angled facial bones, this woman had roundish features, full cheeks and a soft, fleshy pout of a mouth. Instead of Sheila's long straight note, this woman's was a short ski jump sprinkled with freckles. She looked very Irish.

Everything inside of him seemed to go still, then his

heart thundered as his eyes trailed over the red hair, cautious green eyes and the beauty mark beside her mouth.

It was Gem O'Shea.

4

"LUTHER," SHE MANAGED. "Uh...*you're* Luther Matthews?" She sure as heck hoped she got it right this time.

"Cassidy, darling," he announced, waving at her with a manicured hand. "I expected you *next* Tuesday. But never mind! You're as gorgeous as I imagined. Gem O'Shea in the flesh. The same red hair and green eyes. If I don't keep you to myself, Seventh Avenue will steal you away while you're visiting and put you to work on a runway! What a pleasure!"

It was quite a speech, especially since Cassidy was still reeling from a night of sex which, until moments ago, she'd thought she was experiencing with Luther Matthews, who now seemed less seductive and more metrosexual. Not so the guy last night. Pinpricks of awareness assaulted her as images of hungry hands and kiss-bruised lips invaded her consciousness. "Uh...thanks for the compliments."

"Oh, no. Thank *you*." Luther winked, his blue eyes appraising behind horn-rimmed glasses, carrying hints of the flirtation they'd shared on the phone. And why not? She'd given him every reason to believe she'd soon be sleeping with him. Instead, she'd accidentally shared the sheets with a stranger who was still making her knees turn to water. Instinctively, she reached out a hand as if to break a fall.

"You cold?"

Still hot from last night, she thought, realizing that she'd shivered. "Fine."

"Good, because I've got a gazillion things to tell you. The Donatos waylaid me outside court yesterday and made me return my key to their property. Can you believe it? The museum's been working with that family for years and is currently putting together a diagram of the property during that particular era of history! But now we're being treated like thieves!"

She tried not to think of the money she'd taken from Dario Donato's bedside table. "That's just terrible," she managed.

"They are horrible people," Luther confided angrily. "Their son, Dario, works for the NYPD, and he's staking out the place, as if you and I might rob them. And it's your property! Well, next week you'll meet these people and see for yourself."

Given her and Dario's face-to-face, she was relieved when Luther zoomed on. "Give me a minute to finish up with a client, then I'm yours." He grinned. "And I do mean, all yours."

As much as Cassidy loathed men—the ink on her divorce decree was still wet—she'd felt an urge for sex lately. So, when Luther contacted her, like an angel out of the blue, saying he knew pertinent facts about her family history and possessed documents she should see, the new flirtation seemed like icing on a cake. He was decent looking, she saw now, the perfect person with whom to get her ya-yas out, but in a fussy black suit and horn-rimmed glasses, he wasn't her type.

Casual sex wasn't her style, either. Being a one-man woman, she hadn't noticed that Johnny Case, her ex, had been sleeping with incoming freshmen at the college where he'd taught. She'd been the last to know, and ever since, she'd wanted to assert herself, feel hot again, and remind somebody—anybody—that she could knock a man's socks off in bed, which last night had proven.

But what had she done? For a moment, items in Luther's glassed-in office seemed to slide off-kilter. Bookcases seemed to tilt, and the floor felt wobbly. She tried to tell herself last night was a dream, but her mind raced backward in time, and her erogenous zones told her it was real.

She'd thought Luther was expecting her yesterday, on Tuesday, on a flight from South Carolina. Due to a storm, she'd arrived late and gone straight to the Pierre Hotel where the Centuries of Sex Museum was to have reserved her room, but they'd never heard of her, and she'd forgotten to program Luther's number into her new cell.

Convinced she'd gotten her wires crossed, she'd hailed a cab and headed for the bawdy house at Sixty-Seven Anthony Street. After all, Luther had talked ceaselessly of declaring it a landmark, buying it from her and renovating it, then making it the permanent home of the museum's collection.

Making clear that he'd do anything to establish her ownership so she and the museum could make a deal, he'd said he was desperate to show her the place and he had a key. In turn, Cassidy had assured him she'd sell to the museum, and Luther had said he thought Beppe would sell only to the highest bidder. Even the museum couldn't outbid players like Chuckie Haswell, who'd now made his own claim.

After spending her last dollar on the cab fare, at least until she found an ATM, Cassidy had been relieved to find the door unlocked, as if Luther had been expecting her. She'd thrilled with anticipation, wondering what he looked like. Loud dance hall music was playing, and when she'd seen the sign on the door that read, "I'm in here, babe," she'd gotten the picture. He was setting up a bawdy-house atmosphere for their tryst, and he wanted her to play the role of Gem O'Shea.

A shudder shook her shoulders as she recalled the fiery onslaught of wet, deep, open-mouthed kisses that had followed as she'd straddled him. Now the tips of her breasts constricted against the lace of the bra she'd worn last night, and she became hyperconscious of the fact that she wasn't wearing panties, since they'd been ripped to shreds. The tingle became more generalized until every inch of her body was aching, and her mouth turned dry as she recalled how he'd buried his face against her sex.

She'd wanted to turn on the light and get a good look at Luther. Especially since his body felt perfect in the dark… big, broad, rounded linebacker shoulders, washboard-flat tummy, rock-hard abs, steely pecs, bulging muscular thighs. He had hands with long, thick fingers that bore out exactly what women said about the correlation between hand and penis size, too. His movements were so self-assured and controlled that he'd seemed dangerous, albeit in a tantalizing way.

When he'd reached for the lamp she'd stopped him. In the dark, wild abandon could take hold more easily, and the second he'd started stroking her upper thighs, she'd felt brazen.

When she'd awakened this morning, she'd realized the friendly goddess presiding over megahunks had decided to shine on her. The man she'd thought was Luther was lying on his back, uncovered and stark naked. Built like a house. On the phone, Luther had been a flirt but he'd seemed like the brainy type. Maybe too much like her ex, she'd thought. In reality, he was a well-honed, sculpted beauty. Even in repose, his sex was impressive, nestled in glistening black hair. He was so tall that his adorably big feet hung over the edge of the bed, and his face was framed by unruly, silken black waves.

She'd just lain beside him, staring. He'd reminded her of medieval Italian paintings of angels. His olive skin had a glow; his nose was prominent and aristocratic; his lips, which still looked swollen from kissing, seemed impossibly bow-shaped. He could have been Cupid in the flesh. Definitely, he didn't look like a museum curator—more like an adventurer—but then he did specialize in only sex-related artifacts.

As she'd surveyed every inch of his nude form, renewed heat had jolted through her, making her stretch against him sinuously, flexing aching muscles and relishing the soreness, gearing up for another experience to rival the previous night.

Already, she'd been imagining how she'd wake him…by nuzzling her face on his lower belly, then slowly licking his naval, twirling her tongue inside the perfectly shaped depression. Then she'd go lower and blow his mind. Her own was whirling, spinning fantasies of how she was going to spend spare time during her visit, having a no-holds-barred sexcapade with this fine specimen.

Then she'd noticed a gold shield.

Curious, she'd plucked it from the table. "Dario Donato?" she'd mouthed in confusion. Her heart had hammered. Hadn't Luther said the Donatos claimed they owned her property? Moving quietly, she'd replaced the badge soundlessly, then lifted a wallet and studied the cards. The license even had his picture.

He'd chosen that moment to stir, and she'd bitten back a yelp of surprise. She'd slept with a strange man! Someone she'd never even spoken to! She'd thought he was Luther, whom she'd flirted with, at least. She had to get out of there.

He was offering throaty moans of pleasure, as if he was having a hot dream about her. Moving on instinct, she'd pushed away guilt feelings and grabbed the bill on the table, knowing she had no cab fare. Trying not to think of how he'd said he'd left the money there to pay her for sex, she'd edged over the side of the mattress, snatching clothes as she'd tiptoed to the hallway.

Maybe no one would see her. Fortunately, she'd left her roller-style carry-on suitcase right inside the door. "I can't believe this," she'd whispered, panicking when she looked at the doors to other apartments. What if someone came out and caught her naked? Hands shaking, she'd wiggled her behind into the leggings, punched her arms into blouse sleeves, then jammed the panties into her jacket pocket. She was still buttoning the blouse as she lugged the case through the front door, thrusting her feet into shoes as she hailed a cab.

"Centuries of Sex Museum," she'd said frantically.

The driver was eying her blouse, and she'd realized it was buttoned cockeyed. "I can tell you're in a hurry," he'd said, chuckling softly.

She'd smirked. "Just step on it."

"Centuries of Sex Museum," he'd said drily. "Here we come."

She'd perched on a stool in a Starbucks until the museum opened, and now she felt further frazzled by shots of caffeine.

Luther hung up the phone. "All yours," he said, coming forward, the eyes still appraising. Lifting her hand, he made a big show of kissing it.

Great. She'd been leading this guy on for a month, and last

night, she'd been sure they were consumating the seduction. She withdrew her hand and forced a smile. "Nice to meet you."

"Likewise. I thought you were coming next Tuesday."

"I got the day wrong."

He looked ashen. "But your room?"

"I got my own," she assured, her mind flashing once more on the sheet that had been tangled around Dario Donato's hips like a loin cloth. "No problem."

"Here." He made another call, then said, "I've hooked you a room at the Pierre, as promised." He explained that they had an upcoming court appearance with Judge Zhang the following week, then reiterated what had happened in court.

When he finished, she said, "Why don't you show me around?" She hoped she sounded businesslike.

"Sure. First, do you have the documents?"

Nodding, she wondered what Dario Donato would have done if he'd realized the papers were within his reach. Was he honest? Devious? Of better character than her ex?

She could feel Luther's eyes on her backside as she leaned. He thought she was a dish, which was going to make things difficult. "I brought the part of the will that I have, as well as old love letters. Regarding the ownership of the house, they may not be of interest, but I brought them, anyway. My great-grandmother passed the things to Granny Fiona, and she gave them to my mother, Erin Magee."

Hesitating, Cassidy felt suddenly unwilling to relinquish the papers. They were brittle and delicate, brown at the edges, a testament to how many generations had handed them down. Until Luther's first call, the family stories about Gem O'Shea had been just that—stories. Gem was thought

to have been a madam who'd been given jewels by her
lovers, and Granny Fiona had spun stories about her at
Cassidy's bedtime, always against the protests of Cassidy's
mother. "Quit filling her head with nonsense," Cassidy's
mother would complain.

But Cassidy would plead until Granny Fiona described
the dangerous ocean passage, the hard-scrabble life in Five
Points and Gem's time as an escort. According to the tales,
the jewels remained hidden to this day. Maybe that's why
Cassidy had become a jeweler, opening her own shop. Even
now, she believed the lost jewels existed, and the stories had
sustained her through a lonely childhood, after her father
had abandoned her and her mother.

Now the package of papers in her hands were the only
proof she possessed that Gem had really lived. Her breath
caught as she offered them to a stranger. "This is all I have."

"Excellent."

With care born of handling rare objects, Luther took the
pages to his desk. Compelled to follow, she edged behind
him as he took out a magnifying glass.

"Hmm," he said.

"Hmm, what?"

"Some of the papers we have indicate that Gem had only
one lover, not many. I'll get a professional handwriting
analyst to study these immediately if you don't mind."

She was grateful for the help. "Not at all."

As Luther continued his perusal, her thoughts drifted to
Dario Donato. He'd looked like a god. So bronzed that he
could have been glazed with hot sugar, and hard all over.
Slow heat wended into her belly, and a pang of craving
stirred her blood. Oh, she'd thought she'd known everything
about sex. She'd been married for five years, after all.

But now, she got it. She was a dreamer, sure. But she had

a pragmatic side, and she'd always wondered how people lost their heads over sex, giving up marriages and jobs. Thanks to last night though, she understood. She'd have followed Luther to the ends of the earth.

Of course, he'd turned out to be Dario.

Her enemy. Dammit, why did he have to be associated with the one family who wanted to profit from her birthright? Worse, Johnny Case had left her in debt, so just last week she'd lost her second greatest love, her business. Unless the Five Points property was declared hers, she was in trouble.

"Huh?" she suddenly said.

"Being of full age and sound mind," he was murmuring. "Revoking all other wills and codicils made by me at any time…authorize and empower to bequeath the residence at Seven Anthony Street to Gem O'Shea…" Pausing, he sighed. "I wish more of the signature was intact."

"Me, too."

"The last letters could be an *l,* or maybe a *p.*"

It was hard to tell, since the paper had been torn in half.

"Wonder where the other half is?"

"I wish I knew."

"Do you really want to keep it locked in our safe?"

"That would be great." Carrying her heritage around in a suitcase had been nerve-racking. As he locked away the papers, she said, "I appreciate all you've done."

"You're helping us. If we can prove you own this building, then it's ours."

She tried to ignore a twinge of discomfort. Luther was starting to make her feel used. Would he argue for the Donato's case, if he felt that would help his museum? Did he care about the truth? "I'd like to see the roped-off rooms."

If the property was hers, then the items now in the

museum hadn't been the Donato's to sell, but so far, no one had broached the subject, and she wasn't about to do so. She wanted to keep things simple. Declaring the property hers was the first step.

As Luther placed a hand under her elbow to guide her, she recalled how the slightest brush of Dario's skin had solicited shivers. Just his breath, or the stir of air as his body passed hers, had made her come unhinged.

Pushing aside the thoughts, she whispered, "Wow," when she saw the main exhibit. "This was how the house looked?"

"The parlor room. We'd like to get the original bar, but it became part of a kitchen renovation."

"You're kidding."

"Unfortunately, no. It's the kitchen island in one of the apartments."

"The Donatos wouldn't let you take it?"

"Tenants have said they need it. But once you're recognized as the owner, all that will change."

Once more, she felt a proprietary twinge. Still, she'd never have been informed of her claim if it hadn't been for Luther. Vaguely aware he'd left her side, she curled her fingers over the velvet ropes protecting the display and studied the original Asian carpet. It was easily an inch thick, barely worn, and woven in swirling patterns, the dyes still vibrant after a century and a half.

She laughed softly when music started, then shuddered. Spiders could have been dancing to the show tune, doing the cancan on her vertebrae. "A player piano," she said huskily. It was what Dario had played last night. She even recognized the song. But why had he been expecting a woman to show? Clearly, he'd known the legend and had expected his visitor to pretend to be Gem O'Shea.

Her heart skipped a beat. Had the woman he'd expected really *been* a prostitute? Immediately, she rejected the notion. A man who looked like him would never have to pay.

"We found old sheet music on the property years ago," Luther was saying, pulling her attention to the present. "We had it recorded and play it in the museum."

It, too, was evoking memories. She saw Dario's shadow looming above her, his body moving rhythmically, a huge, hot, dry hand cupping her knee, raising it so he could push deeper inside her. A frenzied rush had assaulted her as he'd entered her. Suddenly, she was sure he'd look for her A hand flew to her ear, and she realized an earring was gone. Before she must have subconsciously registered that she'd lost it. Had she left it behind? Or was it in the cab? Even if he found it, he'd have no idea who she was....

She felt a surge of power. In a flash fantasy, she imagined toying with him...calling and flirting with him on the phone. She'd drive him crazy with the need to know who she was. Huskily, she'd remind him of what they'd done. Ask him to take off his clothes. Tell him to touch himself, but pretend it was really her...

Blinking, she wondered what had come over her. She had to quit thinking like this. Dragging her attention to the room again, she took in a well-upholstered settee. Two high-backed, hand-carved chairs covered in blue velvet. A claw-footed gaming table. The original marble mantle had been preserved, and on either side, ornate candlesticks loomed. "I expected it to be..."

"More lurid?"

"Yeah."

"Showing your ankles was a big deal back then."

Seven portraits graced the walls, and the subjects were showing more than ankles. Some raised dresses to their thighs, or wore only corsets. "You can tell the pictures were hung exactly like this," she suddenly said in surprise.

"It's as if the paintings are one, isn't it?"

The first woman was looking at the hand of the second, who pointed to the third. That woman's scarf picked up a trail, seemingly flowing out of the painting, only to turn into a riding crop in the next picture. Any viewer following the trajectory would eventually be looking at Gem O'Shea. "I do look like her," she couldn't help but say.

"You have her hair and eyes," Luther said.

"But not her jewels." Gem's near-naked body was dripping in diamonds, emeralds and rubies. One ornamented hand fingered the strands of pearls looping her neck, the other hand pointed at the floor while Gem's eyes stared at the exact spot. "Wonder what she was looking at?"

"Who knows?"

"Whatever the case, the jewels are real. She must have been wearing them when she was painted." Cassidy sucked in a sharp breath, pointing. A man was standing behind Gem, almost lost to shadows.

"Angelo Donato. The reason the Donato's think they have a claim to the place."

He looked like Dario. She looked at Gem again, and a strange feeling came over her, almost a premonition, as if history were repeating itself.

She couldn't have been more relieved than when Luther spoke, saying, "Let me show you the rest."

After she'd seen the other rooms, she found herself standing in front of a framed newspaper article. "Mr. Ambrose Collier," she read aloud, "the driver, vowed he'd checked the hansom's wheels earlier in the evening. When they disengaged, he was thrown. According to Mr. Collier, an act of sabotage must have occurred. He swore Miss

O'Shea was his sole passenger, although an onlooker claimed two people appeared to be inside. Miss O'Shea's body was retrieved from the East River yesterday."

"So it may have been an act of sabotage?" she murmured.

"Maybe." Leaning, Luther took her hand.

She pulled away. "I should head for the hotel."

"So, you were just leading me on?" He was eyeing her with an urbane expression, as if sex was something he could take or leave, like dessert after a filling dinner.

"Not really. At the time I thought…but then I just.. " If she'd met Luther last night, she'd have felt attracted. Now, she just wanted to catch a cab back to the old bawdy house, take off her clothes, and climb into bed with the enemy.

"You just?"

"Something's…uh, come up."

"Come up?"

The something had been gorgeous, hard and attached to the body of Dario Donato. "Yeah. My divorce," she added. "You know. I haven't quite…"

"Healed? I understand." He paused, shifting gears. "While you're here, you'll want to find out as much as you can about the property," he said, all business. "That's understandable. But steer clear of the Donato family, okay?"

Once more, those huge hands were curled over her breasts, squeezing. "Okay."

"They feel their claim is solid, and letting the courts handle everything is our best bet."

And yet she wanted to feel Dario Donato's hands stroking her skin again. Luther was smart, however. She had to do the right thing—for herself. She had to be brutal, as tough as nails. "I just want to establish my ownership. That's my goal."

"And we want to make the building an historical landmark."

As long as their goals coincided, that was fine. She settled for a nod.

"Steer clear of the Donatos," he repeated. "The son's a cop, and he can probably be ruthless."

She thought of his searing mouth. "I bet," she managed.

"Chuckie Haswell is going to be another problem," Luther continued, oblivious that a shot of liquid fire was now arrowing to her core. "He's got a lot of pull. It's my personal belief that he's forged papers to make it look as if he has a claim to the place. He'd go that far."

She was still thinking of how far she'd gone with Dario. "Isn't he afraid of getting caught?"

"Chuckie will do anything to cash in on the new development opportunities around Manhattan. He wants to build a high-rise on the spot."

She'd barely heard the answer. Panicked when she'd left 67 Anthony Street, Cassidy was just now starting to wonder how Dario had felt when he'd awakened to find her gone. He'd have the glass slipper of an earring, a few hickeys on his neck, but nothing more. "I'm forewarned."

Luther's eyes drifted over her blouse. "If you change your mind about…"

She wouldn't. "Sure."

"It'll take you years to trust men again, right?"

Centuries. Realizing honesty might not be in her best interest, she batted her eyelashes. Dario Donato might have turned her head last night, but during this week, there was no room for error. "I'll call if I need anything."

"Maybe we can have dinner before meeting the Donatos at the courthouse."

She nodded. "Thanks for the tour, keeping the documents for me and the room."

"You'll like the Pierre."

"It's—" Oops. She'd almost given it away—he didn't know she'd gone there last night. No more than he knew she'd wound up having the best sex of her life with a Donato. "Always been on my list of places to visit."

"It's the missing ninth wonder of the world."

Silently thinking she'd discovered that last night, she offered a final nod, grabbed her suitcase and let Luther escort her to a cab. As it pulled into traffic, she found her cell, punched in information for a number, then called.

A woman answered. "Chuckie Haswell's office."

"Cassidy Case for Mr. Haswell."

"I'm sorry, he's…"

"Please let him know I'm in town and making claims against the property located at 67 Anthony Street, which he feels is his."

"Uh…you'd better hold then."

The line clicked immediately. "Mr. Case," he began, as if they were old golfing buddies.

"Mr. Haswell," she returned, making her voice extra-throaty. "I'm in town, staying at the Pierre, and I realized you and I have some similar interests. Care to meet for a drink? Say, my hotel. Six?"

If she was interpreting the pause correctly, she'd just blown the realty mogul away. In the past twenty-four hours, she'd been doing that to a lot of men. It felt good, too. Exhilarating. She was regaining her personal mojo and getting Johnny Case out of her system, hopefully forever. Dark and forbidding, the taste of Dario Donato's skin had been just another truly sensuous temptation. Better than chocolate and white Russians—her favorite drink.

But over. Finis. A one-night stand.

Chuckie Haswell had finally recovered from realizing she was a woman. "Six it is."

"I'll be the girl with red hair and a rose in her teeth," she continued in a breathy voice. Using her thumbnail, she tapped the off button, feeling a rush of satisfaction. "Keep them guessing," she repeated to herself. "A job well done."

As the cab pulled in front of the Pierre, she was thinking that her lapse with Dario Donato was unfortunate, since she couldn't afford to dwell on the delicious experience. She had to recover from it. Forget it, entirely.

After all, Johnny Case had taught her cold, hard life lessons about money and betrayal, and no more men were going to steal what was rightfully hers. As it was, all the inventory had been removed from the cases of her jewelry shop, and unless more money materialized, she'd lose the store. This week, she was going to have to play them all. Luther Matthews, Chuckie Haswell, Beppe Donato, and most of all, his son, Dario.

Sixty-Seven Anthony Street was hers.

None of the men cared about her, only their own interests. So be it. Reaching into her suitcase, she pulled out a letter she hadn't bothered to give Luther. "You know where the jewels are kept, my beloved," she read aloud softly. "They're in the house, in our special place. As long as the house stands, they'll be safe…"

"Look out boys," she added as a uniformed bellman opened the cab's door. The house was hers, and so was everything in it. As she stepped onto a sidewalk under a green awning, she acknowledged that she didn't only look like Gem, but she possessed her spirit.

"Consider me the ghost of Gem O'Shea," she whispered.

5

DRINKS WITH CHUCKIE HASWELL led to a dinner he'd probably thought was romantic, judging by how disappointed he'd looked when Cassidy left him at the Pierre's front doors instead of inviting him upstairs. His attraction had given her an edge, and otherwise, she'd laid her cards on the table, emphasizing the importance of the documents she'd brought to town. Chuckie had evidence that his ancestor, not Angelo Donato, had owned the building, but she could prove it had been willed to Gem.

"By whom?" Chuckie had asked.

"I have a week to find out," she'd returned. "And I will. If your ancestor, Nathaniel, really owned the property, maybe he was Gem's lover."

"He was a respectable man."

"That's what they all say." She'd flashed a smile, thinking of her ex. "Anyway, the Donatos are a wild card," she'd pressed on, remembering just exactly how wild. "If you can prove the place is yours, fine, but if you can't, consider championing my cause. I only want the house for a while. It's…sentimental."

"And you'll sell?"

"Maybe exclusively to you, if you help me stake my claim. Because of the Donatos' squatting rights, and the resistance of the historical society, I'm your best bet."

"When will you sell?"

"As soon as the tenants leave," she'd said, improvising since she wanted to search for the missing jewels. "I'm a small-town girl, so I'd hate to see them inconvenienced, and I want to make sure no work's done on the property until they're out."

"Brice Jorgensen holds the longest lease," Chuckie had said, more aware of the situation than she. "He's gone in six months." He'd paused. "You want me to give up my claim, and spend next week proving you're the rightful sole heir?"

"It's in your best interest."

"You're persuasive, and I'll think about it," he'd conceded. "In fact, you're exactly the kind of go-getter I'd love to have working for me."

Cassidy hadn't exactly taken that as a compliment, but she'd had to strike the best deal for herself, even with a bottom feeder. It was her only chance to jumpstart her business and move on. She tried not to dwell on the potential loss of her adorable store, located in the heart of her town's most popular strip mall. And now every single display case was empty, since she'd sold inventory to pay off her ex's debts. The store had been her dream, fueled by nights when Granny Fiona had plied her with stories about Gem.

"Relax," she coached herself, as she stepped off the elevator. Round one was over. She let herself into the room, and as her feet sank into thick carpet, she sighed with relief. Yesterday, she'd traveled, her night with Dario had been physically charged, and today had been tiring. She couldn't wait to strip, put on her nightshirt and drink the tea she'd ordered from room service before coming upstairs.

Looking around, it was hard not to feel a backlash of guilt, though. This was a far cry from her rustic two-bedroom cottage in South Carolina, with its wild acre of land, wide plank floors and beamed ceilings. Jewels had been her life, but usually she sold small diamonds, engagement rings for regular folks, often kids just getting out of school. Here, she was overwhelmed by opulence. In the mirrored bathroom, she'd bathed in a tub big enough for five, complete with pulsing water jets and an inbuilt bubble dispenser. The main room was more understated, but it, too, had been made for presidents, not a small-town shop owner who'd been married to a teacher at a local college.

Lifting a remote, she clicked a button that said Entertainment Center. Apparently, a menu on television also controlled the music. After scrolling to Classical, she selected a composer whose name she didn't recognize and clicked again. Soft piano music filled the room, coming from surround-sound speakers that had been tucked out of sight. Suddenly, she chuckled. The place reminded her of bachelor pads in movies where, with the touch of a button, a bed appeared, music was piped in, and the lights dimmed. All design features were calculated to lead to sex.

A king-size bed was tucked tastefully into an alcove but within view of velvet-curtained windows overlooking Central Park. One of the walls in the main room was mirrored, and armchairs had been placed on either side of a fireplace. Closer to the door, a table was covered with chintz, and even from here, she could smell fresh flowers from the vase on top. A gift basket contained condoms, lotions and oils.

Suddenly, she ached to use them, and damned Dario Donato for doing more than recharging her body; he'd put a spark of fire back inside her heart. Maybe the romantic part of her life wasn't really over, the way she'd been telling herself. Nothing more could happen with Dario, of course. She was divorced now, and might never remarry, so she had to provide for her own future, which meant getting her property.

Still, horse-drawn carriages were moving along Fifty-Ninth Street, and seeing couples inside, she couldn't help but feel wistful. Too bad marriage had been like a beautiful jewel that, seen under a magnifier, began showing all its flaws. Sex, on the other hand, would be around as long as there were men and women, she decided, thinking of Dario once more.

"How's he going to feel when he sees me in court next week?" Would some hint in her eyes give her away, when they went before Judge Zhang? Would Dario realize she'd been his mystery lover? Had he obsessed all day about their one-night stand? And who had he been expecting? He'd seemed intimate with the person, yet he hadn't realized Cassidy wasn't his…lover? Sex buddy? Fiancée?

She pulled her gaze from the carriages, realizing she was imagining her and Dario riding together, holding hands under a lap blanket. In her mind's eye, she saw the hand disengage and travel to her thigh….

Tonight, she was wearing the perfect outfit for arousing him, too. She'd been blessed with some natural assets, of course, but during the divorce, she'd raised her flagging self-esteem by going on a self-care rampage, regularly working out and giving herself facials and manicures.

After realizing her threadbare jeans and sweatshirts weren't in keeping with the Pierre's unwritten dress code and feeling determined to impress Chuckie, she'd charged the dress in a shop downstairs. It was of a skin-hugging cotton blend and had a tie that knotted under her breasts. Of bright red, the color redheads were told never to wear, it was an exact match for her hair. A tiny red bag still hung from her shoulder, and she'd worn red shoes with spike heels. Her nails, too, were bright red. She'd done her makeup to perfection, something she knew how to do because her mother, Erin, was a beautician with her own shop.

As Chuckie had eyed her, Cassidy had wondered if Dario would be equally stimulated. Now her eyes settled on the phone, and she moved toward it. Sitting on the edge of the bed, she lifted the receiver. It was risky, but she found herself whispering, "It won't hurt just to get his number." She wasn't going to really call him.

She dialed information. "Manhattan. Thirteenth Precinct, please."

The automated operator gave the number, and offered the option to dial direct. It was as easy as pressing a button with a tip of a long, red fingernail.

A moment later, his voice swept her off her feet. Her breath caught as if she'd just been sucker punched. It was sort of rusty, but not at all unpleasant. Whatever hit the back of her knees felt so fluid that she was glad she was seated. Of course, it was only a voice-mail message.

"I'll be checking my messages," he was saying. "Otherwise, you can reach my cell…."

Grabbing a pen from the bedside table, she scribbled the number on a pad. The pulse had gone wild at her throat. Every single one of her muscles felt tense.

"What would I say if I talked to him? That I had a good time?" That sounded trite, but then, she was hardly going to gush about how fantastic some strange guy was in bed. Besides, he was a cop. Maybe he had caller ID. Well, maybe not on a cell phone, she conceded. But surely he could trace her call, and then he'd come to the Pierre….

"It would take him at least a day to trace the call," she argued with herself. That would give her time to change rooms and hide from him. Or flee the city.

Knowing she'd lost her mind, she quickly dropped the

receiver into the cradle, as if she'd been burned. Bringing her feet onto the bed, shoes and all, she laid back on the sumptuous pillows, clasped her hands beneath her breasts, shut her eyes and tried to listen to the music.

But she was still thinking about him.

"Stop," she muttered.

But he was like an unwanted itch that wouldn't go away. "Like poison ivy," she continued.

An image of his naked body filled her mind. Suddenly, she ached with longing, and it was no use telling herself it was because she hadn't had sex for almost a year, since she threw Johnny out. Last night was, quite simply, the best sex of her life, and she had no idea why. They'd just screwed. It had been totally straightforward, no kinky stuff. But there was something special about him…maybe the way he smelled, or the exact tenor of his voice, or the way he moved…

"Tell me what you're wearing," she'd whisper if she called him, she decided.

"Jeans," he'd say.

"Tight jeans?" she'd probe.

She could really see him now, bare chested and dressed in worn jeans. She'd inquire, "How tight?"

And he'd say, "Very tight."

Now she imagined the material lovingly cupping him. Slowly, the powerful bulge was becoming visible under his fly, straining the zipper. "Are they always tight," she imagined herself saying huskily, "or tight because you're so hard?"

His breath was catching now, turning shallow. He was softly panting. "So hard."

"Then you'd better take them off."

She imagined the rustling of cloth, a flapping sound as he kicked off the jeans, then his voice coming through the receiver again. "What about you? Are you naked for me?"

"Oh, yeah."

"Tell me what you want to do to me."

As generalized warmth infused her pubic area, she put a hand there, her heart hammering as she imagined how he'd look, dusky and erect. A soft sound of need emanated from the back of her throat as her other hand covered her breast.

"Turn over," she imagined herself saying. In her imagination, her eyes roved over his firm rear end, his perfect strong, wide back and those huge shoulders. "I'm going to touch every inch of you."

In reality, she was cupping her own breast. When her nipples ached, she sighed and pinched them lightly, but that only make them ache even more.

"Every inch," he was saying huskily. "Is that all?"

Her belly was full from dinner and a creamy desert, and now languid warmth infused her limbs, shooting straight into her bloodstream as if through jets from the bathtub in the other room. Yawning, she felt as if she could fall asleep, yet she was becoming highly aroused.

Dammit, what had Dario done to her last night? Sex was all she could think about now. Using long fingernails, she drew patterns on her own thighs…swirling circles, then zigzagging lines. Once more, she was undressing Dario, but now he was leaning against a wall, and she was the one dragging down his zipper. He was moaning. His hips thrust outward, as if begging for the touch of her hands. She glanced up, just in time to see him raise his arms above his head, and her eyes trailed over his bare chest, from the bones of his ribcage to his bulging biceps, taking in the healthy glow of his tanned skin and muscles coated with dark hair.

"C'mon," she imagined him encouraging urgently.

Her own fingers had slipped inside the leg band of her panties. With a rush, she remembered him ripping her underclothes last night. She could still hear the soft sound as he'd tossed them away. Arching her hips, she pretended he was loving her with his hands, starting to make her climb. The music was lost. Catching her own moisture, she was captured by a dream as she rubbed the swollen nub of her clitoris. Shivering with excitement, she licked her upper lip, tonguing away beads of perspiration.

She was so far gone, she couldn't quite pinpoint the intrusive sound. She was climbing high. Almost there. So close. On the brink…

"Room service!" Hopping up with a frustrated moan, she wobbled a second on the high heels and quickly smoothed her dress. As she headed for the door, she couldn't help but glimpse herself in the mirror, and seeing that she looked totally disheveled, she silently cursed Dario again, vaguely thinking that this was all his fault.

"Just a moment!"

She swung open the door. Instinctively, she gasped and stepped back a pace. There was no tray or roller cart covered with white linen, which meant this wasn't room service. The first thing she noticed when she stared down was the man's shoes, and for a second, she thought Chuckie had come back, then she caught a flash of threadbare denim and realized her error. Grabbing the door's edge, she slammed it shut. Or at least she tried. A foot wedged in the crack as she flattened both hands on the wood and pushed. Equal pressure was being applied from the other side.

The source of the pressure was Dario Donato.

6

"WHO ARE YOU?" she demanded.

Now, that was rich. Keeping a splayed hand pressed to the door, Dario steeled himself against the raspy voice he'd heard uttering urgent cries of delight until dawn. "You're going to pretend you didn't read my badge?"

"What badge?"

This woman was a real piece of work. "You put Sheila Carella to shame," he muttered in astonishment.

"Who's Sheila Carella?"

Did she actually sound jealous or was it just wishful thinking? "The person I thought I slept with last night."

There was a long silence.

"The person I thought took my money," he clarified.

There was another long silence.

"The person who was supposed to come over and have sex with me," he added.

"You're going to have to leave," she returned flatly, "or I'm calling security."

"That doesn't seem quite fair, since you're the thief," he countered. "And besides, I *am* security."

"Not here, you're not."

She was definitely the woman he'd slept with. She wasn't protesting nearly enough, and she knew he was a cop. "I'm getting tired of talking to the door."

"You have other options."

Of course he did. With one push, he could knock her over, but it would be more civil if she invited him in. "Do you really want me to huff, puff and blow the door down?"

"I meant you could leave."

He was no expert on accents, but now he could tell she was from South Carolina, something he'd found out a few hours ago. Last night, the accent hadn't played through all the sighs. "Whatever. Just don't bother calling security. I've moonlighted at the Pierre," he lied.

He could almost hear her mind ticking; she was wondering whether to believe him. It was a tense moment, especially since the answer was no, and it was definitely the wrong time for a door to open behind him. He turned just long enough to catch a flash of silver hair and a beige blazer.

"Is there some sort of dispute here?" the woman behind him demanded.

Dario tried to pull his gaze away from door number one, but he was riveted, studying the contours carved into the wood. He was still registering the unexpected relief he'd felt when she'd first opened the door. As much as he hated to admit it, he'd feared he'd never see her again. After the sex they'd shared, why had she decided to run? Hadn't she been as affected as he?

He'd watched the tapes countless times, unable to stop himself until he'd memorized every movement she'd made while dressing—the sway of her breasts as she'd wiggled into the dark leggings, the tense expression as she'd stuffed the panties he'd torn into her jacket pocket, the trembling of her hands as she'd buttoned her blouse. Each detail was etched permanently into his mind.

All day, while he'd carried her earring in his pocket— jiggling it in his hand as he sometimes did his apartment keys—he'd wondered how long it had taken her to realize she'd buttoned her shirt crookedly. He'd stopped short of dusting his own penis for her prints, of course, but otherwise, he'd used every trick in the book to track her.

Abruptly, he turned to stare across the hallway where the elderly woman was peering at him suspiciously. "Just married," he explained.

She didn't look convinced.

He wasn't exactly a people pleaser, but even he hadn't been immune to the snobby stares in the lobby as he'd cut across it wearing jeans, a black T-shirt and a denim jacket. The woman looked like an Upper East Side type. She probably thought he was a gang member or something. "From out of town," he added. "Honeymoon."

Accepting the explanation, the woman went back inside, slamming her door. Silence came from the other side of door number one. "Let me in," he demanded.

"Why?"

"We need to talk."

"I don't talk to strange men."

He stared down at his foot, which was still wedged in the doorway. "I may be strange, but not in the way you mean."

"That's even worse," she returned. "Strange how?"

He should have guessed. Unlike Sheila, this woman would go head-to-head with him, but then Sheila had surprised him when she'd ended their relationship. "As if you care. If you'd wanted to get to know me," he pointed out, "you would have stuck around this morning."

"I'm going to have to ask you to leave."

So, she wasn't going to directly deny she knew him. Maybe there was a shred of honesty in her, after all, even if her personal records indicated she was in a world of trouble.

As near as he could tell, her husband had finally had enough of her wild lifestyle and walked.

The door behind him opened again, and the silver-haired lady poked out her head. "If you don't resolve this conflict," she informed him, her voice quavering now, "I'm calling security." She paused, drawing up her shoulders regally and added, "My granddaughter marches with Take Back The Night."

As a cop, he'd become acquainted with the marches of antirape activists on college campuses. "Believe me, the woman inside this room has been more than willing."

Since he preferred doing things the easy way, he felt torn, but he also knew he was out of options. Digging into his back pocket, he flipped open his shield protector and flashed the badge. While the woman gaped, he busied himself, wedging his thigh against the door frame, then his torso. Cassidy was surprisingly strong, though, and for the benefit of the onlooker, Dario didn't want to apply force. Using his shoulder, he nudged the door open another few inches, and as soon as there was room, he squeezed inside and pivoted. As he shut the door, he shot a final smile through the crack. "Sorry for the inconvenience, ma'am."

"Oh, dear," she said. "I'm sorry, officer."

He broadened his smile in what his partner always called his baby-kissing, public-relations smile. Then he turned his attention to Ms. Cassidy Case. As soon as he took a better look at her, he wished he hadn't. He wasn't viewing her in the cold light of day—something he could have tolerated—but rather under high-end track lighting and soft-focus dimmers that made her shimmer like a goddess. Yeah, he thought, she looked like she'd come from some distant planet dedicated entirely to sex.

"Cassidy," he found himself muttering, feeling strangely

taken aback, as if the bright red dress was a personal affront, something she'd worn to torture him.

She looked mortified. "How do you know my name?"

She was hardly a "Mr. Case," as he'd been led to believe in court. "I have my ways."

"What are you doing here?"

"Are you always this hospitable? No offer of a drink? Maybe Dom Pérignon? After all, it's the Pierre." Suddenly, he dropped the sarcasm. "Because of the directions you gave me, it took me eleven hours to get here."

"I didn't give you any directions."

"My point exactly."

"Nice to meet you," she returned, her saccharine tone calculated to make clear the encounter was anything but pleasurable. "Since you already know my name, and you're obviously such a stickler for good manners, evidenced by how you just broke into my hotel room, who are *you?*"

As if she didn't know.

"Oh, well then, let me just guess. Mr. Manners? Ann Landers's husband?" She paused dramatically. "Oh, gosh, I don't seem to have packed my crystal ball."

Even if he'd wanted to, he couldn't have spoken. His eyes were too busy, dragging down the seemingly endless length of her body. Was this really the dish he'd slept with last night? It seemed too good to be true. When he'd arrested Sheila Carella, he'd been sure he'd hit the jackpot, but this…. Realizing she was staring at him expectantly, he said, "I thought we might trade techniques."

"On?"

Lovemaking. "Breaking and entering."

"What would I know about that?"

Digging in his pocket, he pulled out the earring. For a second, he hesitated, feeling it roll in the palm of his hand, not wanting to relinquish the one item that had kept him connected to her all day. Grasping a silver hook, he held up baubles, letting them dangle, then he tossed the earring onto the bed. "Why don't you tell me?"

As if she simply couldn't help herself, she slid her eyes to where the earring landed, squarely on a pillow that still held the cradling depression of her head, and he took the opportunity to further study her.

The luxurious dress wrapped perfectly around her, as if held only by a flimsy tie. Just looking at it made him consider catching that tie between his teeth and pulling. Right now, it knotted beneath full breasts he'd fondled through the night, and her hair was really as red as poppies. The video had not told a lie. Looking disheveled, the hair feathered around her face in a haircut that must have cost a king's ransom. It seemed as if the wind were blowing, or as if she were walking along at a fast clip. In reality, she was standing so still that she could have been sculpted from stone.

"I asked you who you are," she said. "Aren't you going to answer me? At least give me some explanation for the intrusion."

"I don't grace idiocy with responses."

"But you'll make an exception for me?"

"Yeah," he said, not bothering to lift his gaze from the dress. It wasn't short—it hung right below the knee—but the recollections of his fingertips hadn't served him wrong, either. Every single curve corresponded exactly to his tactile recollection, and he went over each inch, putting two and two back together.

The legs went on for a country mile, encased in stockings that had a sheen, as if the silk had been sprinkled with gold glitter. The lower part of the dress draped her thighs, clinging, then a sloping line gracefully dropped to rounded cups of knees. Dryness hit the back of his throat as he recalled his hands curling over those knees last night…how he'd slowly pushed them apart, how she'd slowly opened for him.

By the time his gaze landed on red spike heels, he was falling into the male version of a swoon, which meant he was getting awfully hard. "Ouch," he couldn't help but whisper. He might not like her on a personal level—at least judging from all the nasty things he'd discovered about her when he'd done a background check today—but she was one helluva good-looking woman. And when had a woman's loose morals ever stopped him?

She was merely gaping, her pout of a mouth smooth, slick and moist with bright red lipstick. She hadn't budged from her place near the opposite doorjamb, which meant that she was close enough that he was smelling perfume. It made him want to burrow against her, maybe why his gaze dipped again, now to her cleavage. For a second, his face was between her breasts, and he could feel their cushioning softness against his cheek.

"You don't grace idiocy with responses?" she prompted, and he could sense her staring at him.

Coming to his senses, he slowly trailed the gaze all the long way back up her body until his eyes locked with hers. Or tried. Hers darted away as if the fireplace had just become extremely interesting.

"No," he said. "I don't."

"Were you implying I'm an idiot?"

"Take it how you will."

For his part, he felt as if someone had just hit him in the gut with a baseball bat. Breath had left his body, and bands wound around his chest. Her eyes had turned out to be shiny and green, like liquid emeralds, and he'd never seen anything like them. How they'd looked on the tape was just a faint echo, nothing more. For the split second their gazes had meshed, he felt something hard to define…like a lightning bolt had shot from her to him. He'd felt a deep connection, as if their core energies had touched.

He blew out a heartfelt sigh, his eyes on the beauty mark. Why did only the devious ones look this good? He'd spent hours discovering everything he could about Cassidy Case, and she made Sheila Carella look like Mother Theresa. Thankfully, years of practice had made him able to mask his facial expressions, and since coming into the room, he'd been doing his level best to look bored. "Have a hot date tonight?"

He was glad to see that she looked nervous as hell. She had high cheekbones, and right now, one was plagued by a slight, barely noticeable, uncontrollable tick. Her eyelashes were sandy, spiky and fluttering wildly, too, as if they were tiny wings she hoped could bat him away.

"What's it to you?"

"I think you know."

"No, I didn't have a date, for your information."

"You always dress like that for a night at home?"

"Like what?"

"In that sweat suit. Pajamas. Or whatever it is."

"Whatever it is, I'm not at home, anyway," she pointed out reasonably. "I'm in a hotel."

"You're impossible."

"I hope so."

"I bet a lot of people have told you that."

"A few."

She was determined to get rid of him, and would use any means necessary, including acting totally nuts. "You're as crazy as your nearly criminal record should have implied."

"I don't have a record."

The innocent act was wearing thin. Besides, she was too guilty to keep it up. Her cheeks had turned as red as the dress, and her carotid artery was working overtime. As he watched it tick, he realized her heart must be racing a mile a minute. Her skin was almost unnaturally pale, chalky in color like Gem O'Shea's.

Suddenly, he was thinking about how the other woman must have pleased her male clients, and he decided that there must be a gene for sexual know-how, a special DNA possessed only by some women, that Gem had passed to Cassidy.

"Look," she began again, "I really don't know what you're talking about. Or who you are. Or why you're here."

"You're one cool customer."

"What do you think I've done?"

"Besides steal the money on my nightstand this morning?"

"Oh, don't be ridiculous!"

He squinted. He had no idea what he'd expected, but it wasn't this blanket denial. "This has to be the most bizarre conversation I've ever had," he muttered, starting to get genuinely annoyed.

"If you go home, it can't continue."

"It does take two to tango."

"Then leave me to play solitaire."

"I don't see any cards." Before he thought it through, he reached for her, curling his fingers around her upper arm. She wrenched, intending to free herself, but he reacted instinctively by tightening his grip. He knew it was a dangerous mistake when he felt the tension uncoiling inside her—the leap of muscles, the rush of blood, but he was powerless to stop himself. He yanked her toward him, knowing he'd lost his mind as he dropped his voice seductively. "Looks like I'm making you nervous."

"In your dreams."

"I'm nothing if not realistic."

A shallow pant of breath teased his cheek, and her gaze was fiery when it found his. There was a thrill to the moment, something that stirred his blood and made it thrum, maybe because the circumstances were like nothing he'd ever experienced. With her, everything was new. Totally unpredictable. Besides, he knew he had the upper hand. She was attracted to him.

"We might not be in the old bawdy house again tonight," he found himself murmuring, drawing her a fraction closer, "but we are standing in a room made for sin, with a king-size bed just a hop, skip and a jump away. You might want to deny last night happened, Cassidy, but I can't get it out of my mind."

"Your mind," she echoed simply.

She was close enough now that he could feel the heat of her breath on his lips, evoking memories. "It's definitely on one track," he said.

Her lips had parted as if for a kiss. "Which track?"

"The male one."

Angling his head down, he captured her lips. Just like that. It was so easy, and immediately he felt transported somewhere far off, into a dark, heady world where everything vanished but her mouth. The night seemed shrouded in mystery. Pungent with promise. As if its magic could transport them anywhere....

She didn't fight, but she wasn't kissing him back, either, at least not until his mouth turned harder on hers, his lips firmer and more demanding, assuring her he wouldn't take no for an answer. Suddenly, he thrust his tongue, the plunge deep and forceful. Her lips parted wider, taking the heated spear, then hers pushed back, feeling urgent. Probing, he licked the contours of her lips now. As he did, fire hit his loins, and he moved his hips, thrusting.

With a gasp, she stepped back, ending the kiss abruptly with a smacking sound, leaving him breathless as he watched a hand fly to her mouth. Unexpected anger surged inside him. He'd thought about her all day. He wanted her. And he was tired of playing games. "If you think you can really wipe away that kiss, sweetheart," he found himself saying, "it's a little too late."

She swallowed hard, as if around a lump, her expression stricken. "It's you who should have thought of that."

Maybe. The kiss ensured he'd be up all night, craving another taste. "I didn't mind. I'd do it again."

"No, you won't," she whispered.

"Anytime, anywhere," he countered.

Piano music was playing—not dance hall music, like last night, but playful, single notes, all variations on the same melody. Her luscious green eyes still looked as wide as saucers. When she spoke again, the words seemed to catch in her throat. "What do you want?"

You, he thought. In bed. Right now. "Just to talk," he said, although he'd already proven that was a lie.

"About what?"

"I've been looking for you all day." All my life, an unwanted voice in his mind corrected.

"How did you find me?"

It was the closest she'd come to admitting they'd met last night, although not formally. "There are video cameras in the house." Just in case that didn't sink in, he added, "And in the hallway."

"The hallway?"

Given the crimson staining her cheeks, he guessed she was recalling how she'd gotten dressed there. "For the rest, you can thank Homeland Security."

She squinted, and it did wonderful things to her face. Her ski-jump nose lifted, and skin around her eyes crinkled.

"There are cameras all over the city, nowadays," he explained. "I tracked you from my front door, to Luther Matthews's museum, and while Luther was at lunch, I talked to his assistant." He'd studied materials inside, as well. "I found out a few things about you, too."

A steely thread wove through her words. "Such as?"

"Your husband got tired of your spending habits and walked." Only after he'd spoken, did he fully realize he'd been digging intentionally, and he was damn glad that she didn't look too broken up about kissing Johnny Case goodbye.

"You know about my marriage?"

"Some."

She was edging away from him again, and he guessed he didn't blame her, but he hadn't been about to let her get away, at least not without another kiss to remember him by. "Look," she murmured, "I want you to leave."

"And I still think we ought to have that drink."

Her lips were still glistening from the kiss; he'd licked all the lipstick off. "Why would I have a drink with you?"

"I can think of a million reasons." One was the king-size bed. "Would you rather I just shut up and kiss you again?"

She considered. Then suddenly, she spun away, turning on the spike of her heel. He watched as her whole body seemed to whirl on the axis of that slender red dagger. The gorgeous red dress swung around her, exposing heart-stopping thighs. He could only hope he was going to see whatever device was holding up the stockings.

"Don't go away mad," he found himself saying as she headed for the bar.

By the time she turned to face him, her face had composed itself into an unreadable expression. "Ice?"

He surveyed where she leaned against the bar's low-slung countertop, which came only to her upper thighs. "I could definitely use something to cool me down," he admitted, thinking he'd love to trail a cube over her bare skin. "But it depends whether you're serving anything with it."

She lifted a bottle of what looked to be good whiskey.

Leaning his elbows on the wood bar, he added, "And now, if we could just do something about your anger problem."

She didn't bother to look up from where she was pouring. "Like what?"

"Lose it. Because we've already discovered we can play well together."

"You charged in here uninvited," she suddenly began, her voice strained as she pushed a highball glass toward him, then poured herself a drink and lifted it, stopping just shy of her mouth. "And you...you..."

"Kissed you?" he supplied.

"And now you want a drink," she finished.

"Well...*you* broke into *my* bedroom last night," he returned as his fingers curled around the glass. "And you took off your clothes, and so on. I don't know about you, but I ached all over this morning." He flashed a quick smile. "It was a good kind of ache, though, if you know what I mean.

"I'll take that as a yes," he continued after a moment. "My best guess is that you slept with me as some sort of ploy, to get my father's property. So, now I guess we're even."

His little speech had gotten to her. Her jaw was slack, and with her lips parted like that, it was tempting to kiss her again. He wasn't entirely proud of it, but seeing her speechless gave him an incredible sense of satisfaction. After all, he imagined those green eyes had brought many men to their knees. Surely, he wasn't the first. So, moving with slow deliberation, he raised his glass and clinked it against hers.

"Cassidy Case," he said. "Here's looking at you."

7

HERE'S LOOKING AT YOU. Wasn't that what Humphrey Bogart had said to Ingrid Bergman in *Casablanca?* Heat was still curling between them. Sex was stinging the air. While Cassidy knew she couldn't let Dario's physical proximity unnerve her, she'd been lost to desire, touching herself and fantasizing about him when he'd arrived. She'd never expected to see him again, only in dreams, and she'd been right on the brink…but then he'd shown up and kissed her, quoting romantic movies like some erstwhile prince. Now she had to think fast.

"Given your manners," she managed to say, her lips feeling kiss-swollen, "I guess you *would* spend a lot of nights alone watching old movies."

"Not last night."

"Must have been a big break in the routine for you."

"Extraordinary."

Because her cheeks were burning, she damned herself for having such fair skin. No doubt, she was the color of ripe strawberries. By contrast, he looked so self-possessed that it was grating on her nerves. Had he really watched her get dressed on tape? And how much did he really know about her failed marriage? Not only was he killer handsome, he was a good detective, too. Not to mention Beppe Donato's son, she reminded herself. "Last night, I…"

"You?"

Was it really in her best interest to admit she'd slept with him? He knew, of course, but as long as she refused to vocalize it, she'd have him stumped.

He was watching her curiously, and his eyes did the rest of his body justice. They'd been shut this morning, but now, if he said, "undress and get into bed," she'd probably do it, as if entranced by a sorcerer's spell. The eyes were very dark, the color of bittersweet chocolate, and they were big, soulful and smoldering with desire. Framed by thick hoods of brows and surrounded by straight, barbed lashes, they were making her last shred of resolve melt.

A deep rumbling sound came from a broad chest encased in a black T-shirt that cut low enough to expose plenty of unruly chest hair. "Why'd you run off this morning? Afraid I'd bite?"

"You'd already bitten."

"So you noticed."

Her gaze drifted to his neck. "Looks like you're the one who got bit," she said, noticing the hickey on his neck.

"Must have been a vampire. I woke up alone."

"Phantoms?" she suggested.

"A helluva good dream," he countered.

"Don't dwell on it," she recommended. "You're awake now."

"I certainly am." With that, he took another sip of his whiskey.

She could have been running, given how wildly her heart was beating. "Look," she began, wishing she wasn't having difficultly breathing, and that every inhalation wasn't carrying the scent of him. "I've just rethought everything, and now, I do think honesty might be the best policy—" In fact, she'd do just about anything to get rid of him.

He interjected a grunt of disbelief, but she rushed on. "Last night, I thought you were somebody else, you see."

Unfortunately, the words didn't have the desired effect. "Why would somebody else be sleeping in that apartment?"

If he understood the one-night stand had been an accident, he'd lose interest; she was sure of it. "I didn't know it was your apartment," she insisted.

"It's not. I live in Battery Park. But my father asked me to sleep over until our conflicts are resolved."

"See? How could I have known that?"

"So, you came over to sleep with a tenant?"

"No…I thought you were Luther."

"Luther?" He stared at her. "Matthews?"

"He had a key."

He looked incredulous. "There's no way you could mix me up with Luther Matthews."

He had a point there. This guy didn't have a metrosexual bone in his body. Hoping to calm her fraying nerves, she sharply inhaled. Her lungs further filled with something that conjured Christmastime and pine forests. Ten to one, he'd showered before he'd come over. "I'd never met Luther before," she clarified.

When his jaw slackened, she realized she'd jumped from the fryer to the fire. "But you were going to sleep with him?"

"I don't usually sleep with strange men."

Now, she knew she'd misjudged him. He actually looked disappointed. "You don't?"

She shook her head.

"Under the circumstances, why bother turning on a light to make sure it's him? I mean, you'd never met him before."

"It was an accident!"

"Sorry you feel that way."

"No matter what I say, you're going to think whatever you want, anyway."

He knocked back a slug of his drink. "On that, you've got my number."

She took a sip, too, but the whiskey was strong. Just licking it off her lips made her sputter. As she replaced the glass on the bar, she wished the counter was higher, offering her more protection from him. She also hoped he wasn't noticing her hands shaking. "I'm telling you the truth."

"Why should I believe you?"

"Because I'm not lying."

A tense silence fell.

Blowing out a sudden peeved sigh, she pushed away memories of how he'd loved her body in the wee hours, and she wished questions about his relationship with Sheila Carrella weren't starting to niggle. "And whatever you heard about me is probably not true," she added. "My ex was the bad guy, and he wrecked our marriage."

"How?"

Because he looked merely curious, she said, "He slept around, spent way more than we had." She paused. "If you must know. And would you like any other information? My home address? Birth date maybe? Social security number?"

"I have all that, thanks." His eyes narrowed, and for a second, she felt as if he could see right through her, to her soul. "Sorry about your ex," he murmured after a moment.

He'd sounded genuine, and it made her heart tug. "It's not your fault," she said shortly.

"I said I was sorry, not responsible."

"A stickler with words?"

"And for the law."

He tossed back the rest of the whiskey. "So, you were going to have a rebound fling with Luther Matthews?" he guessed.

She was trying not to notice the flicker of his tongue as he tasted the whiskey on his lips, but it was evoking images from last night, all of which involved other places where his tongue had been. "Something like that."

"With no strings attached?"

"Do you always interrogate people?"

"Only if I suspect them of lying."

"No matter what I say, you won't believe me," she repeated.

"Try me, anyway." Reaching for the bottle, he poured another shot, then tossed that back with a swallow.

"Liquid courage?" she suggested. "Am I making you nervous?"

"Quivering," he assured.

She shouldn't have baited him. His expression was intense, the gaze remarkably steady. "Besides," he added. "I figured I might as well fix myself another drink, since you're taking your good old time when it comes to telling me about the jewels."

She gasped. "What?"

"Jewels. Stones. The kind emptied out of your store."

"You know about Gem's Stones?" That was the name of her shop.

"You sold the inventory to pay off your debts—"

"Maybe," she shot back hotly, acknowledging too late that she'd leaned closer to him, within reach. "But what do you know about the two jobs I worked to save the money to start that store? Or how I learned accounting and did my own books? Or built the display cases myself? And painted?"

He looked taken aback.

"My ex-husband's debts," she corrected. "Not mine."

He hesitated a minute, which she guessed was to his

credit. "Sounds like selling the inventory in your store was a smart move, but now you have no income."

Hearing him say it, she felt strangely violated. "Isn't there a law against invading people's privacy?"

"I did everything by the book."

"If not ethically," she muttered.

"The jewels," he repeated simply.

Energy drained out of her. Just as surely as if he'd taken a pin to a bubble, he'd burst her, and now she was deflating like so much hot air. How had he found out about the lost stones? Those jewels were her greatest hope, her legacy.

"I thought you were being honest," he chided.

"I am."

"Doubtful."

She eyed him suspiciously. "What do you know?"

"Everything in the precinct's cold-case files about Gem O'Shea's death. The carriage was probably sabotaged. She was killed. When they brought her from the river, she was only wearing a few diamonds, but she was reputed to have an extensive collection at home. No one ever found it."

"That was the family myth at our house," she conceded. After pausing to consider her options, she told him about Granny Fiona's stories. "My mom, Erin…she owns a beauty shop," she continued in a non sequitur. "She always told me they were tall tales."

That explained the fancy haircut, he thought. "But you don't think so?"

"If the jewels existed, I'm sure someone found them a long time ago. The idea that they've been hidden for years, untouched, is ridiculous. It's like Captain Kidd's treasure. Or Atlantis."

His voice lowered an octave, and if it wasn't for the

thread of challenge underscoring their words, she'd have taken the tone as seductive. "And your husband?"

Whatever his sources of information, they were good. "He's a college teacher, and he spends his spare time looking for antiquities, but…"

"He didn't share your ideas?"

She shook her head. "Like my mother, he just thought they were tall tales."

Dario looked formidable. "You think they're in the house."

Her gut and something in the man's eyes said honesty would benefit her, but she held back again. "What makes you say that?"

"Instincts and…"

When he held up a paper, her jaw dropped. It was the letter she'd withheld from Luther. It had been in her purse, which had been on her shoulder, which… "How did you…?"

"I spent my rookie years arresting pickpockets on the subway. I learned a few tricks."

"I'll say," she managed warily, her mind racing back to the kiss, unwanted heat spiraling through her limbs like a rope of fire. While he'd been kissing her, the man had actually taken the purse from her shoulder, searched it, found the letter, taken it out and read it. "What do you do? Moonlight as a magician?"

"Clowns. Mimes. You name it."

"You read that over my shoulder?" *While you were kissing me?*

"Yeah."

"And you think *I'm* duplicitous?"

"We'll call it evenly matched."

In more ways than one. She was sure that's what he was thinking. She was nearly as tall as he, and last night, as they'd lain in bed, skin to skin, they'd touched at all points. As his eyes dropped down, scutinizing her dress, she instinctively sucked in her tummy, bringing a smile to his lips. Quickly, she relaxed, hardly wanting him to think she was preening. Still, no man had ever looked at her in quite this way. Moments ago, when he'd first seen her, she was sure he was going to simply grab her, force her to the floor, and start making love to her. Those dark eyes seemed almost haunted, hungry to the point of ravenous, as if he could devour her in a heartbeat. Earlier, he'd asked if she wanted him to huff, puff and blow down the door. Now, in the red dress, she felt like Little Red Riding Hood being eyed by the Big Bad Wolf.

His voice was husky. "Maybe we can make a deal."

Warning lights flashed through her system, but everything about this man made her want to ignore them—his looks, his scent, his greedy look of desire that said he was going to take her clothes off. "A deal?"

"You want inside the house, right?"

She was desperate to search for the jewels. "Yeah."

"And my dad wants the deed to the building. Whether it belongs to my family or not, the fact remains that we've managed the property for generations."

"True," she said, now speaking more cautiously, wondering where he was headed with all this, and suddenly glad he knew nothing about her meeting with Chuckie Haswell.

"We deserve to profit when it's sold," he continued.

As much as she didn't want to admit it, he had a point, and probably Judge Zhang was going to conclude that, as well. She'd hoped everything would be awarded to her, of course, but more realistically, she'd expected proceeds from a sale would wind up being split among all parties with claims. "Maybe," she conceded in a noncommital tone.

"If you were able to find the jewels, would you give up your claim on the house itself?"

Her heart skipped a beat. Was he really implying a trade?

Don't be rash, she coached herself. *Feel him out completely.* "You mean, you'd let me search for the jewels, and if I find them, I get to keep them? And your dad gets the building?"

He shrugged powerful shoulders that made her want to ask if he'd ever played football. "Why not?"

She had to be careful. "And your dad would approve this?"

"Why involve him? He just wants the building."

She'd rushed into her marriage with Johnny Case, and it had come to the worst kind of end, making her distrust her gut. Nevertheless, right now her gut was screaming yes. "If I found the jewels, and they were everything they're cracked up to be, I don't see a problem. From various sources, I've found some descriptions, not the least of which is the picture of Gem in the Centuries of Sex Museum. There were emeralds, diamonds, rubies ..."

"I can go you one better."

Her heart was beating a fast tattoo now, and it had very little to do with the fact that the world's best-looking man was standing a mere foot away. "Meaning?"

He smiled, his teeth glistening. "I have an inventory list."

It was too good to be true. "What?"

"Dated 1889, the year before Gem O'Shea died. It was filed with the police, in case of theft, and later wound up in the cold-case file, which is in my possession."

"And I can see it?"

"It depends."

"On what?"

"On whether you want to make the deal."

She wanted to twist and shout, jump up and down with joy, then fling herself into his arms, wrap her legs around his waist and scream with happiness. Instead she stayed stock still. Slowly, she said, "If I really find all the jewels that are listed in the various sources," she began, "including the inventory list, then yes. I'll give up my claim to the property."

She blew out a stunned sigh at how wonderfully well this could work out, as long as Chuckie Hawell didn't step in and ruin things. Silently, she cursed herself for trying to work with him. Apparently, she should have called Dario Donato. "I get the jewels," she continued, mulling it over. "You get the house. That seems fair."

"Almost."

Already in her mind's eye, she was taking apart the place. She'd have to get a crowbar, and some other equipment. Thankfully, Johnny Case had taught her one worthwhile skill: how to dig for artifacts. Now her heart stuttered. "Almost?"

"There's a hitch."

She should have known the offer was too good to be true. "What?"

"When will you need to be in the house?"

"All the time," she managed. She didn't want to waste a minute. "And…I may do some damage," she warned. "I'll need to look behind walls, in the basement, under floorboards."

"As much renovation as the place has seen over the years, I don't think anyone will notice."

"Like I said, I'm ready to shake on it."

He shook his head, then said one word. "Sex."

She blinked. "Sex?"

He nodded. "You can stay in the house all week, but only on the condition that you'll be my sex slave."

Her lips parted in astonishment. "Are you serious?"

"As a heart attack."

He was giving her one. She considered a very long moment. "Can you define slave?"

"Nothing kinky. I'm just talking about consenting adult

enjoyment. Mine's the only bed at the house with any extra room in it, after all."

He was making this sound so reasonable. "And if I say no?"

"Then no deal."

"Let me get this straight. I have sex with you—"

"All week."

"And in exchange, I get to use your case files and search for the jewels."

"If you're nice, I might even help you look."

At some point, heat had begun flooding her whole system. Like a lightning bolt, it sizzled at one spot, then electrified her entire bloodstream. She tried to tell herself the jewels were calling her, not the man. "I don't get involved," she warned diplomatically.

"Me, neither. Confirmed bachelor. My mother's been trying to marry me off for years."

"Seriously?" she asked. "Because I hate men." As if he hadn't gotten the point, she clarified, "I mean, I really hate them."

"I could tell last night," he said drily.

"I've…decided to be alone. But this is just sex for a week, then it's over."

"Is that a yes?"

"Yes." Suddenly, her knees felt weak. "Let me get my stuff," she managed, as if all this was the most natural thing in the world. "It will just take me a minute."

"There's one more problem," he said.

When she looked at him again, his gorgeous dark eyes had settled on the bed. The room seemed dimmer now, but only because night had fallen. Moonlight was streaming into the room, through the windows.

"What's that?" she asked, her voice a husky whisper.

"The sex starts now," he said.

8

THE SEX STARTS NOW? Was he kidding? "Just like that?"

He nodded, and she watched as if mesmerized when he reached across the bar. As one of his huge, dry hands glided over the back of hers, she studied it, liking the size of it, the squarish fingers, the veins that hinted at the corded forearms that had wrapped around her last night. A thumb tucked beneath hers, and as he began rubbing a hollow in her palm, he said in a throaty rumble, "Yeah. Just like that, Cassidy Case."

Inhaling sharply, she darted her eyes around the room, realizing once more that it looked tailor-made for a sexual encounter. The lights were dim, and wide windows framed a gorgeous white-yellow full moon. The mood between them had shifted, becoming calmer. It felt like the hush before a storm, a lull on a darkening sea before gusts of gale wind.

Catching the direction of her gaze, he murmured, "Something sure put a smile on his face."

She took in the moon. "Wasn't me."

"Good. I'd hate to be jealous of the man in the moon."

She couldn't help but smile. "You're crazy."

"As a fox."

In the last moment, everything seemed to have turned on a dime. One minute, they were sparring like sworn enemies;

the next, they were people who'd already spent a night together. In the ensuing silence, something unwanted tugged
at her throat, making it hard to swallow.

She reminded herself that this was just fun and games,
leading nowhere significant, and yet she wondered how it
would feel to make a man like him jealous. It didn't seem
like an emotion he'd be inclined to feel. He was too cavalier.
Easy come, easy go. He made her think of words such as
ambivalence and nonchalance. Everything about him—from
the heavy-lidded sexually charged gaze, to the lithe, predatory movements of his to-die-for body—screamed that he
was born to satisfy many women but to stay unattached,
himself.

Below the window, in the deepening twilight, carriages
were still circling, carrying lovers, and she could hear the
far-off clip-clop of the hooves. Time seemed to stand still.
While much of the city had changed, her and Dario's ancestors would have traveled many of the streets that existed
today, she realized. Had they taken walks in Central Park?
Maybe together? "Gem was riding in a carriage just like
that," she found herself murmuring, thinking of the woman's
untimely death as she nodded toward the window. Somehow, it was as if the past and present were merging.

"What?"

"The carriages," she clarified. "Outside. Can't you hear
them?"

Tilting his head, he listened, then nodded. "Variations,"
he said after a moment.

Was he making an implied comparison of her to Gem,
and to Gem's many lovers? Her heart jump-started, beating
double time, feeling almost painful now, as if it might burst
out of her chest. Excitement sparked, leaping inside her, the
raw energy flickering wildly like a flame in wind. "Varia-

tions on last night?" she managed. "Is that a lead-in to whatever you're going to ask me to do?"

He smiled. "Is your mind running wild with ideas about what being my sex slave might entail?"

She eyed him. "I think I can...vary things."

"I'll bet you can."

Already, she was taking in his open jean jacket and a tight shirt beneath that wasn't going to be hugging his perfect pecs for long. The tuft of black hair visible at his collar caught stray rays from the dim light and glistened. With him right in front of her, it was a lot easier to admit she'd been fantasizing about him all day. What woman wouldn't have done so? Was she really going to share a bed with this man all week?

His soft chuckle pulled her eyes to his face again. He was turned away from the light, so shadows fell over sculpted cheekbones, and the irises of his eyes looked almost black. Faint stubble coated his jaw.

"Did I say something funny?" she asked.

"I was talking about the music." The voice was lazy, as if to say they had all night to talk, but the glint in his eyes said he was thinking of other activities. "Pieces like this are called variations. The composer takes a handful of notes, then rearranges them. If he's good, he can do it for hours. Beethoven's are generally said to be the best, I think."

His thumb was still rubbing deep circles into her palm, turning her insides to mush. Now he reversed the movement, going counterclockwise. When he stopped, the thick pad of his thumb was at high noon, and when she spoke, her voice came out as a faint rasp. "Are you one of the best?"

"Depends on what I'm composing."

"Are we about to do something symphonic?"

"I'll throw in some ballerinas. Maybe a few horses and carriages for the stage."

"You're quick with answers."

"Comes from a lifetime spent getting myself out of hot water."

"I doubt water's the only thing you've found yourself in that was too hot."

"You're quick on your feet, yourself."

"My only talent."

"I doubt it."

"Maybe you're right. I must be a mind reader, because from the first, I had you pegged for the kind of guy prone to get a backside pumped full of some angry daddy's buckshot."

"Not much buckshot in the city, but I've climbed out my share of windows and down a few fire escapes."

She considered, vaguely wondering if she was putting off the moment they'd undress and get back into bed. Was she gun shy? Or building anticipation? "I thought you were a cop. How'd you wind up becoming such an expert on Beethoven's variations?"

"Don't tell me you buy into stereotypes about cops."

"I guess I do. You don't look like a classical-music buff."

"What's a classical-music buff look like?"

"Luther Matthews."

That made him smile. "And what do I look like?"

"The kind of guy who asks women to be sex slaves."

He laughed, and she decided she liked the sound. It was muted, but somehow full-bodied, coming from his chest, then catching in the back of his throat. "I only asked one."

"I feel special."

"Music appreciation," he said, his laughter becoming a muted chuckle. His thumb moved more deliberately now, and she sighed as it stretched from the hollow of her palm all the way down to the pulse point at a wrist she'd dabbed with perfume. "In college, it was a requirement."

So, he'd gone to college. The way he was rubbing her wrist was actually starting to relax her, making her feel freer to express her curiosity. "Did you have a major?"

"Besides wine, women and song?"

"You majored in debauchery?"

"Prelaw. I became a cop instead of a lawyer. You?"

"Special two-year school to study jewels. No music-appreciation courses."

"So, you know jewelry?"

"Don't worry," she returned, her eyes narrowing with pleasure as he continued caressing her wrist. "We've already established that you're never buying me an engagement ring. And in that case, I'll never be in a position to scrutinize it for the three *C*s."

"Three *C*s?"

"Carat, clarity and color."

"You learn something new every day. And it's never too late to learn about music," he offered, his fingers twining through hers. Lifting her hand from the bar, he urged her around it, and her feet seemed to move of their own accord. She felt languid, her limbs propelling her as if by magic. As she neared, he raised her hand another notch, guiding her into a graceful turn that made her dress swirl around her knees.

"You dance, too?"

"Waltz, foxtrot, tango, you name it," he assured, although she didn't believe a word. He tilted his head slightly, as if to better survey her. "But only when the woman's undressed."

"Were you always like this?"

"Like what?"

She considered. He was a type she'd met before. Flirtatious but commitment shy. If he wasn't so sexy, she might be offended by it, especially since she'd never forgiven Johnny Case for his infidelity. As much as she hated to admit it, her anger had become generalized, extending from Johnny to most men. It hadn't helped that her mother still liked Johnny. Even now, Erin Magee thought Cassidy and Johnny were destined to get back together. Finally Cassidy said, "Always after sex."

"Only since birth."

"Ever been married?"

A mock grimace lit up his eyes, making them gleam like black diamonds. "Of course not. But even the best of us can get trapped," he said sympathetically.

"I have my excuses," she defended.

"Namely?"

"Youth and stupidity."

"You're obviously not stupid." He paused. "But you are ancient."

"Twenty-seven."

He chuckled. "I hope we're having sex in the dark."

"I know," she teased, trying not to be alarmed at how much she was enjoying his company. "That way, you won't have to notice my wrinkles and cottage-cheese butt."

His smile really was a draw. Sexy and suggestive without being sleazy. "I swear I'll shut my eyes."

She was standing right in front of him, so close that their bellies almost brushed when she laughed. He had a decent sense of humor. "Why do I think you're lying?"

"Because I am."

"It would be hard for women not to like you."

"They say I'm fun, but not the kind a girl can marry."

"Perfect."

His fingers had twined, dangling by her thigh, but now he disengaged them. His eyes locked with hers, looking serious now, and he began grazing her leg with the curled ends of his fingers. Her heart seemed to be beating in her ears, and yet, at the same time, everything seemed so quiet that she felt the urge to scream. Or…

Take off my dress, she suddenly thought. Inside her, pent-up energy was clamoring for release; she needed something more to happen soon. The fingers crawling on her thigh were raising her dress hem, making her every last nerve jangle in a cacophonic sound that only she could hear, like bells clanging all at once.

"We don't even know each other," she whispered.

His slow smile was as tempting as the devil. It lifted the corners of his lips and perfect teeth gleamed in the near dark. "But you'll never be able to search my house unless you do as I say."

"My house," she murmured.

He shrugged. "Anyway, that's part of the thrill, isn't it?"

"What?"

"Not knowing each other."

"Should we promise not to talk?"

"Too late. You already know my college major."

"A deep, dark secret."

"It was. Usually I tell people I got my degree by sleeping with the dean."

"I promise not to tell and ruin your reputation. But we could stop divulging anything personal now."

"To make things more mysterious?" He studied her another moment, his gaze flickering downward, lingering on the low-cut V of her dress.

She nodded.

Just as she considered reaching for his hand and placing it on her breast, her nipples constricted beneath the cloth. Uttering a ragged sigh, he splayed his free hand on her chest, the heel of the palm landing in her cleavage, the wide span of fingers bridging her breasts, just inches from the erect tips.

"To excite ourselves," he pressed.

"Yeah."

"But there may be personal details I need to know."

"Like what?"

"Like…" Sliding his hand upward, he curled the fingers around her neck and massaged the slender column, tilting her head backwards. Knowing she was probably certifiable, she let it drop into the cradle of her shoulders, and she reveled in the sensations as he stroked more of those maddening circles beneath her ear, then on the lobe. As he charted a course from her jawbone to her chin, she shut her eyes in bliss.

"Relax," he whispered.

"I am relaxed."

"No, you're not, but you're getting there."

"Don't stop."

The whisper was suddenly beside her ear, his breath deliciously tantalizing on her skin. A shiver claimed her when the spear of his tongue dipped, dampening her ear lobe. "I haven't even started yet."

"Then start."

"Sure you're ready?"

"No."

"Ready or not, here I come."

As the thumb skimmed the hump of her chin and found her mouth, the remaining breath squeezed from her lungs. The pad probed, the nail traced, and just as she parted her lips to better let him explore, he tilted his pelvis, so their hips locked. He was getting hard. And warm…superwarm. His belly was moving with hers, their breathing in synch. Her breasts were cushioning against the wall of his chest, which was so hard it could have been made of granite.

"I didn't think I'd see you again," she managed.

"See," he said with a soft chuckle, sounding pleased, as the thumb lingered at the corner of her mouth. "You're already going mushy on me." He toyed with her lower lip until she could feel it swell, begging for a kiss. "But you wanted to?"

She shut her mouth long enough to swallow. Or at least she tried, but an insurmountable lump seemed to have lodged there. "I thought about calling," she admitted.

"Really?" He sounded pleased.

"Only for sex," she assured.

"So, you thought about me today?" he probed, the thumb pressing inside her mouth now. It wedged under her tongue and against the backs of her bottom teeth.

She whispered around it. "I had sex with a stranger. It would be weird if I hadn't thought about it."

For a moment, he said nothing, but merely glided his thumb around her lower teeth, teasing the gums. She suckled as he drew swirls on the inside of her cheek, and her hands drifted down, splaying on the sides of his legs. When she rubbed, his muscles flexed, and his hips tilted again, thrusting upward this time, making her heart stutter, as his erection probed in the folds of her dress. "Yummy," she whispered.

"Exactly what did you do when you were thinking about me today? Touch yourself…"

"Yes…"

Pulling his thumb from between her lips, he slid it under the inbuilt cup of her dress, cradled a breast and applied moisture to the aching nipple. His voice caught. "Here?"

She nodded as her hands circled his hips, then molded

over a tight behind, using it to pull him nearer as she arched. He rolled the nipple between a finger and thumb, slowly working it until her breath quickened, then his other hand sandwiched between them. Bringing the dress with it, it rose. Arrowed fingers dived between her legs, causing her to inhale sharply as he stroked. "Here?" The voice was edgier. "Did you touch yourself here?"

Gasping, she parted her legs, the spikes of the stilettos leaving the plush carpet. The backs of her thighs hit the bar, and she wished the counter were higher, so she could better brace herself. "Yes," she whispered raggedly.

He was inside the thong now, his fingers curving over her pubis, dragging through curls. He cupped her, rocking his palm, then he undulated his hand until she was shamelessly bucking. A stiff finger rimmed her opening, gathering moisture, and she buried a wet cry against his shoulder, tonguing his glowing skin. He muttered something guttural and senseless in return, then pushed a finger in, opening her. For a moment, neither of them moved. Her heart was pounding wildly against her ribs, the blood rushing in her ears.

Withdrawing the finger, he twisted his fist, soliciting whimpers. She melted as another finger joined the first and thrust together, feeling impossibly thick, filling her and making her long for his penis. Leaning over the bar, to better take the pleasure, she tasted the salty flavor of his skin, telling herself not to forget this would never mean anything more. And that meant she could do anything she wished.

Urgently he was strumming her, using a love-slick finger to flick her clitoris, and her hands pushed the jacket off his shoulders, dragging it down his arms. His T-shirt followed. He groaned as she burrowed her hands in his chest hairs, using her nails as she strained for her orgasm. "I want to touch you everywhere," she muttered.

"You have all week."

She'd explore every inch of his body. "You're just the kind of guy I'll enjoy bringing to his knees."

"Do I hear revenge?"

Maybe. For Johnny Case. For all the men she'd ever met who were this gorgeous, but who couldn't be caught. She arched to meet those magic fingers once more, shutting her eyes and swirling in dark sensations, as she said the word aloud. "Maybe."

"Go ahead. Take it out on me," he murmured, his joined fingers pushing deeper, pushing her to the edge. "Hurt me. I really want to see you try."

Suddenly, she cried out, the orgasm quick and shattering. Her hands flew to his biceps and squeezed. She realized his skin was damp now. He'd broken a sweat, and all she could think about was the basket of condoms. She curled fingers over the waistband of his jeans and unsnapped them.

As she reached for the zipper, his shudder and the flex of his hips rerouted her course, and she fondled him through the denim, his moan like music as she pressed her hand flat against his groin. A hand flattened on her belly, and he urged her to turn around. When she did, his bare chest came flush with her back, and heat flooded her as his erection probed her buttocks.

Sensing what he wanted, she leaned over the bar and found it was just the right height for what he had in mind. As she rested her belly on the cold marble surface and grasped the edge, the chill made her shiver. "Is this what you want your slave to do?"

"Oh, yeah," he said simply, his voice thick with appreciation.

"There are condoms in that basket," she managed, but her breath was shallow. Between her legs, she was throbbing. He was panting, pushing her dress upward on her back, and as she dragged it over her head, she was glad he'd seen her in it. It had been wasted on Chuckie Haswell, but this…

She heard him jerk down his zipper, then step out of his shoes and pants. "Wait right there," he said hoarsely.

As if she was going anywhere. She was shivering all over, not from the coldness of the marble now, but from knowing he was finding the condoms…knowing she was positioned to drive him wild, wearing nothing but a thong, stockings that hugged her upper thighs and stilettos.

She heard the rustle of his bare feet brushing the plush carpet as he returned. A hand settled on her neck, traveling downward with a hot caress that made each vertebrae prickle. Gingerly, he drew the thong down, and one by one, she lifted the stilettos.

"You're gorgeous," he whispered.

He leaned, the laboring pants of breath touching her lower back. Rough stubble of his skin grazed her behind as hot, dry hands reached way down and curved around her ankles, molding her calves, then her thighs. Feeling as smooth as glass, they swept over her backside as he released a ragged groan. Trembling palms urged her thighs apart, and as she parted for him, he edged closer, the burning erection finding her and pushing…

Lifting her gaze, she could see him in the mirror, his jaw slack, his eyes nearly shut in ecstacy. He was leaning away, looking down, both hands on her backside, so he could watch their bodies merge, his breath uncontrollable. He was loving this….

Her fingers tightened on the bar as his hands slid beneath her belly, the splayed fingers meeting near her naval. Suddenly, in tandem with the thrust of his hips, Dario half lifted her, half dragged her to him. Enveloped in deepening sensations, she climbed once more, let herself go as each pounding thrust pushed her nearer to the brink. She was drowning as his body covered hers, the hairs of his chest sweeping her back, his heart pounding near her shoulder, his burning mouth on her cheek. "Dario," she whispered.

Roughly, he pushed hair from her neck, then a looping string of scalding kisses rained down. "That's right," he whispered back hoarsely. "Say my name."

She tried to roll to face him, but his arms caught her, holding her like a vise, and she stilled, powerless to move, trapped by his body, but not caring. "Dario," she whispered again.

Hearing his name seemed to drive him mad with lust. His groin was hotter on her backside, and she could feel each slow stretch of muscle as he went deeper. "I'm going to come," she whispered.

An arm reached down the length of hers, his hand found hers, and he wove their fingers together tightly, then he said, "Now."

Three hard, determined thrusts of his body sent them both tumbling over the edge together. Just as quickly, he urged her to turn to face him, swinging her leg near his shoulder, so their bodies never separated. As soon as they were face-to-face, his mouth fell to hers in a tongue kiss. Her arms circled his neck, and she wrapped her legs around his waist, locking her ankles.

"C'mon," he whispered, after a moment, withdrawing from her body and discretely losing the condom. "Why don't we move? I'd hate to waste that big bed."

"Your call," she replied huskily. "I'm the love slave."

He shook his head, those gorgeous dark eyes just an inch away, studying her. "You turned the tables. I'm yours now."

"I can handle that."

"Can you?"

"Sure." But could she? As he stood, grasped her hand and pulled her toward the bed, her heart skipped a beat. As much as she'd felt determined to search the house, maybe she'd been a fool to agree to this trade-off. Could she really sleep with Dario Donato for a week and come away unscathed? For a second, she realized she'd better call it quits right now.

But then he urged her onto the plush duvet, and she hugged him again. "Since I've turned the tables, and you're my love slave now," she whispered, "there are a few things I'd like for you to do."

"Sit on my lap."

She squinted at the non sequitur. "What?"

"That way you can better give Santa your Christmas list," he said.

And so she did.

9

"WHAT DO YOU MEAN, I can handle the arson case alone for the rest of the week?" Pat asked, using a soda straw to shoot a spit wad across his desk to Dario's.

"Now, that's mature," Dario joked as the wad landed on his cold-case file. Not that he'd been reading the file. All day, he'd been drifting, remembering Cassidy in that bright red dress, imagining the wickedly sexy look in those green eyes, which had glittered like the emeralds she'd once sold in her shop.

Now that he'd talked to her, he felt bad about her losing her business. Everything she'd claimed had checked out this morning, when he'd dug deeper. While he didn't like using his badge to further his personal life—the past month had been unusual—his curiosity about Cassidy was insatiable. Her husband had put her into debt, and she'd had the class to clean up his mess, but it had cost her a business she'd loved. It was a story he'd heard many times on the job.

"Men can be pigs," he muttered.

"Come again. That sounded like girl talk."

"Nothing."

"I heard you, but I don't get it. Did you grow a heart overnight?"

"No. And I'm as lazy as ever. The boss took me off the arson case," Dario reminded, returning to the topic his partner had initiated, his eyes drifting over Pat's spiky red hair and street-wise getup—worn jeans, a fake tattoo and an earring. "Because of my transgressions with Sheila Carella, remember?"

"How could I forget? But you've been anxious to stay involved, and night before last, you came to the scene of a fire."

"Do you have any new leads?"

"No." Pat paused. "Uh…rumor has it, Sheila's marrying Bobby O'Harc."

"I'd offer to be the best man, but you hired me first." Rising to stretch his legs, Dario noted the soreness of his muscles and tried to stifle a smile. He'd gotten a helluva workout last night. Definitely better than what the precinct gym offered.

He glanced through a floor-to-ceiling window. At the other end of Police Plaza, he could see a couple coming from the courthouse, where they'd just been married by a justice of the peace. The woman wore a simple white dress, and the man was carrying her, cradling her against his chest while she clutched a bouquet of roses. Emotions tugged at his heart, not that he wanted to examine them too closely.

Realizing Pat had followed his gaze, he raised an eyebrow inquiringly. Pat said, "Are you…?"

"Broken up about Sheila Carella?" Dario squinted, then laughed. "You're joking, right?"

Pat shrugged. "I heard she called you last night and ended your relationship over the phone…"

"Relationship would be a strong word, no?" Dario returned, giving up on working and tossing his pencil on top of a file about Gem. He'd left the rest at the house this morning for Cassidy. A contact at the public library was faxing over news clippings that Dario's previous research visits had missed, and which he didn't recall seeing during his stop at the Centuries of Sex Museum. According to the librarian, Gem had been coming from a wedding at Saint Andrews church when she'd died, and since the church was still standing, records might be on file, if he checked. At the courthouse, he'd copied the original architect's plan for the building, too, which he'd take home to Cassidy.

Home. As many women as he'd known, Dario had never cohabitated, and strangely, he felt a surge of excitement at the idea. "Gossip sure travels fast in precincts," he commented now, thinking Cassidy was his own little secret. "My mother's sewing circle is tighter lipped."

"Your mother's not in a sewing circle," Pat pointed out.

"Busted again," teased Dario. "It was a figure of speech."

"It's not really a rumor," Pat said uncomfortably. "So, don't worry about people knowing. It's just that, uh…Bobby asked me to say something, to…break the ice between you and him. He thinks you're hurt, so he's making himself scarce today. And Eliana's worried."

Dario wished people would stay out of his private business. He couldn't believe Bobby O'Hare was laying low. "My sister?"

"Yeah. She tried to call you this morning."

"She calls three times a day. I can't wait until she gets married. Maybe she'll start calling her husband."

"I don't know why you're complaining. I answered your phone again, and she talked to me." Pat squinted. "You must have special radar for when she's going to call, because you always manage to step away from your desk."

"Telepathy," assured Dario.

"Your sister's afraid you're going to wake up in about five years and realize…"

"I'm the only bachelor left in America?"

He nodded. "And earlier…when I told you Karen wants you to meet us for dinner, you said you had plans *indefinitely.* I mean, you're always up for dinner or drinks. Last night, you were ready to party hardy, but today, you're…"

Daydreaming about Cassidy. "Trying to turn over a new leaf. The boss wants me on cold cases this week, so I'm on cold cases."

Pat didn't look convinced. "Tell me if you're in danger of doing something stupid, buddy."

"Have I ever done something stupid?"

"When it comes to women?" Pat rolled his eyes. "Only every day of your life."

So, he really believed Dario wasn't licking his wounds over Sheila. "You're engaged a week, so you're giving me advice?"

"Sorry. I deserved that Look…" Pat paused. "I really am sorry. It's none of my business. But you're my best buddy. My longtime drinking companion. A skirt-chaser extraordinaire. And I've learned a lot from you. Without your moves, Karen never would have agreed to marry me. Now you're going to be the best man at the wedding. So…I just want to make sure you're all right."

"Sheila Carella didn't break my heart," Dario said again.

But after last night, he was starting to think someone else might. In fact, he was half-tempted not to return to 67 Anthony Street tonight. He'd let Cassidy have the whole run of the place this week. Let her search the property to her heart's content. Give her the bed.

But he knew it was a lie. Lust would win. He'd left her a note, with directions about how he expected to find his love slave when he got home—naked, up to her chin in suds in an old claw-footed bathtub in an empty apartment upstairs. On top of the note, he left the upstairs key, condoms and a bottle of bubbles from the Pierre's complimentary gift basket.

All day, he'd been watching the clock, waiting for five o'clock. He felt like a kid waiting for the bell to ring on the last school day before summer vacation. "If you must know, I have a new running partner already."

Tilting his chin downward, Pat stared at Dario from under heavy eyelids. "You're kidding."

"Slept with her last night." To make sure Pat got the picture, he added, "She was there when Sheila called."

Pat's jaw dropped.

"Just so you know."

Looking impressed, Pat said, "I stand corrected."

"I'd offer to bring her to meet you and Karen, but she may not want to get dressed for a while."

"Anybody I know?" Pat covered his eyes. "No, let me guess. It's Sheila's big sister."

"I wouldn't," claimed Dario. "Her name's Cassidy Case. The ancestor of the cold-case murder victim I'm working on."

Pat shook his head. "The person who might be making a claim against your dad's rights to his property on Anthony Street, along with Chuckie Haswell? I thought that was a guy."

"Nope."

"And doesn't this pose a conflict for you and Cassidy?"

"We're hoping we can work it out in bed. You know," Dario said, flashing a smile. "Like Romeo and Juliet. Warring families uniting through love."

Pat guffawed. "You're serious?"

"Why not?"

"Romeo and Juliet died in the end."

Dario clucked his tongue. "I thought Karen had turned you into a romantic."

"Don't you want to try someone who's not so complicated?"

Dario saw a splash of red, the puddle of a dress on the Pierre's toe-squishing carpet, and how Cassidy had looked in the dark, silhouette in the window, backlit by the light of the full moon—her belly curved, her backside perfect, the aroused tips of her breasts tilting upward. He had to suppress a groan. It was four o'clock, which meant that she was preparing herself for his arrival, undressing and wiggling down into the tub, covering herself in bubbles. He imagined the rosy color of her breasts now, hot from the water, and how the suds would just cover her nipples....

"Dario?"

He glanced at Pat. "What?"

"I said, do you ever feel the urge to get involved in a situation that's less complex?"

Thinking once more of how Cassidy had looked last night, with her feverish, creamy skin looking flushed in the moonlight, Dario slowly shook his head. "Absolutely not."

DARIO WAS ALREADY half-hard as he entered 67 Anthony Street an hour later. Anticipation had built all day, and now he was pleased to see the door to the apartment shut. When he jiggled the knob, he found it locked, too. "Cassidy," he whispered. "You're playing the love slave to perfection."

Peeking from beneath the door, a folded note was visible. Smiling, he lifted it, figuring it would contain descriptions of whatever wild, sensual delights were in store for him. But it said: You were not here last night to protect tenants, so we have no choice but to report this to Judge Zhang. Loud music played all night, and we heard constant banging. Sincerely, Brice Jorgensen, on behalf of the tenants' association.

Thankfully, most of the tenants didn't seem to be home from work yet, but Dario could hear muted heavy-metal music coming from across the hallway, which meant Rosie's daughter, Theresa, was home from school. Probably, she'd been the one playing the music. Shoving the papers from the courthouse inside the apartment, he relocked the door and went upstairs, taking the steps two at a time, determined not to let tenants' complaints sour his evening plans.

Knocking lightly, he pushed open the door of the empty upstairs apartment, and once more, felt surprised at the vacancy. The walls were in good shape, the carpet new, and the two rooms were huge; in a city where many people lived in cramped studios, this had been a bargain. "Cassidy?"

No answer.

His disappointment took him by surprise. Suddenly, he realized he hadn't noticed any of her belongings in the downstairs apartment, either. Had she decided to renege on their contract and stay at the Pierre? Should he call? Let it go?

Retracing his steps, he went into the apartment where he was staying, walked the rooms and found a black roller suitcase tucked neatly in a corner, along with the basket they'd brought from the hotel, containing condoms and the bubbles. Which meant she was here somewhere. Feeling more relieved than he wanted to admit, he started at the top of the building, then worked his way down, until he was heading for the basement.

"Cassidy?" he called as he descended a rickety staircase.

A muted reply sounded, then scraping, as if she were dragging debris. Squinting, he made his way downward, into a dim, musty, windowless cave of a room. Something clinked, and he saw a hole where bricks had been removed, and he realized she was inside the wall. "What are you doing?"

"Searching."

As he neared, he could see her belly crawling backward, coming toward him with her delectable backside wiggling.

Steel-toed workman's boots appeared first, then oversize, baggy cargo pants, which he recognized from the closet of the apartment where he'd been staying. She scrambled to her feet, and just as he realized she looked cute as hell, relief flooded him. She hadn't left; she was his all week.

"I forgot," she said, peering down at a dirt-streaked wrist, the gesture of someone used to wearing a watch. Realizing her wrist was bare, she said, "What time is it? I was supposed to take a bath, wasn't I?"

"So you remembered."

"I don't welsh on deals."

His heart soared, and he couldn't help but grin. She was just as interested in their little game as he. She was wearing a matching khaki shirt with the cargo pants, which were hiked nearly beneath her breasts and held up by a piece of clothesline, which she'd used as a belt and tied in a bow. Her wavy hair, which had swept around her shoulders last night, now looked hopelessly tangled. She'd twirled it into something resembling an animal's nest, then skewered the mess with a barrette. Chuckling, he shook his head. "You look like you're on a safari."

She offered a lopsided grin, her green eyes sparkling, reminding him of bright sunlight on the ocean. Bringing a hand to her forehead, as if in mock salute, she made a show of peering around the basement. Finally, her eyes landed on him. "Looks like I just got lucky and caught something wild."

"Keep at it and you might get luckier."

"Then I'll call it a lotto kind of day."

"I won't mind being your jackpot."

She cracked up. "Careful. Or I might paint numbers on your balls."

"Fine by me. As long as you use edible paint." He loved

sparring verbally with her. She was sharp, and didn't act too coy, like a girly-girl. She didn't pretend to be offended by things when she really wasn't. He'd expected her to look a little nervous about what they were doing, but no one could have looked happier. She seemed entirely comfortable. "Being a love slave suits you."

"You, too." She smiled. "I turned the tables last night, remember?"

His eyes drifted over her. Every inch of her was filthy, and a tool belt, complete with screwdrivers and a hammer, was slung around her waist. She was gripping a flashlight.

"You were supposed to be waiting in the bath. Not getting grungy so I'd have to give you one."

"What?" she asked rhetorically, her eyes glinting with humor. She stalked closer, the tool belt clanking, then she poked him playfully with the flashlight. "You were expecting some prissy woman who smells like powder and flowers? You wanted to see me wearing a little apron and high heels while cooking you a big fat steak and potatoes?"

He shook his head, laughing. There was something so offbeat about her, so unpredictable. "Is that so terrible?"

"Uh-huh. Because I'm too busy to cook."

His tongue found his inner cheek and toyed with it. "You were cooking last night, honey."

Her laughter deepened. "Until everything burned."

Him, especially. But he'd never have guessed that the elegant woman he'd had sex with last night could transform into such a street urchin. "Now you look like something out of a Charles Dickens story."

"There you go again," she chided, crossing her arms over her chest in a way that only served to accentuate her breasts. "More high-brow literary references. Are you *sure* you're a cop?"

"We had to read Dickens in high school," he defended, holding up a staying palm. "After that, I swear I only read stock tips and racing forms."

"No porn?"

His eyes bugged. "A little." He paused. "God, you're nosy."

"Do you mind?"

"Not really." He yanked her close. At the contact of their bellies, she inhaled sharply, the sound attesting to what had already happened between them...and to what was about to happen again.

Not that he wasn't going to take his time and wring out every ounce of sweet anticipation. "You're giving me germs," he complained, peppering kisses over her temples.

"So, you don't like rough, working women?" she teased, bursting into a gale of giggles, clearly pleased with her own ridiculous patter. "Dirty women with tools..."

He couldn't stop laughing. "I have my own tools," he assured, tightening his grip around her waist, so she could feel one of them. Heat claimed his groin, and when their chests touched, he could feel her bra. Suddenly, he wanted to see it. Was it white and frilly? Transparent?

"Ah." She leaned back a fraction, something that made their hips lock more snugly as she whipped out the flashlight. Quickly unbuttoning his shirt, she trained the light on his chest. "You say you have your own tools. Let's take a look."

She was being incredibly silly, and he was loving every minute of it. "Not until you're clean," he protested. "I need to wash every inch of you first. Otherwise, I might get some dread disease and die."

"You're so mean," she whispered, staring up at him and batting her eyelashes. For a moment, he drowned in her gaze, taking in things he hadn't noticed before—their slanted, teardrop shape and the tiny flecks of brown in her irises. He was lost to imagination when her hand unexpectedly slid between their bodies and fondled the most intimate part of him. His temperature shot into the stratosphere. "I like how you touch me," he murmured.

"How's that?"

Her hand felt soft, but her grip was firm. Assured. "Like you like it."

Her voice was a soft pant. "I do like it."

A heartbeat later, he was so aroused he knew he couldn't wait another moment. "You're cute as hell," he found himself muttering, his voice oddly slurred as he gazed at her. "Have I told you that yet?"

She quit stroking him. "No. Do you like the outfit?"

"Almost as much as your little red dress."

"Now I know you're lying."

Slowly, he shook his head. He wasn't. No matter what she wore, she looked amazing. Definitely, she was the sexiest woman he'd ever encountered. Leaning a fraction, he curled both hands over her backside, smoothing her cheeks, exploring the crevice where her legs began. Huskily, he said, "Is there a butt anywhere in these baggy pants of yours? I can't seem to find it."

She chuckled, the sound shot through with excitement. "Do you have some kind of butt fetish? Something weird I should know about?"

He brought his lips close to hers, near enough that he could feel her breath. "Cassidy," he whispered, "I have to inform you of something."

Now she was whispering, too. "What?"

"Every man has a butt fetish."

"Oh," she said innocently. "I had no idea."

"Yeah, right." He sucked a breath through clenched teeth as her hand stroked the space over his pant's zipper again.

Using his hand to cover hers, he curled his fingers, a shudder racking his body as he urged her to apply more pressure. "Harder," he whispered.

A shuddering breath left her lips. The muscles of her fingers rippling against him. "Like this, Dario?"

"I like it when you say my name."

"You said so last night."

"Nothing's changed."

"We're still on a first-name basis?"

"Just kiss me," he growled.

"Where?"

He couldn't wait to see her mouth circling him, his hands threading through her hair and pulling her toward his groin. But he said, "On the lips."

She did, gingerly at first, then by nibbling at his mouth. "Hard day at the office?" she asked, playing the attentive homemaker.

"Terrible, sweetheart," he lied gamely.

"You're home now." She unsnapped his jeans. "Time to relax."

Blood was racing through his system. It was just a game, but it felt good. Maybe having a woman around to greet him after work wouldn't be so bad, after all. "Are the kids in bed?" he managed to tease.

"Are you afraid we're about to make too much noise?"

"Absolutely."

"I sent all our children to boarding school," she promised. "They will never return again. Or at least only on vacations. In fact, they're not even in the state of New York. And I think many people want to adopt them, too."

"It sounds like we're really alone."

"We might as well be on the moon," she agreed, pulling down his zipper.

His hand stopped her. "Like I say, I draw the line at dirty girls."

"I thought every guy liked dirty girls."

"Not tonight. I have my standards."

"I see."

Rezipping his pants, he snagged her shirt and nodded toward the stairs. "What say, I wash you off?"

As they started up, her stomach rumbled and he frowned. "Hungry?"

She looked a little guilty, and he did a double take, further considering her outfit. "It must have taken you hours to get that dirty. Did you eat?"

"I forgot."

"You didn't eat anything?"

She shook her head.

Once Cassidy Case set her mind to a task, she went for it, ignoring all distractions. "Look," he suddenly said, pausing at the top of the stairs, "my partner wanted me to go out to dinner, but I said no. Would you feel like meeting him and his fiancée?" The second he'd asked, he wondered if he'd just crossed the line into something too personal. "I mean, it's no big deal," he quickly added. "Just a quick bite."

"Why not?"

He tried to tell himself this would kill two birds with one stone—fulfill an obligation to Pat and get her fed. Still, he had to admit he was curious about how she'd get along with Pat and Karen.

"Only one stipulation," she said, turning and winding up in his arms.

Her mouth was close. Before she could continue, he bent and kissed her again, and he was pleased to find that her response was immediate. As soft as pillows, her lips crushed under his, remolding to the contours of his mouth, and the dark heat of her tongue pressed between his lips like a tiny blazing sword. When she drew away, she said, "If I'm meeting people, you'd better get me extra clean. I'd hate to make a bad impression."

"They say my tongue works better than bleach," he promised.

"You're on."

Stopping in the first-floor apartment, he grabbed condoms, the soap bubbles and two towels, silently thanking his sister once more for suggesting he bring them. Looping one around Cassidy's waist, he used it to lead her farther upstairs. A jolt of arousal shot through him as they entered the empty apartment and he locked the door behind them. The dead bolt clicked, sounding definitive, as if it were sealing their fate. By the time he turned around, she'd already located the bathroom and started running water. As he entered the room, she finished squirting in bubbles. Then she stood and turned toward him.

"Strip for me," he commanded simply.

She considered a second, then hummed the age-old stripper's song in an off-key tone that made him chuckle once more. He watched as she took a screwdriver from the tool belt. After twirling it before him as if it were a tiny scrap of panty, she tossed it to the floor with a loud clank.

"Sexy," he said, still laughing despite the fact that his voice was straining with need. Stepping forward quickly, he ran both hands into her hair. "Anything living in this nest?"

"Such as?"

He shrugged. "Small birds. Squirrels maybe."

She shook her head. "Only a field mouse."

"Let's see if I can't find him."

"For a city boy, you sure know a lot about critters."

He made a show of leaning and snorting animal sounds against her neck, until she was giggling once more, then he poked his fingers into her upswept hair, as if checking for the mouse. Finally, he unclipped the barrette and set it on the lip of the sink. A mass of red waves fell, untwining from a knot and cascading over her shoulder. His eyes roved over the tendrils now framing her face.

"Da-da," she whispered, kicking off her boots and unbuckling the tool belt, letting it fall to the floor.

For a minute, he could only stare at her. Lifting a hand, he used a finger to swipe away the mud streak that zigzagged across her cheek. She was stunning, he decided. Absolutely beautiful. Her skin was so creamy, the color of something a cat might lap up. "Cassie," he whispered.

Her lips parted with emotion he'd couldn't readily interpret. "You already have a nickname for me?"

"Do you mind?"

She shook her head, but he could see the play of confused emotion in her eyes. Already, they were going deeper than she'd bargained for, but secretly she wanted it. She wasn't going to fight. He tried to smile, to think of something to say to keep up their banter, but he couldn't. The tub was getting dangerously full now, the bubbles threatening to overflow. Unable to stand the tension any longer, he lithely leaned. In a swift motion, he tucked an arm behind her knees, then lifted her, cradling her against his chest. As she squealed, the mood broke, and he deposited her into the suds, clothes and all. She sputtered, "You're crazy!"

Quickly stripping, he kicked off his shoes. For a second, he merely stood there before her, giving her time to look her fill. When she did, her green eyes seemed to darken, turning hot and hungry. Slender fingers slipped over the lip of the tub and curled around it, as if she needed to brace herself.

Seeing that the perfectly shaped nails were still bloodred made him feel like a bull behind a starting gate. Splashing, he followed her into the water, positioned himself between her legs, then began unbuttoning her shirt. "If I'm crazy, you're making me that way," he defended, slipping the drenched shirt off her shoulders.

"Let's push the envelope," she whispered.

His breath caught when he found the bra was more serviceable than sexy. Except that it was black and made with wires that pushed upward, enhancing her cleavage. Just looking, he felt his erection flex against her slippery thigh. In his mind's eye, he was rising on his knees, bracing them on either side of her. Already aroused beyond the point of return, he imagined thrusting his hips, gliding into that deep cleavage. Her flesh would fold around him, creating a scalding hot, slippery tunnel.

He was still eyeing the bra. "I think you're cleaner with that on," he whispered.

She chuckled as he edged into her arms. His hands sloshed under the suds, fumbling with her zipper. "You want my pants on, too?"

"No way."

As he moved against her, waves of heat coursed through him, and sweat broke out, tingling on his skin, making it feel even hotter than the water. The cargo pants rolled down suds-coated thighs that felt silkier than they had last night.

"You'd better hurry," she cautioned, panting now. "Because I'm starved, Dario."

His eyes landed squarely on hers. Only now did he unhook the front catch of her bra. Bracing himself with one hand, he pushed aside the cups, the vision of her nude body making his heart do wild flip-flops. An open palm glided over her slick skin and wiped away thick white bubbles obscuring her nipples. "So am I," he managed. "And after I have my dinner, you can have yours, Cassidy."

With that, his ravenous mouth descended.

10

In the dream, Gem O'Shea was screaming, pressing her hands against the side of the carriage, looking behind her as if someone was there. Who? As Cassidy drifted, images jumbled, probably because she and Dario had lain in bed earlier, reading the files. They'd stopped only when tenants had come by to complain about last night's noise. Now Cassidy heard hooves pounding, and saw a road illuminated by gas lamps hanging suspended from iron stands. Suddenly, the horses reared; the carriage began rattling, its nearly disengaged wheel clattering, and it plunged over the bank, splashing into forbidding waters that churned furiously.

Suddenly, the scene shifted and Cassidy was nervously entering the Chinese restaurant where she and Dario had eaten with Karen and Pat tonight, then she was joking with his best friends, amazed that they were hitting it off. Karen was apparently best friends with Eliana, and Cassidy suspected she'd like Dario's sister, as well. She'd had no idea how to use chopsticks—the only Chinese restaurant in her hometown served with forks—and everyone had pitched in to teach her.

"Don't wear panties tonight," Dario had said as she'd discarded a pair of jeans and decided on a dress to wear while they were preparing to leave.

"No panties?"

"Please," he'd whispered.

"Are you prepared to beg?"

"On my knees."

She hadn't made Dario do so, but she hadn't worn any panties, either. Completely naked beneath a green silk shirt dress, she'd thrilled at the way the night air had felt, then at how easily Dario's had surreptitiously caressed her as they'd enjoyed dinner. All night, Cassidy had wondered what was happening between her and this man. Should she embrace feelings that already threatened to become more than the sexual encounter they'd agreed to share? Or run?

Karen and Pat's company had been an impediment to love-making, and it had left Cassidy chomping at the bit. To offset the feelings, she'd tried to tell herself she was only using Dario, so she could search the house, and also because she needed to do something wild, to get her feet wet after the divorce. Dario was going to keep peeling back layers, just the way he stripped off her clothes, to reveal dangerous potential she'd never guessed she had, a vein of sensual gold only he could tap.

On the way back to Anthony Street, they'd walked hand-in-hand through winding streets of Chinatown. Crowds had surrounded them, jostling and pushing them into each other's arms. He'd bought a fruit she'd never heard of from a vendor, then he'd fed it to her. Tossing away the seed, he'd hauled her into an alleyway and licked juice from her lips until they were both shivering with need.

They'd barely made it inside the apartment before they were tearing off each other's clothes. After unbuttoning her dress, he'd backed her against the door, lifting her into his arms. As their mouths met, her legs had circled his waist, and a second later, he was inside her, his jeans still on, unzipped and pushed down on his hips.

Relief had consumed her from the second they joined. He went deeper than before, the brute power of his thighs propelling him, and her pulse jagged. The demanding thrusts effected her like a catapult, shooting her to brand new heights. The next thing she knew, she was weightless and breathless, flying off a cliff.

Afterward, they'd read the files before making love again in the lumpy bed. It wasn't the Pierre hotel, but they hadn't minded. Now something niggled at her consciousness. Sighing, she tried to roll, then realized he was behind her, his breath a rumble—not quite a snore—his body warm. They'd sunk into a groove in the center of the mattress, and his chest was spooned comfortably against her back, his legs tucked so that his knees locked into hers.

Suddenly, her eyelids fluttered. They batted like wings, then opened on the dark room. Grasping the hand that had settled on her waist, she pushed it aside, along with the covers, struggling upright. "That music," she whispered. Placing a flattened palm on his hip, she shook him. From somewhere far off, a piano was pounding out dance hall music. People were hooting, shouting and clapping, stomping their feet, and tap shoes jangled in tandem, as if women were doing the cancan.

"Dario," she whispered.

He awakened as she had, abruptly sitting, his hand reaching instinctively over her and under the bed. When she realized he'd grabbed his gun, her heart stuttered. Even in the dark, when she wrenched around, she could see that he looked startled. "What's wrong?" he whispered groggily. "Are you okay, sweetheart?"

Maybe under other circumstances, she would have noticed the chiseled contours of his naked body, or the fact that he'd called her sweetheart. Just days ago, she'd been convinced no man would ever call her that again. But she was too intent on the sounds. Her heart was beating out of control, and she was rapidly blinking her eyes, hoping they'd further adjust as she reached for the light.

His hand stayed hers. "Wait," he insisted, grabbing his cell phone and flipping it open.

"What time is it?"

"Two in the morning."

No wonder she felt so tired. "This is what the tenants said they heard last night while we were at the Pierre," she continued in a hushed voice. "This music was playing night before last, too."

"I thought you brought it."

She squinted in the dark. "Why would I do that?"

"I thought you brought a boom box or something," he clarified. "Because you were pretending to be Gem O'Shea."

"You thought *Sheila* brought a boom box."

"You really didn't bring it?"

"No. Even if I had, that wouldn't explain this."

"Did you change my phone ringer?"

"No." She paused. "Could you put away the gun? It's making me nervous. Besides, since we're ghostbusting, bullets will go right through our prey."

He made no move to replace the gun, but got up as silently as a panther. Rustling jeans from the floor, he pulled them on, shoved his feet into shoes, then the gun into the waistband and said, "Don't worry, I know how to use my gun."

"Are you sure?"

He stalked close and whispered in her ear, making her skin tingle with pleasure. "I'm a man."

"Oh, please," she muttered.

"And I'm a cop," he added.

"Don't all you guys take graft?"

"Only in movies. Besides, such activities would only enhance my competency with weapons. Now, stay here."

Instead, she hopped out of bed, ignoring the flattened palm that landed on her chest and tried to push her onto the mattress again. As she fumbled for her clothes, she realized the volume of the sound was increasing. "It's chilly in here, too," she said, the cold making her teeth chatter and her nipples ache. Goose pimples broke out on her arms.

"Right. So get back under the covers. I ordered a new boiler today. By tomorrow night, we'll have heat."

It was the wrong time to figure out that three days had passed. Were she and Dario going to spend only four more nights together, before their fantasy week was over? It didn't seem like enough time.

"It's hard to tell where the music's coming from." She craned her neck. "Probably we'll get a better idea in the hallway."

"Exactly. So, like I said, do me a favor and stay in bed."

"Maybe *you're* still in bed," she returned, stepping into the jeans she'd almost worn to dinner. "Because you're obviously still dreaming. I'm not staying in here alone, listening to this racket."

As she pulled on a T-shirt, his hand curled over her shoulder, this time applying pressure. "It's probably just Theresa, the teenager across the hall. Maybe she's playing a prank."

"To make it seem like the house is haunted?" The idea calmed Cassidy's nerves. It was definitely better than the alternative. "The music sounds real," she whispered.

"It is real. There are no such thing as ghosts," he assured, heading toward the door. "Don't tell me you believe in them."

"You're starting to sound like my mother." Erin Magee had never believed in the stories about Gem. Tonight, the material Cassidy and Dario had read had jump-started Cassidy's mental juices, though, and now they were flowing faster than a river in a storm. For years, tenants had heard music that seemed to have no source, and some claimed to have seen scantily dressed, transparent girls float through the hallways. A shudder zipped down Cassidy's spine. Sidling close behind Dario, she hooked a finger over the waistband of his jeans. "If there are no ghosts, then I'll be perfectly safe."

"Unless there are bad people," he pointed out.

"Oh, yeah," she teased as they crept into the hallway together. "Carmella definitely looked like a serial killer. And Zu and Ling are probably with the mob."

"And Brice?"

"A crime of bad taste," Cassidy continued, further lowering her voice. "Mismatched socks. One black, one brown."

"That deserves capital punishment."

"But we should let him off. Rosie might be able to rehabilitate him."

"If she would. You think he's got a thing for her?"

"Yeah. Judging by how he was acting earlier, when they all stopped by."

"I thought so, too," said Dario. Reaching an arm behind him as if to shield her, he pushed open the door and inched into the hallway, his weapon drawn. As they crept toward the staircase leading to the second floor, the music seemed increasingly muted. "That's weird," he whispered when they reached the landing.

"Yeah," she agreed, glancing over her shoulder, toward their half-open apartment door. "Out here, you can't hear anything."

"The music's fainter."

"But the others hear it sometimes."

"It's coming from inside the walls."

Turning, she pivoted and headed for their apartment again. This time, he didn't stop her when she turned on the lamps. Blinking as she glanced around, she took in the high ceilings and unevenly plastered walls of the cavernous rooms. Pressing her ear to the wall, she skimmed the surface with her hands, feeling vibrations. "It's definitely in the wall," she agreed.

As if sensing there was no imminent danger from which he'd need to protect her, Dario relaxed. Despite the circumstances, she couldn't help but notice that sleep had done wonders for him, tousling dark waves of his hair so that they fell in rakish hanks over his forehead and chiseled cheekbones. His eyes were seductive midnight slits, reminding her of how they looked half-shut in ecstasy, and his chest was bare, his jeans unsnapped. Jet hair tangled between his pecs then arrowed downward, kissing the gun still tucked in his waistband.

"Really," she said. "Put the gun away."

Yawning, he shrugged, put it under the bed again, then came behind her, putting his ear to the wall. Making a fist, he began rapping on plaster as he moved toward the kitchen. Casually, he stroked her side, as if it was the most natural thing in the world. It was as if their physical relationship had gone on for years, rather than days.

He said, "Would you mind getting me the crowbar?"

She'd bought one today, just in case she needed to pry up floorboards. "Sure."

By the time she returned, he was inside a walk-in closet. "Here," she said, following him inside and ducking, but not before she rattled empty clothes hangers overhead. Reaching, she pulled a bubble cord, and a bald bulb snapped on.

Edging closer, she couldn't help but glide a hand over his back as she handed him the tool. He was tanned a deep bronze color from the summer sun, and skin that was as smooth as glass seemed to flow beneath her fingers. Still feeling warm from bed, he turned and circled his hands around her waist, drawing her flush against him.

"We have a ghostbusting mission to complete," she reminded, tilting her head toward the wall.

His slow smile was dazzling, the tilt of his lips endearingly ironical. He swayed to the music. "You haunt me."

"Not as much as your tenants will if you don't find the source of the noise."

"My dad's tenants," he corrected in a sexy murmur, kissing her. The kiss tasted luscious, and his arms wrapped around her were as warm as a wool blanket on a snowy day. For a second, she felt as secure as she had as a kid, and in a flash fantasy, she remembered how she'd come inside from playing in the snow. Granny Fiona would peel wet gloves from Cassidy's frozen fingers, then put them over the heater vent to dry and wrap her in home-knitted afghans.

Her lips broadened into a smile beneath Dario's, and he smiled back. "What's so funny?" he whispered, leaning away.

"Nothing. You feel warm."

"Only because you're used to dating ice men."

"Are we dating?"

"Sort of. We're standing in a closet, anyway."

"It's the next best thing to Aruba," she agreed.

"And that music's still blaring."

"Very romantic."

"Sexy," he corrected. "That's what we're doing here, remember?"

His free fingers traced her waist when he turned away,

as if to say they'd rather linger on her skin. With his other hand, he tapped the crowbar against the back of the closet. "It's hollow. There's nothing back there."

"Take it out."

Before she'd finished speaking, he'd banged the bar against the plaster. A hunk of drywall fell to the floor, then another. After a moment, she leaned, bringing her cheek next to his, and they stared into a black hole. The music was even louder now. "Yeah," she ventured. "It's definitely coming from inside the wall." No ghosts had floated out, either.

"Weird," he commented.

"Keep removing the wall, and I'll get the flashlight."

She was nearly to the closet door when she glanced over her shoulder. For an instant, she was half-tempted to return to him, finish undressing and pull him into bed again, the music be damned. He had an adorably tight butt and as he used the crowbar, the taut, sculpted muscles of his forearms rippled, shot through with cords of veins. Suddenly, he craned his head in her direction, caught her looking, and grinned. "Flashlight," he said simply.

"I got sidetracked."

His bow-shaped lips twisted into a smile she was coming to know very well. It was ironical, bemused, suggestive. "I tend to do that to women."

"Modest, too."

"Only if you take into consideration that I'm the hottest man in the world."

"Oh, let me pause to consider that."

"Better not. You'll be there all day."

Snorting, she rolled her eyes and headed for the flashlight. When she returned, he'd taken out enough of the closet's back wall that they could walk through the hole. "You first," she said, slapping the flashlight into his palm.

"I thought you wanted to protect me."

"There might be ghosts. Or mice. Or…"

He squinted. "Do you really believe in ghosts?"

"Sort of."

"Hmm." Making no other comment, he stepped through the hole, and she followed.

"Wow," she whispered, ducking since the ceiling was only about five feet high, and inhaling dust. The space was too narrow to accommodate them both, and she hooked a finger over his waistband again. They inched forward. The music was even louder now, but it echoed in the crawl space, so its source was difficult to pinpoint.

"The passageway feels long," she said in a hushed tone.

"I bet it runs the length of the building."

"Do you feel that draft?"

"Yeah."

All at once, the temperature had dropped, and now she could see her breath fogging the air. She tried to tell herself the gust of cool air came from outside, but all she saw was dark, cracked, cobwebbed walls. Another tingle of fear skated down her spine, feeling like spiders dancing on her vertebrae. Covering her mouth with a hand to mitigate the musty scents, she tried to joke. "Maybe we just discovered the gate to hell."

He made a spooky ghost sound.

Her mood lightening, she smacked his behind playfully. "I'm serious," she whispered. "I'm thinking of all the movies where kids find caves that turn out to be bottomless pits."

Turning, he suddenly grabbed her. Because his weight caught her off-guard, her knees buckled, but he caught her, chuckling devilishly.

"You're evil," she said in mock consternation.

"You love it."

Before she could answer, his lips were on hers again, even as the music continued. Thankfully, the fire of his mouth was transporting. It could have been five hundred years ago, or yesterday. Time no longer mattered at all. They'd stepped into a strange world, on the other side of the wall, just as Alice had stepped through the looking glass into Wonderland. Cassidy's tongue mercilessly toyed, but his was teasing her to distraction. Hours might have passed, or minutes. She felt all tangled up in knots. Her body had been tingling from head to toe, but fear and pleasure blended now, intertwining.

Suddenly, she squealed, breaking the kiss. Something near her feet had moved. "A mouse," she whispered, her grip on Dario's waistband tightening. Another scurried near their feet.

"They're all over the building," he confirmed.

"Great," she muttered.

"I put down traps. They're more afraid of us."

The only alternative was to turn back, but there was only one flashlight, so she urged him to continue searching. A moment later, they rounded a corner and the ceiling dropped. Crouching lower, she realized the tunnel had stopped cold.

"Dead end," he murmured, tapping the crowbar against the wall, lightly at first, then harder. "This one's solid," he said.

And then the music stopped.

It happened all at once, in midsong, without warning. It was as if ghosts had heard the crowbar and finally knew they were bothering the living.

Dario stared at the wall a long moment, then shook his head.

"The side walls of this passageway must have space

behind them," she persisted, as he handed her the flashlight, gesturing that he was turning around, and that she should lead the way now. "The music is right on the other side."

"Maybe. Sounds can be deceiving. The rooms are like old caverns. I'll come back tomorrow," he murmured, as she crept toward the closet again.

"Don't you have to work? As much as I hate to admit it, the idea of searching this place alone is losing its appeal. A person could die in here and no one would ever know." It was a morbid thought, and she pushed it away, but the inner walls of such a notorious building probably held plenty of secrets.

"I'll take the day off."

For her? "Are you sure?"

"Technically, I'm working, since this might lead to information about Gem's death."

She felt a rush of relief, then excitement. This was larger than her own personal obsession. With Dario's help, she'd become part of a real investigation, one that could lead to answers about her family. "Whatever expertise you can bring to bear would be appreciated."

"You know…" His voice trailed off as they emerged from the closet.

"What?"

"In the papers I brought home with me this evening, there are a stack of original blueprints for the property," he said, heading for the front door. "We haven't had a chance to look at them, since we started with the files, and now it's too late, but first thing tomorrow…" Reaching for a cardboard tube he'd left beside the door, he uncorked an end and pulled out some rolled papers. "Here," he said peeling off the top sheet.

She helped him unroll them, using the crowbar and flashlight as anchors for the corners. Kneeling beside him, she watched as he splayed his fingers, smoothing flattened palms over the top sheet. She liked his hands, she decided. They looked strong and bronze against the white paper, capable and economical.

"This one's a surveyor's map," he said, comparing it to the next sheet, "and this is the original interior floor plan. I always thought there was something weird about the building. Even as a kid. It always seemed…"

"Like there was wasted space?"

He squinted at the papers thoughtfully. "There are hidden rooms here. At least I think so." His eyes locked with hers. "Your instincts were right."

But were they right about him?

His eyes looked a shade darker now, and they were catching glimmers from the dim lamplight. For a second, she felt too open, even more naked than before, although she was dressed now. Still, there were many kinds of nakedness, and Dario Donato seemed to have just as many ways of disrobing a woman. Swallowing hard, she glanced away.

Just as quickly, he grasped her chin. His thumb fit right beneath her lower lip, and slowly, he turned her face to his again, looking into her eyes once more. For the space of a heartbeat, she felt panic. She wasn't sure what he wanted from her, or if it would be too much, or if she was ready to give it, whatever it was. And he seemed to read all those emotions in the blink of an eye.

With deliberation, he angled his head nearer. His eyes were even closer now, looking deep inside her. His mouth hovered, his breath tantalizing. Then he came closer still. Their lips grazed—once, twice. Leaning another fraction, he pressed his mouth to hers. There was no dampness now, only firm pressure and heat.

After a very long moment, he leaned away, and she blew out a shuddering breath. "Nice," she whispered.

"Yeah, but we ought to sleep."

It was the last thing she felt like doing. "It *is* two in the morning," she agreed.

Rising gracefully to his feet, he stretched down one of those impossibly long arms and offered his hand. She slid her fingers across his palm, then felt her heart swell unexpectedly as his fingers closed around hers. With a tug, he pulled her to her feet and into his embrace.

It was the wrong time for someone to pound on the door. In unison, they groaned. Dario lifted his voice, his eyes fixed on hers. "Who is it?"

"The tenants' association," Brice Jurgenson called through the door.

And then Cassidy's cell phone rang.

11

CASSIDY WAS TRYING to follow two conversations at once. "No, really, it's okay, Mom," she said into her cell, catching snippets of the tenants' complaints. Whatever Dario was saying was calming them.

"I can't believe I forgot about the time change," her mother apologized. She was on vacation in California.

"That's okay. We, I mean, I was up anyway," Cassidy managed, still staring through a crack in the bedroom door at Dario. He really did look over-the-top handsome. Tall, slender and well muscled, he had one of those V-shaped torsos that her ex had spent hours in a gym trying to create. Forcing herself to turn away so she could concentrate on the call, she glided bellyfirst onto the bed. She started filling her mother in about her own trip, deciding not to mention Dario. "There's a hearing on Tuesday. A Judge—Judge Zhang— will make a decision."

Her mother was a worrier, and now her voice sharpened. "And everything's fine with the hotel?"

Cassidy glanced at Dario's shirt on the floor. "Great. The Centuries of Sex Museum is picking up the tab, just the way they said, but I'm really glad you called my cell because I—"

Before she could manufacture a lie, her mother saved the bell by saying, "I didn't have the hotel number—"

"Which is just as well because the phones here haven't been working that well—"

"In such a nice hotel?"

"Strange, huh?" Cassidy was almost angry at herself for lying to her mother, but a second later, she remembered why she always did so.

"I wish you'd get these crazy notions about Gem O'Shea out of your head," her mother said on a sigh. "There are no jewels. And no murder. And really, honey, apparently that building has been in the Donato family for over a century, so I wouldn't get your hopes up. I mean, it's nice for a museum to try to help, but—"

"I really believe those things," Cassidy interjected, feeling herself clamming up inside. Whatever excitement she felt, her mother was the first to toss the wet blanket on top of her.

"I'm sorry," her mother said.

"I wish you could be more supportive."

"I know you always feel that way, and I'm sorry, honey, but I think it's good to be realistic. And…well, that brings me to the real reason I called."

Another tiny knife twisted inside Cassidy. Oh, she was used to the way her mother treated her, like a child, but she wished—just once—that her mother would call without an agenda, just to chat. "Which is?"

"Well, I know you won't want to hear it, but—"

"Then don't tell me!"

"Maybe I shouldn't. I mean, I wasn't going to, but now… well, I'm obligated to say something. You see, a couple weeks ago, I stopped by your house, just to check on you…"

"I can take care of myself, Mom."

"Of course you can. But guess who I found outside, sitting on your porch, wearing a cute, pitiful hangdog expression?" Before Cassidy could ask, her mother pressed on. "Johnny Case, that's who. Oh, Cassidy, I know you don't want me prying, but he's taking this divorce so hard. You were so darn mean to him, and he never could understand why. As I told you, I wasn't going to say anything. He made me promise I wouldn't, but—"

"He was at my house? On my front porch? Had he been inside?"

"Why are you so distrustful, honey?" her mother asked, sounding crestfallen. "You loved him so much, and I know he loved you. Your whole life was going so well. Everything was all figured out."

"Every time we had a fight, you sided with him."

"That's not true."

"Mom," Cassidy huffed. "I love you, but I really have to go now. It's almost three in the morning."

"I'm so sorry. I forgot. I thought it was about eleven."

Even that was too late for Cassidy. Her mother was the night owl. She sighed. "It's okay. I'd really better get back to sleep, though."

"Are you sure you're all right?"

"Fine," Cassidy promised.

"I knew I shouldn't have told you," her mother said again. "But I've bumped into him a few times. He was hoping to talk to you when you came home from work. He's so stressed about your financial problems, since he's not there to support you any longer. I mean, he said your store brought in income, but…" Her voice trailed off. "I told him all your news, though," she began again brightly. "He couldn't believe the Centuries of Sex Museum called, and that a twist of fate might change your luck."

Emotions warred within her, among them shame. How much had her mother told her ex? "Look, Mom, I really have to go now."

Relief filled her as she clicked the off button. A second later, warm hands landed on her feet, curling around the insteps. They glided upward, molding her calves and stroking her thighs, then Dario took the phone from her and tossed it aside.

His voice sounded gentle and kind. "You okay?"

There was no hiding her tangled feelings. As she rolled over to face him, she'd felt a surge of anger and dismay. "Yeah."

Propping himself on an elbow, he tucked a fist against his cheek and stared down at her, using his free hand to brush hair away from her face. "So, you didn't tell your mom that your ex wrecked your finances?"

"Eavesdropper."

"A filthy habit, I admit."

"I thought we were trying not to get personal."

"It's impossible not to when you're sleeping with somebody."

"Now you tell me." She shook her head, considering. "Mom really liked Johnny. *I* really liked him. At least at first. He was a teacher at a small college in our area, and he seemed to know a lot, and I guess Mom and I were both a little too impressed. I mean, neither of us have four-year degrees, and he was a teacher." She looked at Dario, deciding how much more to say, and suddenly, she wished he wasn't turning out to be quite so easy to talk to. "In the end, I was ashamed of misjudging somebody's character to that extent."

"You can't know a person until you live with them."

It was nice of him to say so. "Maybe. Anyway, I didn't want Mom to worry, but that backfired. She believes he was supporting me, when it was the other way around. He spent his own money like water."

"Are you ever going to tell her he was a scumbag?"

"Well, it's already been a year, and it's all starting to seem like water under the bridge."

"Only because you're in another man's arms."

"Only for a week."

Leaning, he pressed a quick kiss to her forehead, then studied her. Something in his gaze made her feel compelled to say, "My mother and I…"

"Don't get along?"

"It's not that," Cassidy said quickly. "She loves me. And I love her. But she always worries. And my dad left when I was young, so it's just me and her. Dad didn't want to keep in touch, and I let it go. Mom saw Johnny as the solution, not that he was my dad all over again. She can be a hypercritical, but she means well. She was so sure Johnny was the best thing that ever happened to me, and I didn't want to take that away from her. I wanted her to feel like my life was all squared away. When I got married, it was like she finally quit worrying about me."

"Mothers and daughters," Dario mused.

She couldn't help but smile. "You're an expert?"

"With a bunch of sisters? Uh…yeah. I could have a Ph.D. in the topic. Impressed?"

She laughed, then the laughter tempered to a soft chuckle. She was starting to genuinely warm to Dario Donato. He was quick with answers, and it made her feel good inside. Special. Heard by him. Safe.

"Like I said when we were having dinner with Karen and Pat," he continued, "Eliana and my mom are at each other's throats all the time now. After the wedding, Pop says they may never speak to each other again."

Cassidy's smile turned rueful. "Johnny used to bring up my relationship with my mother. He'd turn our sniping into something more. You know, pathologize it, like we were both nuts, dysfunctional or something."

"But it was typical mother-daughter dynamics?"

"Which *are* crazy," she admitted.

Dario shrugged. "Your ex sounds worse every time you mention him." He fell silent a moment. "He was really at your house?"

"According to Mom." She nodded agreeably, then understood what he was getting at. "Johnny's not dangerous."

When Dario didn't look convinced, she laughed again. "Now you're acting like a cop."

"How's that?"

"You look like you want to arrest my ex."

"He did leave you saddled with his debt, and my guess is, he made a decent salary. What was he spending it on?"

Her lips pursed, she glanced away.

When he spoke, the rumble came from his chest. "You don't have to tell me."

She sighed, her eyes finding his again. Something about him took away the shame of it. "Other women. Girls really. I mean, I only know about one, but suspect others. She was a freshman in his class." Her voice held a touch of bitterness. "As young and doe-eyed as I was when I sat in on his classes."

Dario looked stunned. "He wasn't just a scumbag. He was crazy, toots."

Somehow, he'd gotten a smile to tug at her lips. "You think?"

"Absolutely." He toyed with a tendril of her hair. "You were in his classes?"

"He teaches history and antiquities, and I was interested in old jewels. I supplemented my own schooling by auditing some regular college classes, and his happened to be one."

She narrowed her eyes. "I bet you're a good cop. People must tell you all kinds of things."

Ignoring the compliment, Dario shook his head. "No man in his right mind would sleep with somebody else if he could have you."

"Diplomatic of you to say so under the circumstances."

"Simple truth." A sudden, dazzling smile made his eyes crinkle at the corners. Dropping a lock of her hair, he traced a lazy finger down her cleavage, then splayed a warm hand on her belly. "Ready to get undressed again so I can prove it to you?"

Once more, he seemed to be seeing more than she'd meant to reveal. "Not before you tell me what the tenants said."

"The music is as loud in some of their apartments as here," he reported. "Rosie and Theresa heard it, but Brice said he was awakened by footsteps. Zu and Ling didn't come down. I guess they're still in bed." Inclining his head, he lasered his eyes into hers. "Now, can I restore confidence in your sexual abilities?"

She smiled, then suddenly thought of something. "They used to play panel games in old bawdy houses," she said as he began swirling circles around her naval.

"I've heard about that from vice cops," he murmured, clearly more interested in undressing her. "One woman would keep a guy occupied while another would enter the room by removing a panel of the wall. She'd steal his money, replace the wall panel, and the guy wouldn't know what happened to his cash."

"So, it would make sense if there really were hidden rooms here."

He unsnapped her jeans. "We'll find out tomorrow." He paused. "After we sleep in. Then we'll have breakfast. And then we'll demolish the house. I want to go to the church where Gem went the night she died, too." Earlier, as they'd read the files, he'd told her a librarian had found the information, and even now, she could barely believe the church was still standing. "Sounds like a big day, so I could use a nightcap."

"I polished off the whiskey night before last," he said, "so this is the best I can do." When his mouth found hers, the heat of the kiss entered her bloodstream with the strength of pure grain alcohol. Just like whiskey, it hit the back of her throat, then wended slowly into her belly, traveling to her groin before it curled up like a sleepy cat.

As he gently nudged her lips apart with his, she felt drunk with the sensation. Already, she was dizzy, spinning into a vortex, whirling into the abyss as he slowly eased down her zipper.

"Do me, too," he whispered.

Finding his zipper, she pulled it down, pushing denim over his slender hips. Now that she was in his arms again, she knew sleep would elude her. "The light," she whispered.

"I want it on," he said, sitting up and leaning his back against the wall, his arm stretching for a condom on the dresser. Circling his arms around her back a moment later, he urged her to straddle him.

He was ready and waiting, hard for her, and as she glided onto his length, he felt like scalding granite. Ripples undulated through her. The heat of his eyes matched that of his body as they roved over her breasts. She couldn't believe the heat of their passion, its ease. Raw need was a scent in the air as she settled her palms on either side of his head, using the wall to brace herself.

"We're good together," he whispered, watching her.

"Maybe too good."

"Maybe."

There was danger here, she thought, rolling her hips, grinding against him, taking the pleasure that he was so ready to give. They could take these sensations anywhere… or nowhere.

"Scared?" he asked.

"Of you? No," she lied, then she shut her eyes. The light was on, but now the world inside her mind became as dark as pitch. Desire was winding through her, tying her in knots, coiling and tangling, pulling her toward the inevitable climax. "You?" she whispered, her chest suddenly tight, her breath shallow. "Are you scared?"

"No."

But she didn't believe him, either. Emotion welled inside her and crested like a wave as she rode him. They'd started an innocent love game, but now it was weaving its own spell around them. There was no way out. From the first moment, his every glance had promised delicious sensations, and now he was making good on all his silent promises.

As he cradled her closer, she felt her heart stretch to breaking. His hands trembled, spanning her back as he buried his face against her chest, and tenderness claimed her as she undulated her hips, pulling him deeper inside, so deep that he touched her womb. Johnny hadn't wanted babies, a bombshell he'd dropped after their wedding, retracting his earlier promise to have them. Now, feeling Dario inside her, she felt the call of something she'd forgotten…a dream she hadn't remembered for years.

Crying out softly, she threaded her hands in hair that felt like silk, then she whimpered, rocking against him. He seemed to sense the tenderness in her heart now, and he hugged her close, his hands gentling, as if she was made of something fragile. *I love you.* Unbidden, the words surged to her lips, but she held them back. The impulse to say it was crazy. She barely knew him.

Or did she? Everywhere he touched her, she felt both tender and hot, and as if her heart was breaking all over again. She hadn't yet healed from Johnny, but this man was already ripping open wounds, making her want to trust again, to try at love….

His breath was shaky against her skin, his thighs straining in tandem with hers. He was unbelievably hard now, taut inside her, about to explode. His fingers turned urgent on her flesh, his release imminent. The mouth that touched her mouth was greedy, the kiss so thorough that the man could have believed it to be his very last. Why did she think she didn't know him? What more did she need to know?

They came as she and Johnny never had, at the same second. He was holding her so tightly that his arms seemed to circle her body countless times, leaving no space for a breath. She was the ball, and he was the twine. His heart was pounding against her heart, his lips capturing a sigh from her lips, and a scent rose between them that wasn't him, or her, but their joined selves.

"Now, we can sleep," he said softly, sounding satisfied, urging her lower on the mattress, to share a pillow.

She said nothing, but her arms and legs were twined around him more tightly, like vines growing around a solid tree trunk. She felt like a boat carried on a strong, sure current. That was her final thought as she tipped over the edge of a waterfall once more, into the world of dreams.

12

"Wow," Cassidy murmured in awe the next afternoon. She, Dario and their guide, a woman who'd introduced herself as Mrs. Harrison, stepped through a wrought-iron gate, then beneath the stone archway of a cloistered path, and into the interior courtyard of the church where Gem O'Shea had been the night she'd died. Huge hardwood trees with giant trunks towered over ivy that tumbled from planters, and as they walked under a canopy of sunburst-orange and moon-yellow leaves, the shade made the temperature drop.

As soon as Cassidy shivered, hugging her arms around the raincoat she wore, Dario responded, drawing her to his side. She'd forgotten how much she'd missed receiving public affection from a man. When she and Johnny had first started dating, they'd shared occasional kisses on the street, something that ended after they'd married. Often she'd wound up charging a few steps ahead, while he'd ambled behind. It was as if he was always holding her back. By contrast, she and Dario walked together as if they were one person—his strides matching hers.

Realizing she was comparing the two men again, Cassidy focused on her surroundings. "This is amazing."

"It's one of the oldest buildings downtown," chirped Mrs. Harrison, a birdlike woman with pointy features—a sharp nose and chin—and bright blue eyes that sparkled with intelligence. Looking self-satisfied, she shoved both hands into the pockets of the tweed blazer she wore with khaki slacks. "It's a hidden oasis, isn't it?" she asked rhetorically, guiding them to a door marked Office.

Cassidy had come to the city on buying trips, but she'd never seen the sites through a native's eyes, and all day, Dario had dragged her down intricate winding alleyways that would have been lost on the less observant. The cloistered gardens at the church proved to be another such revelation. While Mrs. Harrison found her keys, Cassidy glanced sideways, smiling at Dario. There was a moment of shared desire, then of intense emotional connection such as Cassidy hadn't felt in a long time. "Thanks," she whispered to Dario.

"For what?"

"Bringing me here. I didn't know places like this existed in the city."

"I could show you a million more," he promised.

"Now, have a seat, you two," said Mrs. Harrison, as she pushed open the office door, "because you're going to need it."

Inside was an oak-paneled room with floor-to-ceiling shelves crammed with leather-bound volumes. Twining his fingers through Cassidy's, Dario urged her to sit beside him on a leather sofa. Feeling their thighs connect, she sighed, suddenly transported backward in time, not to the distant past, but to this morning, when she'd awakened.

As soon as she'd opened her eyes, she'd found him smiling down at her, as if he'd been watching her for a good long while. A bag from a deli was on the nightstand. A mischievous expression on his face, he was waving a cup of coffee beneath her nose.

"Wake up and smell the coffee, huh?" Her muscles tingling as she stretched.

"Undress and you can have it," he'd bargained, his dark eyes crinkling at the corners when he smiled.

"I'm already undressed," she'd returned, smiling back.

"I don't believe you."

"You have trust issues."

"No doubt."

"See a shrink," she suggested.

"But I want to see you."

Slowly, she'd lifted the sheet, giving him a peek. Leaning closer, he'd made a show of scrutinizing her naked skin. By the time they were finished with the full body viewing, another two hours had passed and the coffee was cold, the cream curdled on top. So, he'd taken her to a small, bustling brunch spot in Little Italy, where he seemed to know everyone, from the waitresses to the busboys and the cashier.

Unexpectedly, her throat got tight now. What was happening between them was supposed to be a moment out of time. In a couple of days, 67 Anthony Street was going to be hers, and she had to be prepared to walk out of this man's life. Had desire blinded him? In the end, was he going to be angry at her? Certainly, his father wouldn't approve of her staying in the house, much less tearing it apart as they had much of the day. They'd found nothing. Nor did Dario know that Luther was relying on her, or that she'd met with Chuckie Haswell.

Wondering if she should tell Dario, she shifted uncomfortably, reminding herself she'd done nothing wrong. Her guilt was due to torn loyalties, but she didn't owe Dario Donato anything. She had a right, even an obligation, to cut the best deal for herself.

Pushing aside her thoughts, she surveyed the room. Mrs. Harrison was lifting a plastic-wrapped package from the desk. She came toward them, her movements economical.

"After you called this morning, I went into action," she assured, excitement in her voice. "I phoned Janet Kay, the archivist at the public library, whom you mentioned." Gingerly removing the contents of the bag, Mrs. Harrison placed a white, leather-bound wedding book before them, then opened it, turning the book around so they could read.

"Gem O'Shea," Cassidy said, gasping, taking in the scroll-like script. It was the first signature. Her hands trembling, she grasped the delicate page and turned. "Mark," she continued, "and Lily."

"They were married here on December 23, 1890," Mrs. Harrison said.

"A Christmas wedding," Cassidy murmured. But why had Gem been here?

"This is a very old church, and our rectors have all been collectors, so we have rooms of materials, as you can imagine. I've done my best to organize them during my tenure as the cataloguer." Mrs. Harrison paused. "It'll be thirty-six years when I retire next year. In my experience, it's a rare pleasure when somebody wants a long-lost item. I can't give the book to you today, of course, since my superior has to sign off on transfers of documents, but if you're really…"

"A relative of Gem O'Shea's?" Cassidy finished. "Yes. I am. And I would be interested in having it. It's family memorabilia." Possibly, she'd donate it to the Centuries of Sex Museum for safekeeping. Guilt twisted inside her, and she suddenly wondered what would happen to Luther's collection if the building became hers and she sold to another buyer. Maybe Johnny Case's betrayal had ruined her. The old Cassidy wouldn't have been so afraid about her own future, nor would she have played one man off against another. She'd had more faith in herself, and the abundantly positive powers of the universe. Sex was one of those powers, too, and now as she glanced at Dario, she realized something magical was happening to her. Because of him, she was starting to heal....

"No one here's using the wedding book," Mrs. Harrison was saying. "It's just been filed away. So, I can't see why there would be an objection to your having it."

After all these years, it was astonishing to see Gem's handwriting. It made her seem so real that Cassidy could almost imagine Gem was in the room with them. Her pulse quickened. If Gem had really been in the church, then everything else might well be true, and that meant the jewels must truly be hidden in the house somewhere. Finding the wedding book was even more exciting than seeing the paintings at the museum.

Suddenly, another reality hit her. "She was here right before she died." Maybe Gem had even sat where she and Dario were now.

"Just hours before," agreed Mrs. Harrison. "If newspaper accounts of her death are accurate, anyway. And like I said, once we do paperwork, the wedding book is yours, if you want to take it. Janet passed along information from Mr. Donato, which is how I knew to look for it." Pausing, Mrs. Harrison shrugged. "Family members are always busy during a wedding, then or now, so we often safe keep items such as this. No one ever returned for it."

Dario was turning the pages, reading the names. His index finger settled on the very last line, and he blew out a soft wolf's whistle. "Take a look at that."

Cassidy leaned closer, catching the scent of his body, something pinelike and purely male. "Nathaniel Haswell," she whispered, her gaze darting to his. "Isn't that the guy who's supposedly related to Chuckie Haswell?"

"Sure is," he said, giving her hand a squeeze. "Chuckie's trying to prove he owned 67 Anthony Street."

"Obviously, Nathaniel had some relationship with Gem. Maybe he did own the property and willed it to her."

"Maybe." Dario shrugged, seemingly more concerned with the truth than his family's interests. "Maybe they were…"

"Lovers?" Cassidy asked on a quick exhalation of breath.

"That's what I thought," Mrs. Harrison interjected, her tone becoming a bit smug. "I thought to myself, now, what if Mark or Lily was Gem's child…" Quickly, she shook her head. "And then I thought, no, that seems too far-fetched."

"But why not?" Cassidy interjected.

Mrs. Harrison's beaklike mouth opened in anticipation. "Exactly. So," she continued, rising and returning to the desk, "I checked our files further. Since Mark and Lily were married here, it stands to reason that the same church would be used for other rites, such as baptism and confirmation. A service was said here for Gem after her death, too."

"It was?"

Mrs. Harrison nodded. "She's buried in a cemetery in Brooklyn. Apparently, her mother was buried there, as well."

"I can't believe this," Cassidy said with wonder in her voice.

"I can give you the address. And…" Mrs. Harrison laid a photocopy on the table. "As it turns out, Mark was her son, after all. Further records showed that Gem arranged for the wedding for her boy. The bride's surname was Jordan."

"No father's listed on the baptism record," observed Dario, scrutinizing the paper.

"True, and we'll never know who he was," Mrs. Harrison returned. "He wasn't buried with Gem, and I don't know where Lily was put to rest. Still, it's an amazing find."

"It really is," Cassidy assured, gushing. "I've heard

stories about Gem all my life. And now, it's…almost as if she's come to life."

"History does that, dear," Mrs. Harrison said. "Nothing truly dies. Ideas float for all eternity. Traces of people linger. Some say their belongings even carry their essence."

Mrs. Harrison paused. "Now for the icing on the cake. Janet Kay and I got to talking. In fact, we had so many ideas about linking our archive files that we wound up making a business lunch date. Anyway, once we had Lily's maiden name, Janet was able to go back into the archives at the public library and, as it turns out, she has Lily Jordan's diary."

Cassidy gaped. "You're kidding?"

Mrs. Harrison shook her head. "There was a push about fifty years ago— before my and Janet's time—to track down documents about the Five Points area, and bring them back home to the city where they belong. Archivists were hoping to create a more solid body of information about the immigrant populations who came here in the nineteenth century. Many were Irish, displaced by the potato famines."

Pausing, Mrs. Harrison inhaled sharply, as if to say she wasn't used to talking so much and needed to catch her breath. "Anyway, an ancestor of Lily Jordan's lived in Boston at that time, and she left a box of materials to the library when she died."

"Small world," said Cassidy.

"If you ever want a job with the NYPD," Dario said to Mrs. Harrison, "give me a call."

Mrs. Harrison laughed. Then she said, "If you head over to the library, Janet actually has Lily Jordan's diary. You'll have to read it on the premises, of course, or take the photocopy she's made for you. She told me she wouldn't have a chance to read it before you came—she had meetings this morning—so, whatever you find will be a surprise, I'm sure.

She has no idea if anyone has *ever* read the diary from cover to cover."

"She made a photocopy? And it's at the library? Right now?" Cassidy's heart was beating too fast, but there was no way she could calm it.

"It's not usually standard practice. Usually we'd look over the materials first. But this may help Mr. Donato with a criminal investigation, and you're a relative."

"Great." This was an incredible turn of events, and it was all because of Dario's connections. Feeling a rush of excitement, she sighed. This was the kind of moment that made her sure that, one day, the world's mysteries would all be solved. Wrapping her hand around Dario's biceps, Cassidy rubbed the muscle, feeling a rush of awareness as her breast pressed against his side.

"The diary's waiting for you," assured Mrs. Harrison. "Third floor. In the map room. Ask for Janet. The library's open for another hour. Uh…Janet will recognize Mr. Donato."

Other than the library, the only place Cassidy would rather be was back in bed with Dario, so the innuendo wasn't lost on her. That he and Janet Kay had been an item was confirmed when her eyes found his. Janet must have said something telling on the phone to her new friend. So, once they'd thanked Mrs. Harrison and gone outside, Cassidy said, "Another girlfriend?"

He brushed his mouth across hers in a blistering sweep of a kiss that felt as hot as a winter fire. "How many others do you know about?"

"One. Sheila."

"Sheila wasn't really a girlfriend." He paused. "And you didn't meet."

Cassidy wasn't sure she wanted to know. "And Janet?"

Dario urged her closer against his side while he considered. "I thought we weren't getting personal."

"Maybe. But when we were talking about my life, you said it was inevitable." She squinted, wishing she hadn't gone through so much heartbreak with Johnny's infidelity. "Before I meet her...at least tell me if you slept with her, so I won't feel weird."

"Knowing I slept with somebody would make you feel less weird?"

"Yeah." As soon as the word was out, she understood why. "It...makes me feel that you and I are more intimate, like you'd have bothered to let me know."

"More intimate than her and me?"

Stopping, he turned to face her, and as he did, a lump lodged in her throat. He looked gorgeous at this moment. She wished she had a camera, and could take a snapshot that would last forever. She could barely believe she was hanging around with a guy who looked this good. His dark denim jacket was unbuttoned, the collar turned up against the wind, the thick navy cotton sweater beneath bunched under her palms. Tilting against him, she looked into his eyes. As if sensing what she wanted, he lowered his head and captured her lips, and she stretched her arms around his neck, kissing him back.

When he drew away, his expression was hard to interpret, his voice rough, so low she had to strain to hear. "Would you mind?"

She didn't want to admit it. "Yeah. I mean, I'd feel funny about it. You know, about meeting her."

She sensed, more than heard, his breath catch. She could feel the bracing of his body, too, a tightness in his chest when he inhaled, the sudden flex of hands that found her waist. "We went out a few times. Came close, but we never..."

Should she believe him? She felt more relieved than she wanted to admit, although she knew her emotions were unwarranted. "A long time ago?" she persisted in mock interrogation, as a way of keeping the tone light. "Another century? Yesterday?"

"A couple years ago."

"Just asking." With that, she shrugged, flashed a smile, tapped his shoulder and turned abruptly, as if to say the answer wouldn't have mattered, one way or the other, although it wasn't true.

"Where are you running off to so fast?" he asked, following.

"The library," she tossed over her shoulder, making a beeline toward the wrought-iron gate leading to the street. A few paces later, he caught her hand from behind. She swung around, feeling breathless and sure her face was too naked, too bare. He'd seen how much he was affecting her and guessed she really liked him. Maybe she could even love him. Maybe he'd guessed that, too.

She backed up a step, only to realize a tree was behind her. Bark scraped her back as a long, leisurely arm stretched upward, his palm landing right above her head. Bringing his lips close, as if just to tease her, he didn't bother to kiss her, just let his lips graze hers. His eyes seemed too serious now, dark with emotions she couldn't fathom. Something, maybe a warning, flashed in their depths, prompting her to say, "One look at you, and I know I'd sure hate to be on the wrong side of the law."

His smile was hard to read. "Do I look dangerous?"

"Sort of."

"What are you thinking?"

"Oh, no...not *that* question," she chided. "Isn't that what people always ask when they're trying to start talking about their emotions, or the things we're not supposed to be having?"

"Like what?"

"A relationship."

"Yeah." His eyes were steady. "But I want to know."

She shook her head, wondering how much to divulge. A few days of his company had led her to want more. What exactly, she didn't know. Just more. "I like sleeping with you," she found herself saying. "Eating with you, waking up with you. Dammit," she suddenly added, her voice dropping, "you know this was only supposed to be..."

"An innocent game of shared sexual abandon?"

"Yes. But things...feel like they're spinning beyond my control."

"Beyond mine, too," he said, his voice so husky that she shivered as the finger traced a line around her lips. His mouth followed, his tongue coloring in the line he'd drawn.

"But I don't want to confuse things," she managed to protest, suddenly glad twilight was coming early. It was nearing four o'clock, but already the sky was graying and she could smell nightfall. The shadowy canopy overhead made her feel less exposed until his hand dropped to her shoulder in a caress, and her resolve to keep emotionally distant faltered.

He was watching her carefully, and as if sensing a moment of weakness, he placed both hands on her shoulders, then curled his fingers around them, so they dug into her skin, ensuring she couldn't turn away. "What's confusing you?"

"You know what I mean."

"Yeah." He stepped closer, wedging a foot between hers, forcing her to widen her stance, bracing herself as he pressed flush against her. Hard and warm and male, he drove her back against the tree trunk. His mouth was on hers then—hot, quick, wet. Responsive fire sparked in her belly, ignited and roared as her mind ran wild with possibilities.

Already, she was imagining frantic hands fumbling with her jeans zipper, and hearing the rustling sound of fabric as he pushed away her coat and lifted her into his arms. The memory of how he'd taken her against the apartment door was swift and visceral, and shudders racked her.

The church was behind them, the tree between them and Mrs. Harrison's prying eyes, and now Cassidy's hands were powerless, seized by passion that was a force in its own right. With a will of their own, they molded over his hips, traveling downward. Through rough denim, she could feel the hard bunched muscles of his thighs flinch. His hips arched, and suddenly, she felt him between her legs, the pressure of the erection making her ache. A gnawing craving filled her, and she felt strangely elated, and yet doomed. Having loved this man physically, she realized she'd always crave what they'd shared. There was no escape.

"You're not confused," he said speaking thickly against her lips before plunging his tongue hungrily again—now in a demanding thrust. "You want me. Want this."

Her hand slid between them, over the bulge at his fly. He let loose a soft moan. For a blissful moment, she shut her eyes, and her mind went blank. Just touching him flooded her with a relief such as she'd never felt. Once more, they were going to share passion...bring each other to completion. The last time they'd shared sex hadn't really been their last...

Forcing her lips farther apart, his tongue swept inside her mouth, causing her to tilt back her chin for a stormy assault. Her hand edged away, and she lifted her hips, all the while wishing they were elsewhere...anywhere that passion could have full rein. Another deep guttural sound emerged from the back of his throat as he ground against her, his movements rhythmic and purposeful, the circular pressure making her feverish.

His tongue dived once more, and hers lashed against it. As her arms circled his neck tightly, the hem of her coat swung, further shielding them from onlookers, hiding the unsuppressed surge of lust. Crushed against the tree, she gasped, parting her legs a fraction more, lifting on her tiptoes, feeling near release. Even through the clothes, she could feel his erection separating her cleft.

Her breath catching, she moved with him, the maddening friction bringing her right to the edge, need driving her.

But suddenly, he wrenched away, leaving them both shaken.

She was panting. He looked less shaken, his lips glistening from the ministrations of her mouth.

"I'm not him, Cassidy," he said simply.

For a second, she couldn't imagine what he was talking about. She was aching all over, her heart pounding, yearning for the sweet bliss wrought by the movements of his hips. Vaguely, she was aware of her own moisture, how slick and hot she felt. Frustrated desire was all she could feel, but she shook her head as if to clear it of confusion. "Who?"

"Your ex."

For once, Johnny Case was the furthest thing from her mind. "I never said you were him."

"Sure you do," he returned, his voice low, his grip on her shoulders tightening. "You say it every time you talk to me," he said gruffly. "Every time you look at me. Every time you kiss me. Every time you—" His voice breaking off, he thrust his hips again, making her sigh. "Bring your body to mine," he finished. "And every time we…"

"Have sex?"

"Make love," he countered, his lips close once more, hovering, threatening to descend, his breath slightly labored and feathering her skin.

"We don't even know each other. Not that well."

"Well enough for this."

"C'mon, Dario, let's go to the library. Okay?"

For a second, his eyes darkened, looking thunderous, and she realized he was as aroused as she and just as flinty because of it. "I thought you wanted a week of passion."

"Uncomplicated passion."

"Coward."

"You're not the kind of man who ought to say that," she shot back, her heart still beating double time, the awareness of her erogenous zones making her blind to all else. As soon as the words were out, she wanted to evade his piercing dark eyes. Since the first second he'd seen her, every glance seemed to remove stitches of her clothes, as surely as he was removing the character armor that defended her heart.

His eyes sharpened. "What kind of man is that?"

The kind who had countless girlfriends all over town. Janet, she suddenly thought. Sheila. She'd bet there were hundreds more. "The kind who never settles down."

"I thought you were finished with settling down yourself."

"I am."

"Then why should you care?"

He was twisting everything around. "I need to heal."

"You feel healed enough right now."

"You know what I mean."

"Maybe I could change."

"And you think I should be your test case?" she burst out. Why couldn't he understand? Her heart simply couldn't take any more man trouble. Not now. Maybe not ever. "After what happened in my marriage? No way. I'm more self-protective."

"For how long?" His hands were in her hair now, threading through the strands, his eyes imploring. "Are you going to keep protecting yourself, even if it stops you from exploring something better? Something real?"

"You think this is more real than my marriage?"

"Yeah."

"Why?"

"My gut says so."

"Sex," she forced herself to say, despite the telltale racing of her heart. "Plain and simple. That was our deal, Dario."

His lips parted, but she had no idea why. Was it in protest, or self-defense, or mere astonishment? Or was he about to kiss her again? The flash of heat in his eyes said he was definitely thinking about it. She doubted many women had talked to Dario Donato this way, and he seemed to be excited by the challenge.

"Just sex. So, it's really that easy for you?"

"Yeah," she lied. "Isn't it for you?"

"No."

"What about Sheila? Janet?"

"They were different."

She wanted to pretend he hadn't said it. And yet she wanted to know why. Instead of asking, she said, "We had a deal."

"I'm aware of that, Cassidy," he muttered. Without warning, he leaned, his mouth clamping down on hers again. Hands mussed her hair, and suddenly, his nails were scratching crazy circles on her scalp. They glided down her back, caressing each vertebrae, until each had begun tingling and he was cupping her backside once more. A breath sizzled, pulling through her clenched teeth as he brought her against him, wanting her to feel each inch of him again. The rock-hard, slender muscular length of his body sent her reeling. His weight, his heat, where he was hard—everything. "We need a bed, not a churchyard," she whispered.

"But that's all," he whispered back. "A bed. I'm aware of the deal."

"Good," she managed.

"Make good on it tonight," he said, leaning away, an indecipherable spark in his eyes. As he stood back a pace, she felt his body leaving hers by degrees, but all the impressions remained. Searing heat. Pine scents. Shallow breath. Aroused male flesh. He surveyed her a long moment, his eyes drifting over her, lingering on her breasts and looking hungry. Flashing a smile, as if to say he'd win this argument in the end, he turned and began walking toward the gate.

She stared at his broad back, the wide shoulders, tapered torso, perfect butt and mile-long legs—as she licked his kisses from her lips. Warring emotions claimed her. He expected her to run after him, but she'd never give him the satisfaction. She didn't want the altercation to end this way, though. What was she supposed to do? Beg his forgiveness? And for what? Not admitting she feared her growing feelings for him?

She exhaled a frustrated sigh. Raising her voice, she yelled, "Donato. Quit being a total horse's ass and wait for me."

His steps stilled. Slowly, he pivoted. It didn't help to notice the man was still hard. Oh, it wasn't that noticeable, unless a woman was looking, but she was certainly looking, and she could see the curve under the zipper of his jeans.

"C'mon," she ventured when she'd almost reached him, struggling for a light tone, despite how unsettled she felt. "It's supposed to be a great moment." She'd told him all about Granny Fiona's stories; he knew what finding the wedding book and diary meant for her. "And we may be close to solving a mystery. We did see Nathaniel Haswell's signature, after all. Share this with me."

"Sorry," he apologized, his eyes full of awareness. "I don't know what got into me."

Desire. And she'd felt it, too. "C'mon," she urged, concealing any hint of a plea. She slipped her hand into the crook of his arm and curled her fingers over his forearm. "Is our deal really that terrible?"

"I've made worse."

She feathered her lips across his cheek until she found the heat of his mouth. "Indulge me."

"That," he said, "I can do."

"It's only for a few more days. You'll live."

"You'd resurrect a dead man," he assured.

"Is that what I've done?" she couldn't help but ask. Did he really feel differently about her than other women? Had she, somehow, made sex become more than a game for him?

"Maybe."

Once more, she was glad for the twilight, since emotion welled within her. "Maybe you're doing that for me, too," she found herself saying. "So, let's enjoy it for what it is."

He nodded.

Hugging him more closely as they began to walk, she sighed in relief. They'd avoided a blowout, and things were going to be fine. Wham-bam-thank-you, ma'am. No feelings they couldn't control. No promises they couldn't keep. No shared possessions, knotty entanglements or locked chains that only attorneys could undo.

That had been their deal.

Except that she was falling in love with Dario Donato. And she was pretty sure he was falling for her, too.

13

HOURS LATER, CASSIDY glanced up from some of the photocopied sheets of the diary and caught Dario studying her. Propped against the pillow next to him, she stretched, the muscles of her shapely legs going taut, the hem of a nightshirt rising on tempting thighs. "Hmm?"

He shook his head. "Nothing." When she eyed him, unconvinced, he added, "I can't concentrate when you're beside me, half-dressed."

"You'll live."

"Better if you undress the rest of the way."

Looking preoccupied, she offered a smile, but then began reading again, becoming engrossed. Ignoring the copies in his own hand, he settled his gaze where the slopes of her breasts were visible beneath her shirt. As slow heat ran through him, his lower body tensed. Smoking tendrils curled in his abdomen like jet trails, or like residue left from an explosion of dynamite or gun powder.

The room was warmer tonight—he'd gotten the new boiler installed—but Cassidy looked warmer still. He started to reach for her, but something held him back—either seeing the joy she was taking in reading, or his own conflicted emotions.

He'd never stop wanting her. He knew that now. From their first night together, his response to her had been elemental. Like earthquakes or volcanos, summer storms or avalanches, it was an unstoppable force of nature destined to come to a halt as abruptly as it had begun. Only because she was going to walk away, though. He was just glad he'd been kicked off the arson case, so he'd had time for the adventure.

But Cassidy wouldn't keep in touch. She'd try to forget him, denying how good they'd been together. Maybe that's why he'd been seized by an urge to imprint her with memories as soon as they'd returned home. He'd grabbed the waistband of her pants and pulled her close. In the instant her mouth pressed against his, fire met fire, and in another moment, they were as aroused as they'd been in the churchyard.

"Make good on your deal," he'd challenged.

"You don't think I will?"

"Tease," he'd chided.

A lazy finger had hooked over his belt buckle. "As I said, I don't back out on deals."

"Prove it," he'd whispered, his mind already fogging, his body assaulted by visceral memory and knowing the bliss of loving her was only a breath away.

Emerald slits of eyes had found his, sparkling with intent, then she'd paused, her throat working hard as she'd swallowed, the only show of emotion as she'd unbuckled his belt. The soft, slapping sound of leather and their quickening breath punctuated the silence as she'd released the snap and unzipped him.

As soon as a bloodred nail traced his fly, he'd gotten hard, then her burning hands slipped under the back of his waistband, gliding inside his briefs. Nails raked his flesh as she curled them over his backside, bringing goose bumps. As she'd pushed down the denim, she'd moved quickly, clearly unable to undress him fast enough.

Then she'd dropped to her knees. Just like that. No warning, no fanfare. No tremulous show about how special this was. Just her cool wet mouth circling him. It had been pure heaven. Hell, too. Desire had seized him like an iron fist, and he'd felt he was down there with the demons, flames licking every inch of him. Angels wings had fluttered around him, and he'd felt lifted up, soaring.

Gasping, he'd tried to widen his stance, to brace himself, but that only made his jeans stretch taut across his legs. Trapped and unable to move, straining to spread his thighs, he stretched his hungry hands down, meaning to stop her. Instead his fingers dived, threading across wind-chilled skin, into lush hair still disheveled from the blustery night. Strands ran through his fingers like water, teasing the spaces between, before he closed his fists, his nails raking her scalp as he brought her mouth even closer.

A sound that was hard to define—of need, hunger and even protest—wrenched from his lips. She was taking his whole length, every inch, her tongue swirling, sending slow jolts to his limbs. A hand had landed on his thigh, tracing his taut muscles, then she'd pushed and he'd fallen like a feather, his back slamming the door behind him. Bending his knees, he'd dropped down an inch, then another inch, desperate to lower himself to her level, where she'd been kneeling; he'd have done anything to get closer to the bliss.

She'd been suckling him, her mouth drawing hard, the pad of her tongue exploring each ridge, taking him deeper than anyone ever had, all the way into the scalding, maddeningly wet tunnel created by her lips. When his sensitized flesh had hit the back of her throat, he'd released a sound he hadn't recognized as his own. Animal and primal, it came from a place previously lost to him...a place no woman had found until tonight.

Freeing his fingers from the tangle of wild, red hair, he'd curled a hand around the doorknob to better support himself. His mouth had gone dry, and he'd licked his lips, desperate to relieve the cottony feeling, but in an instant, it was dry all over again. Staring downward, the pleasure made him want to shut his eyes as he pushed away her hair and smoothed it over her shoulders.

"Take off your shirt," he'd said thickly, then groaned, watching as she'd followed his command. Unhooking her bra, she'd wiggled the straps down her creamy arms, her breasts swinging free, begging for his touch. Then her mouth was on him again, her tongue turning lazy—mercilessly flicking under the head of his penis, worrying the rim, teasing and grazing sharp teeth against him until he was raising his hips, silently telling her to finish what she'd started.

Now, recalling the moment, undeniable pangs claimed his groin, making him shift uncomfortably on the mattress. He wanted her again. She wasn't even touching him, but something liquid was swirling around his erogenous zones. What had he gotten himself into? he wondered as his eyes drifted over the waves of her silky red hair. Against the white of the pillowcase, they looked like wild tongues of fire.

Hours ago, he'd watched as she'd playfully touched him until his release was imminent. He'd held back, not wanting the pleasure to end, but then, she'd tickled him, the feathery touch pushing him to the edge, where he'd teetered.

"Please," he'd whispered, stunned to see his own hand tremble as he reached for her. Gently, he stroked her cheek, then her eyebrows, the pad of his fingers skimming her skin, his eyes glazed with need when they'd locked with hers. "Please..."

When she took him between her lips again, a feeling such as he'd never imagined consumed him entirely. There was nothing in the world but her. Nothing would ever matter but her. He wanted a life with her....

Pat would say his love games had finally gone too far. This was about sex, after all. No hearts and flowers. Nothing but raw need. It wasn't anything he hadn't done with countless other women. Janet and Sheila were just the tip of the iceberg, but his heart had remained untouchable and protected. He didn't even have a past love life. No true romance from high school. No lover who'd burned him, leaving him unable to trust. And he didn't want to start such a history with Cassidy...

Still, he only thought about how fast time was passing. It was Friday, which left only three nights until the court date. After that, he'd never see her again. He felt it deep down in a gut he'd learned to trust as much as his own mother.

Cassidy Case was going to walk. Or run. Her marriage had hurt her too much, leaving her touchy, resentful and convinced people would take advantage of her. Many would, too, just not him. Anger twisted inside him, and Dario silently cursed Johnny Case for destroying her. He'd never laid eyes on the bastard, but Johnny was in the way of everything Dario wanted now—Cassidy.

Too bad the best women often got hurt the most. On the job, he'd seen gorgeous girls practically held hostage by controlling men. Sometimes, the men would belittle the women to drive down their self-esteem, so they'd feel grateful and stick around. It was a sick kind of love. Something Dario had no interest in. Abruptly lifting his gaze, he realized she'd been watching him.

She squinted. "You okay?"

He glanced down at the sheaf of papers in his hand again. "Sure. I'm just thinking."

Her voice hitched in a way he was coming to love. "Me, too." She nodded toward the photocopies he was holding. "Did you finish reading?"

Because he hadn't even started, he couldn't help but smile. "Do you really think I was worrying about Lily Jordan's diary?"

"You do have a one-track mind," she admitted.

"I thought it was two."

"Two?"

"Are you referring to sex or food?"

She laughed. "Sex. Don't you ever rest?"

After the way she'd gone down on him a couple hours ago? "Uh…no." Taking a deep breath, he recalled the fun they'd had ordering take-out food afterward, and how they'd fed it to each other. "Having a babe next to me wearing such a slinky nightgown is a little distracting."

"This old thing?"

The nightshirt was worn, printed with pink poodles which had faded with too many washings. "It makes me hot," he assured.

"You're hopeless."

"So true." Staring at the pages again, he forced himself to pay attention. The photocopies were good, catching nuances of the original, which they'd been able to view briefly at the library. A smile curled his lips once more.

"What?"

He glanced from a mess of drywall in the corner, taking in the crowbar she'd been using to hack her way into whatever lay beyond, then he looked into her heart-stopping emerald eyes once more. They were glittering like the stones they'd spent part of today trying to find. "You," he said simply.

"What about me?"

He'd been thinking of how she'd acted at the library. "The way you were sizing up Janet."

Cassidy swatted him with the papers, and he grabbed her playfully, laughing as he hugged her to his side. "Now, you're really distracting me."

"She wasn't very pretty," Cassidy offered, grinning and settling into the pillows again.

Actually, Janet was a knockout. Tall and willowy, with washy blond hair and dark chocolate eyes. "Not nearly as pretty as you," he said honestly, then smiled. "Not smart, either."

"She has three degrees," Cassidy admitted.

"Maybe we should fix her up with your ex," he suggested with mock seriousness. "Wasn't he a brainiac?"

That made her chuckle. "Can we officiate at the wedding?"

"No. We might accidently catch the bouquet and garter."

She made a show of shuddering. "And then where would our sex life be?"

"After marriage, nobody keeps doing it," he returned. Now, c'mon, behave," he chided, changing the subject. "Did you find anything interesting in the other half of the diary?"

She sighed, her eyes turning dreamy, like a sun-touched sea in twilight. "You already read my half yourself," she said. He'd done so while she showered. "But…" Her voice trailed off and she shrugged. "I thought Lily's love affair with Mark was sweet."

"You're turning mushy on me again. I knew a romantic spirit was hiding inside you somewhere. Which part did you like?"

She shrugged. "How they met at the skating pond."

The two lovers had exchanged letters by courier for

months, and they'd dated in a way that no longer existed nowadays, sometimes accompanied by chaperones. "Lily had a wild life story, too," Dario commented. Like Gem, Lily had made a hard passage from Ireland, hoping to be united with distant relatives in Boston. She'd been earning money for the next leg of the journey when she'd met Mark O'Shea.

"Without parents, and few American connections, I guess Lily never had to explain Mark's unconventional family life."

"It couldn't have been easy to be illegitimate."

"Or to have your mother work at Angel's Cloud," Cassidy continued. "But we still don't know much about Gem's personal life, her relationship to Angelo or who fathered Mark."

Pausing, she shook her head in amazement. "Can you believe how New York was back then? Now average buildings are forty stories high. Some even higher. But just a hundred and fifty years ago, much of the city was still farmland. Carriages would have to pull over and wait for pigs to cross dirt roads."

"The bridge and tunnel people weren't even a concept," agreed Dario.

"The who?"

"People from the Burroughs, New Jersey and Connecticut. The ones who come and go through bridges and tunnels."

She grinned. "Is that what you call them?"

He laughed. "Only when I'm mean."

She rolled to her side and propped on an elbow. "You *are* mean," she teased, her eyes glinting with mischief.

"Want a spanking?"

She considered. "What have I done wrong?"

"Looking as good as you is a crime, sweetheart."

She smiled. "They were so in love," she said, speaking of Lily and Mark again. "Don't you think things must have been easier then? Simpler?"

Than lying next to a contemporary woman who could be this intimate with a man, then walk away? He sent her a long, sideways glance. "Doubtful. Gem and Lily escaped a potato famine on dirty ships in the dead of winter, then landed in countries where they didn't know anybody. At least your folks spoke English. Mine only knew Italian."

"You've got a point. C'mon," she added. "I want to read the rest."

"No spanking?" After shooting her a glance of disappointment, he began scanning the pages. Just as the portion he'd read previously, this was written in Lily Jordan-O'Shea's antiquated English and steady hand. "This section's about the wedding," he murmured, absorbing details about Lily's wedding dress. He passed the sheet to Cassidy.

"And Gem's death," he murmured a moment later, causing Cassidy to set aside the sheet, scoot closer and read over his shoulder.

"Oh, no…" Cassidy murmured. "The wedding was so perfect, but then…"

His eyes followed as she read Lily's words aloud. "…I wish my beloved mama had lived to see my wedding day. Trembling, I wait for my husband tonight, the passion of our first night so near. His steps are on the stairs! Shall I leave a candle burning? Oh, yes! Tonight I wish to see all of him. I wish to know everything about love…"

The very next entry described Gem's death, as if Lily had no time to reflect on whatever had happened. "Such an omen for our first day of marriage!" Cassidy read. "I feel such terror! The sadness of my beloved Mark overwhelms him! In one day, he's gained a wife and lost a mother. Worse, we're to keep mum about the loss of his father, too! We can say nothing!

"Dear diary, only to you can I pour out my heart. Mark's father, N.H., was in the carriage with my ill-fated mother-in-law, but none of the papers mention him, nor the retrieval of his body. As we make arrangements today for Gem, we've no idea what to do!"

Cassidy broke off. "N.H. That's got to be Nathaniel Haswell." She quickly continued. "My beloved is heartbroken. His parents both killed! We're in shock, and now we hear rumors the carriage was sabotaged, but by who?"

Squinting, Dario read on when Cassidy fell silent. Lily described Gem's funeral, and a few months after that, divulged that she and Mark were pregnant. For that reason, they'd decided to stay in Gem's old quarters for a while, where Mark had grown up.

"That was the building behind this one," Cassidy said.

Dario nodded. "It was torn down, but the property's still attached. Now it forms the backyard. The garages are there and the trash cans out back." Dario shook his head. "All the property, front and back, was rightfully Mark's."

Cassidy gasped. "Look...now Angelo gets sick."

"With some sort of flu. I never knew how he died. It sounds like there was an epidemic or something."

"He went quickly, within a month."

"And then Mark and Lily's baby was born."

Cassidy shook her head. "What a horrible series of events. Mark was just starting his apprenticeship with a lawyer, too."

"He had good schooling." Despite her life challenges, Gem had done right by her son. "His dad wanted to help him, too," Dario added, his tone causing Cassidy to lean closer. "Look," he added, his finger tracing the page.

"I told Mark to leave things be," Cassidy continued. "I told him we were strong enough to make it on our own. We were together. We didn't need the Haswells' money. The newspapers reported Nathaniel had gone missing while on a business trip to Baltimore, but we knew differently. His poor body was lost to the East River forever. No one was to ever know the truth. It was bad enough to grieve alone, we felt. Worse, since we loved Nathaniel more than his wife, Isme, and his son, Dirk. Gem's whole life revolved around him. He meant more to her than some husbands do to their wives."

Pausing, Cassidy said, "So, Nathaniel Haswell really was Gem's lover, and Mark was their son." She blew out a stunned breath. "But Lily's not using initials to hide his name now. I wonder why."

"Anger maybe," Dario suggested as he turned a page. "She's fed up, letting emotions override judgment."

Cassidy gasped. "And now Dirk has the nerve to show his face here," she read aloud. "Because Angelo's gone, Dirk's claiming Angel's Cloud is his. He found out Nathaniel was the owner, and since his father's been gone a year now, Dirk believes everything belongs to him and his mother. It's not true, though! I know it, and Mark knows it. We have it in writing. Foolishly, Mark told Dirk he could prove the house wasn't part of Dirk's inheritance.

"I begged Mark not to show Dirk the will Nathaniel left for us. Dirk has no idea he and Mark are half brothers! At least I don't think so. And Dirk's mother doesn't know, either, I'm sure! It's all so terrible. Gem and Mark were Nathaniel's family, not Dirk and Isme, but the truth can only bring grief. I'm sure of it.

"I told Mark we can work hard, raise our family. I can take in sewing as I did before, and we'll find another place to live, possibly with my relatives in Boston. Two years ago, they expected my arrival. Surely, they'll find room for all of us now, especially since the baby's come.

"But Mark wouldn't listen, and now he's ridden a mare to the Haswells' residence to confront Dirk and Isme with the will. Alone, I wait for his return, cradling our dear infant…"

Cassidy paused, whispering, "Unbelievable."

Dario offered a soft whistle. "And you said things were simpler back then."

"Now she's in Boston," Cassidy went on. "These three days I can only sit alone and tremble, reliving those dark hours. Where is my beloved? I wonder. My heart cries out…

"From the rear building, where we lived, I could see nothing that night, so I started to go to the front building, Angel's Cloud, where I could better watch for Mark's return from the Haswells'. With Angelo gone, the place was frightening, though. Empty and cold. Vandals had even broken downstairs windows, and they hadn't yet been repaired. The girls who'd worked there were scattered to the four winds. Neither Mark nor I wished to run such an establishment, of course. Without others nearby, we no longer really liked staying in the back building, either.

"Mark hoped we could sell, though, and create a future for our baby. Thinking I'd wait at the neighbor's house, where I could watch for Mark through a front window, I headed down the passageway between Angel's Cloud and the neighboring house, but when I heard horses, I stopped in my tracks. The hooves were pounding hard, then Mark's boots hit the ground. I'd recognize them anywhere. He must have looped the reins around the post, because before I could call to him, he was running up the front steps, shouting, "You will leave my wife and child alone, sir!"

"Dirk had to be following him, and Mark was making a

stir to warn me. Could Dirk have designs on our darling child? Clutching the infant tightly against my breast, I looked to the right, then to the left, unsure where to run. At eye level, a window was broken, but inside looked murky and dark, and I could see little.

"Shivering in the cold, I prayed the baby wouldn't cry, fearing we'd be discovered. 'Lily?' Mark called just as Dirk Haswell arrived, tied off his reins and ran inside. 'Are you here, love?'

"I didn't answer, nor did he wish me to do so. I knew, for I heard the high keen of warning in his voice. Peering through the broken window, I thought I saw his shadow whirl to face Dirk, as he entered, but it was too dark to be sure, the hole in the window too high.

"'My wife and child aren't here,' he said. 'Nor in the back house.'

"'Good,' replied Dirk. 'For it's with you I must settle accounts, and now they'll not see what I'm about to do! Hand over the false will. You've no right to bring lies to the door of decent people. You're Gem O'Shea's son. And like a whore's son, you're prostituting yourself, claiming to be the bastard of a respectable missing man.'

"Mark would never have confronted Dirk, but he wished to protect and provide for our child. Dirk reached, grasping the will, the parchment ripping. Mark clutched the other half, but then a knife appeared in Dirk's hand, the blade gleaming. It whooshed, slashing air, then plunged. A sharp cry sounded. It had gone into the chest of my beloved! I thought I screamed. Or the baby cried. But we must have stayed silent. Dirk's shadow didn't turn toward me. Mark ran. From some other room downstairs, I heard fighting.

"Then Dirk's voice came again—enraged and blood-thirsty. 'Or maybe what you say is the truth,' he shouted. 'If so, it will never matter. No one will know. No one cares about the son of a whore. My mother has connections. Any one of them could have loosened the wheels of your mother's carriage on your wedding night.'

"Mark's voice sounded weak. 'Is that a confession, sir?' he called.

"'As much of one as a dying O'Shea will ever get. My kind are respectable people, with reputations to uphold.'

"'By killing?'

"'No one cares if a whore dies.'

"'Your father was in the carriage.'

"'All the better. That ends his ceaseless whoring, and Mother and I are left with the philanderer's fortune.'

"'You killed them!'

"'Aye. And my mother knew the plot. We knew of what my father did here, and we knew of you. What did you take us for, O'Shea—fools?'

"I was frozen to the spot. Crashes sounded. Bangs.

"Then Dirk roared, 'Where've you gone, you bloody bastard? Where have you vanished to? I've cut you good! Maybe you're even dead by now! Do you really think you can hide from me? I'll find you, I will! Good God Almighty, I know you're here somewhere. Damnation!' Dirk blasted the air with his curses, and I heard more sounds of his mad search—furniture being tossed, armoires opened, lamps broken. He descended to the cellar and returned.

"'Oh, good, my love,' I thought to myself. 'You've hidden from this wretched scoundrel.'

"'Wherever you are,' Dirk shrieked, 'no man can sustain the wounds I've given you, so die wherever you hid. May no one ever find you, son of a whore!' Now Dirk ran to the foyer again, just a fleeing shadow. Feeling the blood drain from my face, I edged toward the street, wishing to make sure he was gone. In the lamps from the street, and from the light of the moon, I could see half the will in his hand, but it was his eyes that arrested me. They were mad and wild, with a killer's glint. As the paper slipped from his fingers, he didn't even notice. He was that far gone. He stared down at his own hands, which were covered in blood. He was holding the knife still, and blood was dripping from it! Mark's blood!

"He wiped blood on his coat front, then he sheathed the knife, and craned his neck toward the door, as if he meant to go inside once more. I prayed he wouldn't. Clearly, my love, although severely injured, had hidden from him, successfully. Hurry, I thought. Please go. I had to get inside and find Mark. I was so scared. And yet I couldn't call out. I had to think of the baby.

"Thankfully, Dirk mounted. Driving a whip to the horse's flank, he took off at a gallop, and I fled inside. Quickly, I lit a candle. 'Mark?' I screamed. 'Mark?' But there was no answer. The baby began to cry, and I cried, too. We went from room to room, but Mark truly had vanished! He was nowhere to be found! He was as elusive to me as he'd been to his possible killer! Where was he?

"Kneeling, I found blood in the floor, in the center of a room. There was a lot of it…too much…he couldn't have survived! It was as if my beloved had simply vanished. It was impossible! And I know Dirk left alone. But where was Mark?

"I retrieved the ripped half of the will and tucked it into my bodice. For the rest of my stay in that city, I feared Dirk would think of it and return. I was terrified and confused. I tore apart the house…not only Angel's Cloud, but the house we shared…and yet, I found nothing! How could a man disappear into thin air? My husband!

"And who could I tell? Where could I turn? Only Angelo had known of Mark's parentage. For years, Angelo pretended to own Angel's Cloud, to cover for Nathaniel. Only Angelo knew of the will. If I went to the constables, what would I say? That Nathaniel Haswell had been the true owner? That he'd died with his beloved, Gem, on the wedding night of their son? And that he'd left the property to the son with whom he'd had a real relationship, Mark O'Shea?

"No one would believe me. Some men had to know the truth, and yet I didn't know their identities. Besides, they'd never admit what they knew. And so now I could only sit and tremble. For the sake of our baby, I knew I shouldn't tarry another day, but I could not leave. I was blessed to have relatives in Boston who could take us in, but for a month I searched. If he were elsewhere, he knew of my relatives, and could always find me.

"Perhaps he is gone to some hiding place. Perhaps God took him straight to heaven when he was killed by the true bastard, Dirk Haswell!

"Oh, dear diary. You are my only friend. For the rest of my life, I must live with this strange secret. A bastard son, a lost heir, two murders, and my own husband vanished, most probably murdered, as well! And by a man too powerful for a person such as me to ever accuse. Surely, given the time that's passed, my Mark could not be living. Oh, may God protect me, and the only evidence my beloved was even in the world, our tiny infant..."

"Wow," murmured Dario, shaking his head. "There you have it. What a story! That infant was your ancestor, and that part of the will was passed down."

"Mark's still in the house," Cassidy said excitedly, already swinging her legs over the mattress.

Dario grabbed her hand. "Where are you going?"

Her face was flushed, and his heart swelled as he looked at her. She was so gorgeous. Her bright eyes glittered, illuminated by pinpoints of white light. "To find him," she said. "There has to be an entrance on this floor somewhere. Every night, music plays from inside the walls. We've heard it. We know there's empty space in there. Maybe Mark did, too. Maybe Dirk stabbed him, and he made it into a hidden passageway, trying to save his life."

"And died inside the walls? Lily would have known about the passageways," Dario countered.

"Obviously not. Otherwise, she'd have mentioned looking there. But she doesn't even consider there might be hidden rooms. I mean, vice cops knew about panel games, but nice girls wouldn't."

"She lived at Angel's Cloud."

"Not really. She lived in back. I wouldn't be surprised if she never entered the front building. She said she and Mark had no interest in such a business, remember? And anyway, we know Gem tried to keep Mark separated from life at Angel's Cloud, too. He was going to be a lawyer. I mean, he wouldn't want to involve his bride in…"

"Okay. I get your point. And that makes sense. But those bones, if they're really here, are over a hundred years old, so they can wait one more day. I say it's a job for tomorrow."

"No way."

"We have a deal," he reminded her.

Sighing, she slid beside him. "And now you need your sex slave for…"

He wanted to say for their own love story. For what they could share in the present, in the here and now. But then, he and Cassidy weren't going to fall in love. Their romance was ill-fated, like the one about which they'd read. "Just sex," he promised.

She rolled on top of him, her vixen eyes like Gem's, at least judging from the pictures in the Centuries of Sex Museum. "I bet you're a lot like her," he murmured.

"Who?"

"Gem."

"Is that a compliment?"

"Sure. I bet she drove Nathaniel crazy with lust."

"Is that what I'm doing to you?"

"Not yet." His hands circled her waist and he smiled. "Which is why you'd better get busy, Cassidy Case."

"Magee," she corrected.

"Magee?"

"I'm taking my maiden name back."

"Hmm." One thing was certain, she'd never be a Donato. *Cassidy Donato,* he thought, mentally trying on the name and deciding it sounded strange. Another sign they weren't destined to be together. He realized she was staring at him.

"Do you have a problem with my decision to be a Magee again?"

Shaking his head, he pulled her closer. "Given the way you make me feel," he assured, as he threaded hands through her hair once more and brought her mouth to his, "you're a rose by any name."

She laughed softly. "Are you sure *you're* not a romantic?"

14

CASSIDY UNTANGLED HER arms from around Dario's neck, then rolled onto her back in bed and blinked in the darkness. She intuited the night outside—heavy traffic, horns blowing, a glimmer of light through a far-off window—and she calculated it probably wasn't even midnight. When she heard Dario's soft snores, guilt and desire twisted, twining like two strands of the same rope.

Getting her bearings, she whispered, "Monday." Hours ago, she and Dario had made love. They'd shared a tender moment, too, recalling their first night together. Had she really thought he was Luther Matthews? And had she really pretended she was Gem, while Dario thought she was Sheila?

She chuckled, remembering her fear when she'd discovered his badge. When she recalled how he'd tracked her down, his dark eyes flashing, she felt the same strong visceral pull of physical longing that kept driving her into his arms. Half-smiling, she thought of their deal, and felt a rush of relief. If she'd actually found the jewels this week, she wasn't entirely sure she'd have kept her promise—to give up her rights to the property in exchange for the stones.

Johnny Case's past betrayals had hurt her too much. She wasn't proud of it, but she'd felt used, and she'd wanted to recoup her losses. Now it was a moot point. No jewels had been found, only passion. Shuddering, she admitted Dario had imprinted each inch of her body, and as craving filled her, she knew it wasn't going to be easy to return home tomorrow night.

Could she afford to tack a few more days onto her trip? She pictured her store—the empty cases once filled with sparkling diamonds—and just as much as she wanted to stay here, she had an urge to hop on the next plane, renew her lease, restock her inventory and reopen. Would she?

Tonight, time had passed just as quickly as the last three days, and now tomorrow's court appearance was worrying her. No doubt, that's why she'd awakened. Was she really ready to do whatever was necessary to make this house hers? No matter how it affected her lover?

Chuckie Haswell hadn't contacted her this week, and she'd put off seeing Luther, but between Lily's diary, the inventory list in Dario's possession and the half of the will that was still in Luther's safe, Cassidy thought Judge Zhang might rule in her favor once they presented all the evidence to him. Obviously, the will had been written by Nathaniel. His and Gem's murders were solved, too, even if many details would never be revealed.

Emotion welled inside her. After only a week, the house had become a part of her. She didn't know exactly when it had happened, but she didn't want to leave. Dario's parents had high hopes the sale of the old townhouse would pay for Eliana's wedding, and since the property had always been a source of Donato family pride, Cassidy hardly wanted to take that away from them. And what was Beppe going to say when he saw the damage? she wondered. Over the weekend, she and Dario had used a crowbar to break through weak spots in the wall, although they'd only found another crawl space that led to a dead end.

"Don't worry," Dario had said. "Whatever happens in the future, the owner will have to renovate."

"Unless Judge Zhang decides the house is Chuckie Haswell's." She'd paused. "Or your dad's," she'd added. "If he sells to Chuckie, Chuckie will demolish it to build condos." A week ago, she hadn't cared. She'd only wanted the highest price for herself, so she could use the money to reopen her business. Now she saw Luther's point of view. Refurbished, the old townhouse would be amazing. It would make the perfect bed-and-breakfast or antique shop.

"It feels like the last thing left of the old neighborhood," Dario had pointed out, further convincing her it could be a viable retail space. When he'd told her tales about playing here with his sisters while growing up, he'd been as good a storyteller as Granny Fiona. Little Italy had come alive with boisterous families, favorite eateries and narrow streets from which older women leaned in the windows with elbows propped on the sills, gossiping.

Dario had said he hated the new construction near the river. He feared the city's older buildings would eventually be destroyed, the historical districts mowed down, and when they'd traveled to other parts of the city, Cassidy could see why. Houses were being demolished, and the air space was being rezoned for the building of mammoth glass towers. It seemed a crime, when townhouses such as this could be so easily renovated. Cassidy envisioned a Christmas store full of ornaments, maybe a quaint tea shop and her own jewelry shop.

She started mentally decorating it again, and when she got to the top floor and began imagining an apartment, she realized she was thinking about a future for herself and a man she barely knew. She tried to cut off the reverie, but she couldn't. Maybe because Dario wasn't really a stranger.

From their first meeting, they'd fit. With Johnny, there had been months of awkward dates and social discomfort, then countless arguments as they'd tried to accept each other's flaws. Sex had never become as exciting as what she'd hoped.

Maybe she and Johnny just had different personality styles, she thought now. She'd been too inexperienced to see it, but she could imagine a younger woman loving how Johnny took control. She'd reacted with anger, though, always wanting someone more like Dario. He'd never order meals for her, or tell her how to park her car, or what to wear to a party unless it was no panties.

Nor did he have to work on having an equal partnership. He just did it. Besides, sex with him was so powerful that Cassidy knew she'd always be willing to work out relational fine-tuning. In his arms, after lovemaking, she felt a sense of well-being that she'd never experienced before.

"Why haven't you found a permanent partner?" she'd asked him at one point.

"I never found the right one."

His eyes had seemed to say Cassidy was his it-girl, and that he was considering telling her. Her heart had missed a beat, too, and belatedly, she'd discovered she was holding her breath.

Maybe that's when she'd admitted she was truly falling for him. All week, as they'd wrecked the place, she'd thought he was overlooking his father's probable reaction to the mess just to please her, but later, she'd realized Dario was as excited as she. A cop on the hunt. Like her, he'd really thought the jewels might be here, and now, maybe Mark O'Shea's body, too. Her heart swelled when she thought of his support.

Other than Granny Fiona, Dario was the only person to believe in the old stories. During their first years of marriage, Johnny had listened indulgently as Cassidy retold them, but later he'd always sided with her mother, saying Cassidy was obsessed with castles in the air.

The stories were true, though—even if she and Dario hadn't found the jewels. The old house was quiet now, but last night, the music had been ear-shattering. All the tenants had packed bags and left this morning, announcing they were staying with friends until they spoke again with Judge Zhang. On the way out, Brice Jorgensen had even delivered a speech about the tenants' association having its day in court tomorrow.

Where had the music come from? And why had she and Dario heard none tonight? Why hadn't they found the passageway inside the walls? Comparing the architectural plans had rendered nothing useful, only that extra space had to exist in the building's interior, and Dario was as disappointed as she at finding nothing. The dead-end tunnel in the basement had to be checked again, but given the layout, she and Dario had thought the opening more likely to be located on the first floor, so that's where they'd concentrated their energies.

Now she acknowledged how much she was coming to trust him. Definitely, he was different from Johnny Case. More complicated and full of contradictions. Guarded but with sensitivity. Smarter than Johnny, but not a guy who'd need to string letters behind his name to feel intelligent. He was seemingly unambitious but—as it had turned out—climbing fast through the ranks of the NYPD. Modest, too, taking little credit. Apparently, he often landed on his feet. He'd been single, and yet he was a family man, close to his parents and siblings.

At first, she'd assumed he was a philanderer, like Johnny, a man whose ego could only thrive on new conquests. Maybe Dario was more like Nathaniel Haswell, though—a one-woman man who hadn't yet found the right woman. Despite his infidelity to his wife, Isme, Nathaniel had loved Gem, after all.

Seized by an urge, Cassidy stretched a hand across the mattress, wanting to shake Dario awake. At the mere thought of passion, white-hot desire flashed into her veins, then ran like a live wire racing with electric current. Sex only, she suddenly thought. Why couldn't she keep it simple? Why did she have to want more?

Shaking her head as if to clear it of confusion, and determined not to dwell on her past marriage, she blinked once more in the darkness, but still saw nothing. Then she tensed.

Fire?

Rising an inch from the mattress, she propped up on an elbow and stared intently into the dark. She could swear she smelled an acrid, crisp scent, like leaves burning in a barrel. She shook Dario. "Wake up." Rolling over the side of the mattress, she grabbed her jeans and stepped into them. "I smell smoke," she insisted. Thrusting her feet into her shoes, she tugged on a shirt, then lifted the flashlight and ran toward the hallway.

Dario was on her heels, his steps sounding uneven behind her as he put on clothes. Something scraped on wood, probably his phone. "Fire? Are you sure?"

"Yeah."

As they ran into the hallway, they both gasped. Someone had opened the back door and cooler air gusted through it, carrying smoke. Was it one of the tenants? An intruder? Muttering an expletive as they ran toward the yard, Dario flipped open his cell and punched in nine-one-one. Cassidy turned on the flashlight, and when her feet landed on the first of the back steps, she could feel heat burn through her shoes.

She flashed the beam, then grasped Dario's arm as soon as he quit talking to the dispatcher.

"Look!"

Shaking his head, he uttered another curse as he closed the phone and shoved it into his back pocket. In the glimmer of the flashlight's beam, smoke seeped from the basement windows looking eerily yellow, tinged with blue.

"Fire trucks are on the way," he said. "I'm going back out front, to make sure they see the place."

"But can't we—" She cut off her words. Do what? she wondered, panic taking hold as her head jerked around. She saw no water, no buckets, no blankets. Realizing Dario's eye had caught something in the yard, and that he was changing the direction of his steps, she followed. Swiftly kneeling, he lifted a stick and poked a rag as she shined the light downward.

"Gas soaked," he muttered.

Horror ripped through her, and a hand instinctively covered her mouth. She spoke through her fingers. "What?"

"Somebody set the fire."

She pivoted as he rose, and he followed her toward the house. "Is there a garden hose out here anywhere?" she asked, speaking over her shoulder.

"No," he said as they entered the house.

"Who would do this?"

"Maybe it's connected to the arsons I've been working on."

Had his proximity to an arsonist made him a personal target? she wondered as they jogged down the hallway. He'd said very little to her about his cases. "You really think somebody's trying to hurt you?"

"Maybe."

"Who?" she asked again.

"Chuckie Haswell," he muttered.

"Chuckie Haswell?" What could he have to do with this?

"He's a suspect," Dario returned as they entered the apartment. She headed for the kitchen and flung open a cabinet. "As buildings have burned along the river front, Chuckie's been buying the property."

She gasped, thinking back to the previous week as she rummaged under the sink, hoping to find a bucket or pan. Anything to carry water. Had only seven days passed since she'd bought the red dress at the Pierre Hotel, meaning to wow Chuckie...seven days since she'd wowed Dario instead? "I thought you were only concerned with Chuckie because he was trying to get *this* building," she managed, but then she realized Dario was gone.

A moment later, he returned with the crowbar in hand. "Chuckie's buying other places, too," he said. "Anything near the water."

"And you think he's behind the arsons?"

"Maybe."

She tried to shake her mind free. Had she had drinks and dinner with an arsonist? A man Dario was chasing? There was no time to deal with this complication now. "No pans," she managed to say, wondering what she should tell Dario about Chuckie.

"Here." Reaching past her, Dario grabbed two rags, ran cold water over them, then shoved one into his back pocket and handed the other to her. "Just in case."

So far, the smoke was outside, and a shudder shook her shoulders when she considered the possibility of a worsening fire. There seemed nothing they could do to stop it. "Let's wait out front," she suggested.

They were almost to the door when she heard the far off sound of sirens. "They're almost here," she added in relief, her nostrils still flaring from the scent of smoke. Although they'd shut the back door, the fire was surely spreading, and with it, her fear. Suddenly, she wrenched. Her breath stilled, her senses on alert.

Dario half turned. "What?"

"Listen."

There it was again. She'd known she'd heard something! But was it really a groan coming from behind them? "Somebody's in the wall!"

Dario came closer, and she could see the sharpness of his gaze as they darted toward the back door and the smoke. "Hello!" he shouted. "Is anybody in here? Can you hear me?"

A call sounded, faint and faraway.

"How did you get in there?" Cassidy shouted in panic, her hands racing over the walls in the hallway, looking once more for any way inside. "We tried to find an opening all week," she muttered, terror gripping her. How could someone else have gotten in when they couldn't? "Who are you?"

Another call sounded, but she couldn't make out the words. It was a man, though. "He must have come in from outside," she said. "Or the basement. I smelled smoke, but I didn't hear anyone."

As Dario opened the back door again, gusting wind hit her face, and her heart dropped when she saw flames licking the ground. Tongues suddenly shot through one of the basement windows, but when she crouched, she could see no fire downstairs. "Can you get out?" she screamed. "Where are you?"

She thought she heard a voice shout, "In here!" Then maybe, "help," but she couldn't be sure. A loud bang sounded, metal on metal, and Cassidy raised her voice. "He's beating on a pipe. He's downstairs."

Turning in unison, she and Dario fled inside once more. Dario went down the basement stairs first, taking the steps two at a time. "Don't turn on the lights," he warned, "in case any electrical wiring's affected."

As the nearing sirens wailed, flooding her with relief, she shined the flashlight, suddenly glad for the wet rag soaking her backside. Pulling it from her pocket, she pressed it to her nose and lips. "Look," Dario added pointing.

Flames were visible in a far corner of the ceiling, near the windows. Smoke was seeping into the room, stinging Cassidy's eyes. The clanging metal rang out, louder.

"He's right above us," Dario said. "Coming closer."

"If he got in, why can't he get out?"

The hammering intensified. *Help.* Cassidy could swear she heard the word again. "Maybe he's stuck in the dark," she added. Clink, clink, clink. The sounds came faster. Helplessly, they listened as footsteps passed right above them. Quickly, Dario grabbed the crowbar, stepped on a chair and began tearing at the ceiling.

"Wait," she said insistently. "Listen."

Looking frustrated, Dario stopped. Another clink sounded. "It's coming from there," she added, focusing the beam. She ran toward the rubble she'd left days before, but smoke was in the passageway, and she jumped back, coughing. When another clink sounded, she gasped. He's definitely in there! A gust tunneled through the passage, clearing the smoke as Dario stepped past her. Where had the wind come from? There had to be an opening up above. Would the wind fan the fire?

The beam flailing wildly, Cassidy lunged. Somewhere overhead, wood groaned, then something snapped. Metal crashed. "A ceiling beam," she guessed.

"Help!"

The man's cry rent the air. For a second, she could have sworn the voice was familiar, but she knew that was only her imagination.

As Dario pulled the wet cloth from his back pocket and pressed it over his nose and mouth, she grabbed his arm, her heart lurching. "No! We can't go any farther inside!"

"We have to get him out."

"Don't!" she hollered, but Dario broke free, twisting from her grasp.

As his body moved away, she felt as if her heart was being torn from her chest. In the dark passage, the flashlight beam looked murky. Icy fear such as she'd never felt slid through her, but against her better judgment, she kept following. Where, though? Days before, she'd explored this tunnel but found nothing.

For a moment, when the beam no longer penetrated the smoke and dust, panic overwhelmed her. Vaguely, she was aware she was endangering her own life, but she couldn't leave Dario. If he went on alone, she might never see him again…

"Get back!" he shouted.

"No way," she returned, pressing the wet cloth harder against her lips, so she'd inhale less smoke.

As if realizing she wasn't giving up, he yelled, "You're right. It was an overhead beam. I can see a guy under it."

Gripping the flashlight more tightly, she raced forward, until the man came into her vision. He was lying facedown on a mud-and-dirt-caked concrete floor, crushed by a wooden beam that had fallen squarely across his shoulders. "Is he okay?" she managed, coming to stand next to Dario and the man.

As Dario felt the man's pulse and tried to ascertain whether moving the beam would further harm him, Cassidy's heart hammered. Her eyes tearing, she glanced around. "Can we get him out of here?"

"I'm used to dealing with trauma victims," he reminded

her as she craned her head, her eyes scanning the ceiling. Another beam had cracked, and its splintered ends angled downward. Her gaze shifted to the floor. The man was wearing a safari-style hat, jeans and a long-sleeved shirt. She couldn't even see his hair, much less his face.

As her eyes traveled toward the end of the passageway, she gasped. Something sparkled in the dirt. When she focused the beam, the twinkle intensified. Despite the danger, she rose and ran toward the spot, squinting. Thrusting down her hand, she lifted the rock. "A diamond," she muttered, studying the stone in her hand. It was at least three carats.

"What?" Dario shouted.

"A diamond!"

"You're serious?"

"Yeah."

Her heart was hammering harder, beating her ribs and making her breathless when she saw another glimmer, this one emitting red sparks. Her lips parting, she inhaled sharply, tasting smoke and gagging as she dropped to her knees and lifted another stone. "One of Gem's rubies," she whispered hoarsely. It had to be! As her free hand slid over the floor, following the sweeping beam of light, she found another ruby, this one smaller.

Apparently, the man had dropped them. But where had he found them? Suddenly, her hand stilled. Her eyes narrowed, then she moved forward at a crouching run, not caring that she was moving toward the fire. Behind her, Dario's voice sharpened. "Come back!"

She didn't listen. Everything she'd been told by Granny Fiona was true. In less than a breath, her hand closed over a burlap pouch. Probably, the man had dropped it as he tried to exit the passageway.

And now she saw why. "I knew it," she whispered.

Although aware of the danger, she still couldn't stop herself. In ten more paces, she'd reached a hole in the wall, hacked by the man lying unconscious behind her. She poked her head inside, and her eyes widened. A large room lay beyond. In a far corner, steps led upward, probably near where she and Dario had been in the closet, listening to the music.

A rat darted past her feet, making her squeal. Leaping onto a stool, it ran across the keyboard of an old player piano. It must have hit a switch, because deafening sounds of applause and dance hall music filled the air. So, that's where the sounds had come from! Stunned, she could only stare. The room was decorated with old love seats and once-plush chaise lounges, now musty and savaged by rodents and insects. In the center, wooden flooring had been extra space gouged out, and she realized the pouch had probably been inside.

"Yes." Flashing the light beam around the wall she saw discolored squares on the plaster. She gasped, recognizing the pattern. The paintings in the Centuries of Sex Museum had once hung in this room, she realized, recalling how a viewer's vision was drawn from one picture to the next, only to land on Gem's finger, which had pointed at the floor. Right where the stones had been hidden.

Maybe Angelo had put them there after her death. Or maybe Gem herself had always kept them in plain sight, for safe keeping, as the letter had indicated. Whatever the case, over the past hundred years, someone had discovered the paintings, removed and sold them, without knowing they comprised a clue. Perhaps one of the Donatos' ancestors had discovered the room, but preferred to keep it secret, in case another hiding place was needed someday.

As her fingers curled more tightly over the pouch, flames filled her vision. Just beyond the room, her eyes landed on yet another revelation…bones!

Cassidy staggered forward with one hand clutched around the flashlight, and the other around the gems. She shined the beam into a musty corner, then gagged. Pushing the pouch into the waistband of her jeans, she secured it against her belly, pressing the wet rag to her nose once more as she knelt. Through watery slits of eyes, she could see the bones were old. "Mark O'Shea," she whispered raspily, her throat aching from smoke as she reached for a fluttering slip of paper nearby, half buried in rubble. It was the missing half of the will. Handling it with care, she backed away, and was nearly to the hole in the wall when the piano stopped.

Suddenly, it was pin-drop quiet. Then she heard pounding feet overhead. "We're down here!" Dario shouted.

The firemen were upstairs. Turning, Cassidy bolted toward Dario. As he shifted the man onto his back, the man groaned, and when she came up beside him, she recognized the char-blackened face. "Johnny?" she muttered incredulously.

Dario's eyes locked with hers. "This is your husband?"

"Ex." Johnny Case looked exactly as she remembered him, with the same deceptively blond-haired, blue-eyed good looks that had once stolen her heart. Spotting a paper clutched in his hand, she snatched it, her heart aching when she saw it. It was a map, showing the opening to the interior rooms. Feeling more betrayed than ever before, she spoke between gritted teeth. "Where did you get this?"

"Everything you told me," he said between wheezing breaths, "led me to find some old papers in Massachusetts. They were supposed to be donated with Lily Jordan's diary, to the library here, but someone had kept this paper…"

"Meaning to come here and look," she finished for him. "The way you did."

Heavy boots were traipsing through the basement, and now three men thundered toward them, down the passageway. She pointed toward the fire. "In there!" Definitely, she was more concerned about the house than the two-timing traitor she'd once married.

"We need a traction board," Dario yelled toward one of them. "This guy shouldn't move anymore until a hospital checks him out."

As far as she was concerned, whatever happened to Johnny Case, he had it coming to him.

"Cassidy," Johnny began, grabbing her hand as she stood. Yanking it, she pivoted, knowing she couldn't get out of here fast enough. When she looked at his face another wave of fury coursed through her. "How long did you listen to my family stories, knowing you were going to come here and search?"

"It wasn't like that," he pleaded.

But it was. "You bastard," she whispered.

Turning, she jogged toward the end of the passageway and the basement, just as another fireman appeared. "We've got a guy upstairs," he yelled. "Found him out back. He was trying to conceal a gas can and some rags that were in the backyard. Looks like he started the fire. Can anybody here identify him?"

Cassidy barely heard. She was taking long strides up the stairs, and when she hit the upper hallway, she sprinted, brushing past more firemen. All at once, she was aware of her stinging eyes and burning lungs. Needing air, she hit the windy night and quickly doubled, sucking deep breaths into her chest. Tears pushed at her eyelids, and she batted her lashes, trying to hold them back.

Dammit, what was wrong with her? Why was she crying? She was sure she'd gotten Johnny Case out of her system a year ago. He'd used her even more than she'd previously suspected, though. He was a specialist in antiquities, and she'd come to his class, telling tales of lost jewels, which he'd used her to find. Had he ever loved her at all? She guessed she'd never really know. Now, she'd never believe anything he said.

The house was hers, though. With the will in hand, and the bones inside, which had to be Mark O'Shea's, there would be no question as to the property's rightful owner. The jewel pouch was still pressed against her belly, and now everything seemed too overwhelming.

Why was life always so bittersweet? Johnny's latest betrayal was worse than before. The jewels were found, proving her right, since she'd always believed their existence to be more than a pipe dream, but now she was supposed to give the house to the Donatos.

The tears started falling, feeling as hot on her cheeks as the fire, and she gasped as strong arms suddenly circled her waist. A second later, she was brought flush against the warm, solid front of Dario's body. Her head lolled back, and she drowned in the sensation, resting into the groove of his shoulder. Flames engulfed her, this time burning with passion. Had her lover really just saved her ex? "You shouldn't have helped him," she muttered.

Dario turned her in his arms. "I didn't know who he was."

Lifting a finger, he hooked it under her chin and used it to bring her face toward his. She looked into his eyes. "You would have saved him anyway."

Dark eyes flashed with sympathy. "Unfortunately, it's my job."

"You can't simply kill the bad guys?"

"No. But I can make sure he gets as much jail time as possible." He paused. "If you want to press charges."

Her heart squeezed tightly. The bastard had been her husband, after all, and it was tempting to let him off the hook. But he'd used her, and run her financial existence into the ground. Envisioning the empty jewel cases at her store, she managed a quick shake of her head. "I'll press charges," she whispered.

"I'll get my partner on the case," he whispered back.

"Not you?"

"I have other things to do."

She squinted, her emotions shaky as she thought about him leaving her alone tonight. Suddenly, she wanted to hug him even tighter, and tell him to stay. "Not on our last night," she managed. "What do you need to do?"

"Get in bed with you," he said.

She almost smiled. "I'd like that."

Their eyes met and held. "Somebody's got to remind you that you've met one guy who's not a class A jerk."

She could barely bring herself to believe it. "You're not?"

Slowly, he shook his head.

"What about all those girlfriends?"

"Right now, I've just got one."

Dario Donato was the best man in the whole world, she decided as her hands found both his. She twined their fingers, squeezing, and a second later, his searing lips brushed across hers.

"We'll get in bed," he promised before his lips settled on hers again. "But first we're going to have to give statements and deal with the medical examiner," he whispered. "It looks like he's just arrived."

15

"It's NOT ACTUALLY our last night together, is it?" Dario murmured in the bedroom two hours later, his throat tightening with emotion as he took off his shirt, then tugged Cassidy's over her head. His gaze briefly settled on her breasts as he trailed fingers down her belly to undo her jeans.

"I don't know," she replied honestly, wiggling out of the pants.

For once, her body wasn't distracting him. He was watching her face, instead. Outside, he'd seen her display raw emotion; it was the chink in her armor, and through it, he sensed he'd find a key that would further unlock her emotional world. "You really just wanted sex for a week?"

"Wasn't that the deal?"

Although her mask was in place again, he knew she wasn't as cavalier as she sounded. "Nobody can do what we have physically, and not feel anything, Cassidy."

"Maybe I can."

"I can't."

"Sheila," she reminded. "Janet." She was trying to look unconcerned, but her smile was forced now. "And how many others?"

"Tons. But they don't matter now." Studying her, he was sure they never would again.

She surveyed him, as if from a distance, a knowing expression in her eyes that he was starting to find irksome.

"A week with me has sworn you off all other women?"

"Maybe," he admitted. "And quit looking at me like that."

"Like what?"

"Like you summed me up the instant we met, and haven't been proven wrong yet." He paused. "I like you, Cassidy," he continued. It was an understatement, but she knew what he meant.

"You're speaking in the heat of the moment."

And she'd make any comment to undercut what he was saying about his feelings. "Not really. And you're still half-dressed."

"Not for long."

He wanted to kick himself for starting the conversation, since she obviously didn't want to hear it. "You…feel so right," he pressed on, anyway, his hands circling her waist.

"You'll forget me quickly enough."

"Like hell."

"You're only after the conquest," she ventured.

"Meaning?"

"If I say I want more, you'll lose interest."

"No way."

"Way."

"What makes you so sure?"

"The fact that I'm definitely leaving is the one thing that makes me different."

"Not true."

"What's different then?"

Your hair, your eyes, your face. The fact that he knew he'd never get tired of her, but whatever her effect on him defied analysis. "You keep me on my toes."

"Exactly. And if you knew you had me, that would change."

Biting back a curse, he damned Johnny Case for what he'd done to her. Now that he'd seen the other man, his animosity had intensified. "At least your ex is in a cell tonight."

"Hopefully for longer."

She was prosecuting him. That meant she'd let go of past feelings. Once this evening's events came to light, her mother would start siding with her daughter instead of Johnny, as well, and that would be good for Cassidy. At the station, Pat was questioning Tim Jones, the man the firemen had discovered in the yard. Tall and skinny, with a shaved head, Tim had sported an ominous tattoo around his neck that was fashioned to look like barbed wire. Apparently, at age eighteen, he already had a long rap sheet and some of the arrests had involved arson.

Dragging a splayed hand over his hair, Dario glanced toward the closed drawer of the bedside table, which held the jewels, then he turned his attention to Cassidy again. Love would heal her, he told himself, not recrimination, which was what Johnny had dished out in hopes of better controlling her.

"If it's just sex you think you want," he found himself saying with a reasonableness he didn't truly feel, "then I'll be happy to give it to you."

Now she sounded flirtatious. "You *will?*"

"You bet."

"Only until tomorrow," she reminded.

He nodded, but he knew he'd use whatever he could to reduce her to putty in his hands, including a body she clearly found irresistible. Already, he was imagining pushing her to the limit, making her plead with him, begging for more. Dammit, she hadn't done anything wrong, but they were both being punished, he decided now. Johnny had messed with her mind, and now she didn't trust herself to find something better with another man. It wasn't fair to either of them.

She was so perfect, too. Every inch of her body was mouthwatering, and now Dario was craving her like a dangling sweet treat. "The panties," he whispered, giving up on any talk about emotions, his eyes burning a trail from her face downward, lingering on her breasts before studying a triangle of blue silk. Beneath the patch, he could see a faint outline of bunched curls, and scents just as tangled were rising from her body, making his nostrils flare. "Come hither," they seemed to whisper.

She shot him a coy look. "The panties?"

"Take them off."

"Like this?" His heart hammered as she stepped from his grasp, hooked a long red nail inside the scrap of material and drew it downward. As it slid over her thighs, it looked like a tiny blue wave cresting over creamy skin, and as he watched, he felt his chest tighten. The material was as light as wind, and by the time she tossed it away, he was breathless. Already, he was envisioning touching her, toying with the moist curls she'd just uncovered, which were within reach. Wet, slick and tight, he imagined how she'd feel closing around his finger, how her lips would go slack as she took the pleasure. A pang coiled at his groin, pulling him close, as if by a magnetic force.

"There," she whispered. "Does this work for you?"

Hell, no, he wanted to say. He wanted more than her body. Why couldn't she say something stupid and girlish and flowery, for once? So many other women had flattered him, experienced heartbreak when he'd ended relationships, and now he was on the other side of the fence. "It'll do," he said, the roughness of his own voice surprising him.

"Liar," she said, offering a tremor of a smile. "You love it."

And she was right. He did. As much as he hated to admit it, he'd almost liked seeing her cry earlier, too, since it brought out his protective instincts. While holding her, he'd felt like she needed him, and like he was becoming the man he was meant to be. He wanted her to stick around, maybe even move here. He wanted to talk about it, at least.

His eyes skated over her body. "Haven't you ever started to want more?" he couldn't help but ask against his better judgment.

"Obviously. I married Johnny."

"Screw Johnny. I mean, now."

"Yes and no."

Frustrated, Dario suddenly wanted to hit something, maybe put a fist through a wall. A man could only take so much. Cassidy Case Magee was starting to make him wish he was in the precinct gym, wearing boxing gloves, instead of watching her strip. *That* was definitely unlike him.

"What are you thinking?" she asked.

The million-dollar question. "That usually naked women turn my head."

"I'm not?"

"Sure you are," he returned, knowing pounding a punching bag would never get her out of his system. "But you're going to have to let somebody care about you again someday," he added, closing an inch between them. The instant he molded his hands over smooth hips again, his anger vanished and he was reveling in how she felt—all fine silk, soapy water and polished marble.

"Johnny never cared about me, not really."

So, she understood that. "Other people might." Dario saw people harmed by vice every day—whether by greed, lust or plain old selfishness. "I don't want you to be a victim. Don't let a guy destroy your life."

"Like most women?"

He arched a brow, thinking about how her father had left her and her mother. "Men can be jerks," he agreed. "But my mother did all right." Beppe Donato was the kind of husband who remembered birthdays and sweated his daughter's wedding. Cassidy's ex had been like a steamroller, though. He'd flattened a life Cassidy had tried to build, and even now, the man was unrepentant.

She was studying him, her eyes suddenly glittering like the stones she'd found tonight. "And the someone meant to love me would be Dario Donato?"

It was hard to tell whether or not she was mocking him. "Why not?"

"It seems unlikely."

If Cassidy let him, Johnny Case would move right back into her life and rip it apart again. She had no reason to believe Dario could be different. "Oh, you've got my number."

"The quintessential ladies' man."

"Like I said, there's only one woman right now."

For a long moment, he stared into the liquid slits of her eyes, fringed by dark, spiky lashes, then he leaned to nuzzle her neck, marveling at everything that had come to light earlier. All the jewels on the inventory list had been accounted for—diamonds, rubies, emeralds and pearls.

He'd started to ask Pat to drop by and take the stones to the precinct for safekeeping, but Cassidy had begged him not to, arguing that she wanted to be alone as soon as possible, after the medical examiner left, saying he'd return again in the morning. Since Dario wanted to be alone with her, too, he hadn't been about to argue. Besides, she'd said he could defend them against any robbers who might attack them before morning, which was true. Still, he'd given in against his better judgment, only because he wanted to be back in bed....

Angling his head farther down, he swept his hair against her chest, burrowing between her breasts, then he swirled his tongue around a stiffening tip. Catching the nipple between his teeth, he held it, tugged, got hard when he heard her heart thudding beneath his ear. It hammered wildly as he flicked his tongue. Her hips swayed gently forward, the provocative brush of her belly making him catch fire.

"Touch me, baby," he ordered, groaning as slender fingers threaded through his hair, massaging his scalp. He pulled his mouth to her breast once more, and as the pad of his tongue lapped a distended tip, her other hand traveled lower, scraping his jeans zipper with a sharp thumbnail. Flattening her palm against his bare belly, she glided it lower until he felt pressure where he most wanted it. He gasped, his breath turning ragged as she began exploring him through the denim, stroking the thickening ridge. Within a moment, he was sure he was going to burst the seams. Making an O of his lips, he exhaled a whistling sound, blowing on a nipple he'd lathered with his tongue, soliciting a shiver.

"That's right," he muttered thickly, his eyelids slamming shut as he rose to full height, his hands settling on her silken hip to steady himself as his eyes rolled back in ecstacy. "If you insist on making this our last night together, Cassidy, then—"

His voice cut off as her fingers clenched around him, squeezing his stiffened length. As blood engorged him, fiery liquid heat shot into his lower belly, swirling like a whirlpool. Waves of fire washed over him, and his skin prickled as a guttural male sound of need lodged in his throat. Something inside him took flight. Undeniable yearning claimed his whole being, pushing his hands downward, around her backside.

"Then?" she said huskily.

He'd completely forgotten what he'd been saying. "If you're leaving tomorrow," he repeated, "then you'd better make it good tonight."

"Right back at you."

"It'll be a night you won't forget," he promised.

Earlier, he'd dressed so quickly that he hadn't worn briefs, and now, as she tugged down the zipper, every inch of bliss felt like torture. As the tab hit bottom, Dario gasped once more, bursting through the opening of his jeans, released from the constraints of fabric.

"C'mon," he muttered nonsensically, not even sure what he wanted her to do next, only relieved that he was this much closer to getting what he needed...what he had to have. For a second, he didn't even blame Johnny Case for the way he'd mistreated her, not that he'd ever behave that way. But Cassidy brought out the animal in a man. Dario wanted to tell her, but he couldn't find words to describe the craving. It gnawed at him like an addiction and made him feel wild.

She was pushing his jeans over his hips, exposing a burning erection. "Let's get you out of your pants," she whispered, playing Gem O'shea once more.

"Is this what you want?" he asked throatily, although he knew it was because of her shallow breaths and the shaky tremors in the hopelessly soft hands now banking his bare hips.

As he stepped out of his jeans and kicked them away, her hands were on him again—silk on silk. A breath sucked through her teeth, sharply audible as she fisted torturous fingers around him, gripped tightly, then moved her hand like a piston.

Something raw hit the back of his throat. It felt like sand

or dust. A pang of greed twisted his groin, and he bit his lower lip in agony, or bliss, he'd never know which. Either way, he tasted blood, and to soothe the wound, he licked his lips. In the next instant, they crushed down on hers.

As her tongue dampened like a healing salve, he tried to be gentle, but her touch was excruciating. Savagely, he responded, pulling her head back. Hot lips tempted, then trembled, parting as his tongue darted. Licking as fast as flames, he could swear he saw red-and-orange forks of fire. Blue hues hazed in the periphery of his vision as her tongue glided along his.

Ready for branding, his lips marked hers. Never breaking their kiss, he urged her two steps to the bed. As her back hit the mattress, rough, greedy hands slipped under her knees, and he raised her legs, urging her to part for him.

"A condom?" she asked shakily.

It was too late. Slick moisture covered him as he pushed each greedy inch inside, muttering, "I'm healthy. So are you. I want it this way."

She must have, too, because she only caught the rhythm, moving in synch. Her first orgasm came an instant later, and his mind blanked as nails dug into his shoulders, scratching a path all the way down his back to his buttocks. Her next took longer, and he reveled in every breathtaking second of the wait. She was shivering, shuddering as darkness overtook them.

Love was blending into love. Arms and legs tangled. Taut nipples brushed and tongues meshed. Perspiration was turning their skin slick and they slid over each other as if lathered in soap. He didn't care where he ended and she began…didn't care when he came still buried inside her. Deep down, maybe he wanted to make her pregnant. That way, she couldn't leave him tomorrow. She'd be forced to deal with him forever….

They drifted. He wasn't sure, but they must have slept for some time. Their hips were still joined when he awakened. As she strummed slender fingers down his spine, he began to move again. Every inch of his body met every inch of hers. Time slowed. Only his hips moved. She brought her knees up once more, rocking her in the cradle of his thighs. The whole house was silent, except for sounds that belonged to their shared darkness—soft whimpers, panting breath.

"Is that good enough for you?"

For their last night? No, he thought in protest, letting his hips do the answering, driving harder against her, deepening his thrusts. The pure silk of her legs wrapped around his back then, those shivering thighs bracing against him as her ankles locked near the small of his back. Digging in her heels, she brought him closer still.

Everything went black when he felt her come again. In that instant, a thousand women passed in his mind, their faces flitting in an endless array. Tall, dark beauties in suits. Petite blondes in sports clothes. Trashy temptations wearing fishnet stockings and spike heels. Then he saw Cassidy again, wearing that gorgeous red dress. Cassidy...beneath him now, her skin flowing under him like water.

Gasping, his hips went wild as he exploded. He was lost, coming and coming, sure the heady sensation of release would never end. No one had ever felt this good. Instinctively, he knew no other woman would leave a mark like hers.

When he caught his breath, he whispered, "Tell me you'll change your mind and give us more than a week." When she didn't respond immediately, he covered her mouth, kissing her, and although she'd drained him, he thrust his hips again, as if to prove they should never be apart.

"Maybe we can work something out," she whispered back.

But he wanted everything nailed down right now, all the specifics discussed, a contract signed and sealed. Damn if he'd let this woman walk out of his life, he thought. Still, relief filled him. She was willing to continue seeing him. He rolled, dragging her on top of him and hugging her tightly as her legs dangled down the lengths of his.

As he began to drift once more, he was vaguely aware of the house. It was as if, after finding the stones, the will and what was probably Mark O'Shea's body, the house's hidden recesses had shut down for the night, like a shop closed for buisness. Having no more secret tales to tell, its ghosts had vanished. No skittering feet had activated the old player piano concealed in the walls, as if out of respect for whatever was happening between him and Cassidy. The past was past, for the house and maybe for them. A smile curved his lips as he burrowed against her warm body....

Or pillow, he suddenly thought.

As he rubbed his cheek against something as soft as cotton, he smelled floral-scented detergent mingled with Cassidy's skin. Rolling, he blinked and glanced around. He was alone in bed. It was morning! Grabbing his cell from the nightstand, he opened it, checked the time and sat up. "Eight-fifteen?"

Court was in forty-five minutes. He had to shower and dress. Last night's intensity had knocked him out cold. Now...

"Cassidy?" Her bag was gone. He was on his feet in a flash, his worst fears realized as he strode through the apartment. *She* was gone. Surely, she wouldn't miss court, he thought. Then the probable truth hit him. Yanking open the bedside drawer, he stared inside. The will, the inventory list and jewels were missing. She was going to be in court, all right, making sure his father didn't get the property.

"Damn," he whispered. Had he really expected her to

keep her end of their crazy deal? To give him sex, if he let her search for her beloved stones? It had seemed like an adventure, an inconsequential game with the sexiest woman he'd ever laid eyes on.

"Pat would have a field day with this." Countless women had turned his head, but it had taken Cassidy to airlift him and spin him around until he felt like he was inside a tornado. By rights, she was supposed to give the property to Dario now— or to his father. And of course, she'd decided against doing so.

For a moment, he merely stood in the middle of the room, unsure of what he felt. The deal had been crazy, sure, and her enthusiasm had captured his imagination. Now he felt... wistfulness, maybe. Defeat. He felt the way he did when a perp got away, as if the good guys were losing ground, and the bad guys were destined to win in the end. Johnny Case had so disrupted Cassidy's ability to trust that she'd become untrustworthy herself. She wanted payback, but it wasn't Johnny she'd hurt, it was Dario. And herself.

He sat on the edge of the mattress, wishing her scent wasn't everywhere. Every breath was pure torment. Imprisoned in his lungs, he was sure it would haunt him for years, just the way ghosts had seemed to haunt the house. Damn if the supposed ghosts hadn't turned out to be Cassidy's ex and a bunch of mice. And now, the only thing left of her was going to be the tapes he'd made of their first night together.

The imprint of her head was still on the pillow. White on white, it was only an indented mark, like footprints in the snow. She'd left without a word of explanation. How could she? Lifting the cell, he flipped it open and punched in her number.

"Cassidy," he said when her voice mail activated, "You're gone, but I imagine you plan to see me in court in less than an hour. Since you've got the stones, both halves of the will and the inventory list, you'll have no trouble making Judge Zhang rule in your favor. I'm a big boy. I can take it. But my family's tended this property for years. It was ours. If you found the stones, you were supposed to give the property to us. So, when we see each other in court, let's pretend we never met."

Abruptly, he hit the off button, ending the call. At least he'd salvaged his pride. With Cassidy gone, it was all he had left.

16

DARIO GLANCED TOWARD the courtroom door, not knowing what he'd do if Cassidy walked in. When his eyes caught Eliana's, she hunched her shoulders in an exaggerated shrug. She glanced toward Judge Zhang, then at Dario again, lifting her hands. "Where's Pop?" she mouthed. "Ma was supposed to meet me, but she didn't show. We were going to go over last-minute details about my dress. The hem's too short. It just doesn't look right, and she picked up your tux, by the way."

It was hardly the right time to discuss the wedding. Leave it to his big sister not to notice he was heartbroken. He turned his attention back to Judge Zhang. The events of the past week had been divulged, and now the judge was about to make his final determination about the property's ownership. Usually, the judge took his time, but today the proceedings had moved quickly due to Luther Matthews who was talking at a fast clip. As much as Dario needed to hear every word, and as much as his mind kept straying to Cassidy, he found himself frowning at Eliana. "Did you call Ma's cell?"

"I got her voice mail."

"And Pop?"

"He said they were fine, and on their way, but he wouldn't tell me anything else."

The motions of Eliana's hands communicated her anxiety. Ever since her engagement, she'd started gesticulating in a way that would showcase the rock on her left hand. Now she seemed to have forgotten the ring completely. "I hope they're okay."

So did Dario. His parents were in good health, and while he hated to think something bad could have happened to one of them, they were usually punctual. "You did talk to Pop?"

"Yeah. And he sounded fine."

"You still want me to stick around?" whispered Pat, who was on the other side of Dario.

"Might as well," Dario said under his breath. "We've got Chuckie Haswell in our sights."

"He's got a helluva lawyer," continued Pat, who'd been up all night working the arson case. "I'll give him that much."

Tim Jones had admitted he'd been hired to start fires, not only at the Donato's property, but all over town. When questioned, the middleman who'd hired Tim confessed the payee was Chuckie Haswell. Shortly afterward, around six, Pat had turned up two witnesses who'd seen Chuckie talking to the middleman, and by seven, Chuckie had been arrested. Within the hour, however, he'd posted bail, but that wouldn't matter in the end. With the information they had, Dario figured they'd get a conviction.

Still, Chuckie had the nerve to enter the courtroom and continue arguing that the very property he'd tried to burn last night was rightfully his. Probably, in his twisted imagination, he'd convinced himself it was. That meant he had the right to do whatever he wanted with it, including destroy it. Johnny Case had turned out to be even more devious. Despite the statement Cassidy had given the police last night, Johnny claimed she'd told him the property was hers, and that he could let himself in to search it.

Pat whistled softly. "Cassidy's not even here."

Dario could have kicked himself. On his way to the court-house, he'd told Pat the whole story over the phone, and of course, Pat had told Eliana. His partner and sister were as nibby as the gossiping women in their old neighborhood. "It was a week-long thing," Dario muttered, wishing his chest didn't feel quite so tight. A part of him wanted to leave the courtroom right now, find Cassidy, and demand an explanation. Last night, she'd said they could work things out, but then she'd disappeared.

He tried not to berate himself, but he should have known she was lying. He was a cop, supposedly an expert in deviance. Why hadn't he guessed she was using him all along?

"You let her rip apart Pop's property?" whispered Eliana in disbelief, shaking her head. "He's going to kill you. The woman must have really done a number on you, little brother."

"Mmm-hmm," he said under his breath. Briefly, he shut his eyes, and his mind filled with images of her. "She was supposed to give us the property," he reminded, "if she found the jewels."

Eliana snorted. "And you believed that?"

Yeah. He had. But had Cassidy really just played him? Pushing away his emotions, he shrugged. He wanted to call her, but his pride wouldn't allow it.

"She must be gorgeous," offered Eliana.

"Sexier than Sheila Carella," agreed Pat.

"Like I said, it's over," Dario muttered, and now Cassidy was the last thing he wanted to discuss. She was probably on a plane by now, or in South Carolina unpacking. She'd left Dario and let Luther Matthews do all her remaining dirty work. He was making a good job of it, too, as if he couldn't get the property signed over to Cassidy fast enough. He'd even brought a museum guard, pictures of the jewels, and a handwriting expert to testify to the will's authenticity. Not to mention the inventory list, which was really the property of the NYPD.

How had she accomplished so much in such a brief amount of time? Had she even thought of him during that time? Of how he and his family would be affected by her claiming the property? Of how hurt he'd feel in the end?

But no…her only thought had been for herself. She was as selfish as her ex. And Luther Matthews. Every few seconds, the man's eyes were darting toward the door, as if to say there were a million places he'd rather be.

"Here," Luther said, pacing in front of Judge Zhang's bench. "As you can see, we also have the complete will, written by Chuckie Haswell's ancestor, Nathaniel Haswell. Clearly, the property was a gift to Gem O'Shea. Because they died together, she was never able to take possession, but it was definitely meant for her, and in turn, for her son."

Pausing, Luther shot Chuckie a long look. "A man most probably murdered by Dirk Haswell."

"That's absurd," countered Chuckie. "You can hardly believe Lily Jordan's diary."

"Maybe not," returned Luther. "But the will has been authenticated." Gem O'Shea's jewelry, which was inventoried by the New York Police Department over a century ago, has been retrieved, also, and the judge has pictures. Everything has been accounted for. Surely the bones found this morning must be Mark O'Shea's."

The medical examiner had returned to finish last night's job just as Dario was leaving the house. In the interest of truth, Dario had passed along the information. Just because Cassidy had burned him, didn't mean he was going to turn the tables and do the same to her.

"On behalf of the tenants association," Brice Jorgensen put in, "I'd like to say that we're glad to finally have the matter cleared up. Obviously, something very strange was happening in that building. Now, whatever the outcome, we hope we'll be able to stay in our homes until our leases are up—"

"Duly noted, Mr. Jorgensen," said Judge Zhang.

"Judge—" Pat dragged a hand over his buzz-cut red hair. "Once more, I feel compelled to point out that Mr. Haswell was arrested this morning on charges involving the attempted arson of the property in question."

"They're trying to frame me in order to get my property," Chuckie snapped. "It belongs to me. I assure you I'm being set up by the police! Officer Donato's father is the one who—"

"Careful, Mr. Haswell," the judge interjected. "Accusing law enforcement officers of wrongdoing while in a court of law isn't advisable." He turned to Luther. "So, Mr. Case did not make it to town, as expected?"

"Ms. Case. And yes, she did…" Pausing, Luther sent Dario a glance, making Dario wonder how much he'd been told about the affair. Whatever the situation, Luther probably knew the truth regarding Cassidy's real feelings for Dario, if she had any. "Ms. Case couldn't make it this morning. She sent me on her behalf, however, and the papers are in order, as you can see. I'm hoping we can have a speedy determination, since it's a very busy day for me."

"Wait a minute," interjected Chuckie. "I admit I was arrested this morning, but the behind-the-scenes machinations regarding this property have been unbelievable. Ms. Case came to town last week, all right. She called and asked to meet for drinks at the Pierre Hotel. When I arrived, she was dressed to the nines, in a bright red dress and spike heels. The works," Chuckie clarified.

Dario's body tensed as he registered the betrayal, now realizing he'd never wondered where Cassidy had been the night he'd tracked her to the hotel. He'd been so blown away by how she'd looked in the dress that he'd only asked in passing.

"She said the Donatos were a wild card," Chuckie continued. "She said she didn't care about the museum's interest in the property, either, in spite of what Mr. Matthews is saying now. She wanted money. Just like me, she wanted the best business deal, and I was impressed. She promised she'd sell to me if I helped her stake her claim. Like everybody said, she wanted inside the house, to look for the jewels, which she found, but she didn't tell me about them when I met her. She told me she wanted inside the building for sentimental reasons."

He flashed a sharklike smile. "But that woman doesn't have a sentimental bone in her body. It was all about getting what she wanted. She'd do anything for it, too. Drinks led to dinner…"

Judge Zhang considered. "And then?"

Chuckie looked torn. "And then dinner led to her room upstairs."

"That's a lie," Dario couldn't help but mutter, suddenly hating the weakness Cassidy Case Magee had revealed in him. He was hardly proud of the anger flashing along his nerves, but when he imagined a slimy weasel like Chuckie Haswell pawing Cassidy, he felt positively sick.

"How do you know?" asked Chuckie.

"I was there that night."

Chuckie was loving every minute. "Before or after me?"

Dario shook his head in disgust. "You're an animal, Haswell."

Chuckie threw up his hands, as if to say this was only

further proof the NYPD was out to get him. Dario barely noticed. He was still trying not to imagine the worst—Cassidy clinking champagne flutes with Chuckie, hanging on to his every word, undressing him in her room at the Pierre, just the way she'd undressed Dario.

He thought back, but he could remember no trace of the other man in the room that night—no scent of cologne, or sight of a lost sock or tie. Definitely, he hadn't smelled a man on her. But then, the red dress had completely captured his attention.

Vaguely, he was aware Judge Zhang was speaking to him.

"Are you sure you don't wish to retract your statements, Officer Donato?"

Hell, yes, he wanted to say. He wanted to retract the whole past week. Instead, he'd corroborated the truth—testifying the stones had been found on the property, as well as the other half of Nathaniel Haswell's will. Abruptly, he shook his head, knowing what determination the judge would have to make. "No, sir. Everything I said is true." And by virtue of that, he might as well have signed over his pop's property to the woman who'd used his body for a week, then vanished.

"All things considered, I'm naming Cassidy Case the sole proprietor of 67 Anthony Street," said Judge Zhang. "All tenants will remain in residence until the end of their leases, in accordance with New York law."

Eliana gasped, and without a word, Dario slid a hand under her elbow and began steering her from the room. "We'd better get out of here," he muttered. "I can't vouch for what I'll do to Chuckie Haswell in a one-on-one. Luther, either."

"Ditto," said Pat, who took up the rear as the three headed down a center aisle and into the hallway.

"Meet you outside," Eliana said. "I've got to find the little girls' room."

"Me, too," said Pat.

"You might get arrested," warned Eliana.

"Thanks for the tip. I'll use the little boys' then."

Dario kept going, wanting to avoid Chuckie and Luther, but mostly because he needed air. Using his shoulder, he pushed through brass revolving doors, and then the air hit him hard. While it was sweater weather, the wind felt gusty and carried the first sharp, acrid taste of winter. Just as he sucked a breath deep into his lungs, he could swear he smelled her. Her scent pooled, eddying low in his belly. He turned.

"There you are!" she exclaimed.

She was right behind him. Anger surged when he saw her face, and vaguely, he thought she had no right to look so damn beautiful—her eyes narrowed against the wind, her cheeks pale. Just by surprising him, she was making him see red. He'd been here, after all. But where had she been?

"Did you talk to him?" she asked breathlessly.

"Who, Luther? Chuckie? Oh, yeah," he said acidly, not bothering to let her answer, his annoyance intensifying when he saw the feigned, innocent expression. "You look like you've seen a ghost," he added, and suddenly, he guessed she had. "So, you didn't plan on running into me again, did you?"

"Of course I did. I was looking for you. What's going on?"

As if she didn't know. "You didn't get my message?"

"What message?"

So, she was really going to play dumb. "Court's over, doll. You got everything you wanted. The stones. The property. And if you hurry, you might catch your friend, Chuckie Haswell, before he goes back to jail to keep your ex-husband company."

She blinked as if he were a stranger. Before he thought it through, he'd grasped her shoulders. Almost immediately he emitted a soft, telltale breath, almost a gasp, his fingers loosening their grip. Suddenly, he was both stroking her sweater and damning himself for it, knowing he couldn't afford to let her reopen the wound she'd gouged in his heart. Against his will, he ran a hand upward, along the side of a smooth, silken cheek. Windswept hair across the back of his hand—red on white, like a rose on a sheet— and it felt as astonishingly soft, just like a petal.

"I tried to get here," she said weakly, still seemingly breathless, as if to prove she'd run all the way here.

"But you didn't quite make it, right, Cassidy?"

"Look," she began. "I—"

"Whatever you did, I don't care," he murmured, and he really didn't, not anymore. But he had to kiss her again. Just once. Angling his head closer, he paused before their lips brushed. Her breath was mingled with his, carrying a mint scent. He hovered, committing the sensation to memory, knowing he'd never feel it again.

"Sex for a week," he whispered, his voice gravelly. "That was the deal, right? And you played it well, Cassidy. Didn't you? All the way to the hilt. You're a real pro. In the end, you put Gem to shame—"

She tried to step back, looking as if she'd been stung, but he tightened his grip, holding her fast. "Chuckie said he enjoyed that gorgeous red dress every bit as much as I did, and Luther argued your case brilliantly."

She was shaking her head. "No! I only told Luther to keep the—"

He used a finger to silence her. "I want to remember you the way you really are."

"How's that?"

"Sexy as hell. And totally out for yourself."

"That's not true," she said, shaking her head.

"I won't forget the way you pretended to be upset about Janet and Sheila. Meantime, you were meeting Chuckie… Luther."

"You can't believe that."

Now she was going to deny the obvious, exactly like Johnny Case. "Your ex screwed you over," he continued, "and now, you're passing along the goods. But don't worry," he said, his voice lowering, "I can take it. I see this every day at work. What goes around comes around. Call it what you will. Divine Karma. Tit for tat. Whatever the case, I want you to know…you're the best " He trailed a finger down her cheek. "I enjoyed every minute we spent together." Nothing would detract from that.

"You've got everything wrong."

"That's what Johnny said last night, wasn't it?" He flashed a smile that didn't meet his eyes. "And I guess you learned that from him, too."

"You think I was with Chuckie?"

"I know you were. But you can ask your friend, Luther. I'm sure he'll fill you in on the details when you pick up your precious stones."

"I'll do that," she managed to say.

"Meantime," he began, leaning another inch toward her lips, "this is goodbye."

He kissed her then, and beneath his, her lips felt cool and firm, parted more in surprise than passion. Slowly, he increased the pressure, already feeling the heat course between them. If one more second passed, instinct would take over. Already, he felt compelled to pull her against him, wrapping his arms tightly around her waist. He wanted to rip off her clothes, unbutton her jacket, reach inside, and strip off whatever was beneath. Instead, he broke the kiss abruptly, pivoted and headed down the courthouse steps.

For a moment, he heard nothing. Then high heels. She was running after him. Right before she reached him, he hit the lowest step, raised his hand to hail a taxi and glanced over his shoulder. Something in his expression stopped her in her tracks. Her own eyes were gorgeous, a jewel-like green that sparkled with uncertainty. Hair blew wildly around her face, the red strands whipping her cheeks. Her jaw slackened, and her lips parted as if she was about to speak.

He didn't let her. "Stay away from me," he said as a cab pulled to the curb. He got in, slammed the door and gave the address of his apartment in Battery Park, which he hadn't seen in a week. It was an apartment that, thankfully, would carry no reminders of Cassidy Case Magee. She'd never even been inside it before, just as he'd never seen the interior of her home in South Carolina. This seemed further proof that the week had been only a mirage. A passing indulgence. A sexual encounter taking place in a moment out of time.

He didn't look back.

"YOU ARE NOT EVEN MY SON," Dario's mother chided a week later, in the hallway of the church where Eliana was getting married. Wearing a grim expression, as if to say all her children were married now, except for her wayward, youngest son, she brushed at the shoulders of his tux, smoothing imaginary wrinkles.

"This could be you, going down the aisle, Dario," she continued. "But no. You have to follow in the footsteps of Angelo. Thank God—" his mother crossed herself "—that terrible place has finally left our hands for good. Now, maybe you'll find a nice girl."

Taking advantage of the narrow window, Dario leaned

quickly and kissed her cheek, hoping doing so would make her change the subject. "You look beautiful, Ma." And she did, dressed in a gold dress, similar to those worn by the bridesmaids.

"Humph. Don't distract me. Maybe your luck is about to change. Maybe you won't send away another girl who was going to be my daughter-in-law."

Dario groaned. "Cassidy Case wasn't going to be your daughter-in-law, Ma."

"Magee," his pop corrected. "And that's not how it seemed to me when she came to meet us last week," his pop said, sidling next to his mother.

"She snowed you two, just the way she did me," Dario offered gruffly, although he knew it was lie. Later, he'd discovered he was in the wrong. Cassidy had been late to court because she'd been trying to strike a compromise with Beppe. While Dario had been sleeping, she'd been busy approaching his folks with a plan to start a commercial venture in the townhouse, comprised of small boutique-style shops.

They'd reached an agreement to manage the property jointly, too, and she'd hoped to work out an arrangement that might help the museum, also. Luther had double-crossed her, arguing for her to get the property, when she'd asked him to make sure Judge Zhang understood she wasn't intent on keeping it. Later, after it was hers, and she'd refused to sell to Luther in fury, it had become clear that he'd really had her best interest at heart, and Dario guessed she'd forgiven the curator.

Now, no one knew what would happen. Cassidy's plan had been a better proposition than if the Donatos had been awarded the property, and then sold, since the house would have continued to produce revenue for years to come. In addition to showing how the venture would pay for Eliana's wedding, Cassidy had talked to his folks about keeping space available for her living quarters, which would provide in-house security, as well.

The impromptu meeting had run on too long, then Dario's folks and Cassidy, traveling in separate cabs, had gotten stuck in traffic. Now his parents were convinced Cassidy had meant to include Dario in the deal, and that she'd imagined living with him, once she was in New York, with an eye to marrying him.

Of course, that's what his folks *would* think. They loved him. Good Italians, they wanted their kids married off. And as far as they were concerned, every female in Manhattan had been chasing Dario since birth. Cassidy hadn't, though. He was the one who'd tracked her down and inserted himself into her life while she was trying to heal from a relationship.

His stomach flip-flopped when he recalled the look of hurt on her face. He'd left four voice mails during the week, hoping to apologize, but she'd never returned the calls. Anyway, she was back in South Carolina now. A lawyer had contacted Beppe, saying Cassidy had changed her mind. The deed was Beppe's, in accordance with what she'd called "an undisclosed deal between myself and Dario." Now the Donatos could do whatever they wanted.

Legally, it had been accomplished overnight, leaving Dario's mind reeling with if-onlys. If only he hadn't brought up Chuckie or accused her of lying. But he had, hadn't he? In the end, he'd been the one without any trust. Always, when he awakened now, he'd imagine she was naked beside him, then he'd recognize it was only a lingering dream.

"I'll see you inside," he said abruptly to his mother. "I'd better line up with the other ushers, and Eliana needs you more than I do right now, Ma."

"I already said goodbye," his mother said, tearing up. She stretched on tiptoes, kissed his cheek, then kissed his father. "It's time for me to go in. I'll see you gentlemen at the altar." She quickly patted Dario's shoulder before starting down the aisle.

At least the past week had been a madhouse, Dario thought, as he pushed open the door to where the ushers were lining up, his father close behind him. His chest got tight when he saw Pat. "Hey, buddy. You're next in line, after Eliana."

"Not until spring. Karen just set the date."

"Congratulations."

The next few minutes passed in a haze. The week really had been crazy. Eliana's dress hem had to be lengthened at the last minute, and one of the bridesmaid's shoes had been dyed the wrong color. He must have been completely out of it, he realized, seeing a man from their social circle among the other ushers. He could have sworn he wasn't a member of the wedding party, but then, he'd been so caught up with Cassidy....

As his turn to walk down the aisle neared, he glanced at his father, who was preparing to give away Eliana. As Pat preceded him, to walk with Karen, Dario couldn't help but wonder if he was ever going to join the ranks of his married friends. Probably not, he decided. He didn't even want sex at the moment, not unless it was with Cassidy.

Eliana's wedding planner, a woman who'd done little more than graciously take orders from Donato females, nodded at him. Telling himself to ignore his own soured love life, since it was his favorite sister's big day, he stepped through a door, into the hallway. A second later, he was facing the long, white runner, and was stunned at the sea of smiling faces looking his way. Crooking his arm, he forced himself to smile toward one of Eliana's childhood friends, Melissa Keating, whom he'd be escorting.

"Cassidy?" he said aloud, half believing his mind was playing tricks.

She looked stunning in the bridesmaid's dress, a floor-length gold gown that made her upswept red hair dance like flames. His eyes left her face only for a moment, seeking his sister, but she was nowhere to be found, of course. She was behind him, waiting to walk down the aisle herself. So, his favorite big sister had trumped him on her very own wedding day. This explained the extra usher. *I'll be damned.*

Cassidy was surveying him, her gaze wavering with uncertainty until he put out his arm. The second hers slipped into the crook, peace filled his heart. It was risky, but he couldn't help but say it. "Welcome home."

"Good to be back."

It was that simple. The rift repaired. And as they walked to the altar, he knew he'd be next in line, after all, and the last of his crowd to marry. When they'd almost reached the pulpit, his eyes widened. He could swear Gem O'Shea was seated in the front pew, right next to his mother, and then it occurred to him that it had to be Cassidy's mom. Given his lack of priors, Johnny Case was headed for plenty of community service, instead of jail, but it was probably enough to make Cassidy's mom see the light about her daughter's relationship. Finding the jewels had changed everything. Cassidy had been right. And leave it to his own ma to set about matchmaking.

"My folks must really like you," he whispered before they parted at the altar.

"Not as much as *you* like me," she returned.

The service went by in a flash. As much as Dario tried to attend to his sister's vows, he couldn't wait for the ceremony to be over, so he could hold Cassidy again. As much as he liked his new brother-in-law, he was gaining more than a brother today. Cassidy was in his life again, and he was fantasizing about how her mouth would feel. Forget everyone, he decided. He was going to find some hidden nook in the church....

"What made you change your mind?" he asked once they'd traversed the aisle once more and he'd grasped her hand, pulling her through the front door and down a sidewalk. Seeing that the back door of an empty limo was unlocked, he opened it and urged her inside. Soon, the driver would arrive, to take them to the reception, but they had a few minutes.

"Sex for a week was pretty good," she murmured, seemingly noting the tinted windows as she snuggled next to him, "and the plan I proposed to your folks was brilliant, if I do say so, myself. I've forgiven Luther..."

"No more talk about other guys."

"Jealous?"

"Like I said, you turned the tables on me. Sure I am."

"Show me."

His mouth was on hers in a flash. As a hand rustled the hem of the gown upward and glided it high on her thigh, his tongue thrust possessively between her lips. Arching, she gasped in response, clearly missing their passion as much as he. He urged her on top of him. The gown bunching around her thighs, she straddled him, and he inhaled sharply as his hands grasped her ankles. Her legs were bare, as smooth as glass when he began gliding them upward on her calves, then her thighs.

"I need you," he whispered. Inside. Deep.

"I need you, too," she whispered against his mouth.

"Really?"

"Uh-huh," she managed breathlessly, the words coming on a soft pant of excitement. "Which is why this sex for a week thing got me to thinking."

"Funny," he muttered, heat flooding his groin, "because I can't think about anything right now."

"Not even me?"

He shook his head. He could think only about her hand, which was gliding between them, burrowing in the folds of his slacks. He darted his eyes around, then pressed a button and secured the only unlocked door. It was risky, but he had to have her. Leaning his head back on the plush leather, he gazed intently into her eyes, and hers burned back at him, the green irises blazing. Then her mouth brushed his, a spark of fire, and her hand massaged him, driving him wild with the touch he'd been so sure he'd never feel again.

"Cassidy," he begged, overwhelmed that they were together. "I want…"

Her kiss silenced him. "I know."

She wanted it, too. With a quick glance through darkened windows, she urged the slacks down on his hips, then poised above him. Sucking a breath through his teeth, he glided his hands higher…then higher…and gasped audibly when he felt her silky backside. No panties.

"You've forgiven me for not trusting you?" he asked.

"Have you forgiven me?"

"Yeah."

"Then ditto."

"Rose and Brice got together."

She smiled. "But Johnny got off the hook."

"Sort of." Now he was smiling back. "Wearing an orange jumpsuit and collecting litter in your hometown will probably make him look less appealing to the girls he chases."

She laughed softly. "True."

"Chuckie will probably do time."

"Good." She surveyed him, and something in her eyes made him think about Gem's last night. Somehow, it seemed fitting they were sealing their love in a carriage of sorts, even if, unlike Gem and Nathaniel, they were going to live and prosper.

"Like I was saying," she continued in a deep murmur, lowering herself, her wet, slick warmth surrounding him, making him cry out, "when I thought about sex for a week, I got to thinking."

He could barely find his voice. She was so beautiful, and the thrusting, rhythmic movements were making his pulse race. Tightening his arms around her waist, he hugged her close, burying his face against her chest and whimpering, "About?"

"Sex for a lifetime," she answered, threading splayed fingers into his hair.

His throat felt raw. "When do we start?"

Her arms wrapped around his neck, and her hips rocked even more deeply against him. When they were completely joined, she went very still. Suddenly, he lifted his face and found her eyes. "We already have," she told him gently.

"Then love me, Cassidy Case Magee," he returned.

She began to move again, her hips sending shudders through them both, and as she did, as if it were really their own wedding day, she whispered, "I do."

* * * * *

On sale 5th December 2008

STROKES OF MIDNIGHT
by Hope Tarr

Becky Stone's horoscope predicted that the New Year would bring her great things, but she never expected the first thing she'd experience would be *truly great sex*! Or that her New Year's fling would have the power to last all year…

KIDNAPPED!
by Jo Leigh

She had a secret desire to be kidnapped and held against her will… but when heiress Tate Baxter's fantasy game turns out to be all too real, can her gorgeous bodyguard rescue her in time?

MY FRONT PAGE SCANDAL
by Carrie Alexander

Bad boy David Carrera is the catalyst she needs to release her inner wild child. His daring makes Brooke Winfield throw off her conservative upbringing. But will she still feel that way when their red-hot exploits become front-page news?

HER IRISH ROGUE
by Kate Hoffmann

Recently dumped Claire O'Connor is ready to try anything for love, even boarding a plane to Ireland! Now irresistible Irish innkeeper Will Donovan means to be the one to mend her broken heart.

FREE

2 BOOKS AND A SURPRISE GIFT!

We would like to take this opportunity to thank you for reading this Mills & Boon® book by offering you the chance to take TWO more specially selected titles from the Blaze® series absolutely FREE! We're also making this offer to introduce you to the benefits of the Mills & Boon® Book Club—

- ★ **FREE home delivery**
- ★ **FREE gifts and competitions**
- ★ **FREE monthly Newsletter**
- ★ **Books available before they're in the shops**
- ★ **Exclusive Mills & Boon® Book Club offers**

Accepting these FREE books and gift places you under no obligation to buy; you may cancel at any time, even after receiving your free shipment. Simply complete your details below and return the entire page to the address below. You don't even need a stamp!

YES! Please send me 2 free Blaze books and a surprise gift. I understand that unless you hear from me, I will receive 4 superb new titles every month for just £3.15 each, postage and packing free. I am under no obligation to purchase any books and may cancel my subscription at any time. The free books and gift will be mine to keep in any case.

K8ZEE

Ms/Mrs/Miss/Mr...Initials ....
BLOCK CAPITALS PLEASE

Surname ....

Address ....

....

....Postcode ....

Send this whole page to:
The Mills & Boon Book Club, FREEPOST CN81, Croydon, CR9 3WZ